THE MEMENTO

A NOVEL

CHRISTY ANN CONLIN

DOUBLEDAY CANADA

Library and Archives Canada Cataloguing in Publication

Conlin, Christy Ann, author
The memento / Christy Ann Conlin.

Issued in print and electronic formats.
ISBN 978-0-385-66241-3 (paperback).--ISBN 978-0-385-68616-7 (epub)

I. Title.

PS8555.O5378M44 2016 C813'.6 C2015-906220-9
C2015-906221-7

The author would like to acknowledge the support of the Canada Council for the Arts and the Province of Nova Scotia through the Department of Communities, Culture and Heritage.

Canada Council for the Arts Conseil des arts du Canada

Lyrics from the following songs appear in the novel:
"Down by the Salley Gardens," William Butler Yeats (1909 set by Herbert Hughes to melody of traditional Irish air "The Moorlough Shore"); "She Moved Through the Fair," Irish traditional; "White Coral Bells," American traditional; "Slumber Boat" by Alice Riley (1898); "Connemara Cradle Song" (Irish traditional)

Excerpts from "Rappaccini's Daughter" by Nathaniel Hawthorne (1844) appear in Chapter 10, Part 1.

Part II epigram poem by Yosano Akiko translated from the Japanese by Kenneth Rexroth, *One Hundred More Poems from the Japanese*, 1976.

Scripture quotations in Part II, Chapter 1, from the King James Bible: Matthew 10:32-33; Luke 15:10 and 1 Corinthians 5:11.

Book design by Five Seventeen
Cover Painting, *End of Spring* © Marie Cameron
Printed and bound in Canada

Published in Canada by Doubleday Canada,
a division of Penguin Random House Canada Limited

www.penguinrandomhouse.ca

10 9 8 7 6 5 4 3 2 1

For Andy Brown
&
Millie Laporte

The memory is a living thing—it too is in transit. But during its moment, all that is remembered joins, and lives—the old and the young, the past and the present, the living and the dead.

EUDORA WELTY

Part I

Part II

Part I

But we can't possibly have a garden-party with
a man dead just outside the front gate.

"The Garden Party," KATHERINE MANSFIELD

A ghost must speak in D minor, though on this point
Gluck, Mozart and Rossini differ.

ANONYMOUS, *Extracts from the Diary of a Dilettante*,
THE HARMONICON, LONDON, 1828

1.
The Twelfth-Born

I WAS TWELVE.

That is the year I must tell you about.

The cicadas buzz on this hot August afternoon as the season draws to a close. There is a mirror by the big door here at Petal's End but I have not looked in it this summer. I am not yet ready to see what might be reflected. It's a tradition in these parts to have a mirror outside by the front door. You can take a peek before entering. Not to see how fine you are looking but to see what's at your back. Even those who don't believe in the Mountain traditions will hesitate a moment before taking such a mirror down, and to this day you'll still find them mirrors on the century houses in Lupin Cove and across the mountain. There's an even older story, though, which most have forgotten. The mirror is there so if you've been to a funeral you can see if the dead followed you home, which they will do if they have business yet to resolve with the living. But there is no story about what you are to do if a dead one is there behind you in the mirror. Marigold Parker, the grand matriarch at Petal's End, was afraid of the hobgobblies, as she called the dead. She checked the mirror in the evening, for that's when she said they came around. They'd slip in the door behind you or come in an open window. They would get inside you and fold up your soul with their long spindly fingers, she told us. The old story was wrong, Marigold said. Ghosts were not confined to the funereal period—the dead kept their own schedule.

Grampie advised we pay no mind to Marigold, but nonetheless keep an eye on the mirror. We had one over at Grampie's cottage, where I lived with him as a young child. The mirror was by the door when he moved in and it stayed there, for Grampie believed in tradition. But Grampie was never afraid of what we might see behind us. Best to know what is on your heels, he would say.

Grampie's father had been a poor dirt farmer who supplemented his living with beehives and making turpentine and furniture polish. My great-grandfather bought the place from the Parkers when they were selling a few pieces of what they called their vast *demesne* at Petal's End after the Great War. The Parker money was endless and flowed down through the generations. They parcelled off parts of the land to returning soldiers. Out of compassion, people said. Out of pity. They practically gave the land away, expecting only gratitude in perpetuity as payment.

Grampie was in the next war, but he never spoke of that—only his limp told the story. He was not a young man when he went off, but the army would take who they could get in those last few years, Grampie said, even a farmer and a gardener. So many younger than him died, and their bodies would often not come home. This drove him to enlist, thinking it would lessen the sorrow. He was wrong about that.

Grampie called himself the accidental artist. Ma told me he found his gift for painting when he drew for the army. They called him a war artist, but he never showed me a single sketch from that time. He come home to Lupin Cove a changed man and went back to work at Petal's End as a gardener, his leg not fit for walking any distance. His eyes looked the same but they could see different.

It's easier to rest here in my chair with the years heavy on my bones than to rise and stand by the door. There is a mirror in my mind's eye, and my recollections lure me into the harsh light whether I want them to or not. The birds sing, high and clear. It is June. It is the last day of school before summer vacation. It is also my birthday. I am twelve that day. Grampie is three years dead and I live over at Petal's End with Loretta, the longtime housekeeper tending the place for the Parker family, who don't come no more but insist the estate be kept like they'll be taking up residence any day. They are more phantom than alive, for we rarely see them.

The bus brings us down off the mountain, away from the rocky shores of Lupin Cove, down to the valley. When I get off the school bus I avoid them kids at school who laugh and point. Those kinds of people, they never change. What I learned is that all them idiots in the halls of school are the same people you meet in all the halls of life. I keep my head down. They laugh at my clothes, at my scar—they say I'm the girl who got knocked on her head, the girl who lives in the shack over by the bay where there is nothing but lobsters and rocky beach and the strange island that seems to float on the waves. I stopped going to school for a time when I lived with Grampie, the day they strapped a boy in front of the class to scare us good. No sir, I will not go back, I told him. They tried to make me but Grampie said I was staying home and he'd teach me what I needed to know. It wasn't until he died and I was living with Loretta that I went back, to make her happy.

Loretta was from down in the valley and came to work at Petal's End when she was a young woman in need of sanctuary. She worked as a kitchen maid and babysitter at first, moving up to housekeeper and cook, doing a bit of everything as she got older. Good help was hard to find after the war. Grampie got her the job. Loretta owed my grandfather for a long-ago kindness, she said, even though the man was never one who kept score. She was the same age as Ma, and they both had babies when they were unmarried girls. Loretta had been shamed for having a baby unwed. Unlike Ma, she gave her baby away, and she never directly spoke of it until the summer I was twelve.

On the last day of school we do crossword puzzles and word searches and play silly games. The teacher talks about summer vacation plans. She says it is Fancy Mosher's birthday and she makes the class sing to me, although the only voices I hear are hers and Art Comeau's. Art and I have grown up together and travel back and forth on that godforsaken bus. Art is my only true friend. This summer, we'll be Loretta's helpers at Petal's End and we want nothing more than for the school year to finish up and to get working. The Parkers are actually paying us, a real summer job, not just picking berries. There is much to do, what with the rumour Lady Marigold Parker is finally coming back. No one gave Loretta any information about when or if any other Parkers would be coming out with her. That's not on their mind, keeping us abreast of their plans, no sir. They're fighting, we know that much, the Parker women are feuding. But that summer day in the classroom Art and I are just excited thinking how Petal's End might come back to life, alive again with all them stories we'd grown up on, the parties and the exotic visitors from all over creation.

I'm on the steps at school waiting for Art, eating my sandwich and the birthday cookies Loretta made. Art is in the music room helping the teacher tidy it for summer. He is late and I am almost finished lunch. Other kids are off on the lawn under the deep shade of the red maples, eating and laughing, happy in the way summer makes people. The solitude of the concrete steps is where I feel best. I chew on ham and fresh lettuce leaves, lettuce from the kitchen garden at Petal's End. Loretta and I started it from seed and it came early. We grow all our own vegetables in the summer. I'm thinking about that when Ma arrives.

I hear her car before I see it, the muffler about to go, Ma gunning the gas. She has a relic of a car. It's not intentionally an antique. Ma won't ever buy anything new or full price. The enormous lilac hedges are blooming between the school building and the parking lot. Through the blossoms I watch Ma park. She shuts the engine off but she doesn't get out. Cigarette smoke trails out the car window.

I didn't see my mother much after I went to live with Grampie in his home called the Tea House when I was three years old. They took me from her, out of the back seat of her car in a ditch full of flowers on the side of the road rolling down into the valley. We'd been on our way to return her booze bottles. Ma was blind drunk, she didn't see nor hear the police sirens or see their big hands reach for me in the back seat, where I was lying with a concussion and a cut on my cheek swirling from my lip right across my cheekbone and into my hair. Grampie said later it was like a stem, my mouth a red flower. It faded pale white over the years, but if you look careful it still weaves its way through the lines on my face. In the tender evening light even those wrinkles diminish but the scar remains. It's the way of the evening, when form and time lose shape.

The Tea House used to be called the Woodcutter's Cottage, built for the man who cut wood for Petal's End back when the whole place was heated with wood and coal. I don't recall his name. But when I was a child it was called the Tea House because people came to take tea with Grampie. A house takes on the way of its dwellers. For years I thought it was just a social thing, but later I learned that when they came with their teacups and their fearful sad eyes they came for dark reasons.

It's blistering that last day of school as I stare at Ma's car, smoke hanging in the air. The valley offers no relief, not like over on the bay shore in Lupin Cove where huge tides sweep in cool breezes and the stark sun disappears inside mists and clouds. Then with a puff the haze will clear and unfurl an endless banner of blue sky streaming overhead. I sit dumbly on the steps finishing my lunch like I'm expecting Ma, but I am not expecting her. It's not the car she crashed when I was three. This is the sixth car since that one. Finally, the rusty door flies open and out she lunges. She's done up for the weather in a tight summer dress with a black bra hanging out, and she comes strutting over in her high heels with long hair piled fantastically high, dark Mosher eyes all lined, big long lashes, red lips a line of sunset cutting through her cheeks. Fifty-seven years old. Seeing her from a distance, it does seem time screeched to a stop for her. She never got fat like lots of ladies, not even having twelve kids. But up close Ma is a skeleton. Her slinky walk is how she keeps her balance in them castle-high shoes, hips swaying side to side. Her face is lined from too many smokes, too much booze, from my brother dying. She looks like she walked out of the past, in what were once her best out-on-the-town clothes, now faded and dated, dyed black hair frizzing out in all directions. Ma had two kinds of outfits. Her working clothes, simple cotton dresses she sewed herself, for picking fruit and vegetables and cleaning houses. And her going-out clothes, the tight, sexy ones accompanied by heavy perfume and makeup. She wore her going-out clothes for weddings, funerals, picnics, parties and bars.

Ma sees me right away, not that it would have been any better if she'd gone strutting and swaying all over the school property singing out *Fancy Mosher, Fancy Mosher, fucking little Fancy Mosher.* She's holding her own, flouncing toward the stairs, but she's teetering real bad. Ma stops to light up another cigarette and lets out a horrendous cough and I know she is back on the gin again, singing her gin songs, the rattling cough and throat clearing. The only time she yells is when she's drunk. Near the bottom of the steps there is some dirt and grass where her heels have speared the lawn and I hear the familiar click click as she comes up the stairs, her cheap sunglasses covering her eyes.

I see Art coming along then, rambling at first, but the second he spots Ma he breaks into a run. She continues up the steps, clinging to the railing, and stands in front of me with her hands on her hips. Art comes up behind her, not sure what to do. He's winded. It's hard to catch your breath in thick clammy air.

Ma lifts up her sunglasses and rubs her eyes, liner smudged, crooked. You could tell how much gin by how straight the line, how smudged the shadow. She must have been crying all the way down the mountain and into the valley. Ma knows better than to come here. Loretta already told her to stay away from me for the summer, on account of what Ma did in early spring. Yet here she is, only two months later, tap tap tapping to see where she can get in. I rest my eyes on the sky. It's no panic for me, Ma like this. It is her normal state. It's just that her man, Ronnie, usually reins her in. Where could he be? I start humming.

Ma opens her mouth and a slow purr comes out of her. "Fancy, you got a sweet voice, and you sound like one of them red birds your Grampie loved so." She takes another wobbly step. "You're special to me, Fancy. You know you are, don't ya, Honeysuckle? I waited so long for you, and you were born when the air was sugar fancy, flowers as far as I could see, my summer baby. The rest of them was all born when it was cold. But not you. You were born in the heat. Early in the morning when the sky was on fire and the air was so humid it was crawling in the windows." She gives a burp and a laugh comes out of her mouth as she runs her hand up and down the railing, her fingernails tinkling on the metal. She sits down right close to me, playing with the curls falling down by her eyes as she did when she was young, but the gesture's not beguiling no more. She strokes my knee. "Today is your day, Honeysuckle. You are the twelfth-born. I counted off them babies until I had you. John Lee was my first baby. Then two, three, four, five, six. You see, I knew about the story and the numbers. Seven, eight, nine, ten, eleven. And they stopped coming. But oh, I waited. Yes, I did, I waited ten more years just for you. Your father, he said I tricked him, getting my fancy baby but not keeping him around. Isn't that just like a man? A lonely man is an easy man. But I needed a twelfth because of the Mosher ways. You know what your grandfather could do with his teacups and paints. He could have helped me. But he said no, he would not talk to my baby boy. It wasn't my fault, what happened." Ma's voice stops like she's crashed into a cliff.

She sees me staring at her smeared makeup and whatever softness was in her voice slinks away.

"Don't you look at me like that, Fancy. You know what those paintings were about." She takes a deep breath and smiles so sweet I can feel the teeth rotting out of my head. Ma lurches up as though she suddenly remembered she needs to be somewhere even though she's not sure where that might be. Art's behind her with his hands out, in case she falls. Her arm drapes on the railing and she slouches back. She won't be upright for much longer.

I don't know what she's speaking of, going on about my grandfather and whatever shameful secret she thinks I'm in on. Grampie was a painter. Folk art, they call it. Grampie had a garden and he cut firewood and trapped animals. He kept bees and made wildflower honey. And for as long as he was able he made turpentine and furniture polish as his father did, to bring in extra. But above all else he was an artist. Everyone knew that. He painted pictures on pieces of board and driftwood and stones, anything flat. People came from all over to have him make one for them. They'd bring a teacup, and I thought they was doing a trade for his art. He called his pictures *portraits*, some smiling, some looking right crazy, some woebegone, some tired, some asleep. Pictures of people sitting in gardens, and at tables, and on occasion there was nature surrounding them. Sometimes there was an object: a cane, a truck, a chair, a coin, a building far behind. Grampie said he painted what was in their eyes, what came off their tongues. When he wasn't painting portraits he was painting on the walls of the house.

In his bedroom he had a painting of my grandmother. It was his favourite. Her wrinkled, smiling face he treasured so. Bright sparkling sunlight surrounded her as she sat under the pines, blowing him a kiss like she did when they went into the forest to collect berries. I loved to stand in the doorway and look at her. Just after she gave birth to my mother she got a terrible joint disease and she became bent and twisted, except that gentle look. My grandmother died long before I came to live with Grampie, from her illness wearing her down over many years. She was his heart's song, he called her. After she died they found him at the kitchen table with the teapot, the cups set, staring at her empty chair like he was waiting for her.

One of my earliest memories was Ma saying Grampie should put advertisements for his portraits in the paper. Not everyone could do what he did, she said, because he had a rare gift. Grampie said that was ridiculous and most people wouldn't want one glimpse if they knew where his inspiration really came from. He shushed her, the way he would, waving his hand slow through the air, like he was clearing smoke. *For some people, Marilyn Mosher, there is no point in seeing, and you are one of them people.* There was no more talk of advertising. After he retired from gardening in Evermore, the garden at Petal's End, Grampie made enough to get by with his portraits. He gave up the bees and collecting pine sap for turpentine and just did his art. He wouldn't charge a price for the paintings and he wouldn't make an appointment for anyone. People would leave an offering in a wooden box he had on the table, and they'd leave the teacups they had brought. The people never stopped coming.

The sign was on the house by the door, and he had painted it in clean black lines, with fuchsia morning glories coiled around the letters.

SAMUEL MOSHER

PORTRAITS

BY CHANCE

But the narrow lane to the house snaked through the forest, with no number or sign, so if you didn't know where to turn, you would never find Samuel Mosher. When someone did find us, he'd shoo me away. It was confidential, he said, giving someone a painting. *Some things are private, Fancy*, Grampie would say, *and privacy is to be respected. All the problems in the world come when we go against the natural order respect lays out*. Most people who came left happy with their paintings, but some left crying. Grampie would stand with me on the verandah at the front of the house, and we'd wave as they drove away. He'd glance in that mirror by the front door as we went back into the Tea House.

As Ma got older she wanted to be like her father, for he was peaceful despite what he had seen. And he was able to make peace for others. She was unquiet, angry she never saw the world. Grampie never wanted to leave Lupin Cove again. Aside from the war, he spent his entire life here. He told her you could find the world in a teacup if you took the time to look, that there was no need to travel. Ma said she never got the second chance she deserved, that she'd spent her life being judged, tripping on it each step of the way, slaving for others. You could only talk to her on her terms. Ma was furious Grampie couldn't fix things. Or wouldn't fix things. She kept waiting. But he had the nerve to die on her.

Before Ma worked as a maid over at Petal's End, she made her living working on the shore picking dulse and collecting fish in the weirs. Grampie told me that. Ma hated to speak of the past so

Grampie kept the memories for her and shared some with me over the years I lived with him. After Ma quit being a maid, she went back to work on the shore for a time. Then she wouldn't go beyond the beach, nowhere near the salt water, and instead worked on farms picking fruit and vegetables as each season unfolded. At dawn, if she wasn't parched from drinking, she'd pick buckets of water lilies and fish trout at the lake, selling her harvest down in the valley stores.

In earlier times women took their children right out into the field, but no one did that by the time I was a young child, except Ma. No one minded for I was no trouble. My earliest recollections of life with my mother are of playing and running about, napping on a blanket in the shade. Ma would have lunch packed for us and she'd sing as she worked. When she wasn't doing farm work she'd make wild fruit jams and pickles and pies. Grampie had pictures in his album of us selling them by the side of the road and at tourist shops. He said Ma was as famous for her jellies and baking as she had once been for her needlework. She made her own labels. She'd embroider her name and the name of the jelly or jam, and she'd glue the muslin label to a glass jar with a shiny metal top, wrapping a thin silk ribbon around it. Everyone said it was a tie between how good her preserves tasted and how pretty them jars were. We'd go all over the mountain and the valley to her secret spots for picking wild berries. Ma not only had two kinds of outfits, she also had two sorts of smells—the sweet fragrance of sun-warmed skin and berries, and cigarette smoke, hairspray and rose perfume. In those early summers of my life it was mostly the berries, and the earthy rich scent of her hands that would stroke my hair and show me how to make flower garlands we'd wear on our heads. I have fragmented memories of other times, when she would make home deliveries to men and I would sit in the car waiting for her. When she'd come back Ma would reek of liquor. She'd light up a cigarette and the smoke would slither through the car and out the windows in an all too familiar way.

In the winter we'd sit by the fire while Ma taught me to embroider samplers, pictures with your name and date stitched. Young girls did these long ago to demonstrate their domestic skills, when embroidery was needed to put names and dates on clothes and linens, sacks of flour and grain. But then times changed and samplers were nothing more than pictorials to please the eye or stitching for decoration. Grampie told me when Ma worked as a maid at Petal's End she'd done designs and stitching on their linens. He said I never had any interest in doing that even when I was little, just making my embroidery pictorials. Ma would show me how to stitch those same flowers we'd picked and played with in the good weather. She loved my pictures. But none of it lasted, and Grampie said each summer ended with her mind darker, leading us into cold, harsh winters. So it went on until she crashed the car and they took me away.

Except there Ma is on my twelfth birthday, still thinking she knows best, never wanting to accept that her own bad choices were what made life bitter and broken.

"You look at me," Ma says.

I do as she bids. Her eyes are undulating red jellies.

"He did, he did it for so many. Your grandfather sipped the tea and he saw their faces and he gave that to them, those they left behind. But he wouldn't for me. No ma'am. He wanted to punish me. He said John Lee never came to him, not once. I never got nothing. I brought his baby cup, that small mug with the silver moon and the golden stars. I gave it to your grandfather, I put it in his big hand myself and watched them paint-stained fingers take it away. You seen it there, Fancy, I know you did. Be a good girl now and you tell your Mama. You tell her the truth. I won't be mad. You need to believe, that's all. You didn't believe in the spring but you were not yet twelve. It was too soon. But the time has come."

My scar burns but I don't touch it, just pull my hair over my face. It's like we are together again, me in my pink dress picking wild blueberries by the train tracks at sunset when I should have been in bed. Ma holding me up so I could try to grab a handful of the pink sky. Tears fill my eyes.

"Don't you cry, Fancy Mosher. Don't you dare," Ma whispers. "I'm the one who deserves to cry. You listened to your Grampie for too long. He took you from me. Now he's gone and you can listen to Mama again, and make me happy. Loretta will fill your mind with stories that are corrupted. But you know I'll tell you true. John Lee might have died when he was only six years old but he's more alive to me than you are. I see him there in my mind each moment of the day, my dearest treasure. And time and time again lying there on the rocks."

I remember seeing that baby mug sitting on the shelf. *That was your little brother's*, Grampie said. *We keep it as a memento. He was a sweet child.* At that moment I do want to make her happy, because she never was, not for long, not even when my hands were full of the pink sky and she'd laugh like it was the most adorable thing. And now, I think, all she wants is a cup and I can't give her no cup.

"Oh, John Lee, little Johnny Lee." When she says my brother's name this time she starts crying in a horrible, small, breaking voice. Art takes an awkward step up but stops when Ma puts her smudged face in her hands. She lifts up her head and looks me right in the eye and waggles her long finger as she bawls. "What you don't know is that you're just like your Grampie. Oh yes you are. You're the twelfth-born, just like him. Today you turn twelve years old. But this is my day." She stops crying and barks at me. "And this year you *will* see what your Grampie could see and you will see your little brother for me and you goddamn *will* speak with him because that is what you were born to do. It's the only reason I had you. Jesus had twelve disciples and so twelve is no ordinary number. Your grandfather said I wasn't supposed to tell you. He made me promise. But who went and made that bastard lord and master?"

Ma's chanting. I'm standing up, shaking, and Art is now beside me. Kids have gathered at the bottom of the concrete staircase, watching us, whispering, giggling. Ma is weeping. I can't keep up with her.

"Oh, Mama," I whisper. "What can I do so you'll stop crying?"

"That's right, Fancy. Help your Mama. You will see him. You will see my little boy and you will make it right between us. It wasn't my fault. John Lee will forgive me. He already has, I know it. He was his Mama's boy. He just can't tell me himself. But he can give you a message, if you find him."

Ma puts her finger up to her lips. "Hush-a-bye," she coos, just like at Grampie's burial. "Don't you dare cry, Fancy Mosher."

Art is my protector, standing between me and Ma in all her raging drunken glory. He is a young boy, tall and thin and brave. He tries to be a barrier but Ma shoves him out of the way with her strong hands as though he is no more than a reed in a pond where she is picking water lilies.

Art had come to Petal's End to live with his grandmother, Yvette. Art was kind and he was rational. He noticed the small things. He was the type who would glance through a small gabled window and in that moment see the shooting star in the sky. When we walked in puddles when it rained he never went around them, not even when he was a grown man. He went right through in his rubber boots, me walking ahead in bare feet, listening to his ripples. Grampie said we shared the ability to understand in a glance.

Art understood that this was extreme, even for Ma. She'd been bad in the early spring but not like this.

In a flash my mother had my head between her hands, her rank breath in my face, the smell of cigarettes in my nostrils as she ran her nicotine-stained fingers over my scar, repeating as if in a trance that she didn't mean for it to happen, she didn't know how it happened to John Lee, she should have been there.

Art was pleading in his songbird voice, "Mrs. Mosher, Mrs. Mosher, let Fancy go. You need to sit down. You need to sit down. We need a time-out here, a time-out."

She hated being called Mrs. Mosher. She was never married, for one thing, and said she'd never marry, for no man would keep her down. Being called Mrs. Mosher made her feel Stone Age old, and there was nothing she liked less than age wrapping its bony arms around her. *Marilyn. My name is Marilyn Mosher*, she'd say. But Ma kept talking like Art wasn't even there.

"Jesus wept, Fancy, *he* wept for the little children, just like I'm weeping now. I'm only taking back my word, Fancy. I'm not *breaking* it, just taking it back. Grampie, he'd understand, surely he would, just as sure as you are the twelfth-born and that's no baker's dozen but a clear ringing twelve. You came into this world not even crying, just taking in a big gasp of air, and I knew. You can take things back from the dead in a way you can't from the living. The dead forgive . . ." Her face twisted up, a face wanting to crawl off and bite. She rubbed my scar like she was trying to erase it. "The dead forgive, not like you . . . people. Praise be to the dead."

No amount of powder could hide how thin her grey skin was. All at once I experienced the rush of Ma holding out her trembling hand with yellowed fingers, the cigarette, burned to the filter, falling on the step, Art's hand on my back, the principal opening the door behind us, his voice a thick ribbon running along the bottom of Ma's desperate words.

2.
Hear the Wind Blow

The principal came dashing out, the secretary right behind him. She took me and Art inside. Ma was screaming about my birthday and that they had no right to keep her from celebrating. We waited in the office for Loretta to come and get us. Me with my hands tight together and Art sitting close beside me, the heat off his brown skin soaking into my arm and thigh. Art knew better than to talk.

My eyes were closed and my thoughts were trapped birds, darting about as I tried to comprehend what had possessed my mother and made her crazy. The last time I'd seen her was in the early spring. Ma wanted me for supper and overnight. It seemed so promising, as everything does in that season when the whole world is bursting to life. Ma was off the gin for most of the year and she was embroidering and baking pies and cakes again. Ronnie told us Ma had been sober all winter when we bumped into him down in the valley at the grocery store, the week before Ma showed up to plead for me. "Marilyn's been dry as the dunes in the desert," he said, all proud. Least we could do was be friendly to her. Her own damn daughter most of all, for a child owed her parent that much, Ronnie lectured, as Loretta and I stood in the baking needs aisle.

Ronnie was a long-haul trucker who brought up flowers from way down south where the palm trees grow for stores to sell here. He showered Ma with bouquets until the moment she died. Ronnie had loved her for years from afar, but Ma only let him move in after the car accident when they took me away and she had no toleration for solitude. Normally Ronnie couldn't stand the sight of me but sometimes I'd catch him staring, for he was seeing glimpses of my Ma when she was young and tender. Ronnie called her his saltwater rose. What others saw as reckless he saw as courageous. He was the only one who could get Ma to take a break from drinking and call out the best in her, get those hands steady enough so she could make her pies and pickles and do embroidery, the things she treasured until the end. Ronnie was her knight in shining armour arriving in a white transport truck full of flowers. But of course Ma's dry spells were like summer—glorious with promises of forever until one day the sky turns chill dark blue, the air turns cold and deceitful leaves spiral down, dried-up promises turning to dust.

Ma came over to Petal's End to invite me herself. She was extra polite and minded her manners. She left her beater of a car grumbling in the driveway. Maybe she thought we would not open to her knock. But Loretta opened the door and stood listening. Ronnie would be the chaperone, if only Loretta would be kind enough to let me come for the night, Ma said as she stood eagerly at the doorway. "Loretta, of all people, you should understand." Ma's voice was breaking.

It wasn't that Loretta liked Ronnie, only that she didn't dislike anyone. *There's the Lord in all people*, she'd say. We believed her and

Ronnie when they said she had been off the gin all year. Loretta believed in forgiveness—hate the sin but not the sinner, she preached. It had been heavy on her mind that it wasn't right for her to keep a child from her mother. Loretta had a deep look of pity. Ma was so calm and contrite that Loretta was off her guard—she relented.

Loretta's voice reached into my thoughts and brought me back from the spring to the principal's office. "Girly Miss, I tell you, it's never a dull moment. And Mister Man, what would we do without you looking after our Fancy?"

I opened my eyes. Loretta was beside me. I hadn't even heard her come in the office. She took my hands and looked at my scar. "Oh my glory! We'll put some ice on that," she said. "Don't you worry, not even for a minute."

"I don't need no looking after," I said.

"Well, Girly Miss, you'll just have to put up with it, isn't that right, Art?" She squeezed my hand and I stood up. I was almost as tall as her that summer. I had no idea if she knew what Ma had said or what the principal had told her. But if anyone knew what Ma was ranting about, it was Loretta. She was avoiding my eyes. "You and Art get out to the car. Hector's there."

Ronnie's truck was in the parking lot beside a police car. I looked around, worried Ma would leap off the roof screaming, wrapping herself around my neck, telling me to talk to the dead. There was no sign of her. I was glad Ronnie wasn't around either. He blamed me, as though it were all my fault. But you don't ask to be born.

Hector was leaning against a car near Ronnie's, watching the grade nine class go by. He was examining the girls in their bright summer clothes. They were all giggling. Hector was dazzling to look at. There was not a woman who didn't feel some sort of swoon for him. Loretta had made him the hired man earlier that year. He lounged on that fine long shiny car like he was the only owner it had ever had, but in fact it was the Parkers' car. Old Rolly, he called it. It had been the Colonel's car and was sitting in the carriage house for years, but Marigold got Hector working on it. Or, rather, he got her to let him work on it, when Marigold decided she was well enough to come for the summer. It did not occur to Hector that no one with an expensive antique car like that would be in greasy work clothes and a ball cap.

Hector's father, Clyde, had a farm on the mountain, inland from Petal's End, to the southwest on the Flying Squirrel Road. Clyde had occasionally worked at Evermore a long time ago, but mostly he farmed with draught horses, and they had fields of strawberries and you could go pick them, looking out over the bay as you filled your berry baskets. We'd see Hector there, working in the fields, and he'd give Art and me mints when Grampie or Yvette took us over. He was always working on some old-time car of his own, and back then it was one he called Old Stu. Loretta had a car and Hector kept that running as well. He took care of all the transportation needs. Long ago Grampie had helped Loretta get her driver's licence but she was a nervous driver and drove rarely.

Hector had been someone I noticed from the corner of my eye, but that summer he went to dead centre. He was wearing aviator sunglasses, likely thinking they would hide his gawking at the young girls, with his slow easy smile. He tipped his hat at us when we came over.

"Long day, I hear. Well, don't let that bother you. It's cooler over in Lupin Cove and we'll be there soon. You're just as well out of this place where people think they're better. Nothing good ever came of living down here. School never did anybody no good, no offence to the school system." Hector laughed like that was the funniest thing and he gave us both a mint and opened the back door to the car. "Don't you worry about what anyone thinks, Fancy. They're all idiots here in the valley."

I nodded and touched my scar. We were bound together, those of us from the mountain.

Hector knew about crazy parents. When we was very young there was Petal's End Gala Days in mid August, the same time the Parkers would have their big summer garden party. It was a magical time of year for children. They'd have horse pulls at the community hall before it burned down. Clyde would go with his big workhorses, their manes braided, harnesses polished and bells jingling. One year we was sitting in the stands, me and Art and Grampie and Ma and Ronnie. Even Yvette was there with us. Hector's uncle, Eldritch Loomer, who was jealous he wasn't left the family farm, kept making low comments as Clyde was getting his horses ready to pull more weight. Eldritch was sitting at the bottom of the stands and it was just a murmur to us in the back but Clyde could hear every drawled insult and curse. Suddenly he dropped the reins and left his horses there hitched to the weights and come running and started pounding away on his brother. Blood was flying and people was screaming and taking their kids. Clyde would have these fits of rage and they'd only last a few minutes and he'd have no memory. His sore bloodied knuckles and the police would tell him the tale of what he done. When Hector got older he started to be just like his father. You see, what runs in the blood runs in the blood.

When Loretta came out of the school Hector was telling us a story about his father chasing the workhorses when they got out of the barn because he forgot to close their stalls, and how he heard his father calling to them, Lloyd, Floyd, Harold and Jim. They had boy names, Hector said, because Clyde viewed them horses as his true sons. Loretta was with a policeman and he walked her to the car. Hector opened the door for her and the policeman called Hector by name. His troubles with the police had started when he was just a boy. Hector helped Loretta into the car and closed the door, tipping his hat to the policeman, and off we went through the valley and up the mountain.

We drove toward the mountain and Loretta discussed her summer plans for us as though Ma had never come to the school, like it was just a normal June day. She and Hector began their regular good-natured bickering about household matters, making the odd comment to Art, who also seemed happy to pretend nothing had happened. The breeze floating in through the windows smelled of fresh-cut grass. I tried to make sense of what had just happened. Ma had just picked right up from that night in the spring.

Once details between Ma and Loretta had been finalized, I'd ridden my bicycle over from Petal's End one evening after supper. It was a beautiful spring night. Ma's house was painted different colours because she could only afford to buy the discontinued paint, the leftover cans. My mother greeted me at the door without any of her usual makeup on, not a bit of jewellery. She was in a ratty bathrobe and her hair was in curlers that looked like they'd been in there for a few days. She had that odour of smoke and booze and hairspray, and her hand shook when she lifted it from the doorknob. I asked her where Ronnie was and she said he had to go off and haul some flowers, she had the dates mixed up. She hugged me, too tightly, and tried to keep from crying.

"Oh, Fancy," she said, "I'm a bad mother. I baked for you but it didn't turn out so well, Honeysuckle."

"You're not so bad," I said. "No one can stitch like you, Mama." She was a horrible-looking mess. I put my arm around her and took her inside. She sat in a chair picking at her fingernails while I put the kettle on.

"Well, you can stitch like you was born with a needle in your hand, Fancy Mosher, and you ain't even twelve years old. Almost but not quite," she said.

We ate the cookies she'd made. She had forgotten to put sugar or baking powder in them and they were flat and bitter. I knew she'd used a cookie cutter, a steel bird-shaped one, because it was on the counter, but the shapes were all wrong from her hand shaking so. They was birds that would never fly.

We was out on the screened-in verandah after and the embroidery picture Ma was working on was stretched in her hoop on the table by her chair. I had brought my hoop along, a night garden by a pond with tall swooping willows and water lilies. Ma picked up her embroidery. She pretended she didn't notice me watching as she started slowly pulling the mauve thread through, colour Ma was putting into the sunset sky behind the green floss treetops. She was making a flock of dark birds swooping through the sky with one split stitch after another and, unlike her cookies, those stitched birds looked like they would always be flying.

While she'd drink cheap wine and dirty-tasting gin, Ma only used the finest silk flosses for her work and had them mail-ordered. She poked her finger and a stain of blood spread over the tight Evenweave fabric she was working with. Ma swore and put it down and took a sip from her teacup full of gin. She sat looking out at the stand of silver birches and crossed her arms. "Your needlework is near perfect. You got a gift for it, Fancy." She studied my satin stitches in the flowers I was making. "I never seen someone who didn't need to work with a pattern. It just comes right out of you. Watch your shadows, though. They don't fall right. The sun or the moon has to be behind to cast a shadow."

She lit up a cigarette and blew the smoke out in rings and puffs, beautiful and deadly. After a time she smashed it out in the ashtray and started stitching again. "Ain't nobody got use for this no more but that's no reason to stop, Fancy. Maybe them Parkers will get you doing their linens again. But I don't know who they think they are, having you work there so young. They're making fun of me, that's why they offered you a summer job. You'll find out, yes you will. Them Parkers are bad. Nothing good will come from spending time there. Look at me. It all went wrong when I started working at Petal's End, only sixteen years old, I was. Your

Grampie had me looking after my poor crippled mother and waiting on them snobs at Petal's End. How was a girl to have any fun, I ask you?"

I didn't reply, for that could turn her, if she felt you was prying. It was best to keep stitching while she bounced around from one topic to another. There was a shake in her voice, from the weird blend of anger and fear that ran through all Ma's conversation.

"There's no one to wait on *me*. Ten other children and litters of grandbabies and none of them even so much as visit. And they pretend you weren't never born. I'm just a pariah, Fancy, that's all I am. They abandoned me, one after another.

"I would have gone and caught you a fish but I wasn't up for it. I hope you'll understand. I know how much you always liked a butter pan-fry with a bit of lemon and parsley. You were the cutest thing when I'd take you out in the boat on the lake. You'd clap your little hands when I'd haul in a fish. It was a miracle how long you could sit in that canoe without saying a word. You always understood you had to be patient. You liked most when we'd wade in for the water lilies when the sun was rising. The best time to pick them, you know, when the day is fresh. Remember that? I'm sorry I didn't cook you supper, Fancy. I'm all worn out from years of cooking and stitching for the lot of you. Ronnie does most of the cooking now, God love the man. A good man is hard to find, and you should stitch that and hang it on your wall right in front of your goddamn nose. You be careful over at Petal's End. That place was always full of shady types coming and going."

"They're paying me, you know. It's not like I'm going to be a slave for the Parkers. I'm old enough for a job. Art's helping out too. They told Loretta to hire some help but they didn't want any strangers. That didn't leave her with much choice. But Art and I are both almost twelve. We ain't babies. I'm surprised Loretta didn't try to hire you back, Ma. She thinks the Parkers will come out again this summer, and it will be busier than it's been in a long time." My eyes stayed on the embroidery, trying to make sure when I put the shadow in it fell right.

"I wouldn't go back and work there if it was the last place on earth. They paid me too, you'll recall, and it wasn't worth a penny. It always ends in heartache and tears over there, and it don't matter a shit how gorgeous it may be, goddamn mansion. Loretta was always willing to bow down and do as she was told. She gave her own baby up. Can you imagine? It's always like that, poor young girls having to give up so much. But I wasn't going to pull out my spine and dissolve into a helpless jellyfish. That's the sort of help the Parkers like. It's peculiar enough up there that won't anybody even notice. It's no wonder they don't come out. That place is full of bad spirits. You be careful. What your grandfather thought sending you there to live when you could be with me I'll never know. You watch your six, as your Grampie used to say. You be careful around that Marigold. She's a wily one. Sweet elderly lady, my precious arse. And only poor Loretta with all her useless prayers to protect you." Ma kept stitching and snorting. "A frail woman half dead coming out to a big empty house?"

"But Marigold's an old lady. What harm can she do anyone? Dr. Baker says she's well enough now to do as she pleases. And anyway, Grampie always said that whatever happened to Loretta was because she never had family to help her." The lime-green leaves were on the embroidery trees now.

Ma took a swig from her cup. "Dr. Baker would say that, the arse. He's just trying to curry favour with the old bat. He's no different than his father and probably not even as good a doctor. And your grandfather was right about fat old Loretta, I'm being too hard on her. Nothing for her but the turds life has placed in a bowl at her feet. But you watch those Parkers, every single one. They'll try to use you, mark my words. What runs in the blood runs in the blood, and that, Fancy Mosher, is the truth. You look at me."

Her voice was hard and hollow now, and the soft wreck who

had answered the door was long gone. It was clear it had been a mistake to give her one more chance.

"What runs in the blood runs in the blood. Do you understand? Your Grampie must have told you."

The only thing I understood was that she hadn't changed at all and that she'd fooled even her beloved Ronnie. We said nothing further, not even good night, and I left her there looking out into the dark, scared of old ladies, humming to herself. I went into the room that had been mine, where so many children before me had slept. I put myself to bed, imagining a flock of birds, the starlings that Grampie liked, swirling up in the way they did at twilight, bending like a long black ribbon through that early sunset. I counted every bird in my mind.

Hector's loud voice burst through my thoughts, a town crier proclaiming to Loretta and Art what a fine machine Old Rolly was. He then moved on about Old Stu, about how they didn't make them like they did back in the day.

Loretta wagged her finger at him. "You talk as though you were in the first car factory there ever was, you fool. You're only nineteen years old. Now don't you go getting any ideas, Hector. This car will be parked just as soon as we get back. The only reason we're out in this car is there wasn't room to put us all in your pickup truck and I'm not driving around with anyone in the back. Nice and slow, Hector, please and thank you. Don't strain the engine. Marigold wants this machine running smoothly when she comes out. She wants everything to be just so."

"When you get to a certain age wanting your own way is understandable," Art said.

Loretta turned around and she looked back at Art. She was so short she was like a child herself peering over the edge of the front seat. "Why yes, that's true, Mister Man. It's more when you get to a certain age you want things the way you remember them. That's what Marigold is after this summer, a bit of life how it was, and still is, in her mind."

"Eighty-five, isn't she?" Hector looked at Loretta. "My grandfather lived to be a hundred. Marigold says she wants the car ready in case she needs to go somewhere. Or for company. No offence to senior citizens. Just seems you get to a certain age and it's kind of like you're young again except you ain't. You're just travelling around in your mind. And looking in the mirror seeing what only you can see."

"Hector, sometimes you speak the truth." Loretta sighed. "Only sometimes, mind you. In the end, it is Marigold's decision to do what she pleases with Petal's End and we'll be respectful and do our jobs. It's not our place to disagree. I remember the day she hired me. She supervised each blessed detail at the house. You have no idea. Marigold swept around and we did as we were told. At nighttime she looked as though the day was just beginning, not a hair out of place, her clothes immaculate. There was a butler way back then and he was always at her side. Mr. Long. I never saw the man smile once, not even when he got his Christmas bonus. He took nothing stronger than hot water with a teaspoon of lemon. There used to be a big gong in the small back courtyard by the kitchen that a guest had brought as a hostess gift. If Marigold was up before the help she sent Mr. Long out to give it a smash. We'd all awaken thinking the world was coming to an end for we'd only just fallen asleep. He dropped dead one day just as he was to ring the morning gong. We'd fully expected him to live forever. He was laid out in his coffin looking just the same as when he was alive except his eyes were shut and for once he wasn't standing up. All us girls were afraid to look at him for fear he'd open his eyes and order us straight back to work. 'You know your places, girls.' Those were his favourite words."

"My mother wasn't afraid of him, I bet." Of course I was curious hearing Loretta talking about the past, but mostly I wanted to prod her about my mother. It was odd that Loretta was acting like nothing untoward had happened.

Loretta paused for just a second before she swallowed and replied. "No, Marilyn was not, much to his consternation. That day in the funeral parlour Marilyn stood by his corpse and made faces when the undertaker wasn't looking. We couldn't help but laugh. It's best to remember your mother, Fancy, when she was well, although short on propriety as she always has been."

"I haven't heard you like this, Loretta, since you and Art's grandmother came to the church charity bingo and got into that punch someone spiked with pear wine."

"Hector, I did not drink the punch. You're mistaken. Anyway, children, in the good summer weather there was no end to the parties and events Marigold put on. A stream of guests and family from all parts of the world. There was a large staff living at Petal's End back then. We worked from dawn until dusk, all of us wearing uniforms, with Sundays off. We could hardly wait for winter when it would end. Marigold would be out in the Water House making her soaps and flower waters until all hours of the night, and she expected us to work just as long. The Colonel was always telling Marigold she should leave a few things to chance. In his spare time he enjoyed spontaneity. Marigold despised it.

"When Marigold telephoned last night she was already speaking of a garden party. 'You're caught up in a second wind, Mrs. Parker,' I said. 'Loretta, this is my *final* wind and we best make haste while it blows,' she said. Most people don't change. Hector, slow down please. Do not come up so fast behind that car. Thank you, my dear."

Art put his hand out the window like he was patting the wind. "I guess the wind blows for all of us someday."

"Well, ain't we got us a little poet back there."

"Don't mock, Hector, my young man. Art might be only twelve but he understands more about life than most ever will. Slow down, please. There is a speed limit." Loretta put her hand to her mouth and held it there.

Many years later I realized Loretta was nearing sixty that summer and already her time-gone-by was circling back to find her. She was being brushed ever so soft to the other side of that wind Art was stroking.

3.
The Memento

I HEAR GRAMPIE'S voice in my head still. And your voice. Once, a long time ago, you asked me what I was afraid of and I told you I wasn't afraid of one single thing. That was not true. I was afraid of many things but talking about them only made it worse. I was never afraid of the dark, nor of animals, or creatures that howl in the night. But I was afraid around my mother because there was no fixing her. Stiff and old in my chair, I am only afraid now of what will be in your eyes when I see you, if you come out from wherever it is you are waiting. Afraid of the judgment, I suppose, same as what Ma feared she'd see in my eyes. It's the details, isn't it, that we remember? The eyes, the sound of the voice, the scent of the air, the way the light dapples through leaves onto the grass, or the perfect shadow of the winter branches on the snowy field, and how the child's footprints on the sand are always washed away. This is what we remember.

These fingers of mine, they curl, the thick yellow nails I can't trim no more with such stiff hands. But these hands do not tremble, not even with the age all over them. They are held tight together now as I rock, taking a break from my stitching. I've done a lovely sun with this floss, and my shadows are perfect.

Petal's End was where I wanted to be as we drove from the school and over the valley floor, past the farms, the big sky stretching above the fields and orchards. A haze was hanging over the land from the fierce heat. It was like we were in one of my embroideries, peaceful and perfect, with cattle and sheep grazing in the gentle June fields, some farmers still working with draught horses. We smelled something putrid come in on the wind then as we drove up behind a big truck. It hit a bump and an animal leg was sticking up, and there was another bump and the load shifted and a furry head jostled up and down, and another hoof. A truckload of carcasses. It made me think of crazy Ma again and filled my mouth with thick bitter drool.

Hector swore and he hit the gas. We roared by the truck in Old Rolly. Hector gave the finger to the driver as we passed, shouting that a farmer should know better and he had half a mind to call the police when we got back and report his ass. Loretta was gagging and she said nothing about how fast we were going. Hector sped along, careening up the mountain and screeching through the sharp turns, up and around the oxbow switchback where Ma had put us in the ditch, away from the stench and the sweltering valley, up and over the mountain on the Lonely Road, the car purring along by fields of buttercup, clover and Queen Anne's lace. Their sweetness filled the car as the bay appeared before us, a strip of blue and the sky beyond and the island. The island never looks to be in the same spot. Sometimes it's as though it's moved right close to shore and other times it seems to be drifting away, as though it don't want to be an extension of Petal's End. And sometimes it disappears in a fog bank, all but the top. On a clear day it can look either like it's floating on the water or descending from the sky, long like a man's old-fashioned hat, forest and meadow on top but almost entirely surrounded by soaring jagged cliffs. We drew nearer to Lupin Cove.

❧

At Ma's I had woken in the middle of the night in a cold sweat, surrounded by darkness. The spring peepers, them tiny tree frogs, were singing in the swampy part in back of Ma's, near the falling-down barn she'd once kept her horses in. Far off I could hear lonely coyotes, their yips and yowls coming from the woods, and the wind blew in the spring leaves. But inside Ma's house I heard singing, too. I didn't know who it was at first. There was faint whispered words all run together. I heard footsteps, you see, these gentle steps, right slow, but I could not tell whose footsteps they were. My bedroom door swung open. There was glossy singing and a soft flowery breeze brushed my face, but it wasn't coming in the window, and I knew there was something right in front of me, searching for me. Shaking, I reached out to the lamp on the bedside table and snapped it on, but there was nothing there and the singing had stopped. I turned out the light and lay back down, eyes wide open, and as soon as I did the singing started again. I heard shuffling in the hall, a dull light getting brighter, and there was Ma in the doorway and she was singing in a tremulous voice, *Baby's boat the silver moon*. I smelled gin. *Sailing in the sky.*

I squeezed my eyes shut and when I opened them there she was standing over me with a candle and a picture of my brother. Her hair was a huge crazy halo with some curlers hanging down like broken bits of wing.

"Do you believe? I know you're awake. You turned your light on. I wouldn't come in and wake up a child. John Lee was here. I am sure he was here but he ain't looking for me because I can't see him. He's looking for the one who can see him." Her voice was a rough whisper. *Baby's fishing for a dream, fishing near and far.* It was no song she ever sung to me. "Can you see him? Has he come visiting?" She took a sharp breath and whispered, "Can you see him, Fancy, can you see your brother?"

I said yes because he was in the picture she was holding.

Ma gasped and tears streamed out of her eyes like silver rivers in the candlelight. "Praises," she said. "Praises. Does he forgive me? Does he know how sorry I am? Ask him. You're almost twelve now. You can ask him for me. You can see him."

I realized my mistake. Ma thought I could see John Lee, not just the little boy in the photo. His tender face in the soft light seemed to be saying, *Our Ma is a nutbar, sister-I-never-knew, so just count yourself back to sleep.* Ma kept talking and crying, and it made no sense to me, but even in my confusion there was a frosty shivering horror that come over me realizing Ma thought I could talk to my dead brother. She was a reckless drunk but she'd never been demented, beset with visions. There is a quiet terror that fills a child when they realize that their parent has gone over the edge and won't be clawing their way back up again.

I could have lied to her and made up a story and she'd have gone away. But I didn't even think to lie. I told Ma I could see him in the picture she was shoving in my face, that there was no ghostly business in my bedroom. The photo was moving in her trembling hand and it looked like his sweet eyes were shifting in the flickering light.

I waited for her to get right mad but she didn't. She shuffled off, crying and singing her lullaby. *Hush-a-bye, don't you cry.* It was quiet, not even the coyotes howling or the peepers singing, just Ma and her drunken lament. She knocked over a chair and broke a glass and she was swearing and howling again like all the world was lost to her. *Holy Mother Mercy*, I prayed, *Holy Mother Mercy and Dear Grampie come and save me.* Neither of them did.

It was hours I lay awake in that bed, even after she lurched off to her room, calling my name and John Lee's name and swearing at Grampie.

When dawn slipped golden in the window I was up and dressed and back on the lane to Petal's End. I put the kettle on and made tea and toast and was sitting at the table when Loretta came into the kitchen. She put her hand on my shoulder as she bustled by but I did not want to talk. Later in the day she found me asleep over my homework in the sitting room off the kitchen. I woke up when she came in.

"Was your mother on about anything?" That day Loretta held my eye, searching for what I knew.

"She came at me with a picture of John Lee in the middle of the night, babbling and singing and stuttering. She scared me. Ronnie wasn't there. She lied about that. I think she wants to know how John Lee died. Doesn't she already know?"

Loretta's face went flat. She sat down beside me and took my hand. "You don't pay any attention to her, Fancy. It was a mistake to let you go there. I'm sorry. Give me strength. There's just no place for a soft spot with Marilyn and I should have known better. I remember how she was back when I first met her, when John Lee was alive, and how different she was, such a sparkle to her. You have to understand. There was not a person she didn't captivate even if she irritated at the same time. This was the problem. Her beauty was unearthly, and beauty is a burden. I could hardly look at her then for the loveliness, just as I can hardly manage the wreck of it now. Headstrong and impatient with everybody but animals and children. Your grandfather had his hands full with her. Do you understand?"

Even only eleven I understood completely. The expression on my face was all Loretta needed to continue.

"Marilyn was just a child herself but she was such a good mother to John Lee. We all loved him so. She'd take him fishing in the canoe, just like she took you, over at Little Blue Lake. They were always down to the shore as well, collecting shells and seaweed on the dulse tide. When I first started working here she'd bring him into the kitchen, only four years of age but sociable and jolly, playing with the cat. John Lee would look at your mother with such adoring eyes and she'd look right back at him with a wink and he'd giggle so. He'd sit on my lap and I'd read him stories. His skin was soft as a butterfly's wing and smelled like spring violets. Marilyn would let me hold him as much as I wanted. I have never forgotten her kindness that way." Loretta closed her eyes and took her hand away from mine and covered her mouth with it, pushing the stories back inside.

There seemed no words I could speak to comfort Loretta but I was compelled to try. I cleared my throat, but her eyes popped open then, the grief swallowed back down for the time being.

"Well, there is nothing to be done, Fancy. She's back drinking. She hid it well this time, but now we know. Marilyn will die of the drink. She's already drowning in sin. Terrible things happened to her but she refuses any help. She has turned from the Lord. I'm sorry to tell you but it's the way it will be. We should not speak of John Lee. It's not right to speak of a dead child like she did." She squeezed my shoulder. She was satisfied Ma had not told me everything, and she didn't invite me to speak further of it.

Loretta enjoyed nothing more than stories about the good old days but she was never one for talking about the bad times. Until that summer she had always been private that way. She was sentimental about cooking and baking and sewing. She went out to her prayer group every week, talking about good deeds. She was true and loyal and ever steady.

❧

As we approached the village Art started singing some French song he learned from his father, *Demain s'il fait beau, j'irons au grand-père*. Normally his singing calmed me but right then those words brought me back to the car. He kept going and I got more and more anxious. The more he sang the more I thought of Grampie and his songs, and Ma and her strange lullabies. Loretta started discussing Marigold's favourite baked desserts in a very serious tone and finally I'd had enough. The endless stream of their ridiculous talk and the stink of carcass had contaminated any chance my birthday had of being salvaged.

"What was Ma talking about today being my twelfth birthday and Grampie having special powers?" I inquired from the back, my voice loud and angry. Art stopped singing.

Loretta didn't turn around. "We'll talk about that at home, Fancy. Not another word." She had never used such a threatening tone before. I didn't dare disobey.

We passed the village and a salty breeze was blowing in over the water as it came into the harbour at high tide. Lupin Cove was quiet and still most of the time, no bustle about, and if you didn't know schooners had once docked there long ago in the age of sail there was nothing to give you even a peek into that time. The village was faded, like it still is now, hardly anyone about, as though they'd all closed their doors and left one day, never to return, just as it was up at Petal's End. Only those who knew the history could picture it. The wind ruffled the water like lace at the edge of a bedsheet. There was a thin fog coming in with the tide, coming so quickly that when I looked up the island was gone.

We dropped Art off at home. "You take care of Yvette, Mister Man, and we'll see you tomorrow." Loretta gave him a wave.

Art looked at me but I closed my eyes and kept them shut. I didn't know who to trust any more. It was like they was all in on it. In the quiet of Lupin Cove my heart was a pounding drum, and the thoughts in my head fast charging, all them memories of Grampie painting, them people looking out of his portraits and on the walls of the Tea House, John Lee's cup sitting on the shelf. Did

Grampie ever hold that cup or sip out of it? I couldn't do as Loretta said and remember Ma when she was well for she was scarcely so while I was with her.

We drove up the road. Without lifting an eyelid I could feel the turn as my body rolled into the car door. I had no use for my eyes right then, just as I don't need them now to know you're still listening to me. Petal's End was home to me, as frightful as some folks thought the vast house was, way off on the mountain in the forest by the bay. Things smelled familiar. I thought of how I missed the Tea House, Grampie's fresh-baked bread, the sharp thick odour of his oil paints and turpentine, the scent of the wood stove in the winter. I felt sick to my stomach with longing. I pushed Grampie and our lives together out of my mind and sat in the back of the vintage Rolls-Royce, feeling the car moving through the imposing wrought-iron gates and by the huge chestnut trees in front of the stone walls like guards, driving over each and every bump of the long lane. Them raging words of Ma's scrambled in my ears, the foul valley air lodged in my nostrils. Finally we plunged into the deep piney woods Petal's End Road ran through. Off in the forest there were broken pieces of marble, statues that had long ago fallen over and broken. The pieces would glow white at dusk, as though they might pick themselves up and put themselves back together when the moon came out. Petal's End wasn't on no modern maps.

They built Petal's End back behind the forest and away from the water to keep it sheltered from the winter winds, but that didn't stop the fog from creeping out from the forest. It kept the world away, and that was how the Parkers liked it, especially after Charlie killed himself. They liked privacy for personal matters and publicity for public matters. Charles Parker VI. The newspaper called him "The Scion" when he died. Charlie Parker, as he was known to those of us at Petal's End. Charlie was a small man, fragile and reed thin, and he liked gardens and roses, dancing, and beautiful women and men. He was nothing but a disappointment to his big, strapping military father.

A long time ago the first Lord Parker had come across the water from the Old World. Petal's End was created—a thousand acres of forest and farmland, and even an island in the bay with massive four-hundred-foot vertical cliffs, part of the ancient basalt headlands. On an antique map of the estate hanging in the grand library it was marked Parker Island but it was only spoke of as *the island*. They had a lighthouse there and a family who kept the light and had a small farm on the island top. The Parkers went over for the occasional summer picnics and whale-watching trips. Lord Parker wasn't born a lord, as the story goes. His people made money and then he bought himself a title. By the time I was a child the Parker family was already fading into history and stories, and Petal's End was a mystery set back behind the woodland, the island a place where no one went, the lighthouse burned down and replaced by an automated one. The Parkers had another grand house in the city where they did most of their business. When the grandfather was grown and had become Colonel Parker, he went back to the Old World doing who knows what and he brought back Marigold, a young woman who liked dancing and singing and strolling in the gardens and spending her time with artists and at galas. The Colonel was much older than her and he wanted a proper wife. Marigold was built to last, he would say, pretty and dainty and durable just like fine bone china. Grampie said she was from a family of aristocrats with no money but an endless supply of prestige. Marigold didn't have any idea what she was getting into, coming across the ocean, but once she was here, she rose to the occasion and never went back.

As we drove into the estate I felt sick to my stomach and tried to conjure up soothing thoughts about my life at Petal's End. Loretta and I were accustomed to the quiet. In the winter Hector would come and plow out the lane, and we'd stay in the back part of the house with the wood stove going. On stormy days I'd read and write and stitch. Sometimes in the summer I'd creep into the big house and play the piano. Pomeline Parker, the Colonel's eldest granddaughter, had given me piano and singing lessons until they stopped coming out. The piano was kept in tune and it seemed that I should make an effort to play in case one day Pomeline did come back. There were times when I played and the air in the gardens would lift up and ripple and swirl, as though a fine lady had walked by with perfume, and a slight shiver would go up my spine and down my arms right into my fingertips that would be icy on the ivory. Fear shook me, and I forced myself to look, just as I had at Ma's that night, but it was only ever the breeze blowing the curtain, and the sun casting a shadow in from the beauty bush growing near the window. I remember laughing at how superstitious I was, just like Marigold and her hobgobblies.

The Colonel died when I was five, the year before his only child did. We think the Colonel got mauled by a bear. It was his own fault, having a bear as a pet. They said it was Marigold's fault. If she'd let him keep his raptor birds he wouldn't have had a need for playing with a bear. He had a wildcat too, not so big, and in tree branches it looked almost like a house cat. But it weren't no house cat. That was clear when it leapt down and chased a guest through the meadow, hissing and making an unearthly noise not like any normal meow. It came in a big crate off an airplane from somewhere far away. When the Colonel was found dead his throat was chewed and they never knew if the bear or the cat did it.

Charlie, the heir, he died playing with a rope. It was just the ladies left, Marigold and her daughter-in-law, Estelle, and the two granddaughters, Pomeline and Jenny. Pomeline was sent off to boarding school but she was home every summer. Jenny was home-schooled and they went through at least two teachers a year and not one would come to Petal's End. Most of what she learned was from her grandmother. Marigold had a stroke a few years after Charlie died. Loretta said the depression that blossomed in her after losing her only child caused it. It shocked her system, made everything constrict. After his death her hands were permanently clenched together and hung so low it seemed she had been forced to carry a stone about for the rest of her days. And so the family stopped coming.

Estelle had never come any more than she had to. She was a nurse a long time ago, and they say she married Charlie for his fortune, but when he died the whole lot went to his mother. Then she hated Petal's End and the country more than ever. Estelle kept thin with coffee and cigarettes. She had been pretty once upon a time, and her looks lived on in Pomeline.

They brought Marigold out once, in a wheelchair. It was like half of her face was stuck in a leer and the other half was stuck in anguish. Marigold seemed to shrink, the way the elderly do, getting shorter, like the earth itself in her precious garden had reached up one fine summer morning and curled fingers round her ankles and started tugging her down. Dainty don't always hold up to aging. Jenny and Pomeline and the doctor carted Marigold about, out in Evermore, and she looked around, smirking at half of it, raging at the other.

The bumpy lane, the thought of the Parkers and their tragedies, my birthday ruined—the entirety of the day made the bile rise in my throat and I gagged. In a daze, I heard Loretta tell Hector to stop. He slammed on the brakes and my stomach lurched as I pushed the door open and threw up all over the wildflowers growing at the edge of the forest by the road, the bitterness spewing forth. Sweat dripping down my temples and Loretta rubbing my back. Exhaust fumes made me throw up again and Loretta told Hector to shut the engine off. All went quiet except for a draught that came right up and tickled the leaves. My hands went clammy. A bird called out, a red bird, its trill long and clear, and Loretta and I both watched it fly down and perch on a low branch gazing at us.

"It's Grampie," I said. Loretta's eyes got great big and she said I was exhausted by the horrible shock to my system with Ma coming by. The bird sat on the branch and sang. Loretta shooed it but it took no notice of her. A surge of great hurt flooded over me. Was it Grampie in the bird? I do not know, but it sang out once more and flew down the lane, as though we were to follow, as though there was no turning back. I wiped my mouth on the hankie Loretta passed me and pulled the car door closed.

We came out of the lane in sight of the house and the stark sunlight made me squint. There was a row of laburnum trees off to the south, just starting to bloom and hang with their poisonous golden chain blossoms—we were not allowed to climb those trees. I fixed my eyes on the yellow flowers as the vehicles from the Briar Patch headed out in a convoy. The Parkers had hired the garden centre to do all the gardening and lawn mowing. They came five days a week in their trucks and vans, wearing their uniforms and hats and tool belts, waving and smiling but never making much chitchat, maybe warned to keep to themselves and ask no questions. Art was the only one who spent much time with them. The Happy Helpers came as well, a cleaning service, with two vanloads of girls in uniforms, whispering to themselves, biting their tongues. They'd been warned too, it seemed. They also came five days a week, as though the Parkers were in full-time residence, when really it was just a big empty house and sprawling grounds, waiting for a party that never started, for guests that never arrived, a family who was missing.

Hector parked at the carriage house. He ran around but Loretta was already getting out. He held the door for me. "Miss Fancy Mosher," he said, holding out his hand. I put my hand in his and as he pulled me out he gave me a tight squeeze. "Don't you worry. You forget about your Ma. You're a big girl now."

Loretta nodded at Hector. "Thank you, Hector. You are helpful in an emergency, I'll say that. Fancy, you need to relax. Come along to the house. We'll have some birthday cake and lemonade later. Hector, make sure you put the car back, and don't go disappearing. There's cookies and I will put on some tea, if you want, and you can come help yourself."

"Well that's awful kindly of you, Loretta, but I'd be happy with cold water. My father never takes a glass of water. 'Did you ever see what water can do to a nail?' he says. 'What it can do to steel? Rot your gut. I wouldn't put water in me if you paid me, unless it's diluted with a shot of bourbon.' He swears if the well runs dry he won't have a new one dug. Nothing I like more than drinking down a big tall glass of water in front of my father. Makes him shudder." Hector snorted as he shut the door to Old Rolly.

"Good enough then, Hector. Just come to the kitchen if you want a drink."

"I have a few things to do but I may come by later. Now you all go and have a quiet afternoon. It's just too damn busy down there in the valley, and it reeks. He should know better, transporting dead animals like that, uncovered and all. It's against the law. Must have been on his way to the incinerator. I don't know why he just didn't burn them on his farm or bury them. Kind of disturbing, ain't it, seeing that. Nothing like the fresh air to clear that out of your system. Sniff a few flowers. Don't let any of it bother you, Fancy."

"Too late for that," I mumbled under my breath. I started walking back to the house.

Hector let out a low whistle and starting crooning. "Fancy's looking all grown up, not like no twelve-year-old. She don't talk nor walk like one neither, oh no she don't!"

That got Loretta's ear pricked right up. "Lord, give me strength. Hector, how rude. She's still a child I'll have you remember."

I went in through the kitchen door at the back of the house, Loretta close behind me. "Fancy, you pay no attention to Hector.

Don't encourage him. He's a fine worker but he likes the girls. At least he's pleasant, not like his father. That man would rather impale himself upon a pitchfork than say a pleasant word. I never understood why all the girls were crazy for Clyde. There's more to a man than looks. There's kindness, but that can be just as deceptive. Listen to me go on. I don't know what's come over me today." Loretta set her purse down and reached for her apron.

The air in the kitchen was a tonic. Big thick walls and the deep-set windows kept the heat of the day outside. I heard the clock ticking. I said nothing, just got myself a glass of milk. I wasn't going to rattle on and pretend nothing had happened. Worse, I feared I would start screaming and never stop if I even opened my mouth. Loretta was fussing, retying her apron, fiddling with lists on the bulletin board. In the rear of the house there was a housekeeper's sitting room, and a corridor leading to a staff living room and bedroom and bathroom, and a flight of stairs that went up to the long hall where the servants' quarters once were. All those rooms were empty now except for the room I had. The house was a maze of staircases and halls, corridors so the staff could move without being seen, all of it connecting. It was easy to get lost, and the only ones who knew it well now were the children, me and Art and Jenny and Pomeline. We used to play hide-and-seek in the house while Marigold napped. It was easy to hide from grown-ups in such a big house.

I stomped upstairs. I took my shoes off and the hardwood was cool on my feet. Then I sat on my bed, which was as old as the house itself. For a second I considered running back down and through the mansion to the front door to look in the mirror there but I was too tired and angry to move. Creaks and groans threaded through the stillness. I could always tell who was coming down the halls at Petal's End. Everyone had their own way of walking, and the floor had a special squeak for them all. Loretta made a lot of noise coming up the stairs, her thick body pressing down on the floorboards, bracing herself on the walls, clomping down the hall. She knocked on my door. I said nothing. The knob turned. Loretta stood there with an ice pack.

"Fancy, I'm sorry. I know you are angry. You should soak your feet. And put this on your scar."

I slapped the floor with my feet so hard it made them sting and I crossed my arms with as much force as I could muster.

"We were trying to protect you. I understand you're upset."

"What was Ma talking about? First the awful ranting in the night and now this? Why won't you tell me, Loretta? It ain't right to hide the truth. That's what you always told me, but you're a hypocrite." I spoke to my dirty toenails at first, and when I raised my eyes she didn't look away. Outside the window I saw Evermore, calling me out to where I could sit quietly within those stone garden walls.

Loretta came and sat beside me, the bed sagging underneath her. She passed me the ice pack as she surveyed the bed. "Let's hope I don't break it. It's been here for years and I suppose it can take the weight of old Loretta, don't you think?" She took my sweating hand in her cool ones. "It's true about your grandfather . . . he did believe what your Ma said. And all who came to see him believed it. What you believe is true, that's what I think now, although I didn't back when I was young. I suppose it was inevitable it would come out."

"Do you believe it?"

"It's not for me to believe or not. I know your grandfather saw what he said. But then the artist sees many things we cannot."

"Why didn't he tell me? I still don't understand."

"He didn't want to frighten you. Samuel never even talked to me about it, not directly. He would say he had to go tend to his business. He helped people is what he did. He knew all the shades of sorrow, he said, but then, that's a part of life, isn't it? That's all I know."

But Loretta did know more, and suddenly she couldn't seem to stop talking, trying to make sense of it all, as much for herself as for me. "Fancy, it's hard to explain to someone who has never lived through a war, the way it changes people. We were in solemn times with news of people dying every single day. The soldiers were in a sea of death. Your grandfather came back a changed man. He felt such shame for leaving your grandmother in the first place. She was crippled up early in life with the arthritis that came over her when your mother was a girl. It's why they never had another child. You know that."

I did know that. My grandmother was so crippled up she could hardly walk or use her hands by the end. Ma had cared for my grandmother while Grampie was at war and worked at Petal's End at the same time. She was only a teenager taking all that on. But I didn't want to tell Loretta what I did and did not know.

Loretta was looking at the wall now, seeing a story written there only she could read. "We have to remember the past in a frame of compassion or we end up in misery. Even at Petal's End life became simple for a time during the war, so they said. I didn't start working here until after it was all over, and things had gone back to extravagance. I was raised plain, as I think you know a bit about. Marigold was making up for what she saw as the lost years now the Colonel was back from the war too. They were having a disastrous time finding help. All kinds were moving to the city for work. I'd had some . . . difficulties."

Everyone knew she gave her baby away, even if no one talked of it.

"Your grandfather was acquainted with some people down in the valley who understood my situation. He knew people all over, from his paintings. He made the arrangements with Marigold. Your grandfather picked me up in his truck and drove me up from the valley. It was a beautiful summer day, much like today. There were so many people scurrying about and they got me settled. I was hulling strawberries when Marigold came into the kitchen to meet me. Mr. Long and his scowl were at her side, and she had little Charlie by the hand. He was four years old, same age as your brother.

"Then Marigold spoke to me in front of all the servants in the kitchen. She told me part of my duties would be to assist with Charlie, and that I did the right thing for a girl who finds herself in such a situation. 'There are good married people who cannot have children who are able to provide the most suitable environment. Others could learn from your selflessness,' she said. Words left me, if you can comprehend it."

Loretta's face flushed and she still kept avoiding my eyes, which I was grateful for.

"And before I could burst into tears, who else but your mother sashayed into the kitchen from the pantry where she was gutting a fish. And in her loud voice Marilyn called out, 'Why, has anyone seen John Lee? He must be out in the garden. I brought him over to play with Charlie, as you asked, Mrs. Parker.' She was holding a big bloody knife with that look she had, you know the one, Fancy. Charlie waved at her and she winked back. And off Marilyn sauntered. There were a few titters, and Mr. Long's brow got so low we could hardly see his eyes. To this day I remember that horrid silence. Then Marigold left without continuing to embarrass me. You see, your mother did the work of three girls, and they could ill afford to let her go. She was indispensable. And your mother, being who she is, took full advantage.

"There was a girl who worked here at the time. She is long since dead from a lung ailment. She gave me a tour of the gardens when I arrived and she told me how a few years after the war ended was when your mother found herself in her predicament."

Loretta looked down at her hands as though she would weep and my anger sagged. She kept talking, paying some kind of debt to me with her revelations. "Your mother never showed me much patience, Fancy, but she was the only one who understood how hard it was for me. We needed jobs and you'll put up with a lot when you have to. People like Marigold can't help themselves. I've come to see this. Marigold thought she was being benevolent. She paid for your grandmother's funeral. And your grandfather's. She felt she was generous taking me in and letting me work and live here all these years."

"I know what Marigold is like," I whispered.

Loretta took my hand in hers. "I know you do, Fancy. I'm telling you all of this so you'll appreciate that when you came along your grandfather was determined to make sure you were cared for, and that you were sheltered as much as you could be, just as he did with me. When you had the car accident he felt like he'd failed, and when you went to live with him at the Tea House he wanted things to be simple and light." Loretta was swinging her feet like a girl. She patted my hand. "But Fancy, it wasn't for discussing with a child, what your mother was going on about today. People understood he had a special way. He called it a little family memento, and he had us promise not to speak to you of it."

"That's the problem with you adults, not ever talking about nothing when it needs talking about, keeping all these stories secret. And what about me? Being the twelfth-born?"

"It's just a story, Fancy. Your Grampie wanted to protect you."

"Well don't you think he should have told me? What if I was walking along and all of a sudden somebody comes crawling out of the ground? What if some ghost grabs me and throttles me? Ma keeps going on about John Lee. What if he's some angry demon child out to get her? Ma talks like he's all mad, like she's afraid, that she's got to make amends with him before she dies or he's gonna get her good."

"Don't go talking about demons."

"Well, Marigold will be here soon talking about the hobgobblies. Maybe she sees stuff too. Maybe there are hobgobblies roaming around."

Loretta took in a deep breath and blew it out slowly, as though she was thinking of the right words. "Your grandfather did the best he could, that's all there is to this, Fancy. He should have told you earlier. I should have. But we didn't. I suppose we thought your mother would just let it go as she got older, that Ronnie would help her. But we were wrong. She can't let go of John Lee dying young. When you lose a child you spend the rest of your life hearing their voice and seeing glimpses of them around every corner."

"How did he die? No one ever talks about that."

"You know he drowned down on the beach. It's why she finds the ocean unsettling. Your mother wasn't paying attention. She'd quit Petal's End by then and she was running wild. Oh my, your hands have gone stone cold, Fancy."

They had. I was shivering, too, in the warm summer air. My stomach felt queasy again. "People are going to think I'm crazy like Ma."

"No one knows the family story of the twelfth-born, just your mother and me. Oh, there have been rumours, but as the older people have passed away so have the speculations. Ronnie doesn't believe any of it. He thinks your grandfather is to blame for all your mother's problems. He might be right, to a point. There's no perfect parent."

There wasn't nothing to argue there, for right then it seemed to me Grampie should have done a lot of things different. At least Loretta wasn't pretending otherwise. Her forehead had creases I'd never noticed before, and the crow's feet by her eyes seemed to have deepened.

"Marigold came to visit your grandfather when Charlie died and he gave her a painting. Your mother held that against your grandfather, one more item on her list of grievances. He wouldn't see Marigold when she wanted to go back for a second visit. He wouldn't tell me why, but they had made the arrangement you could come here. Marigold seemed indebted to your grandfather. Many people feel that way. People assume when your grandfather died his memento went with him."

I wondered what she wasn't telling me.

"Your mother is trying to change the past, and how can you blame her? But no one can do that, not your grandfather, no one. As your grandfather said, sometimes those who pass on need to be left in peace."

Loretta stood up and went to the doorway. "I'm making you a ham dinner for your birthday. Your favourite. It's in the oven now. You'll surely feel better after that. Strawberry shortcake for dessert with whipped cream. Just relax until supper. You're only just twelve, Fancy. You are not your mother or your grandfather. Life goes quick enough. You'll have fun helping out this summer, you and Art. "

"Grampie has John Lee's cup, the one Ma was talking about. It's in the Tea House. I saw it there on the shelf. Maybe he talked to John Lee."

Loretta turned and looked at me. "You need to let well enough alone. Do you understand me?" She shook her head and went down the hall, the stairs squeaking as she descended. At last it was quiet again, only the far-off birds sang, the smell of early summer hay caught up in the wind blowing south over the mountain fields.

I followed Loretta down into the kitchen a while later. She was hulling strawberries, and the aroma of baking ham basted in maple syrup filled the kitchen.

"Go get some fresh air, Fancy. Your days of going barefoot will be over soon enough. Have fun with Art. He's a special one. He's a good man," she said.

Even in my bad mood I laughed at that. "He's just a boy, Loretta."

"Oh, he might have a high squeaky voice but he's got a sense of right and wrong. Art knows when to step up, that's all I know. It's not how you speak that makes a man, Fancy. You best learn that."

She pointed with her knife toward the table to a white envelope with my name on it, *Fancy Mosher*, in Grampie's perfect penmanship in black ink. "That's for you. I should have given it to you earlier. I wasn't even going to give it to you for it might just make you more confused. But it would be wrong to conceal it. Your Grampie wanted you to have it when you were twelve. He wanted to tell you himself, my dear. I wish he had told me more. I'll call you when supper's ready. These onions are bothering my eyes." She was still hulling strawberries but I didn't point that out to her.

I clutched the letter to my chest as I went barefoot over the walking path to the walled garden. It had just been worked on by the Briar Patch people, the grass trimmed up neat. I pulled the door to Evermore open and closed it behind me and turned around. It was a different world in here, dense and lush, the high stone walls sealing the garden off like it was a kingdom unto itself. And if there was a Princess of Evermore it was Jenny, but she was in exile in the city.

I ran as fast as I could over the path, by the Water House where Marigold made her flower water and herbal remedies so long ago, by the kitchen and herb gardens, the cutting gardens, the rose gardens, the gazebo where Marigold once danced with her son. For a moment I was afraid I'd see Mr. Charlie dancing there, blue in the face, his arms dangling, dancing to music only he could hear. But there wasn't no one there. Evermore stretched on for five acres, with formal gardens and statues as well as groves of trees and pathways, secret tangled corners and nooks. It was easy to get lost there, or to hide. I kept going, past the big fountain gurgling away, by the huge hedge labyrinth the Colonel had put in for Marigold when they got married, by the lily pond where Jenny's swans were paddling along, the empty chairs on the deck of Margiold's Atelier where no one sat any more, and along the path at the far west end of the walled garden to the tall cedar bushes growing in an oval surrounding the Wishing Pool. To the southeast was the path leading to the Parker Family Cemetery, where tombstones stood with curious carvings, the weeping willows and their cascading branches, the hand and fingers with one pointing up: "Gone Home," the chiselled letters said. The only new stone was the one for Mr. Charlie, made of red granite. There was the no fear in me of a graveyard since it didn't seem the dead who found the Moshers spent much time in the regular places where phantoms lurked. They was teatime spectres, and the thing to avoid was cups, I told myself as I kept going, slipping in through the cedar hedges to the small Wishing Pool at the centre where goldfish swam.

There was a marble bench inside the cedar enclosure, with flowering dogwoods on either side. I sat there, crying finally. The sun was softer in the late afternoon and it sparkled on the polished gemstone border that encircled the pool. That was Charlie Parker's passion as a child, gathering up the jasper and agate and amethyst and quartz from the beach, polishing them and placing them by the Wishing Pool. You could pick one up and make a wish and throw it in. When he died Marigold had some of them scattered on his grave.

I opened my letter. The paper was smooth and unfolded without a sound.

Dear Fancy,

If you're reading this then I have passed on and Loretta has given you my note because you have turned twelve. We all pass on, Fancy. Do not be sorrowful. But not everyone who turns twelve will have your experience. You are a twelfth-born Mosher. I suspect you knew I did not take tea alone and that my paintings were not simply from my imagination, although we Moshers do have fine imaginations. If you look back now perhaps it will make more sense. I do not know if you'll have this family memento. I tried to protect you as best I could. If it has come to you, the only way you will know is if you believe. And perhaps you will not. But if you do there will be a visitation.

It's never the same in any of us, so the story has gone in the family. They found me through a teacup. I only saw them across a table after they were gone a short time. My grandfather, he needed their shoes, and he'd walk at low tide and draw their words in the sand, and he only saw them a long while after their time of parting. How it will be for you I am not sure. Perhaps you will never know. But there was that day not long ago when I sensed a stirring in you. You saw something in the maple trees, I am sure of it. But here's the thing. The dead will find you, if they want you and you want them. And if they come, they come for truth.

Your mother is a broken woman and does not understand. One does not go calling to the dead, for even if you could call them, sometimes the dead do not come back to forgive. She will ask you to do something and you must not. There are some secrets that best remain untold.

It's a quiet night as I sit writing this. I can hear your breathing up in the loft. Jake is restless. The moon is small and high as a night bird flies across the dark western sky. The night bloomers are strong this evening and the wisteria is almost growing through the open window. Live your life well among the living, Fancy Mosher, for that shapes the life you will have among the dead.

Remember that I love you. Remember what I have taught you, for you have already learned so much if only you will remember.

Grampie

A big fat fish jumped up into the air and the sun glimmered on its golden body. It fell with a splash and I stood up, startled, the letter falling down on the polished stones. I didn't know what Grampie taught me except for gardening and the names of trees and flowers and making my bed tidy. How could I remember what I didn't know? He taught me how to call the birds. How to keep the house. How to read and write. How to sing. How to be still. They'd all played a terrible trick on me. Ma bringing me into the world to fix her mistake, and Grampie for not telling me none of this when he was alive. Loretta, for helping him keep the secret. But it wasn't even that clear-cut, which made it all the worse. I had a gift, what my mother and grandfather referred to as a memento, like it was something collected on a horrible holiday a long time ago. Whatever happened to my first-born brother, which only my Grampie and Ma seemed to know, and concealed from me.

The water in the Wishing Pool settled. Would Grampie appear in the water and tell me what to do? The Mosher eyes staring up at me were my own. I grabbed handfuls of the small gemstones and starting throwing them in, handful after handful bashing the water, getting more and more angry and yelling until my throat hurt and I lost my balance and fell right into the Wishing Pool. There I sat, quiet and wet, like some horrid little statue.

4.
The Tea House

When I came out of the garden Loretta had my birthday supper set on the verandah off the back of the house. She'd gone and made the table pretty with a lace cloth and a vase of flowers and a basket of fresh-baked rolls wrapped in white linen. She had china plates and what she called sassy lemonade, lemonade with strawberry syrup served up in pink Depression glass. My hate was skulking away, and trying to haul it back was wearing me out. Plus the idea of chucking questions at her when she didn't want to talk made me feel ashamed. Loretta had told me more in one afternoon than in all the time I'd known her. If I pushed she might fall apart and that made me nervous, for she was all I had holding things together. She didn't even ask me why I was wet. "Don't drip on the floor, dear," was all she said, and she went back to smashing berries and whipping cream for my cake. For now we could carry on like I'd never found out about my apparent kinship with the deceased, or, as it seemed, their affinity for me.

I went up to my room and put the letter on my bed. In the bathroom I dried off and braided my hair. I came back downstairs in a smocked sundress. Loretta was waiting, relieved to see me tidied and proper. It was the time when day and night come together, when the light is soft and you can catch a glimpse of the young in the elderly. The evening glow blurred the revelations—the memento, and what I had read in the letter, none of it seemed real.

We made what Grampie always called idle natter as we ate supper. It was best that way for Loretta now looked pained, as though the delicious ham was giving her cramps. She needed a good sleep, she said, we both did. Where we sat we could see the grey flagstone walk leading around the corner of the house to the Annex, the northwest part of the house, the part they closed up after Charlie died. Grampie and Loretta remembered when it was used as a convalescent hospital long ago, during the war. They were overcrowded in the hospitals all over. The Colonel offered the Annex, as it hadn't been in regular use for decades, not since before the other big war, when Lupin Cove was still a bustling place of importance. It found new life as a place for the war-weary to take respite and relief. Some of them were restored, some stayed crazy, and others died and were taken away in a long black hearse.

Colonel Parker said it was the least he could do for the men. I guess it was from feeling guilty about whatever it was he did in the war. Of course he got some big tax break and they put up a huge statue of him down in the valley at the hospital and that statue is there to this day, although no one aside from me and the historians much remembers him no more. Nothing about him seemed like a warrior, more like a businessman, but he loved his parades and his uniform. When his mind started to go it was all he would wear as he marched about tending to his matters of consequence. The stories we heard about the Colonel and his war only made mention of chemicals, some factories, things made for the war, for the killing.

Grampie said the soldiers' souls were in a state of fatigue after what they had seen. He would visit at teatime during the week, and for some he made paintings, grisly paintings with crazy eyes, which he never gave them. I'd always wondered about those paintings, and as Loretta and I celebrated my birthday with a quiet ham dinner, all the stories Grampie told me, the things I had seen in my young life, all was taking on new meaning. I always thought he had listened to their stories and then gone back to the Tea House to draw out what they described to him, the artistic inspiration, if you will. But as I chewed on my fresh-baked roll and drank my strawberry lemonade, it was clear it was another thing entirely.

It was supposed to be temporary, the Annex being a convalescent home, but after the war they brought them back every summer. It was more a holiday home for soldiers who never got better, the fresh shore air and its healing properties. Marigold made them all participate in a choir and they'd perform at the garden party, standing there on the gazebo singing like dippy old dogs. People referred to it as the Invalid Choir, and they were known for ballads and hymns. She would also take them to the Atelier in the walled garden and teach them still-life drawing. It kept Marigold busy. Charlie said the reason his father had the men there so long was for this exact reason.

They finally stopped coming near the time Jenny was born. Estelle didn't seem to worry at all when Pomeline was a child, nor did Marigold. Sometimes you would find young Pomeline, with her golden curls and her pretty dress, holding the hand of a stricken time-worn man as she guided him through Evermore, looking at the fountains and the statues. The small staff still at Petal's End was the ones who looked out for Pomeline. Charlie was barely around then, off on travels with his friends, avoiding his wife and his mother. Estelle would just lounge around in a lawn chair with a book and a drink and a cigarette, and Pomeline could do as she pleased. When Charlie was at the estate he would usually find

Pomeline off in the garden or lost in the house crying, and he'd fight with Estelle about it.

When Jenny was born it was a different story. Estelle had a bad womb is what people said. Jenny was her miracle baby after all the lost ones. They all thought Estelle would prefer Pomeline, with her beauty and her music, but it was like it all got reversed. It seemed in Estelle's mind Jenny had all of Pomeline's graces, and Pomeline, she had all of Jenny's jagged personality and sickly pall. Estelle had complained about the soldiers and finally Charlie had taken her side, telling Marigold it wasn't safe with young children. He knew the men were harmless but it was disturbing for youngsters. It wasn't healthy. Estelle had her way, even though she was a nurse who was supposed to have compassion. That's how she had come to Petal's End, working as a nurse in the Annex hospital.

Loretta went into the house to get my cake. I never liked a birthday party and that was just as well considering we had almost no one to invite. I waited for her to come back out, fixing my gaze on a smattering of starlings collecting in the sky.

We weren't ever, ever supposed to go in the Annex. Even Grampie had told me never to set foot. That was on account of the one time we did go and the horror we found in the far room. When they closed the wing up after the sick soldiers stopped coming for the restorative country air, they locked the door and left it. They had no need for that much space and it was easy for the Parkers and everyone else to forget about it. Except for us kids, of course. Especially Jenny. And so that summer day came when Art and I went sneaking in the door. There was a painting of a landscape, all mists and blues, with a key hidden behind it, but we didn't need that for the door was open a crack. That was what called us in. We crept down that long hall past all the cobwebs that were out of reach. There was a whirring sound, getting louder and louder as we went down. There was closed doors on either side of the hall and we opened them up one by one. The noise was coming from the last room, the patient salon that had once been a spacious drawing room. The door was open. There was a sudden scream and then a piercing wail. We peeked in. The curtains were pulled and the light was dim. A fan whirred, circulating a horrific odour. Marigold was restraining Jenny and Charlie was swinging from the chandelier, his toes just grazing the floor. His face was purple.

Photographs were spread out on a nearby table like a deck of cards, as though Charlie had been playing a game of solitaire or blackjack with ghosts, drinking wine from a crystal glass. We ran in thinking we could do something but there was nothing to do except cry. Marigold backed up, hauling Jenny with her, and she crashed into the table. Nothing shatters as spectacular as a quality crystal glass. I was silent, a dark horrible shudder crawling up my limbs. Then there was a parade of adults coming in and hauling us away, Estelle righting the table, picking up the larger pieces of glass and the mess on the floor, screeching as though she had lost her senses, clasping all of those photos like they was the most important thing in the world, barely noticing the children.

When I was a small child we'd tell ghost stories on the beach by the bonfire. I knew many from my mother, from the fishermen in the village. We'd tell stories of the pirates who'd roamed the bay, the pirate who'd left the beheaded sailor behind over on the island. We didn't share as many ghost stories after Charlie died. Estelle wanted to tear the Annex off the house but Marigold refused. It seemed odd that she wanted to keep such an awful memory alive in there, but eventually I understood that she wanted Estelle to remember, never to move on. The door stayed locked, the Annex shut up, locking in its memories and ghosts. It was the place we was not to go, the long dusty wing, the last place Charlie Parker ever saw.

I sat at the table, transfixed by the Annex. What if Charlie was in there waiting for me to come see him? I couldn't ask Loretta about that. There was only one time later that anyone ever spoke of the Annex. Marigold had come into the kitchen to discuss the menu for a dinner party with very important people. Estelle come in behind her. Loretta turned to the cupboard and I just kept washing the dishes. They were fighting over the Annex. The argument went as it always did between them two no matter what they were quarrelling over, with Marigold's voice ice-thin and Estelle blowing and thundering. She started hollering that Marigold should let that godforsaken mausoleum be torn down. Marigold slapped Estelle and said it might be the place Charlie died but it was also the place he and Estelle had fallen in love. "You should show more respect, you gold-digging opportunist." That's what she called her, and it shut Estelle up for a long time. The Annex remained, vacant and avoided.

Loretta came out with strawberry shortcake and a sparkler flaring in the middle. She normally just sang hymns and she approached "Happy Birthday" as though it were a selection from her hymnal. "Here's to a hopeful year, Fancy," she said. We ate and Loretta chit-chatted about making jams and picking berries, and her plans for the summer and how charming the gardens looked. She didn't ask me about the letter and she didn't eat her cake. We brought in the plates and she said I could go entertain myself while she finished cleaning up the kitchen.

In my room, I put the letter in my backpack, tucking a flashlight in there as well.

I went back into Evermore when the shadows were starting to fall. Vesper bats were just taking to the sky. Summer days trick you into forgetting night is coming. I walked through the garden to the east wall back by the gazebo. The forest pressed in on that door, and the only opening in the dense brush was the narrow trail to the Tea House. This had been the path for the woodcutter years before, and then we Moshers had used it. It was much darker in the woods. Soon Loretta would come out to call me in for bedtime so I planned to be quick.

I'd been on that trail hundreds of times and could travel it with my eyes shut. It was quiet except for the flutter of the tree birds I was disturbing. Or the slumber of the wood spirits, for I was in such a state of sorrow and resentment it was sure to disturb them as they sang their twilight lullabies. When Art and I was little we made up a story of creatures living in the woodland. They weren't people or animals, nor ghosts. If you came into that ancient woodland crying or breathing hard or stomping they'd see you, and you'd hear them if you listened proper. It was their breath that rustled the leaves, not the wind. And it wasn't no proper rustle but the branches and foliage babbling, a susurration, as Grampie described it. We was sure the forest air held their moist breath, scented with emerald moss and dewdrops.

Far off I heard a coyote call. I went fast and smooth toward the opening in the forest ahead. I pushed aside the branches and there was the Tea House. The property had grown wild the last three years. Loretta never told me I couldn't come here, and I did a few times, coming only to the edge of the woods, looking at our quaint house and the forlorn gardens. But it hurt too much to step out, and I'd turn and run back to Petal's End. It was just a place of memories, and it was easier to leave them there undisturbed rather than carry them with me. But that night I swear I heard the house calling as I went along on the soft floor of pine needles and plush mosses.

I knew Grampie and John Lee's cups must be in there. Loretta said the house was boarded up to keep Ma out. On my birthday I was thinking Loretta had misspoke—it was for keeping me out. Grampie's clothes were gone, I knew because I'd helped pack them. There would be no shoes I could slip on and take down to the beach and see if I was that kind of Mosher.

I took a step forward, back into that world, into the high grass, and another step, looking for Grampie's gardens, now tangled with flowers and weeds, the lawn now a meadow. Grampie pastured sheep and goats so we never mowed an inch, but those animals were long gone. Now I was wading through the grass and hay, the tall red clover and buttercups and blue columbine. His pickup truck was rusty and abandoned, weeds growing right up through the stick shift. But the grasses was much lower near the house, like they was afraid to grow too close, and I went around to the front verandah. I saw Grampie's bird feeders, paint peeling off, empty. There was wild roses along the side and the old peony garden he planted for my grandmother when they were first married. He called the peony the fairy blossom for sprites and said such beings was drawn to it. A flower, Grampie had told me, is the easiest thing to underestimate. *The peony, for instance, its leaves are thin and long, and the bud is an insignificant hard ball covered in green with ants crawling on it, and then it bursts forward into splendour. The peony can live for over a century, but who would know that, looking at the fragile petals? The peony blooms for itself. You move it and it refuses to bloom out of spite and will bloom again when it suits. But a peony always brings good luck, even if it begrudges.* The peony garden he planted in Evermore blooms still. Roses, Grampie said, are a different creature. *They need us. The more you cut, the more they bloom. A rose tended blooms for decades. The peony needs only the affection of the sun and the butterflies.*

I could hear Grampie then, in my heart, slow voice singing to the granddaughter who come to the old man like a stunted peony. *Hear the wind blow, love, hear the wind blow.* Our rocking chairs were gone so I sat down on the verandah floor. In those last days when he was sick I sat out there alone, within calling distance in case Grampie needed me, reading my books while I hummed and whistled, *Angels are coming to watch over thee, so listen to the wind coming over the sea.* Grampie wanted water from time to time, or for me to read him a letter or a book. And sometimes he'd ask me to sing. He had been dead three years but it was like Grampie had gone away on a trip for he was still sharp in my mind. Those were the best years, those six ones with Grampie.

What I grew up knowing about my brother John Lee wasn't much. It was from the snippets Grampie had told me, for Ma rarely said his name in my presence. In the house right off the front door there was an old-fashioned parlour where Grampie would receive his customers when they come about paintings. This was where Grampie and I would sit on Sunday afternoons. It was also the room where my grandmother's body was laid out, and then finally Grampie himself. And John Lee. It was both the death room and the living room. Grampie was from the old world and he had no use for funeral homes or embalming. He kept some framed photos on a small table in the parlour. There was one of John Lee with my mother, holding hands on the beach. In a cherrywood frame was a picture of me as a baby sitting on Ma's lap in a rocking chair. Grampie said having me brought her youth back for a time. From that picture you would never think she was forty-five. And you would never think that adoring smile was not for me but for herself, finally having a twelfth-born child.

One Sunday when we'd been sitting in the parlour reading, my grandfather had looked at Ma's photos. She'd come by drunk the night before and I'd heard them arguing, then the door slamming. She was on his mind that whole morning and he couldn't take his eyes from her in the pictures. "Remember your mother like that, Fancy. Remember her laughing. She loved her children, although she was not fit to raise them after John Lee. I always thought of Marilyn as a lake that had no still water. It was a marvel she could sit for so long and stitch. Before your grandmother's hands were twisted by the arthritis she played the fiddle and tried to teach your mother. She stopped for fear your mother would fling the fiddle across the room."

The fiddle was in a case on the shelf and no one played it after my grandmother passed on. Grampie looked at the case for a spell before he continued. "Marilyn was best when she was occupied doing things that spoke to her. The house used to be full of her cooking and singing. And she'd make sketches for her embroideries. I always wondered where she got her ideas for she was never still long enough to study or contemplate her surroundings. But she just absorbed it. It was your mother who was always filling the bird feeders and whistling their calls.

"We should never have let her keep working at Petal's End when I came back from the war but we were not thinking clearly at that time. Too much fell to your grandmother and your mother. But your grandmother felt Marilyn was too cooped up here in this cottage. She said Marilyn was afraid of me when I first come back, that she was frightened to be in the room with me for the look on my face when I thought no one was watching. We let her keep working there, but it was a mistake. Your grandmother blamed herself that Marilyn ended up with the baby. We welcomed the child. Your mother would never answer any questions and we knew better than to even ask. We'd never seen her happier."

I could hear the silken leaves outside as they rubbed together. "We wept when his small body was brought here and laid out in the quiet of this room. I did not expect you, Fancy Mosher, as you came so late." Grampie closed his eyes and eventually stood up and went to the verandah to smoke his pipe.

The last summer Grampie was alive I was out there on that verandah one afternoon while he was sleeping when a fragile, aged man come around. It was late August and the cicadas were screeching as the day drew in. I'd been finishing an embroidery that I'd been working on all week, a picture of Grampie napping on the sofa because that was all he'd been doing. I took the embroidery inside and put it in my bedroom, grabbing a book from the shelf, and returned outside. And there he was, this man. Lots of people come by to see Grampie and for portraits—it wasn't unusual to have someone in the yard. But this one didn't say a word, wouldn't come out of the shadow of the grand sugar maples. My book was almost finished, a story about orphan children living alone near a mountain they called Old Joshua, gathering herbs and flowers. There was a rustle so I looked back at the man, who I then saw had dark smudges under his eyes and looked bent out of shape.

"Hello," I rang out, and he stepped far back into the heavy shade. It was blistering hot. It was clear to me he was embarrassed. Some people didn't want anyone knowing they were coming to the Tea House and they'd only come at night.

Grampie come out then. He was bent over, his hand on the door frame.

I pointed. "Must be looking for a picture . . . probably don't want to disturb you, Grampie. Folks know you're not feeling well."

Grampie looked at me and out into the yard at the tree and then back at me. He braced himself as a big hacking cough erupted from his mouth. I went over to him with my glass of water and he took a sip and spit it out. Jake started barking in the house. "I see, Fancy," Grampie said, and went back inside. I searched the whole yard but the man had gone off. They did that more often than not.

Grampie was resting in the parlour and I told him the man had left but I expected he would come back. Grampie nodded without opening his eyes. "No doubt he will return if you saw him. You're a good girl, Fancy," he said. "You don't scare easy and nor should you."

The next week we were inside around the same time of day and Jake started barking and panting out front. I went out and that same man had come by. His head was turned in my direction but the shade was so thick he was hard to decipher. Grampie came out quickly when I called for him but hurrying made his cough bad. He tended to the dog, patting Jake. Grampie said the dog was getting delusional with old age. "Oh yes," he said, "it gets to some dogs like it gets to some people." If you spoke to him and stroked him Jake would settle right down. It was being alone he didn't like. A dog's not a solitary animal.

I pointed out to the tree line and Grampie took a gaze at the sugar maples. "You're sure, Fancy?"

"I'm no delusional old dog, Grampie."

Didn't he start laughing, but it led off into a coughing fit. He wiped his forehead and went back in the house, each step an eternity, going right by the mirror at the door. When I followed behind Grampie I looked in the glass but saw only my tanned skin and the branches of the maples. I turned my head real quick to check the woods but the man was gone. There was only a red bird balancing on one of the fireweed spires. Round and round the Tea House I went but there weren't nobody there at all, and the bird too was gone when I come back.

Grampie was on the couch. I brought him some bread and butter and a cup of tea. "You're a brave girl. I'm glad for that. You'll need to be brave." There was a vase of browning peonies and he let his eyes rest on their petals, ruffled and delicate. The fragrance was cloying. Grampie's eyes were closed as a long trill came out from the forest. *When's your cough leaving, Grampie?* I had been asking him all summer. He would hack deep and low. *Soon enough, Fancy*. He'd already made me promise not to say one word to Ma that he wasn't feeling well, and she hardly came to call so that was no trouble. He said arrangements were already in place. That I wasn't to go get her until his time arrived, and I was to fetch Loretta first.

Later, when I come into the parlour to clear up his dishes, he was there, no cough, lying on the sofa like he was sleeping as he usually did after a snack, but there was a stillness in that room that I did not recognize. I washed up all the dishes, dried them and put them in the cupboard, Grampie's teacup with the ferns and red birds beside the other teacups and the pot, the plates. I wiped down the counter and hung the dishcloth to dry. I swept the floor clean, making the house neat and tidy, the way Grampie and I liked it. Jake was lying by Grampie and he didn't move as I went through the house. The air smelled like faded turpentine and beeswax. I went out on the verandah. The cicadas were buzzing. It was when I looked at our chairs, Grampie's big chair, and my little one. When I knew he wasn't making supper ever again, and we would never sit there while the sun went down, watching the shadows reach for the walls of the Tea House, tears slid down my cheeks.

Jake come and sat beside me wagging his tail. Together we went through the forest on the path to Petal's End to get Loretta. When we come back, Ma was sitting on the porch and she stood up. It was like she knew he was dead. Loretta made me stay outside while she went inside with my mother to see Grampie's dead body.

Hush-a-bye, don't you cry, Ma cooed as we stood in the graveyard on Flying Squirrel Road and they threw the soil on Grampie's coffin. There was no proper funeral. He was laid out in the parlour at the Tea House, as he desired. We had a short graveside service at his burial. People come from all over and the cars lined the narrow dirt road.

Grampie was buried fast because he didn't want no embalming. We all understood the desire to rot back into dirt. I threw in my flowers as the dirt thudded down on that wooden box, the abiding peonies and the longing roses, and Ma wrung her hands and lit a cigarette, her lipstick smearing on the butt, watching me. *Don't you cry, hush hush hush-a-bye, poor little Fancy Mosher.*

Grampie dying was the worst thing that could have happened, but he'd foreseen that, which is why he had arranged for me to go from his to Loretta's care. Ma would never contest it and Grampie knew that. They shovelled in the dirt as we stood there, Ma and Loretta and me and Ronnie, and my ten brothers and sisters and all them nephews and nieces and people I didn't know, people who wouldn't stay because Grampie's will left everything to Loretta. He'd made arrangements with his lawyer years before. The family faded away again once Grampie was laid to rest. But that day we was all there, my estranged family, my dead brother John Lee in his grave beside Grampie and my grandmother and their parents before them.

When the burial was done and Loretta had led us through hymn singing, she took me along to Petal's End. There weren't no reception after the burial. Grampie never liked standing around eating finger sandwiches. After supper Loretta took me over to Grampie's to get some of my things. Ma got there before us. She'd taken a saw to several of his bird feeders. Loretta locked the doors then started the car again but I could still hear Ma rambling as she came lurching over to the car. "This place should be mine. You know it should, Loretta. He didn't leave me nothing. He even took my daughter, the twelfth-born. That's a sin, to take a child. It all should be mine."

Loretta put the window down. "It should be no such thing, Marilyn. Your father bought you the house you live in and this he left to me. You'll do well to stay away, that's all I know. Give me strength, oh Risen Lord. You are not fit to be a mother, as much as it pains me to say so, and you know it does."

Ma's eyes were huge. "Loretta, you know what the truth is. Jesus wept. She'll believe. You know she will, Loretta, you know. It's in her nature to believe. You aren't any different than me and you can pretend, and you can go about with your hair covered and your quiet ways and living the spinster life, but you ain't no different. How can you take Fancy away from me, knowing what you do? You're putting a curse on me."

Loretta gripped the steering wheel, saying over and over, "Pay her no mind, Fancy, pay her no mind," like she was praying, hailing Holy Mother Mercy, her face steady, but Ma had got to her. Then she suddenly got out of the car and pointed her finger at Ma, looking down her arm and over her outstretched fingertip like she was taking aim.

"The truth? I do know what the truth is. And *you* gave your *word*, Marilyn Mosher. On your father's grave you will keep that word. Let the dead bury the dead. He did everything he could for you. May the Risen Lord have mercy on your soul, Marilyn, for you are well down a road which has but one destination." Loretta kept her hand up like she was warding off evil.

Ma, in her tight top and skirt, wobbling on her high heels, looked at Loretta's small hand before shifting her gaze to me, the smoke from her cigarette going straight up. Ma was crying as she swayed back to her car and got in. I cried too. I could feel her longing for her father. For, despite her hostility, Ma relied on Grampie to keep her steady and now he was gone. The place was rank with her fear.

We listened to her car go roaring down the lane and up the hill to her house. That's when I got out of the car to find Jake. We were taking him with us to Petal's End. He was stretched out in the painting studio in the sun, where he liked to be, at the foot of Grampie's armchair. When I called his name he did not move. Loretta had Hector come over and he buried the dog out back by the white pine trees.

The twelve-year-old me stood on the verandah of the Tea House thinking of that man in the trees and of Grampie's letter. Who was he? Had it only been shadows? A feeling came over me. It was confusion, the rampant confusion you feel at that young age. But with the windows boarded up, the calm of the house felt beyond reach. I closed my eyes, scattered thoughts of Loretta and Grampie hiding things from me, of Ma using me, when a quivering high voice come out of the forest. *Fancy Mosher*, it said, rising on the end of my name, a question. I could hear steps, slow and steady. Out of fear I whistled, trying to drown out the steps and faint humming, and there was a sweaty hand on my wrist and I screamed, opening up my eyes, shaking off the hand. Art leapt back and fell down hard on the verandah floor.

"Oh, Art, what you doing here, you idiot?" He was even more scared than me, wide-eyed, looking up at me. "Sorry. You looked like you were in a trance, and I didn't want to scare you."

"Well, you did just that. What are you doing here?"

"I figured you'd come here. After today, after finding out . . ."

"You checking up on me?"

Art took the letter that I held out to him and read it, his hand shaking. He looked around as he gave it back. "So it really is true. What did your Grampie think you saw? Do you think that anything will come looking for you? Are you afraid? We should go. We shouldn't be here."

"Do you think I got any answers, Art? It's all just so mixed up. I don't know if anything will come calling. Of course I am afraid. What secrets are they still keeping?"

Art let out a nervous laugh, and at the same time I heard a rustle at the back of the house. "Did you hear that?" Art shook his head as I took off running. There was nothing there, just the boarded-up windows of the painting room. I ran to the woodshed and pulled out the rusty screwdriver shoved through the latch, grabbed a hammer, went back to the house and started prying at the nails.

Art cleared his throat and squeaked, "Do you think you should do this?"

I ignored him and kept pushing, loosening the two nails at the bottom.

"If you come all the way over then help me, Art. For my birthday present. That's all I want. Think of this as my party."

Together we pulled the board off. It wasn't hard to push the window open and I pulled myself up and went in, Art close behind me. We were quiet as cats, being twelve and thin and nimble. It was dark in there but the bit of sunset coming in the window glinted off a few of the teacups on the shelf. I heard and felt warm breath by my ear. It spoke, and it was Art again, and I whacked him. "Stop scaring me. I keep thinking . . ." But I didn't have to finish, for he understood.

I took out the flashlight from my backpack and shone it around the room. The walls were covered in Grampie's paintings. There was the lingering scent of oil paint and turpentine, smells that diminish but never disappear. I went into the kitchen. It was warm inside from the sun beating down all day. On the top shelf was the fancy china set, *Blossom Time*, and on the bottom shelf, where I'd washed and put it three years ago, was my grandfather's cup. And there too on the shelf was John Lee's little cup.

I came into the painting room, Art behind me like a caboose. He went over to the window. "Let's go. It doesn't feel right in here."

"Don't be afraid of the dark, Art," I said, turning to go up the stairs, the flashlight beam lighting up the embroidery I'd done, hung up on the wall. I studied it: Grampie carefully stitched, lying on the sofa. I went up the stairs, two at a time, and stood in the doorway of Grampie's bedroom staring at Grampie's bed, stripped and bare, and above it, the painting of my grandmother blowing me a kiss from her crippled hand, the sunshine all around her. Art was calling to me, his voice even higher than normal, fright right through him now.

I stood paralyzed in the desiccated air, staring at the painting, Art still calling to me, inching closer, probably thinking something bad had happened upstairs because you don't go upstairs in a dark boarded-up house at sunset. *Please*, I prayed, *please let my grandmother start talking, give me a message*. I called to the memento to come right then. But it was just a painting, of course. Defeated, I turned and shone my light down the stairs, and just then there was a flash of white at the bottom. I had the sharp sense that something else had come in through the window behind me and Art, and that it wasn't me doing the looking, and my heart started pounding and I started whistling.

I swallowed hard and followed the flash of white, but there was nothing waiting for me at the bottom of the stairs but a mirror and my big eyes looking back at me. My flashlight guided me to the kitchen and then back to where Art was now waiting by the window outside. He looked like he was going to cry when he saw me, and I gave him Grampie's and John Lee's teacups, holding them through the open window. Art stood there gaping at me, his arms folded on his chest.

"Just take them," I said. There was a creak behind me then, and heavy breathing on my face. "Please. Please, Art, take the cups. Did you hear that? Take the cups," I said.

"I don't hear nothing but your breathing, Fancy. You sound like Jenny Parker, like you're having an asthma attack." Art was afraid as he looked at me, and slowly I realized what he was afraid of. Me. Art was scared of me. He backed up even as he held out his hands and took the saucers, not letting his fingers touch the rims of the cups, holding them away like they was contaminated. I heaved myself out the window but my dress caught on the sill and I tumbled out, crashing down on Art, smacking my head against his, my ears ringing as I rolled over in the grass, stars in my eyes. I rooted like a goat, my hands coming up with pieces of cup, crying now, calling out for Grampie, his name as sharp on my tongue as the piece of broken china that cut into my finger, and I sat back up.

"I'm no believer," I screamed out. Art reached over and pried my fingers open. They were slippery with blood.

"It's fine. Look," he said, his voice urgent. "Fancy, look." In one hand I held pieces of the saucers, in the other, the teacups, chipped, the handle broken off Grampie's, John Lee's untouched, both of them smeared with my blood. They were okay. "We need to get going. Your grandfather wouldn't like us here. He wouldn't have wanted it like this. You know it."

I sat there with the china and he nailed the board back to the window, and disappeared while he took the hammer back to the woodshed. I wrapped the teacup and saucer pieces in my sweater and put them in my backpack.

Art went through the woods with me, through that overgrown trail back to Petal's End. It was dark by then but our feet knew the land better than our eyes.

"What was that song you were whistling in the Tea House?" he asked me, weakly.

"I don't know. Must have been the song Grampie sang to me."

"No," he said. "I never heard it before."

"It felt like something was in there looking for me."

"Maybe we woke up the wood spirits, Fancy. Maybe that's it. The hobgobblies."

We said nothing more as we passed through the garden door, pulling it shut tight behind us.

Art followed me through the garden, saying he would get one of the old bicycles and ride it home. The bikes were in one of the carriage houses and Hector had them all tuned up.

"What are you going to do with the cups? Do you think—"

"I don't know, Art. I don't know if I'm like Grampie." The moon was low and we were now by the Wishing Pool, closed in by the cedars. I took the cups out of my backpack, kneeling by the water. A frog croaked. The moon was rising.

"What is it?" he asked.

"It just occurred to me that Grampie looked no different lying on the sofa napping than when he was dead."

"What's that got to do with anything?"

"I don't know." I scooped the moon water into both cups, disturbing a frog who splashed away. The water was clear and I sang, *Angels are coming to watch over thee, So listen to the wind coming over the sea*. The uneven stones cut into my knee as I lifted Grampie's teacup to my lips and took a sip. I took another sip, this time from John Lee's cup, still singing, *Hang your head o'er and hear the wind blow*, and I saw a small face behind my shoulder, reflected in the water, white like the moon. Art was beside me, and I could feel his warm breath on my cheek.

"Can you see him?" he whispered. "Is Grampie here? John Lee?"

It was still, and an owl called out. Art's hand snapped out and flipped the cups from my grubby fingers. They shattered on the rock edge and fell to the bottom of the Wishing Pool. "What are you doing?" I screamed, not caring if Loretta heard us, or if I frightened either of them. *They* should *be afraid*. *I am Fancy Mosher, seer of the dead*, I thought.

Art's voice broke. "Oh, Fancy, let it go. You aren't like him. And he said it wouldn't be the same for you so you don't need any teacup anyway." He leaned into the water looking for the pieces of teacups and saucers, his tears slipping into the water, the whole pool awake and rippling away any possible reflection.

"There was something there but you scared it away, Art. You ruined everything. Maybe it was Grampie. Maybe he was visiting. To tell me why Ma wants to talk to John Lee. Or John Lee come to speak for himself, to explain. But you went and ruined it."

I ran all the way to the far door in the wall of Evermore. Art ran behind me calling my name but I was the fastest. The path became illuminated as the garden lamps snapped on. There was a shape standing in the dark of the magnolia tree by the service door. I stopped, Art banging into me for he'd followed immediately as I'd bolted out from the cedars. Hector came out from the shadows. "What in fuck trouble are the two of you getting into here in the garden? Hope you're being a gentleman, Arthur." Hector winked at Art, and his expression changed as he saw Art's red eyes. "Well, I guess crybabies don't get up to that yet, no offence, Art. Fancy, you being mean to him? Loretta's looking for you. Good thing she didn't hear all the commotion, Girly Miss and Mister Man, like old Loretta calls you. What do you think she'd call me?"

"Arsehole," I said, and he rubbed his ear like he heard wrong and started laughing. Art didn't laugh and neither did I but the tension was broken. It was nothing more than childish imaginings. The moon can make you think the craziest things.

"Well, Loretta don't strike me as the swearing kind. I'm sure she's got a nicer name than that for me, even in private."

"What are you doing here? I thought you left for the day."

"A handyman's day is never done, don't you know. Just doing some extra chores," Hector said. "Art, I'll take you home. Fancy, you should get in there before Loretta thinks we're up to no good and blames me." He lit a cigarette and leaned against the tree as he winked. There was a belch and Hector waved his hand. "Well, Jesus, Buddy, come on out. Don't hide behind a tree like a pussy." Out stepped his short friend, Buddy Mote. He was the same age as Hector, nineteen, but he was already balding. He had a thin moustache, and no matter what he said it came out as a whine or a snort. "Buddy's helping me out with them lawnmowers. Don't see why the Briar Patch can't bring their own but who am I to question?"

Buddy burped at Art and gave me an up-and-down. "It's a weird place up here," he said, looking at Art and over to me, up and down, up and down.

"It's no weirder than you are," I said.

"Fancy's had a long day. Don't you mind her, Buddy. She's a real nice girl."

I left them all there and went around to the kitchen door. Art came behind me calling he was sorry but I told him to go, and I could hear his footsteps stop as I slammed the kitchen door closed.

Loretta was in her nightgown, reading a book in her sitting room. She looked at me standing in the doorway and gestured at a chair. I told her I was done for the day, that I lost track of time in Evermore. She could tell I was upset but she didn't pry, and I left. In my room I could hear her climb the stairs and come down the hall to my room for the second time that same day. I sat on my bed thinking about them broken teacups.

"Girly Miss, it's been a long day. You should get some sleep. Don't fret about this. I'm so sorry. I never should have let you go to your mother's overnight in the spring. It set her off. She's been waiting, the poor wreck of a woman. This is my fault." Loretta went down the hall and came back with a warm facecloth and washed my cheeks and eyes.

"I want to know if I'm like Grampie, Loretta. Why wouldn't Grampie help Ma?"

"Because knowing any more about John Lee wouldn't have helped her. Or any of us. What could be done? Unspeakable things happen to the young and old."

"Well, maybe if I could speak to John Lee then Ma would stop hounding me. Maybe I could try. At least Ma told me the truth, and you and Grampie never did."

Loretta looked tired and stiff. "Don't be like your mother. She told you the truth for selfish reasons. You must pray for strength to carry on, that's what you must do."

"I went to Grampie's house. I took the cups. They got broken." I cried more and told her how angry I was with Art.

"Oh, Fancy, don't go looking for it. Part of me believes that perhaps your grandfather just imagined these people, these visitors. And I don't mean he was crazy. You know how these artist types are, seeing inspiration in all his surroundings. That's how I mean it. You know how some people say the birds talk to them, how they see things in the clouds? Well, your grandfather, he saw things in teacups, at the tea table. You've got that same spirit in you, in your great dark eyes. It's for the best that you broke those cups." Loretta gave me a smile but her lips fell back down like they was too haggard to care what Loretta wanted out of them. "You must try to go about your life the same way as you have, no different, my dear. Your grandfather, he didn't go looking, you see. And you don't need to either, Fancy. Go to bed and say your prayers." Loretta kissed me on the head and left.

I put Grampie's letter on the bedside table and prayed to Holy Mother Mercy to come in my dreams and tell me how to see the dead. I prayed to the stars and the sky. When you're a child you believe such things can hear you. You know with absolute certainty the twinkling star is twinkling only for you. *Keep me safe*, I said in the dark. All night it seemed there was a voice out there singing, that maybe some spirit had been following me around. I decided what I believed in was the Grampie I remembered, and he was there beside my bed, not a dead Grampie but the one I knew, with his cheerful, wrinkled face, his dentures white, his low grumbly voice singing, *Hear the wind blow, love, hear the wind blow.* The curtains were long and slender white on either side of the window, and the moon moved across the sky as smooth as a petal blown over the surface of a pond. I could almost feel Grampie's rough hand softly graze my forehead as sleep drew me in.

5.
Margaret and Hector

ART AND I spent the next morning picking strawberries in the kitchen garden, relieved to have the wreck of my birthday behind us. We did not speak of the day or night before. In the early morning the letter had been there on my bedside table. I had taken it and crawled under my bed, where a piece of the wooden floorboard was cut as a lid, with a metal hook, to cover a small compartment. I kept special stones in it and a lavender peony sachet for good luck, to keep the good fairies about. I put the letter in there, where it would be out of sight and out of mind. And so it was, as we picked and ate those succulent strawberries until the sun was coming up on high noon.

On our way back through the garden we cut tall flowers and took them in a gathering basket to the house. Loretta was in the kitchen bustling about, writing things down on lists and sticking them to the bulletin board for the house and estate staff, which was me, Art and Hector. There were lists she did up for the services they contracted out, as it was called: the gardeners, cleaners, roofing and electrical services. There was a big chalkboard on one wall where she wrote out her own schedule and personal lists. Loretta was worried that the Parkers might appear in the doorway, ringing bells, at any moment. We were out of practice with real people.

I went into the flower-arranging room off the side of the kitchen. There were shelves with every kind of vase and flower-holder, from the smallest bud vases to enormous silver pitchers and all sorts of jardinières. Along the far wall was a wide counter for arranging flowers and a sink for rinsing stems and knives. I heard Loretta and Art talking away, the muffled sounds a familiar comfort. I took a big full vase and struggled down the hall connecting the back house to the main residence, pausing at the door to the Annex. There was a small mirror across from it with an ornate frame. I was waiting to hear a sound coming from inside, but there was nothing. No singing or rustling, nothing but the usual creaks of the house. I did check in the mirror but there wasn't no one or thing standing behind me, just the locked door and the window beside it.

I continued down the hall, out the door that led into the grand hall, and put the flowers on the big round table with the gleaming marble surface. The table faced the massive front door. It was opened to the screen door Hector had put on for the summer. It was later in the morning and the torrid air was coming through both the door and the windows. We always opened them up in the early morning so the fragrant brisk air would fill the house, and we'd shut up them later against the approach of the heat. Marigold wouldn't let the windows or doors stay open at night, due to her superstitions. Loretta must have forgotten to close them up.

Right off the grand hall was the music room. The door was open and sun streamed through the lace sheers hanging in the tall southern windows. In the room were Marigold's prized Queen Anne armchairs with elaborate embroidery seat covers: a black background and an intricately stitched array of flowers and birds in deep, brilliant colours. This was my mother's fine work. Marigold had loved to sit in those chairs, resting and contemplating or listening to Pomeline's sonatas. Loretta said Pomeline was taking her exams for the music conservatory at the end of the summer but I didn't see how that would be much different from any other time Pomeline was out over the years. She'd sit in there at that piano, the music pouring through the rest of the house, shimmering and rising through the rooms and halls, even reaching the servant quarters. Despite my occasional lessons with Pomeline and practices by myself, I never could truly relax when I was in any part of the main house alone. It felt like an empty stage, just waiting for the Parkers to come back and start performing.

My understanding of the past was very different since Ma had come to my school with her gruesome news flash. Standing at the door looking at the Queen Anne chairs took me back three years to when I had moved into Petal's End with Loretta. That first day, Loretta toured me through the grounds and the mansion. I remembered my first time seeing the music room. I stood by the piano while Loretta pointed out the chairs to me and explained Ma's design was to reflect the estate—the gardens and creatures. The Colonel loved the chairs as much as Marigold and had gone so far as to have Ma brought up from the kitchen and presented at a reception when guests inquired about the embroidery. The high-backed chairs was taller than I was. The air had wafted in through the front windows, aromatic with the lavender and rosemary growing around the stone pathway in front of the house. Loretta had announced then that I must never play in the main part of the house. It was forbidden. And she told me why I was to take the rule seriously. She took me back out into the hall, to the bottom of the enormous oak staircase. Loretta put her hand on the carved wooden banister post as she said how John Lee and young Master Charlie had come sailing down the banister one summer day when

Marigold had been reposing in the music room. The door was closed tight. The boys weren't supposed to be playing in the main house, certainly not John Lee. He was not permitted in this part, only the kitchen or the playrooms and nursery, or in the garden. Some other children visited but poor Charlie was so timid he would only play if John Lee was by his side. Charlie and John Lee were the same age and the best of friends even though they was total opposites. There was a new nanny, Loretta said, but no one could find her. She'd left the children unsupervised.

Charlie and John Lee had come cruising down the banister in a gale of laughter. They were playing tag and had decided to hide on the main floor in the music room. They tumbled in the door and onto the soft silk carpet at Marigold's feet. The story went that her eyes flashed open and she was yelling, *How dare you come in here, John Lee. The servants' children are forbidden to play here!* Marigold rang the bell for the nanny but it was Loretta who came running. Marigold shrieked that John Lee was not to be left to run about the property like a stray dog. Charlie started shouting how John Lee was his best friend.

After that story, we never played games in the big house, not even with Jenny. And now three years later I was working throughout the house as a maid.

After I made sure the room was tidy and the flowers set perfect in the hall, I came back to the kitchen. Loretta was on the phone. "Oh yes, I see, yes, oh really, yes," she kept saying over and over again. Art was hulling strawberries and I put on an apron and started helping him. Loretta was going to make jam. Even when the Parkers didn't come out they still wanted Loretta to make preserves and send them to the city for the winter.

Loretta hung the phone up. "Well, the Parkers will be along any day now, not that they've settled on a day." Loretta didn't get annoyed—she got concerned. She liked a fixed schedule. She started getting the huge Maslin pots ready for cooking the jam.

"That was Dr. Baker calling on behalf of Marigold. They've hired a girl to help Marigold out. He says it would be too much for me or you, Fancy. Pomeline is so busy practising for her piano exams she can't help her grandmother as much as she used to. Jenny isn't capable, of course. Apparently Marigold is doing very well, though. She's a tough old bird. She'll attribute it to the herbal remedies and teas she has taken over the years, and her hardy constitution. Maybe there's something to it after all, children. Don't be fooled by how fragile she looks. We should never judge someone on their appearance, that is the truth. They've hired Margaret Armstrong. You'll remember her from Bible School."

Art locked eyes with me from across the room as he dried his hands. I took the plates of sandwiches out of the fridge and put them on the table. "Oh. Yes. Bible Camp Margaret," I said.

Loretta was inspecting the strawberries, making sure we hadn't cut too much fruit off with the hull. "Well, was she a nice girl?"

"She's lazy as a pet raccoon."

"Fancy, really, that's not pleasant."

"Well, it's true. She's not much of a worker."

"Her father owns the store that sells furniture and vitamins and swimming pools. And he has a private nursing home now, too. That must be how Dr. Baker knows them." Loretta put her hands in the prayer position and looked at me and Art over her glasses. "Margaret will be here after lunch. You can show her around. There won't be much for her to do yet. I'm sure she is a wholesome girl if Dr. Baker has hired her. You know how he is. She's going to the vocational school in the autumn, doing the certificate program to be a nursing home attendant. This will most certainly be a good job to get experience attending to the old." She shook her head and chuckled.

"I hope Margaret likes seniors more than she likes children. I don't think she liked working at Bible School," I said.

Art shot me a laser eye. You see, until the previous summer when we was eleven, we had gone to the Summer Vacation Bible

School each August. Margaret had been a camp counsellor. She paid us no mind for most of the summer, and from the way she treated the kids who did catch her eye we were grateful we were invisible. Until one day near the end of camp, when we was waiting for the rickety school bus to take us home. The minibus was run by a number of churches, and after we got dropped off in the morning the bus would clang and bang away to pick up other kids going to the Christian Canoe Club, Gardeners for Christ, or out for full-immersion baptisms at the lake camp up on the South Mountain. At the end of the day it would rattle back to get us at camp, where we'd spent the day learning Bible stories and hymns under the old-growth hemlocks, and playing godly games of hide-and-seek and statue tag where we froze in the shape of Bible characters. I got in trouble every summer for swearing and telling ghost stories about the night-creeping hobgobblies at Petal's End and the headless sailor over on the rugged island off Lupin Cove. It was so easy scaring them valley children, their great big eyes and round mouths. I felt bad when the little ones were scared but it was funny when the older kids got even more afraid. Art had stories too, ones he learned from Yvette, about the *duppies*, as she called them in the place she come from, nasty spirits of the night wandering around with chains and animals not quite right in their animal minds.

Margaret was a sixteen-year-old girl then, whose come-hither look was wearing out from overuse. Her voice was nasal-sounding from her allergies, and being a heavy girl only made her breathe harder. She was allergic to pollen, she said, to summer itself. She'd cock her hip and flip her hair. She didn't have a bit of interest in children. We was pests to her. She'd take bug poison when we'd act up and wave it around like she was going to spray it in our eyes, sometimes misting our hair in it. Once Margaret sprayed it in a glass of water when a young bucktoothed girl called her a fatty-cake. She gave the girl the glass of water and ordered her to drink it right up or she'd put the poison in her eyes. The little girl didn't know what to do because she was told over and over to obey the grown-ups. A teenager was a grown-up to the girl, and she started crying as she went to take a sip of the poison. Margaret started laughing. "Only kidding," she said, taking the glass away. "Who doesn't like a joke? If you're stupid enough to be tricked then you get what's coming to you."

The bus was late that day and it was terrible hot, even in the shade. Art and I had gone to get a drink of water from the lunchroom in the administration building. When we got there the screen door and the inside door were both locked. As we stood there thirsty in the wicked heat there was a groan inside. We looked through the window and saw Margaret kneeling in her navy blue work skirt. The student minister who ran the program was standing with his eyes closed tight and his fleshy pink man part going in and out of Margaret's mouth. The white blouse she wore was unbuttoned. Her big boobs were jiggling up and down. Margaret's eyes were shut too and her bangs were hanging in her face. Art and I had seen nothing like that before. The minister had his hands in her mousy hair. Even through the window we could hear him saying her name, *Maggie, Maggie, Maggie.* We never heard anyone call her Maggie. She got mad if you gave her a nickname, but apparently she changed her rules for romance. Margaret suddenly glanced up toward us when Art took a step back. We didn't know if she'd seen us, with the hair in her eyes and the minister going at her like he was trying to pump the life out of her, and just then it was like he was having an attack because he started shaking and thrusting and gasping, all red in the face, and we went running off, waiting down in the shade, praying we'd hear that consumptive bus pull up. It didn't.

Margaret came strolling down through the hemlocks with the minister. He was holding a Bible and they looked all earnest as they discussed the good Lord, except they was flushed and sweaty.

"Scorcher of a day, isn't it, children. Be good. Don't sin," he chuckled, fanning himself. He nodded at Margaret all formal, and off he went through the gates.

Margaret came over to us, let out a big breath, her mouth open wide like a dragon, and bits of her bangs flew up to show us her eyes for just a second before her hair closed back down over them. Margaret smelled salty, like a starfish that's been in the sun too long. She held up a finger straight and stiff like she was going to slice us open with it. "Don't you say a word. Do you hear, you motherfucking whore bastard?" She poked Art. "And you too, brown boy. Or I'll take care of both you, I really will. First I'll freeze your eyeballs and then I'll chop your head off just like that pirate did to his sailor. You'll just be drifting around forever, stuck here, and no one will even ever see you. Bet you wish you never told me that story, Fancy Mosher."

The minibus finally came rattling in, the muffler half hanging off making an angry terrible growl, the driver beeping. We took the steps in one leap and the bus driver hollered at us to slow the hell down. Margaret walked away, and when the bus passed her on the sidewalk we didn't look at her. The last week of camp the student minister didn't come back. Word went around that he got caught with another one of the camp counsellors, a thin girl with short red hair and big green eyes and great big boobs. A boob man, I told Art on the way home the day we found out.

Margaret didn't even look at us after that. She didn't come back the next year, either. I guess she'd thought she was the only one. She worked in her father's furniture store selling sofas and vitamin pills. She had a reputation with all the kids, and probably with some of the adults, but not Loretta. And Dr. Baker was mostly in the city so he didn't know much about her neither. It seemed to me that even if they did know they both would have wanted her to have a second chance, that good honest work might restore her. Margaret wouldn't have cared if they did know her reputation.

She was fine with how she was, like being bad made her mysterious in a way her big body and her crooked teeth and the pimples on her cheeks didn't.

We didn't tell anyone. No one keeps a secret like a child. Sharing the secret binds you together. Art and I had an unspoken pact between us then about secrets. When you threaten a child and tell them that if they don't keep the secret something wicked and terrible will happen, they believe you. They won't go and ask a grown-up for help for they believe there is none. It's an invisible wall they stand behind, peering through to the other side where there is safety, a safety they can't reach.

In the kitchen, Loretta looked at us now, her hands folded, like she thought we were about to confide in her, but we did not. We made the praying hands and she led us in grace as she asked for health and friendship and harmony in the moment, in the day, through the nights and in coming summer if God in Heaven and His Son the Risen Lord was willing and merciful, Amen.

"Did you give the list to Hector, Mister Man?"

"Yes, first thing. But he wasn't too pleased about going for groceries. He said he's the mechanic."

"Well, he is the mechanic. And the chauffeur, and the handyman, too. He keeps forgetting that. We all do a bit of everything. It's not like the days gone by. Look at me. I was in charge of the housemaids back when I was just a bit older than Margaret. Hector's busy making up some list for Estelle. He thinks I don't know. She still thinks she's going to sell the place but Marigold seems to be having a second wind. Anyway, we'll get that jam done up. The berries look beautiful. I remember when we made all kinds of jams and jellies in this kitchen."

"I thought you were in charge of keeping the house clean," Art said.

"I didn't start out that way. I would do cleaning. Sometimes they'd need help in the kitchen. Good help was scarce. *Any* help was scarce. Fancy's mother and I both worked in the house, but the last year she was here Marigold moved her into the kitchen full time and she'd do cooking and the laundry." Loretta's tone had changed.

"Ma said she hated working in the kitchen."

"Your mother wasn't easy to work with, as you can imagine, but as I told you, Fancy, she was the hardest worker. Even Mr. Long said if you wanted something done right the first time to ask Marilyn Mosher." Loretta chewed her sandwich fast, and I knew there was another thing she didn't want me to know. "There's nothing I like more on a summer day than one of my tuna sandwiches, if I do say so myself. You did a nice job with the flowers, Fancy. That will be your job this summer, filling the rooms with fresh flowers. But you'll need to go close all those windows you opened. That was helpful but you must remember to close them before noon. And when Marigold is here you must not open them at night. We must follow her rules."

I gave Loretta a look. "I didn't open them. You opened them when you got up, didn't you?"

"Maybe it was the hobgobblies," Art said.

"Art, we'll have no talk of Marigold's superstitions. And Fancy, it's fine if you opened them, but not fine to tell stories. It's nice you're trying to help but I don't want you running around the house. It's not allowed. You know that. Go shut the windows, Girly Miss."

We all got on with our chores. I hadn't opened any windows, you see, but I wasn't going to argue with Loretta. She must have forgotten. She was getting older, and my birthday had taken a toll on her. I went back into the grand hall. I looked around and I listened for what I'd heard in the Tea House, telling myself even as I did that it was nonsense. There was a muggy breeze blowing in, carrying whiffs of ocean that lingered after I shut the front door and pulled the windows closed in the music room and the study and the day room. I remember thinking Loretta must have been distracted with all her worry about the Parkers coming and about what would happen to the house now Marigold was elderly and Estelle was vengeful.

Back in the kitchen Art was now mashing up strawberries. Loretta had gone out to hang laundry on the line at the back of the house. I started smashing up another huge pot full of berries. Art looked over at me, eyebrow raised. "Maggie?"

"Maggie indeed," I answered.

"Maybe she was born again."

Loretta came bustling in with glowing red cheeks. "Fancy, did you close the windows? Art, how are the berries? We'll do two batches. Let's get the burners on then. Fancy, run out and tell Hector we'll need more pectin when he goes to town. I'm sure he's still out there. See if you can catch him. And I hope Buddy isn't hanging around. He doesn't have good sense. And bring in the rest of the laundry off the line. There's another basket out there. And if you have some time, maybe you could start an embroidery for Marigold, a new sampler for her to have when she arrives. She'd be overjoyed . . . maybe a serene garden scene with her in it. You're so talented with stitching people." There was nothing that made Loretta happier than a long list of tasks to get through, chores that ordered her day.

Hector was working on Old Rolly again, trying to get the wheel off, pounding with a hammer. The car looked perfect but he fussed with it anyway. He said his father told him an old car was like a woman of a certain age, kept in fine shape only with regular maintenance. Loretta said the Colonel was a car aficionado just as Hector was. Estelle wanted the cars sold off, but Marigold had insisted they stay just where they were. The same fight between the two of them ladies, but there the cars sat because Marigold was still in command.

There were three carriage houses, one large one and a smaller one on either side of it, creating a courtyard. It had a curiously pleasant smell, a blend of gas and oil, paint and varnish, and old wood. I stood there, listening to Hector bang away. No sign of Buddy. Hector didn't notice me. Hector had always lived on the mountain on the Flying Squirrel Road. He couldn't bear to leave. Going to town was as far as he wanted to go. Who needs the world out there when you got the whole world around you here? he would say. I suppose more than anyone he understood why Marigold held so tightly to Petal's End.

When I turned twelve I saw a new side of Hector. He was the grown man that Art was not, and I was a girl waking into a woman. Oh yes, he was an arse, I'm sorry to say, but it was easy seeing past that when you were either a young girl or an elderly lonely lady. Hector had a slow quiet drawl, a long purr slinking between his full red lips, just like all the men in his family. It was hard to know what he thought, except that he was sure he was always right about everything. He'd smile and do just as he pleased. If he was wrong he found a reason to justify it. Hector was no different than the Parkers. That day in the carriage house I watched his muscles as he swung the heavy hammer to knock the tire off, the clang ringing out, the small butterfly tattoo on his bicep. His ball cap had fallen to the ground and he'd taken his T-shirt off. His sweat blended with the smell of oil and gas and it was intoxicating to me.

"What are you staring at there, Girly Miss?" There was nothing sweet and innocent about how them words sounded coming off his tongue.

I jumped and my face flushed. "Loretta wants you to pick up pectin for her jam. She forgot to put it on the list. She wants you to go soon. She was worried you'd just go and disappear."

"She does, does she? I see. Isn't that just like a woman. Well, I guess I can head down now the afternoon has drawn on. Don't that woman ever rest?"

"Loretta's got rest on her end-of-day list."

Hector laughed at that. "Loretta's a good woman, don't get me wrong. You should try living with my father. At least I don't have to work for him any more now I got this job. But I got some big plans with my friend, Buddy. I won't be needing nothing from my asshole father soon." He was scrubbing his hands and arms with some kind of spicy citrus cream for removing grease. Then he rinsed in the big set tub and washed again with soap and water. Beside the sink were some ropes and chains hanging on wall pegs and beside them rusty metal leghold traps hanging from hooks.

Hector combed his hair. It was so thick and wavy, I can see it now, after all this time. "Well, guess who grew up this year," Hector drawled, looking at me in the mirror. I saw his eyes in that reflection looking at my body. He didn't even try and hide it now we were alone. I blushed again, his eyes on mine, his low laugh when he saw my fingers touching my scar. Hector was too young then for the cigarettes to have stained his teeth or his fingers, and there were no lines yet around his eyes or mouth, but there was a dark look he'd get. "Want to come to town with me, Fancy?"

"I'm bringing in the laundry now. Art and I got work to do. Hector, you should get going or Loretta will get agitated."

Hector pinned me with a big long stare. I suppose it would have been good if I'd been frightened and run away like he was the big bad wolf but I had no fear of Hector. That summer it was more like a fascination come over me.

"So, you aren't scared now, a big girl like you, all that nonsense with your mother? I know what she was going on about, what your grandfather did. Don't be ashamed. He helped people. I guess it's time you knew. I thought you did."

I waited for him to say more, but when he didn't I knew Hector knew only part of the secret—he didn't know the other secret hiding inside it.

"Marilyn's not all bad. My father liked her. I remember her bringing you over to the strawberry field when you were small and how you'd run up and down the rows. You was the cutest thing, you was. She was always running after you. I used to pick you bouquets of buttercups and daisies. I guess you don't remember." He winked at me and grabbed a clean shirt out of a bag hanging on a nail. "She was good with the horses, Marilyn was. Shame she can't look after them now. My mother married a farmer, thinking she was going to live a soft life. She lived to learn the truth about that one." Hector took a few steps until he was standing close to me, his T-shirt in one hand, using the other to touch the hair by my temple, pushing it out of my eyes. "You got other things to worry about now you're twelve."

I heard Art calling my name. He stood at the open door of the carriage house like a shadow at the edge of a painting. Hector was pulling his T-shirt on over his head. I walked over before Art could step into the garage and we walked out onto the cobblestone courtyard.

Hector came out after us and scuffed the stones with his workboots. "This'll be needing some work soon enough. This old-fashioned masonry costs a lot of money. But they just throw the money away, those Parkers."

"Did you add pectin to the list?"

Hector spit on the ground. "What are you, Art Boy, the butler now? Yes, I'll get the goddamned pectin. I got better things to be doing than grocery shopping. And you should be out here working with me, doing real work. I know your father ain't around to help you out and he was an asshole anyway, from what I hear." Hector laughed. "But still, Art, you should be working out here. Tell Loretta you don't want to be no pussy. Look how that worked out for Charlie Parker, living his life as a pussy, or should I say pansy? Loretta's either got you doing her errands or helping out them gardeners. What do you want to be, Art? A flower or a man? Estelle's asked me to make up a list of all the things that need done around here, the big jobs, you know, the wiring, the foundation. That colossal house ain't got no real insulation. The last time they modernized the place was after the first big war. Don't know how you haven't frozen to death in the winter, Fancy. I mean, Loretta's got enough padding on her to survive an ice age. You're filling in but you're still pretty skinny."

Art rolled his eyes. "Fancy, Loretta wants you to bring in the clothes. She wants us back at the house."

"Yes, Mr. Butler, yes, she'll get to it, won't you Fancy. Holy fuck, boy. You have to stand up to women, don't you see? All these women walking around here with the opinions of a ten-foot man. Loretta might be small and wide but she's got the determination of an ocean liner, she does. Oh well, if they shut this place down she can have a bit of relaxation. Maybe that's why they have a staff of kids running the place. Nothing Estelle would like better than to see this place bulldozed. Can't blame her, right, Art Boy?"

Art blushed and looked down.

"What's he talking about, Art?"

Art shrugged his shoulders and didn't say anything.

"Well, I'll tell you if the butler ain't going to. Art was out helping me a few weeks ago, after supper. It was the day Estelle came out with Dr. Baker. Remember that, Art? We heard them back around by the old wing, the Annex."

"We didn't mean to hear them, Hector. We were watching the starlings lift out of the trees. That's why we were back there. We weren't listening in on purpose."

"Well, I didn't know it was wildlife hour. Starlings should be shot. Pests. There's pigeons roosting in the back of the house. Those I definitely will shoot. Why are we talking about goddamn birds? Anyway, we heard Dr. Baker and Estelle having it out." Hector was enjoying how the high and mighty had been careless enough to be overheard. "I thought maybe there was a coyote or some such beast coming around. They ain't done nothing back there, talk about needing maintenance. That back wing, they either got to fix it up or tear it down. And that's just what Estelle wants to do."

"That's no secret. She's been going on about that for years, Hector."

"We went out back there and they didn't hear us, did they, Art?" Hector looked at him but Art was looking at the sky. "Oh, they had a monster fight going on. They should have been in Evermore arguing if they didn't want nobody to hear. Probably drunk as lords to go at it like that. Estelle kept going on about how Marigold's not in her right mind and Dr. Baker should sign papers so Estelle can be her guardian and lock her away."

I was chewing my lip. I didn't want to know anything more, and Art was looking away. "Well, that ain't nothing new. I gotta go take the clothes off the line."

Just as Hector was going to continue, Art started talking, like he thought if he told me Hector would shut up. "Dr. Baker said that Marigold could do as she pleases, that she was doing fine for someone in her eighties and she could make her own choices. He thought it would be good for her to come out, and Pomeline could come and stay with her, and Estelle had to accept that this wasn't her place. That's what he said. And that Charlie was weak and certain kinds of men are like that. He called it *an affliction*. I never heard it called that before but you learn something new every day. Anyhow, Dr. Baker said it made Estelle go all crazy. Estelle said it was going to be hers soon. Dr. Baker told her that the estate would go to Jenny, not her, when Marigold passed. Estelle looked like she was having one of her migraine attacks. Next she got all disturbing saying how she wished Marigold would just die because the money is hers and she certainly deserves it after all the suffering she's gone through, all the horseshit she's had to put up with through the years, how nothing was what Charlie had promised. 'I have been betrayed,' she kept growling."

Hector was nodding. "It might do Estelle good to let loose, if you know what I mean. That's half her problem. She's too uptight, that one. The doctor was saying, 'Time passes, Estelle, time marches along. Things change. People make their choices. You have to accept this.' Talking like that in his goddamned doctor voice, talking right down to her like he does to everyone. I don't know why they're all so crazy about him, like he could walk on fucking water."

"They didn't mean for us to hear, Hector. And Dr. Baker's nice to us. He likes Marigold."

"Mr. Man of Medical Science and all, with his stethoscope around his neck and his prescription pad, like he's ready for the next heart attack or emergency, although I don't think he'd even remember what to do any more because he don't even seem to really work, just fusses with the Parker women. He's stuck up, that's the problem. At least Estelle's practical."

"Well, no one's asking you, are they, Hector?"

"What a mouth on you, Fancy. Don't backtalk me. I'm your elder."

I couldn't imagine Dr. Baker saying anything like that. Hector was jealous. He was jealous of anyone with more than him.

"Who knows what's going on there, but something is. Probably what got to Charlie Parker. The truth can kill, my father says. It's a lethal weapon so there's no point in even telling it," Hector said.

That was enough for Art. "It doesn't matter what we heard. Mr. Charlie's dead and he's been dead for six years now. Just leave it alone. All these old people having problems from the things they did when they were young. This doesn't have anything to do with us."

"I just thought you might want to know," Hector said. "Art, he don't want to grow up. But we did hear all of that. Sort of puts things into perspective, don't it? You might not like it, Art, but it's the truth. Not everything's stars and birds singing and violins playing."

I'd also had enough, and whatever I had felt in the garage for Hector was gone. "We got to get back to the house. Margaret Armstrong's going to be here soon."

Hector let out a whistle. "That's who they hired to look after Marigold? I wonder how them saddlebags of hers are doing. Shame to see those on a woman. She's only eighteen. Her mother's like that so must be where it comes from, runs-in-the-family sort of thing. Margaret don't got much of a sense of humour, not like you two. She's got some mouth on her, too. Now I'm going to town to get these damn groceries." Hector winked at us and started walking to his pickup truck.

Art and I ran to the house. We stopped at the door, both of us, composing ourselves before going in. We didn't want Loretta to ask what was on our minds. She could always tell.

"Why didn't you tell me what you overheard, Art?"

"It didn't seem right. It was a private conversation."

"But you did overhear. You can't change that."

"I don't like this growing up and finding out everyone's an asshole, Fancy."

It was the truth. Art looked miserable. I had never heard him swear before. His high voice made me laugh. He looked hurt, like I was laughing at him the way Hector did all the time.

Art opened the door but looked back at me as he stepped inside. "It's none of our business." He disappeared into the house, and as I started in after him I heard a swishing in the bushes. I turned around. There was another rustle, and a chill went through me. Just then Loretta called from the kitchen and I ran inside, slamming the door behind me so whatever was out there, or if it was just my imagination, would be left behind.

6.
Come, Margaret, We'll Tell You a Tale

At Petal's End we could hear a car long before we saw it come through the woods onto the expansive oval drive. The velvety air seemed to amplify sounds and words. If you lived at Petal's End you discovered the only private conversations were ones you had in your mind.

Art and I sat waiting on the verandah for the sound of the car that would bring Margaret. We had sassy lemonade poured over crescent-moon-shaped chunks of ice in frosty tall glasses. There wasn't no plastic at Petal's End. We finally felt carefree, and the conversation with Hector had evaporated, swallowed up by the puffy white clouds. It was easy to pretend right up to the last minute that Margaret wasn't really coming. Art was in a rocking chair, humming. I had brought out my needlework but it was stifling hot so I set it on the table. It was an embroidery pictorial of Marigold asleep in her bed surrounded by flowers, the size they call a miniature. Her face was disconcerting as I'd stitched the way she looked after her stroke. I didn't know why it had come out that way and I was done with it for the day. We enjoyed our afternoon solitude until we heard a far-off car engine. Finally it pulled out of the woods and looped around to the front door.

Margaret's father didn't get out or shut the car off. He barely stopped as Margaret got out. Apparently, driving her to the first day of her new job was a mighty big inconvenience. We heard him say to call ahead of time when she needed a ride home so he could schedule it in. His voice was instructive, a tone used for giving orders to a dim-witted employee. He drove off just as soon as she had shut the door, her hand still on the handle when the car started rolling forward.

"Asshole," Margaret hissed, waving and smiling as the vehicle circled toward the wood.

She turned around with her hands on her hips. Margaret's dull brown hair was now bleached blond with frost tips, her long bangs greasy and hanging in her eyes. Her skirt and blouse were baggy except at her hips and chest, where they pulled wire-tight to accommodate her. "Holy fuck," she said, walking up to the big mock orange bushes. "I thought this place was a joke. But it's real. Can you believe it?" She looked at us like maybe we hadn't observed our surroundings. I rolled my eyes at Art and watched Margaret as she ogled the place. She didn't seem to have any bug poison and she hadn't called me a whore bastard or Art a brown boy so it seemed we were off to a good start. The heavy makeup on her cheeks was melting. And she was wheezing. The pungent air was going to be hard on her.

"Don't stare. It's rude. Didn't anyone teach you any manners living over here? I've got severe allergies. Just make sure you don't bother me. I didn't come over here to look after brats."

The second she looked at us, those eyes glinting behind the mess of bangs, I saw her on her knees back at Bible School. Art did too and his cheeks went crimson. It was curious to me how my feelings stayed put in my chest most of the time but they seeped right out of Art. It was impossible to know what Margaret was thinking with her hair in her face. She could look out but you couldn't look in.

"Where is Loretta? Dr. Baker said I'm supposed to meet her and she'll train me." The mowers behind the walls of Evermore started up, and Margaret's eyes followed the noise. "What a monstrosity if I ever saw one. You'd think they'd knock this place down. Oh my God. Look at them creepy things." She pointed at the stone gargoyles hanging off the roof, shielding her eyes from the sun.

"The Colonel had them made for Marigold. She's afraid of hobgobblies. She won't sleep on the ground floor in case they come in. And she don't want the windows open downstairs. Jenny's just like her."

Margaret snorted. "Is everyone here crazy? What's a hobgobbly? Maybe that's what you two are."

Art laughed. "We don't know. Some sort of bad spirit."

"Well, I don't care. You both would believe in anything, telling all your ghost stories and crap. I don't believe in that any more than I do the devil. Just stories grown-ups tell to keep kids in line, that's all. Who needs a house this big? They should make it a museum or a hotel. Or knock it down. Better yet, burn it down."

"You keep saying that. Better not let Marigold hear. You sound like Estelle, her daughter-in-law."

"Yeah, I hear she's a bitch. My father said that. Well, he didn't say she was a bitch but I knew that's what he meant." Margaret snorted. "What do you call Marigold and Estelle?"

"The Missus Parkers. That's what they like. We only call them Estelle and Marigold when they're not present."

"I hear you had some trouble with your mother, Fancy. Word gets around. Better not grow up like her. But you won't be able to help it, being a Mosher. Heard she came by pissed out of her mind at the school this week and they had to take her away."

I stared at Margaret and she started brushing at her skirt like there was lint on it, though there wasn't a speck.

"We should be getting you to meet Loretta," Art said.

Loretta wasn't in the kitchen so we took Margaret through the long passage into the main house. We showed her the imposing rooms on the main floor, went up the grand staircase and down the hall to the bedrooms, then to Marigold's set of rooms. We didn't take her to the third floor. Most of the rooms were locked up tight and you needed one of the big keys that hung down in the kitchen. Margaret didn't talk at all throughout the tour, just looked at the paintings, at the great big pieces of furniture, the mouldings on the ceilings. Petal's End could take the words out of almost anybody's mouth.

Loretta had snacks ready for us in the kitchen when we came back. She was writing on the blackboard and she brushed her chalky hands on her apron before she shook Margaret's hand. "We're pleased to have you here, Margaret. It's very quiet now, but I'm sure you'll have plenty to do."

"Yes, ma'am." Margaret sat down.

"Dr. Baker said you are skilled with the elderly. You'll need patience here. He thought you'd be the perfect helper for Marigold. And of course your experience at the Bible School."

I saw Margaret's head turn, ever so slight, but I ignored her, as did Art.

"Hector will drive you back down to the valley after your visit, if you like, seeing as you're just here today for acquainting yourself with the place. I will call and let your father know." Loretta poured her lemonade and Margaret perked up at the mention of Hector's name.

"So it's just him and you, and these two?" Margaret wrinkled her nose. It was hitting her how odd it was.

Loretta didn't even seem to notice. "Well, don't be fooled, these two are quite useful. But there's the Briar Patch people and Happy Helpers, too."

"Well, I don't mean to be rude, Loretta, but I never heard of anything like this, a great big place and all the work to keep it going with no one even living here."

Loretta dabbed her lips and forehead with a napkin. "My dear, this is the way it is. The Parkers have their ideas. They nearly did sell the place a few years back, after Charlie died. That's when then they started to disagree, which I am sure you will hear plenty about once they arrive. Just don't pay any attention to it. They'll sort it out. We always wait out their clashes as we wait out bad weather."

The kitchen door opened. "Hello, big house," Hector called as he came in with the groceries. Margaret giggled and looked down. "Well, hi there, Maggie," he said as he put the groceries on the far end of the big table. "And the pectin, just as you ordered, Miss Loretta."

"Sit down and join us, Hector. Take off your hat, for goodness' sake. The Parkers will be here soon and you'll do well to remember to take your hat off. And Fancy, you'll do well to wear shoes. This isn't a barn."

We all started laughing.

"I'm serious, children," Loretta said. "I take it you know Margaret, Hector?"

"Well, just by reputation," he said as he took off his hat, tipping it as he did. His tattoo looked darker inside the kitchen. Margaret looked positively delighted by Hector's comment.

"I should tell all of you, now I have you gathered together, that Marigold will be coming out tomorrow." This explained why Loretta was breathless. "Sometime after lunch, Dr. Baker said. I don't know who is coming with her but we'll need to have rooms ready in case. Fancy and I can take care of that. The piano was tuned earlier in June, so if Pomeline is coming that's ready. Marigold was going to wait but when Dr. Baker said he'd hired you, Margaret, she didn't see the point. Remember how important it is to respect their rules. And stay away from the Annex— that part of the house is not safe. The support beams are unstable and the floorboards are weak.

It's full of black mould, and Dr. Baker says the air isn't fit to breathe. Avoid all of the locked rooms, for that matter. When the Parkers are in the house we stay out of the way unless they need us. Fancy and Art, will you show Margaret around outside? Marigold will be expecting to take her promenades so Margaret will need to know her way about. You should draw her a map. We used to have them printed up. One of Marigold's visiting artist friends did a map. It was worthy of framing. I haven't seen one in years. At least we don't have animals to tend to. Does anyone have any questions?"

Margaret grinned but not in her regular rude way. It was hard not to like Loretta, unless you were Ma. "I think you pretty much covered every single thing, past and present and future."

"Marigold is speaking already of having a garden party. We'll hope that is nothing more than a notion."

"What kind of animals were there?" Margaret asked. "I like horses."

"Well, my dear, there were sheep and cattle grazing and chickens running around. There were horses and carriages and such, but that would be going way back."

It was nice to see Margaret actually interested in a topic and not ridiculing the place.

"Colonel Parker used to have all kinds of exotic creatures, too," I said. "Now it's just the swans on the pond, and some ducks. The swans have babies. Cygnets, they're called. But don't go anywhere near them. Swans are like attack dogs around their babies," I added.

Hector chuckled. "You listen to Fancy, Margaret. And there still happen to be peacocks in the forest. My father said he had to shoot a few that came over and were eating up his garden. They eat down to the goddamn stem, excuse my language."

"Hector, please. As far as peacocks go, I haven't seen one around here in years. Maybe off in the woods. Marigold hated them. They were always eating her flowers and perching up in the branches." Loretta sat down, picking up a small fan from a basket on the table.

They were lying all over the house in trays, another relic from the days of yore. I got her a glass of water and she looked grateful.

"Yes, the Colonel liked the strangest things for pets. Marigold preferred cats, but his falcons ate some of those. There were rabbits at one time, too. The Colonel gave a pair to Charlie for Easter when he was a baby but Marigold turned them out. She couldn't stand them in the house. Then they just started breeding and breeding."

Margaret giggled.

"That wasn't the half of it." Loretta was fanning herself full force now. "I can tell you a story about a garden party about seven years after the war ended. Mr. Charlie was about six years old. Fancy's mother was still working here. There were rabbits hopping all over the property at that time, not just peacocks strutting about. It was a huge party and there was a whole area in the walled garden with activities for the children who came. Your brother, John Lee, was there, Fancy. Charlie was shy to such a degree it was painful speaking to him. He'd cringe when the Colonel would address him. But John Lee would talk to anyone, shake anyone's hand. What a sturdy little mister he was. The colonel called him *my fine little man*."

"Ma always said Charlie was timid because his parents was so bullheaded they flattened out his personality," I said.

"That does sound like something Marilyn would say. She was working in the kitchen during the party. I was out in the garden with the children. There was a mime and a juggler and trays with tiny fairy cakes for the children. And croquet and a magician and a special marionette play performed in the gazebo. Of course, once the rabbits started hopping out of the thicket the children only wanted to chase them about with carrots from the snack table. Charlie had the biggest carrot and he was holding it out to this large white rabbit.

"And out of the sky came this huge falcon, swooping down with an ungodly screech. It grabbed the rabbit by the neck. It was dreadful. Charlie was still holding on to the rabbit. He lifted about a foot off the ground. John Lee was yelling, 'Let go, Charlie, let go of the bunny!' Charlie was petrified. John Lee gave a jerk on his leg and Charlie came tumbling down to the lawn. What a thud his head made. We could hear the falcon's huge wings beating as it rose in the sky, blood dripping down."

"Marigold must have had a fit," I said.

"We heard her screaming as she ran across the lawn, and she sounded just like the great bird, but who wouldn't seeing their son dangling from talons like those? The Colonel dashed over with his huge leather arm cover. The falconer was running beside him. Well, that great raptor came screeching down to him with the rabbit in its beak. The Colonel held up his arm and the bird landed. I can still see those talons gripping the leather and the Colonel holding it high. 'Have no fear,' he said. 'This is a trained bird. I assure you he is under control. Isn't he splendid? He must have escaped from the mews. Control has been restored.' He had such a queer way of talking. I can hear him still."

Hector slapped his leg and tried to say something but he was laughing too hard to get any words out.

Loretta shushed him. "Hector, please. It might seem funny to you but it was frightening for everyone. Except the Colonel. He never really did think beyond his own pleasure. Anyway, Charlie threw up right there on John Lee's lap. 'Buck up. No one likes a sissy,' the Colonel said to Charlie. Can you imagine? The Colonel had no patience with his son, poor thing. I took the both of them into the house. Charlie had a concussion from hitting his head."

"I bet Marigold had it out with the Colonel. I bet he let that bird out on purpose. Jenny said he had that sort of sense of humour."

"Yes, Fancy, he did find that sort of thing entertaining, oddly. Anyway, this was a long time ago."

Margaret and Hector sat there as though they were waiting for another story, enraptured. But it was like someone had flipped Loretta's work switch. She put the fan down and stood up. "How these stories keep flooding back. There's nothing but songbirds now.

Hector, the gardeners were asking about the fountain, something to do with the plumbing? They left a note for you in the carriage house. And if you could take Margaret home later? Children, take Margaret about and give her the history of the place."

Hector nodded, put his ball cap back on and left. By the time we got out he was gone, and we went around back to the south side of the house. It opened up onto a trellis garden and a big swath of lawn for croquet and badminton and lawn bowling. I looked over to the stone walls of Evermore, but unless you knew what was inside it didn't look like much.

"What's that, an animal pen? I thought Loretta just said there weren't any animals around. I hope the Colonel isn't still lurching around like some zombie."

I frowned, ignoring Margaret.

Margaret persisted. "Loretta sure can talk. She's got some crazy stories. She must get lonely in that big house with just you to keep her company, Fancy."

"Fancy's good company," Art said in his high voice. "Loretta just likes to keep people informed. She doesn't normally tell stories. It's been a busy few days. She's stressed out."

"Well she seems nice enough. My father said she used to be a religious fanatic but she doesn't seem that way to me. You must like living over here with her and not your drunk mother, Fancy. So who's the other daughter, besides the one who plays piano?"

"Oh, that's Jenny. She's the same age as us. She almost died being born early. Jenny has health problems, troubles with her lungs and her eyes. She had a virus in her brain. Isn't that right, Fancy? And she's got her own religion."

We were almost at the big door to the walled garden.

Margaret snickered. "A twelve-year-old preacher with her own church . . . that's all I need. This place is crazy. Don't you see that?"

We knew it was unusual, but it was familiar. And Margaret didn't seem to be no authority on what was normal and healthy. "Jenny lives for coming out here. We play with her. She's a bit touched in the head but she's always been that way. You just have to let her have her own way. We don't mind. She doesn't have much of a life."

"Well, she's got lots of frigging money. And you're getting too grown up for playing if you're twelve."

Jenny's favourite game was Dead Body and she'd get the three of us playing it whenever she could. One of us would have to pretend to be dead of a tropical illness or a plague. The dying was the first part of the game. When the dying was done and you was lying in the grass in the final position of your death throes, the two living would carry the dead body and heave it onto a marble bench by the garden, with a bit of help from the corpse. Jenny would do the sermon, followed by lullabies we used as hymns, dancing about until the body would rise. Jenny's mother had a fit when she caught us at it once and blamed me and Art, the country children with our queer ways. That only made us laugh for it was Jenny who come out from the city with her queer ways. Jenny was the first to speak up and tell her mother it was her idea. She relished shocking Estelle but it was impossible to do—Estelle was convinced her frail little girl was pure and innocent. Even when she saw her do something right in front of her. It was amazing.

My mouth was dry and I smacked my lips as we walked. "There's nothing wrong with playing, Loretta says . . . being carefree. You know the garden party Loretta was telling us about? It would be in here." I pushed the door open and there was Evermore.

The fragrant thick air wrapped around us. I pulled the door shut. Margaret put her hands on her hips where the nylon skirt pulled tight and looked around speechless, under the spell of Petal's End just for a moment, even pushing her bangs away for a clear glimpse. "No one's going to believe me."

"Well, that will be fine with the Parkers. They don't like people talking about their business so you best be careful what you say in case it gets back. Jenny calls it her garden. She's possessive like that."

"Doesn't that make you mad, Fancy? Jenny sounds like a spoiled bitch, if you ask me." No one had asked Margaret, but that never did stop her from offering her opinion.

"Jenny don't intend to be mean . . . most of the time. She tries to be nice but she don't really understand how."

"Fancy can whistle." Art looked over at me. "And she can do embroidery."

"Those are useful skills," Margaret said, "if you're a fucking bird or an old hag. Don't you two watch television or anything like normal kids?"

"There are no televisions at Petal's End. Marigold don't want no new stuff. She don't trust it. This is where we come and play. And this is where Jenny likes to come. Marigold and Estelle don't like Jenny down on the beach." I didn't bother whistling but I spun around with my arms out, and Art joined in.

We gave Margaret the tour, taking her to the gazebo. Margaret took in the latticework. Its intricacy reminded me of embroidery. We told her how Marigold had loved dancing with her son and that the Colonel never had time for dancing. Margaret rolled her eyes and when we showed her the hedge labyrinth she said it should be cut down. It hadn't been trimmed yet and the seven-foot walls were ragged.

"When it's pruned up you won't say that." Art held his hands up. "If you fly over it, it looks like a rose. There's an aerial photograph of the estate in the library. There's four ways in and at the centre there's a white marble bench, if you can find it. The Colonel had it made as a wedding present for Marigold. She never, ever goes in. She says the hobgobblies hide there."

"The Colonel was forever going on about the war. He seemed to be in made-up days all the time, by the end. He would walk around apologizing to people no one could see."

"Did he really have a pet bear?"

"Well, it lived in the woods and he fed it. Marigold said he spent more time following the bear around in his last years than he did with her. Maybe he tried to dance with it and that's what set it off."

"That was the problem," said Art. "He thought it was his pet."

"Grampie said no wild animal is ever your pet."

"Well, he should have told the Colonel that. It chased Marigold about the estate. They set a trap for it. No one could walk in the forest. Marigold was right to be upset, Fancy. It tried to kill her," Art said.

"Yes, it was in league with the hobgobblies, she declared. It was one of their representatives. Imagine. Don't go scaring Margaret."

"I'm not trying to scare anybody," Art said. "But it did try to kill her!"

"How do the two of you manage when you aren't together?" Margaret made a face. "It's like listening to one person with two voices. Down in the valley no one really cares what happens over here. I'm just here to look after the old lady." She looked over her shoulder.

"The Colonel's family built Petal's End way, way back. They owned all the land over on the mountain in the days of sail, before the trains and highways. Loretta says the first Lord Parker was a lumber baron. Petal's End and Lupin Cove was so different a long time ago. In the past they used to dredge the harbour, and it was a lot deeper, that's what Grampie said."

"I can't imagine. You two are like little history teachers. I bet that's your favourite subject at school. It always made me want to poke my eyes out with a pencil."

Art looked hurt. "Well, we just thought you might like to know a bit about the place to help you understand Marigold. When the ships stopped coming was when Petal's End started being mostly their summer place. The Parkers have a big house in the city. That's why they let the Annex be a mental hospital during the war, because they didn't need all the space," Art said.

"The Colonel got money for it. Tell the truth, Art. Parsimonious, Grampie called it. One way they knew the Colonel had dementia was when he started throwing money away. Marigold put a stop to that."

"How'd the old lady get sick?"

"After Charlie died she had her attack," I said.

"Stroke. The proper name is a stroke, Fancy."

"Fine, Art, a stroke. When your veins get too tight. Marigold shrivelled up on one side." I thought of my embroidery and how I needed to fix her face.

"Well, my veins are getting tight just listening to the two of you. I'm only eighteen and I can feel a stroke coming on."

We didn't bother taking Margaret to the family cemetery or to the Wishing Pool surrounded by the cedars where the broken teacups was lying at rest in pieces at the bottom of the water. We came back by the long perennial beds. There was butterflies everywhere.

"There's all kinds of rare types," Art said. "One of the gardeners told me that. And heritage variety plants, too. He says the butterflies like the air here. He calls it a microclimate." A butterfly fluttered to the stretch of lupins. It had a border of white and black at the edge of its blue wings. "That's the Melissa Blue. The blue lupin is the only flower with the nectar they like. The gardener says their larvae eat the leaves. It's got gossamer wings," he added.

"I don't know what that means."

"Silky. Ma uses that word for embroidery floss."

Art nodded. "You can't touch their wings though, or they can't fly. They'll die if they can't fly."

We walked out of the garden and Margaret glanced around hesitantly again, like she wasn't sure if any of this was real. "What happened to the son, Jenny's father? I mean, I heard what happened to him, in the end, but what did he do?"

She didn't like history but she sure liked the gossip. "Oh yes," I said. "Mr. Charlie. He seemed to spend all his time travelling. He was nice, quiet. He helped with the family empire but he didn't seem to have a real job. He didn't come over too much that last year."

"I guess he just came back to kill himself, did he?" It seemed there was constantly things Margaret could make fun of.

It was a scandal but it had faded out of sight, out of mind. Not out of our minds, though. You never forget the sight of a dead man.

"The whole place is creepy. It was back here, right?" Margaret waved her hand at the west side of the house. The air felt cold to me despite the swelter. And it wasn't fun no more. I didn't want to be talking of the dead.

Twelfth-born, I was thinking.

We were just past the carriage houses then. The summer sun was still high but had moved through the sky. It must have been close to suppertime. Only the roof of the west side was visible where we stood. Margaret started walking toward it. We hesitated, but followed close behind.

"That was the mental hospital that Loretta mentioned was mouldy," Art explained. "Marigold called it the asylum. She said that's what Petal's End was, a sanctuary. There was a swimming pool back there once, a black-bottom pool. It was filled in a long time ago. Loretta said she could hardly remember a pool being here. None of the Parkers are swimmers. They like croquet and badminton." There was only a slight depression in the grass in front of the abandoned wing of the house.

We were around the side of the house now, where the lawn ran down a steep hill, and a high, ornate wrought-iron fence with a heavy gate blocked the wing off from the rest of the property. The far end of the neglected wing was against the forest. It wasn't built that close but the forest had grown in to meet it.

"It's so creepy. Estelle is right to want it torn down. You mean to tell me that two snoops like you never come back here?"

Still we didn't tell Margaret. I knew it was making Art sick just remembering.

"Can you get into it from the main house?"

"Yes, but the door is locked. One of the old soldiers had a heart attack playing croquet. There was only a few left by then and they moved them all at the same time when he died, back down to the valley to a place for seniors. That was when Jenny was a baby." I knew the key was hanging on a nail behind the painting in the hall leading into the kitchen. Jenny had shown it to me once. She didn't say a word, just lifted the painting, her huge blue eyes moving to and fro like they was on either end of a teeter-totter. We heard Loretta's shuffle and her voice calling us and Jenny let the painting bang down.

Margaret pushed through the gate. It creaked and Art jumped. We followed her. That's what children do. They follow, even when they know they shouldn't. There were stone benches, the remains of garden beds and a marble bird feeder. Lupins were growing around the edges and the Melissa Blue butterflies were flitting about, more petal than insect.

There were dusty blinds and sheer yellowed curtains in the windows. "Which room did he do it in?" Margaret looked at the far end.

I pointed. "In there. That was the entertainment room for the patients. He was hanging from the middle of the room where the light was." My heart was pounding thinking about it. It was a warm spring afternoon and the lilacs were all in bloom, and the lily of the valley. They had all those flowers at his funeral.

"Is that so?" Margaret laughed. "Chandelier Charlie. Maybe they should make it a hotel and call it that, Chandelier Charlie's." Margaret laughed like a maniac and she licked her lips as though she was trying to savour her own chortles.

Art was staring at his feet.

"If anyone catches you talking that way, Margaret, they'll ship you right back down to the valley and your daddy, so you best think on things. You shouldn't talk that way about the dead. They wouldn't like it." I didn't know why I said that. The words just come out of my mouth.

Margaret held her breath then, just for a moment, and she tossed her hair. "Well, I didn't mean anything by it. He couldn't have been much of a man, my father says. Leaving his family behind."

"Well Mr. Charlie died and there ain't nothing we can do about it, and talking bad don't make it better."

Margaret's voice was low. "Did they see him hanging there? Who found him?"

Art's eyes stayed on his feet. "We shouldn't talk about it. It's not respectful."

"Jenny and her grandmother found him. And then I came in . . . and then Art. The door was open. We went in to play. We would sneak in. Jenny was first there. The rope was long. He was dangling there, the tips of his toes on the floor, like he was going to start dancing. Charlie's face was purple and black." I wanted to scare Margaret, and Art knew it.

"Fancy! We shouldn't be talking about it. It's not right."

Margaret wasn't smiling any more. "That's no story for a girl your age to be telling, Fancy Mosher. It's disgusting. I don't believe either of you were there." She took a step back from us.

I thought she was going to cry and it made me feel powerful. I wasn't myself. "Well, then, you shouldn't go asking, Margaret. Jenny says this place is haunted, that Charlie comes out at night, looking for who hung him there." I was making that up now, to scare Margaret. Art hated it when people made stuff up, but of course he was thinking now that maybe this might be true.

"Well, there was no one to blame but himself. Maybe Charlie comes back now, looking for himself." Margaret laughed, but we didn't laugh back and she stopped. She pulled her bangs down. "Maybe someone strung him up in there. To get his fortune. Maybe Estelle did it."

"Marigold owns the whole lot of it so I guess that didn't work out for too good her." I thought about the picture Grampie did of Mr. Charlie. He was pointing his finger in it, maybe judging those looking at the painting. Grampie saw him. I knew that now, and Art did too. It's why Marigold was never the same, knowing Charlie knew something. Something he told to Grampie.

Art's voice was the lowest I ever heard it in my life. "We should go back and see if Loretta needs us. I've got to be getting home soon. I have to help my grandmother with supper."

That was when I noticed one of the windows was open just a crack. They saw it too.

"I thought you said no one goes in there," Margaret said.

"Loretta must have done that. For air circulation. There's black mould. It can infect your brain." I didn't know if that was true but it come easy off my tongue, like I was protecting the place from Margaret, or Margaret from Petal's End . . . I couldn't tell which. Margaret wanted no part of it and that was probably wise, but Art and I, we were already deep within the world of Petal's End, too far in to get out.

"You know, at Bible School they said your family has the devil in them. That's what the ministers say, Fancy."

I understood later that Margaret was mean when she was afraid, but at that time it caught me off guard.

It brought out the same in Art, anger caked on top of his fear. "There's no need to talk to Fancy like that, Margaret. She's just a kid."

"And what are you, a big man?"

"You better be careful, Margaret. Maybe I can see things, you know, tell them what to do." I kept looking at that window opened a crack. Charlie's bowed head appeared in my mind, his face like crushed pansies.

"I'm just teasing. You two can't take a joke. You never could." But Margaret was serious, her lips pulled in and twitching slightly.

I ignored her and walked over to the Annex. Inside, I heard a low swishing from one of the windows.

"Did you hear that?" I looked at Margaret.

Margaret took a step back. "Hear what? You're not funny, Fancy."

"Fancy?" Art's voice was quiet.

It started again. It wasn't no joke any more. I looked at them at the top of the hill by the fence. I heard Margaret say, "Why is she acting that way, Art?"

"I don't know. You shouldn't have brought us back here. You shouldn't have made us talk about what happened to Jenny's father. You have to do what you're told here, Margaret. Fancy, let's go." Art was almost in tears.

I heard it again, swish, swish, like the curtains were blowing. But there was no breeze. The sound stopped again.

"It's probably Loretta. Or you're imagining things," Margaret said, her voice tense. She marched right down beside me, to show me how stupid she thought I was being. Her hands were shaking, and she rubbed them together while I stood there. I could have sworn she heard it too, but she was looking at me, and though she couldn't hear it she knew I was not lying. I began whistling to make myself feel brave, and Margaret bolted and run up the hill screaming I was a freak who should be locked up.

Art was calling after me to come back but I went right up to the window and put my eyes to the crack. I couldn't make nothing out except for the white wall across the room. There was an overturned chair.

"You're whistling that song again, Fancy," Art called out to me. He called again as the hair on my arms prickled up like needles in my flesh. If I was older would I have looked again?

Something darted away from the window. It had been looking out at me. I opened my mouth to scream but nothing came out. There was no time of day I could hide from whatever set after me on my birthday, not morning, noon or night. I ran toward Art, and together we sprinted around to the kitchen door.

Margaret had a cigarette in her jittery hand and was struggling to light it. "I hate this place already. Fancy, why did you do that? Why did you go act all psycho?"

Just then Loretta come rushing out the door and Hector come loping over. "Mother of God, what the hell are you all up to? I could hear you all the way back by the cars even when I was hammering on metal."

"Yes, what's the hollering out here for? Margaret, what is going on? You can't be smoking back here when the Parkers come. It's not proper. You have to obey the rules." Loretta followed Margaret's gaze in the direction of the Annex. She gave Art and me a severe look. "Hector, take Margaret back down to the valley. I'm sure she's had enough for today. And we'll have our hands full with the Parkers tomorrow, that's all I know." Loretta went back into the house.

Hector laughed. "You kids can't stop getting into trouble." He looked at Margaret. "It's not so bad working here, even if they're trying to scare you off. Fancy and Art aren't afraid of things most normal kids are. Though it might get scarier when the Parkers get here. I shouldn't speak too soon. You haven't met Jenny yet." He walked off to get the truck.

Margaret blew a big smoke ring followed by two small ones right through it, some sort of peace offering. She needed us if she was going to make her job work here, or she'd be going right back to her father. Margaret acted like she was never scared but I could feel way underneath it all that she was. I didn't know if I would be seeing the dead some day but I did know I could smell fear like Jake could smell a stranger.

"Art, it was a fan, that's all."

"Well it must have been some big fan to scare you like that, Fancy."

I didn't tell him that when I was down by the window I felt a puff of air on my cheek, not wind from a fan. A breath, a putrid breath.

Margaret gestured to my hands. "Look at you, Fancy. You're covered in goosebumps and you're shivering. I didn't mean you had the devil in you. It's just what other people say. I thought you should know."

"It's chilly standing in the shade, that's all, with the cool breeze," I said. But there was no shade, you see, as we stood in the middle of the yard in late-afternoon sun. And not even breeze enough to stir the gossamer wings of the smallest blue butterfly.

7.

Down the Long Dark Hall

ONLY THE sound of a breeze tickling the treetops came in the window screen of my bedroom. The air felt lifeless and each breath I took felt forced. My room was usually a comfortable, safe place in the dark, but that night nothing was the same. What had I been thinking going near the Annex with Margaret and Art? It was forbidden. I had always kept my word, but ever since Ma had come to school I was sneaking about, like she infected me.

Loretta was right that I should just let it go. Grampie was an old Mountain man with curious ways, that's all. But thinking about him made me want to cry, questioning every moment we spent together. Nothing about our lives at the Tea House was as I remembered. Grampie spent most of his time looking right at ghosts. While I was in the house making a cake. It was astonishing he could do it, and that he hid it. He was having tea with the dead while I was reading or filling the bird feeders or building a fort with Art in the woods. He would never have put me in danger . . . would he? He was trying to protect me, but not telling me had left me defenceless and alone. It was like there were two parts of me arguing that night in the oppressive air. Betrayal throbbed in my chest, but then a voice would remind me that Grampie hadn't asked for the memento any more than I had. It was something he inherited. It was our bloodline. He'd hoped it would never get passed down, but Ma made sure it did. And so he tried to shield me. When people asked him why he was a painter, Grampie would put his hands in his pockets and rock on his toes before he replied. And when he replied he always said the same thing—it was beckoning, and he could either follow it, or spend the rest of his life trying to look the other way. Those were the choices.

You can run but you can't hide. Grampie would always tell me and Art that. I wondered if that was what Charlie was thinking when he walked into the room in the Annex with a piece of hemp rope in his hand. He would have taken the time to get the chair, to knot the rope. Was he humming to himself, keeping away the thought of what he was going to do? Or was he picturing it the whole time? Was he thinking he could run but he couldn't hide, and the only way out was to hang himself? Did something beckon to him? That stupid Annex was a tomb for the past, keeping it dead and alive at the same time.

It was awful for a young girl to be lying in a bed with her head jumbled up with such thoughts, but I was no typical young girl, as I'd recently been told. Maybe it was standing there in the dark beckoning to me right at that moment. I turned on my light fast so if it was leering at me it would be caught with its hand in the air. Nothing but walls with faded flowered paper. On my nightstand was the embroidery hoop with my pictorial of Marigold without a face as I'd pulled the stitches so I could redo it more cheerful. The small glass lamp, my tattered clothes on the chair, the worn Persian rug. I was compelled to get out of bed. If there was anything beckoning to me in the Annex, I would confront it. It was better than lying in bed waiting for it to come.

I took the flashlight from the drawer in my bedside table. I went ever so quiet down, down, down the stairs, not making a creak, hearing Loretta snoring from far off through her door as I slipped my hand behind the painting and felt the key, the key I was not to touch.

What I learned, you see, is this—what goes around comes skipping right back around because there ain't no circle that don't want to close. Such is its nature, and we cannot defy our nature, although we do try. Sitting on this verandah now, I know this as truth. And this is why you have come, even if you still linger out of sight.

I thought of the story of the pirate who chopped the sailor's head off, leaving the headless body to watch over his treasure, treasure you can only find on a full summer moon in silence, because uttering even one word will collapse the hole and you'll never see what's inside. That night I crept from my room I was silent, my twelve-year-old mind following that pirate's rule of keeping quiet in the midnight hour.

There was a long window just before the big door leading to the Annex. The moonlight was falling in through the pane, through the yellowed sheer curtains. The key went smooth into the lock. I turned the doorknob and pushed open the door with a squeak. I left the key in the lock and nudged it a crack more, squeezing my thin body through, noticing how my breasts got in the way, and I sucked in my breath to shrink them back, searching for my body of just a year ago, the body of a child. I stepped into the darkness of the long hall with the doors on either side all along to the end, the rooms all closed except the one at the far end, the door to the patients' salon. The dank air was rife with mildew. They hadn't sent the Happy Helpers in here to clean with any of Grampie's turpentine and honey furniture polish or their lemon and orange oil and their lavender and vinegar window spray. The moonlight was spilling down the wall and over the floor at the end of the hall, as though it was trying to escape out of the room. I heard the vibrating again, the fan sound, but when I listened closer it was more like the breath of an angry little animal. I took a step. *Oh, no, Fancy Mosher, go back, and keep your word about not sneaking.* I took quick steps, one two three, then I was beside the moonlight on the floor. My own breathing, my foreign whistling in my ears, and then a soft whir. I inched further because I had given myself my word that I'd go and see what was in that room, and Grampie said you must stay true to your word.

My feet were white in the moonlight, and my small fingers were slivers of cold marble. *Hush-a-bye, don't you cry*. My lips made the shapes of the words. I was trying hard to whistle a familiar tune but I kept unwillingly returning to the melody I'd never heard before that summer. I was looking in the dark room and feeling the breeze from the fan, shivering, and I heard a slow, faraway singing, a thin voice falling into a whispery song. I couldn't tell if it was far away in the room or far away in my head, and suddenly I was trying to whistle again, my lips pulling into a circle, but I couldn't get air out. My lips moved like the mouth of a fish tossed on the dry dock, mindlessly opening and shutting. In the dark of the room there was a bridal veil and it was streaming out and words I could not understand were blowing from it.

My fists squeezed tight and I felt the flashlight still in my hand and shone the thin beam in front of me. It was just a fan and the curtain blowing in on the wind. I shut the fan off and took a few gasps, bending over to calm myself. Composed, I stood up and tilted my head back, and there was the big hook in the ceiling where the chandelier had been. The rest was the same as when we'd found Charlie there. There were chairs all gathered round and a movie screen stand, waiting for a show that would never come again, an old movie projector on a shelf, some papers, a Tiffany lamp in the corner, a worn leather sofa and a rectangular mirror over it, reflecting my flashlight, and then suddenly a glimpse of a face, with white swirling around.

I heard my name being called and I broke out of whatever stupor the room had me in and went fast down the long creaking hall with my feet flying. I pulled the door open to the light and Loretta was there, waiting in her tented granny nightgown, what she called her nightdress, her arms folded, a big sigh, and the skeleton key I had left in the door lock now in her fingers. In my head was the blurred melody, the half-formed words of a song I couldn't catch. There was something in there, and it had followed me from the Tea House, and that something had been peeking out the window earlier in the day, waiting. Loretta was protecting me, keeping whatever it was at arm's length, for as long as Loretta was there it was possible to not quite fully believe that the dead would come singing. And as long as I did not believe so absolute and pure, they would be nothing more than hushed melodies and snatches of whispered words.

8.
The Arrival

THE PARKERS was over two hours late. The sun was cooking our flesh. While we waited, Margaret complained how stupid it all was. She must have felt my eyes on her for she turned to face me. She took a step back.

Loretta went inside to the kitchen, saying how the devil loved idle hands. She was worn out from being up in the night with me. All she said in the morning was no matter the trauma of my birthday I was to bear in mind the importance of keeping my word. Margaret went with Hector back to the carriage house.

In the shade of the verandah I told Art about the new embroidery I was working on: Pomeline and Jenny playing in a meadow of daisies. I told him I might stitch me and him into it . . . a keepsake for Pomeline when she went off to the music conservatory in the autumn. He thought that was kind. Then I told him about the Annex. Art said he'd thought plenty about the matter and I should forget all about it. No one could see the dead, he lectured. We were twelve now and shouldn't entertain superstitious stories. No disrespect to your Grampie, he added fast. But Art didn't believe a word he was saying—he just wanted to believe. And wanting to believe's not the same thing at all.

"Your Grampie said dead people would find you. But you keep looking. You don't need to follow everything that waves at you, Fancy. You're frightening Loretta. She already told me what happened last night. She thinks you were sleepwalking. She's getting old, Fancy. It's just that Margaret got you all wound up about the Parkers, from forcing us to remember Charlie."

We heard the far-off rumble of an engine and I went calling for the others to come back. We stood in a line as the long black car with tinted windows gleamed through the leaves and turned into the drive.

"Well, ain't it good to see Dr. Baker is still driving Mr. Lincoln," Hector said. He was all cleaned up, wearing a short-sleeved shirt.

"Looks like a hearse to me." Margaret watched as the car came around toward us.

The car rolled to a stop and idled in front of us, the tinted windows reflecting our faces. I wondered if anyone was even in there. Maybe what was looking for me could drive. I wondered if whoever was in the back was looking out at us, wondering if *we* were real. We'd mostly observed the Parkers from a distance. They seemed to have crawled out of them paintings of landscapes and galas in the big house. Marigold in the gardens, Mr. Charlie and Estelle, the Colonel marching in his uniform thinking he was back in the war, and Pomeline sitting on a marble bench writing in her journal. When she wasn't playing the piano or singing she was skipping through Evermore or writing in her journal. Mostly lyrics and love poems, Jenny said. That was back before Pomeline locked her journals so Jenny couldn't pry.

Estelle thought we was strange country children, that we'd corrupt her precious child. Even back then we could plainly see how little Estelle knew her own daughter. It was Jenny picking rose thorns off and leaving them on the stone bench where her mother liked to sit. It was Jenny who would feed her lunch to the swans. Jenny who would drop her dishes on the stone path. She said she liked the sound of things breaking. And she never pretended she didn't do it. She was accident-prone, Estelle and Marigold would say. Jenny's skin was thin, and it affected her grip. Jenny would just stand there, hiding in plain sight behind her big thick glasses, her crooked grin for me and Art. She didn't even mind falling. The pain of it reminded her life wasn't a dream, she told us once.

Hector cleared his throat. "Christ-on-a-stick-shift, I can feel the winds of time passing over me." Sweat trickled down his chin. Margaret snickered. It was like they'd pulled up to the wrong house. Art and I started laughing from nerves.

Loretta shushed us. "They'll be out soon enough."

Hector wiped his hands on his pants and boldly walked over to the car. He opened the back door. "How you all doin' in there?" he said. "We got the place all spiffed up for you. Welcome to Petal's End. No time like the present, as my daddy likes to say."

"Hector!" Loretta gasped, but as she spoke a white gloved hand drifted out and into Hector's callused palm. He guided Mrs. Marigold Parker out of the car in her elegant summer dress and her blue sapphire pendant the Colonel gave her so long ago. Her face was still tight and droopy at the same time. From under the great brim of her summer hat Marigold gazed around Petal's End as though she was waiting for someone else to come running down the steps to greet her.

The car engine finally turned off. We heard angry voices through the open door. Estelle and Pomeline. Marigold shuttered her eyes, an irritated look coming over her. Estelle appeared with her regular facial expression, which suggested she was about to start yelling. Art thought that's why she looked strained all the time, because she was always shouting inside her head. She took handfuls of pills for her colossal head pains. Her expression screamed that she had been born into a cruel world that forced her to endure imbeciles. She was a good nurse, Loretta told me once, because Estelle never doubted and never strayed from a course once she was on it. Her face was elegant on the rare occasion she was in repose. It was an embroidery picture to me, as though her features had been carefully put on by expert fingers. It was when Estelle opened her eyes and spoke that the loveliness frayed.

That good-looking part of her reeled Charlie in. The rumour was Charlie only married Estelle because she was pregnant with Pomeline. Ma said Nurse Estelle got along so fine with Dr. Baker that it seemed odd when she hooked her star to Charlie's instead. An unlikely match, my mother said. Charlie didn't like the ladies, just his mother, until Estelle come striding through. The Colonel wanted his son married and so Charlie did what was expected. There was nothing Marigold could do either but keep smiling.

Margaret was rubbing her eyes in wonder. Pomeline Parker was next out of the car, her long blond hair glittering in the sunlight. She had on a sapphire ring that Marigold gave her, just like the one she gave to Jenny. Her beautiful hands with them long graceful fingers made just for playing the piano. They were her future, she would say. The only one without a shiny blue stone was Estelle.

Pomeline gave Marigold a black cane with a silver rose handle. "Look at you children, growing up so fast. Fancy, we'll do piano lessons. Loretta, you'll have to put up with us. You've probably enjoyed the quiet summers without us here but we won't make too much fuss and bother, will we, Granny?"

Dr. Baker was right smack behind Pomeline, shaking our hands with his dry palm, his hand soft and gentle like his words, saying how wonderful we kept the place. He was like the mayor greeting his citizenry. He had this way of taking your hand, squeezing it a bit as he looked in your eyes like you was the only person alive who mattered.

Marigold squeezed Hector's shoulder and reached up to pat his cheek. "Clyde. Oh, Clyde, how lovely to see you."

Estelle stood beside the car, her index finger on her temple. "That's not Clyde. It's his son, Hector. Hec-tor. It's not practical for you to be staying here, Marigold. Nor is it safe. We have some hard decisions to make. You're not going to live forever. That's apparent to everyone but you, it seems." Estelle had usually been able to keep her hatred wrapped up in a thin paper of civility in front of the help. "H-e-c-t-o-r," Estelle said again.

"Yes, of course it is. Hector. Clyde's your father, isn't he, darling?" Marigold said. She was still holding Hector's hand. "You look just like your father, young man, exactly like him. Clyde worked for us on occasion. He had that funny expression he used to say. 'Don't it slice you right up.' He had such a country way with words. And he was constantly singing those shameful love songs to his horses."

"Oh, I'm a bit like my father and not much like him at the same time. I'm good with engines, like he was. Me, well, I don't sing, but if I did it would only be to a fine-looking woman." Hector laughed, and I noticed his big hands, so careful with Marigold.

Marigold took a few steps toward the house, running her eyes over the line of us, finally landing on Loretta. Marigold chuckled, "Oh my goodness, Loretta, you haven't changed at all. I told you they couldn't keep me away. Soon we'll be promenading the gardens singing the songs and canticles I loved so well as a girl. Making rosewater and soaps, entertaining guests. Sipping iced mint tea. Eating Lady Dundee cake in Evermore and sipping Campari and lime over crushed ice before dinner. Loretta, I do hope you'll make some rosewater and pistachio ice cream. We have enjoyed the jams and jellies and vinegars you've sent to the city. And of course, my herbal remedies—it's the herbal remedies that are keeping me alive. Some traditions are worth preserving, aren't they? It will be just as it was, steaming up the Water House."

Estelle looked up from her perfect fingernails. "So this is who will be running the place this summer, a bunch of children? Loretta, you have your work cut out for you. Marigold has invited her cousin Harold Prescott and his wife to spend the summer. I don't know if she's told you that bit of news yet. She's also planning on reviving the garden party again, in mid August. It defies all good sense. Marigold, it's ridiculous. I'm sorry but you simply must understand that we are obliged to let some things go. Honest to God, I'm so tired of this. There hasn't been a party at Petal's End in years." She paused. "I'm dying of thirst."

Marigold tapped her cane. "Well, Estelle darling, perhaps you should have a drink before you leave, which, my dear, I'm sure will be soon. Loretta, I'm sorry I couldn't come out for the sensational spring flowers."

"Well, Mrs. Parker," Loretta said, "you are on time for the summer blooms."

Estelle let out a dramatic puff of air.

"Really, Estelle, I understand you don't enjoy flora and fauna. Concrete and asphalt are more your taste. That's perfectly fine, of course. Each to their own. Brutalism, I believe, is the architectural term. There was a marvellous program on the radio about modern architecture. I do enjoy the radio in the winter. I'm sure it's very engaging for you, these contemporary perspectives. I am a holdover from a more genteel time. No one likes an intense woman. It's coarse. Try to have a bit more *sang-froid*. You really must learn to relax. Isn't that so, Dr. Baker?"

Dr. Baker nodded. It was hard to tell if he was just humouring her.

"And yes, Loretta, we will be having houseguests, and we will be having the garden party. I'm sure Harry and his wife, Sakura, will be happy to help. Outdoor enthusiasts, both of them! He met her when he went off to exotic parts of the world to research and he stole her away. So romantic. She showed him how to eat with chopsticks. Doesn't that sound adventurous? I'm sure she's a darling, just like dear cousin Harry. Sakura means cherry blossom. Isn't that precious? I missed the cherry blossoms as well. What comfort it brings to close my eyes and imagine Petal's End flowering, knowing that even when I am not here the gardens continue on." Marigold yawned. "I'm parched myself. Nothing like a bit of time with family to bring on a long, dry thirst. A tall cool glass of lemon balm tea is just what I need. With a few rose petals."

Estelle massaged her jaws and opened her mouth to speak, but Dr. Baker interrupted.

"This is no way to start the summer. Estelle, Marigold has decided what she wants to do. Let us please stop this." His tone then made me think of what Art and Hector had said they'd overheard. "The place looks beautiful. Well done, Loretta and Hector, for such well-executed preparations."

Loretta said Dr. Baker always had a pleasant bedside manner, right from the time when he replaced his father, the first Dr. Baker, and come here to work in the final years they had the summer hospital retreat. He and Charlie were a fine pair of chums, she said. Charlie was handsome and charming, and Dr. Baker was the calm and reliable one. Dr. Baker wasn't a crazy-person doctor, but after his father retired they brought him out for the general health concerns of the soldiers.

"Mrs. Parker?" Loretta was tired from the theatrics. "You'll be wanting to meet Margaret Armstrong." Loretta put her arm behind Margaret and moved her forward.

"Margaret, darling, how do you do? I'm sorry for all of this. We Parkers can be a bit tempestuous. We'll have a wonderful summer, the two of us." She pinched Margaret's cheek. "You could have lovely skin, darling. I can make you a tincture to help make things smooth, to settle those blemishes. Such a pity Agatha isn't here. She knows the old ways. I have a passion for botanicals, a special understanding that Agatha has inherited directly from me."

Margaret tried to do some awkward curtsey thing.

Estelle took out a cigarette. She was rooting through her purse when Hector rushed over to her with his big silver lighter and she blew out a thank-you, waving him away.

Dr. Baker patted me on the head. "Fancy Mosher. Are you in trouble yet?"

I giggled. There was something boyish about him.

I asked where Jenny was and Pomeline answered. "She's in the city. She hasn't been feeling well. Obsessing over things, as per usual. She's into snowflakes now, you know. No, wait, that's her winter symbol. She has a crystal snowflake Granny gave her that she wears around her neck but she's changed it for a silver locket with a rose petal. She says flower petals are summer's snowflakes."

"Pomeline. Please. It's not your sister's fault she's delicate. She was born under different circumstances than you so, please . . . you know better."

Marigold glared at Pomeline. "It's perfectly fine Agatha has such an imagination. How else is one to have an inspired life? Creativity is a gift. She's a very clever girl. Pomeline, you simply are not patient enough with her, the poor frail thing. You're six years older than her and you should be setting a proper example."

"Oh Granny, you indulge her as much as Mother does. You know she prefers Jenny."

"Jenny then, if you insist, although Agatha is a more graceful name. It was my mother's name. She was a woman who understood tradition, as Jenny does. Jenny's interested in more than just the piano. She wants to come out and learn what I did out in the Water House. She isn't interested in picking flowers like most young girls, and I certainly don't understand *that*, but she was always more practical than you, Pomeline. Jenny appreciates my expertise. You'd do well to find some purpose for your life, not just pounding at the keys all day. Margaret, you'll adore my sweet rosewater. We'll be brewing some of that up. You can take a spoonful a day and it will clear up your skin in no time at all. I used to make a serum to calm the skin from rosehip, lavender and calendula. And, oh, to make some lavender soap. I used to have my own cottage industry. We'd go wildcrafting for wood violets and lady's slippers."

The heat was crushing and we were relieved when Marigold turned toward the house. She stopped, resting on her cane, her face trembling. She was staring at me. I was squeezing the little embroidery I did for her in my pocket. I had redone the face and now was anxiously rubbing the stitches. Marigold gasped like she was having an attack. She lifted her hand and pointed, her top lip twisted. My heart throbbed in my ears and the tight air closed in. Suddenly a cardinal sang out, and the sounds of summer come rushing back. Pomeline and Dr. Baker and Loretta hurried over to Marigold.

Dr. Baker cleared his throat. "Now, my dear, what is it? It's only Fancy Mosher. She's grown up so much in a year."

"Why yes, Mrs. Parker, it's just Fancy," Loretta said.

Pomeline was frowning. "She's frightened to death, Granny, look at the poor girl."

Marigold shook her head and snapped out of whatever had seized her. "Oh. Yes. I don't know what overcame me. Fancy looks like her mother. No doubt she's a Mosher." It didn't sound like no good thing to be.

Pomeline took her grandmother's arm and Marigold didn't seem to even notice. "Granny, you're tired from the journey. You just need to rest. We should get you out of the sun."

"Fancy Mosher. My but you have grown up, darling. You frightened me. I didn't know who you were. I thought you were a hobgobbly," she tittered. "Look at how strong you are. I was quite an athlete when I was a girl. Award-winning, you know."

Estelle was correct—Marigold wasn't right in her head. Loretta waved at me. She wanted nothing more than to be in her kitchen.

I stayed close to Art. A terrible shy feeling come over me now that our peace had been invaded.

Marigold reached out her finger and ran it over my scar. I wanted to pull my head away. "I'm glad Loretta is taking proper care of you. Someone had to. I can make you a salve for that. You look so pretty, just like your mother. She had perfect skin. The first time I saw her I thought how beauty can be such a curse."

I bit my lip as I slowly handed Marigold the embroidery.

"Well, isn't this utterly charming. I see your mother did teach you something useful. What fine stitching. Fancy, darling, what a gem of a gift." She handed the picture to Margaret to hold. "We'll have tea at four o'clock. We'll see you, Estelle, when you bring Agatha out, which I hope will be soon." Marigold fluttered her hand. "Come along, Margaret, my dear girl. We'll be good friends. You'll laugh at my stories. What a nice outfit you have on. You're lovely and plump! You'll have to teach Pomeline to eat a bit more. She takes after her mother that way. She's so thin, if she falls I worry she'll break."

"Granny, really!"

Marigold continued like she didn't hear Pomeline. "That won't happen to you, my dear girl. You're just delightful, nice and round like a popover. Men like a woman with substance. I met my husband back in the old world. He was there visiting his family. He preferred curves on a woman, but as you can see I was a disappointment to him in that regard."

That sweltering July afternoon Marigold went up the stairs, trailing her words behind her like a cape, one hand on Margaret's and the other on the railing. Marigold glanced in the mirror at the side of the door and then resumed her slow step. Like she'd been working here all her life, Margaret opened up them big doors, escorted Marigold through, pivoted, without even looking at us, and pulled them closed.

The rest of us was still in that blistering sun. Dr. Baker opened the trunk. Art and Hector took the bags and went in the house.

"I don't see the point in you staying, Dr. Baker," Estelle said.

Dr. Baker looked directly at Pomeline, lingering a moment, then shifted his gaze to Loretta. "I'll be driving out from the city on a regular basis, just to keep an eye on Marigold. She is still suffering the effects of the stroke, as dramatic as her recovery has been. Pomeline will help, and I'll help Pomeline, if she needs anything."

"Yes, after her dramatic recovery." Estelle was back to rubbing her temples.

"Mother, please don't start. I don't see why Dr. Baker has to go to the city with you. Granny will need him, even with Margaret. It's not like she's a nurse."

Dr. Baker touched Pomeline on the shoulder. "I'll be back out every few days. Don't worry, my dear. It's not that long a drive. Margaret seems capable, very robust." He lifted up his hand and said firmly, "Estelle, I am telling you Marigold is perfectly fine, and a quiet summer away from the city—"

"Away from me, you mean," Estelle interrupted. "And what, really, do you know about this, David?"

I thought again of the conversation they'd had by the Annex, and Hector's surmising. Pomeline turned and went inside.

"I don't mean to interrupt but I've got some cold lemonade and strawberries and cake, if you'd like. It's cool in the house. And there's supper to get." A piece of Loretta's grey hair was sticking out of her bun and she poked it back into place, sweat rolling down beside her eyes.

"We're heading back now. But thank you, Loretta." Estelle smiled at her as though only Loretta understood what Marigold was putting everyone through. Estelle opened the passenger door. "Jenny will be out at some point. She wanted to be her grandmother's caregiver but I told her that was crazy. On that, at least, Marigold agreed with me." Then all in one move she squished out her cigarette with her high heel, got in the car and slammed the door.

Dr. Baker got in the driver's side. Off the black car went, sliding through the forest. The trees seemed to have inched closer toward the house while we weren't looking, their tops brushing the speckless summer sky. Piano music streamed out the mansion's windows. As Loretta and I walked to the house, I realized I was whistling the piano melody, and it was the same one I'd heard in the Annex the night before, the same song I'd heard at Grampie's . . . now soaring from Pomeline's fingers.

9.
The Maids

Calm returned as soon as Estelle and Dr. Baker left. It wasn't the same, but it fooled me—the summer air, the way of our daily routines. There's great comfort in predictability, Grampie would say. All good in a garden comes from habit and all good art comes from the same, he'd remark when he went off to the outdoors or to his painting. Through the long years I have lived I've found comfort in the routine of the day, the rising and setting of the sun, things that never fail you. Art and I did our chores and ate our meals and spent our spare time riding bikes and roving the beach and playing in Evermore. I cut flowers each day for the house. We opened the downstairs windows each morning and closed them by noon. Loretta cooked meals and we served them in the dining room, on trays in Marigold's rooms, or on the verandah. Marigold took her daily walks with Margaret, and sat in the shade in Evermore, looking for her vitality, she proclaimed. She'd sip her teas and take her pills and tinctures. She went to bed right after supper and in the morning she slept in. Sleep, she preached, was the best healer. Margaret served her breakfast on the balcony of the bedroom, looking out over the grounds.

I'd sit with Loretta in the evening doing embroidery and we'd watch the day fade into night.

But underneath the tranquility there was a certain restlessness. I'd be sitting by the lily pond and there'd be chatter in the leaves, and yet when I looked there'd be nothing there. From the corner of my eye there'd be a flash in the perennial flower beds but when I gazed upon those lofty flowers there were only hummingbirds and butterflies. When the birds sang I would whistle along, and sometimes it seemed a muffled voice sang with me. When I'd stop and cock my ear there was only birdsong. It was at them times the memento seemed believable.

Loretta did not want to discuss it any more. She kept herself busy, never looking at me for too long. Art would notice me listening and peering around my shoulder. But he too said nothing, not then anyway. It became easier and easier to let the peace of summer, them lazy days, just waltz us from dawn until dusk. Before long I had stopped looking over my shoulder altogether.

Dr. Baker came out every few days as promised, and he'd chat with Loretta about domestic matters before heading off for discussion of intricate family politics—the management of Marigold and Estelle—with Pomeline. Their lives moved back behind closed doors. We were told what we needed to know when it pleased them. Marigold was determined to have the garden party, and Pomeline was helping. Dr. Baker looked after the back and forth with Estelle. He was the only one who could stand her, Art and I decided, because he was a man of medicine.

Loretta and I would have our breakfast outside at the table near the kitchen door. The early air was refreshing, but the sun started licking at the edges and by noon the freshness was spoiled. There was little rain in July and by mid month the land was parched. No one knew when Jenny was coming and no one spoke of her. The city was a world away, and not even the loud ringing of the heavy black phones could bring it to us. We began to forget Jenny and her mother. If it wasn't for the constant piano music flowing through the house, and the glimpses of them Parkers through doorways and in various parts of the garden and grounds, we might not have known they were at Petal's End.

Pomeline moved through the house like flickers of light coming in the deep-set windows of the mansion. At first I'd see her outside, or walking along a hall singing these cheery songs, or skipping over the stepping stones as though she was a young child again, twirling like she was dancing with someone we couldn't see. One afternoon shortly after Pomeline arrived we was out by the lily pond. Art and I had been lying on our backs playing a game of finding shapes in the clouds and we heard Pomeline singing in the distance. She strolled over and sat down on a bench nearby, caressing the daisies in her hand and crooning in perfect French as she sat in her wide-brimmed sun hat. I could not understand a word. Art told me later she was singing about love—*amour*, he said.

Margaret was with Marigold all the time, and we'd only see her when she was leaping out of her father's car in the morning, or in passing as we gave her a tray or watched her take Marigold to the garden, or sometimes in the car with Hector if he drove her home. When Marigold would nap through the mid-afternoon Margaret came outside for her break, sitting out talking to Hector, if he was around, smoking cigarettes. She kept away from us.

Time itself lost the meaning we put upon it, and it was a shock to us when Pomeline came down to the kitchen to tell us that, now two weeks had passed, Marigold was settled and wanted to start a choir in preparation for the party. Marigold insisted on calling it a choir even though we were such a small group. From then on we'd spend every afternoon in choir practice in the music room. I started hoping Pomeline would remember our piano lessons but she hadn't mentioned it since the first day. She was distracted by her coming piano exams. She abruptly stopped walking in the garden and her colour began to wane from being inside most of the time, intensely focused on her relentless cadenzas and arpeggios.

I came into the music room early for our first choir practice and I was a bundle of nerves, for I'd heard the piano far off in the house and recognized the tune right away. Pomeline was alone at the keyboard. She lifted her eyes to meet mine. She was playing that now familiar song again, the one that kept revealing itself to me. When I asked about it she said, "Oh, you look so alarmed, Fancy. It's just a song Jenny loves. Granny sang it for us when we were children, a song from her childhood, she said. Granny sang it to Daddy, too. He couldn't stand it. Granny said her nanny sang it to her as a child. I suppose it is somewhat creepy, like a lot of old songs are, terrorizing children to sleep. We aren't doing it for the garden party, have no fear." She put her head down and launched into a spectacular piece for a few moments. "'Wedding Day at Troldhaugen,' opus 65, number 6 . . . isn't it breathtaking? It's for my examination." Pomeline didn't wait for me to answer and she seamlessly switched to a ballad she said we were to sing for the garden party.

I didn't worry no more. The music I kept hearing must have been tucked away from when I was little, nothing more than snatches from my memory that was so sharp they seemed to play outside my mind.

Just when singing was added to our day, Marigold had Pomeline tell us she wanted to start doing needlework in the late mornings before lunch, and I was to join her. Margaret would bring her down to the front sitting room and we'd work there by the French doors. It was unusual, as Marigold didn't do much stitching. She just held the hoop in her hands as she rocked in her chair and watched me, admiring my herringbone ladder stitch and my lazy daisies and French knots.

Margaret wouldn't let on but I knew she was impressed by my skill with a needle, for she could hardly take her eyes from watching my fingers. She was acting like some senior maid and Art and I weren't worthy even of her notice, unless we was doing something wrong. When I passed her in the hall she'd tell me to put on shoes, and to slow down or speed up, the opposite of whatever I was doing. Margaret had no interest in learning embroidery stitching but Marigold insisted she try and do a sampler. I explained what Ma had told me, that it was what young girls did long ago, to show off their skills. I saw her watching me from under her bangs. It was the speed I could stitch at that Margaret liked, how fast my flowers would appear, and how perfect. Margaret and Marigold marvelled how I didn't need to draw no picture on the muslin, how I just stitched the picture waiting in the fibres. I could put in stitch after stitch with my eyes closed, letting my fingers take control. Even the colours I picked without thinking, pulling the floss from the basket.

And now with my eyes dim it is no different. It focuses the mind, and when you are old that is helpful, for the mind begins to fracture. Needlework was my only way to feel close to Ma. I always knew it give her a satisfaction, too, that she passed something along to me, although I did not understand the significance for many years.

The first day Marigold called me into the sitting room to join them she looked at me careful before she spoke. "Marilyn had a way with a needle, Fancy." Marigold's voice cracked when she said my mother's name. "There was a time when most of the linens were embroidered by Marilyn Mosher. Now it's all done by machine, but back then it was done by hand. It's long out of fashion, but here at Petal's End we don't concern ourselves with fads." Her tremor was barely visible, as though Petal's End was rehabilitating her.

❧

Deep in July I took a vase of fresh flowers up to Marigold's room just after breakfast. A light rain had fallen in the night and I'd been soaked from the raindrops falling off the leaves as I picked the flowers. I had to change when I got back. I was late coming up and hurried along to her room.

When I walked in the door Margaret was helping Marigold pull on thick support hose, which she wore to support her bulging veins. Her white hair was braided and pinned up on her head.

"Oh, how stunning, Fancy. Put them right here on the table beside me. I admire midsummer flowers but there's nothing quite as special as the first and last flowers of the season, the mayflowers, and the October roses. I see you've been cutting the Lord Black of Swallow's Hill. I worship the tea roses. I did a hybrid once, for my husband. I called it The Colonel Parker. But it had a fishy odour so I let it die. Charlie's rose garden is doing well. They are keeping them splendidly. Arthur is a great help in the garden, they tell me."

She moved over to her dressing table where she looked at me in the round mirror. Margaret came over and helped her with her makeup. There was a magnifying glass on the table that Marigold used on her own so she wouldn't get the lipstick and eye liner crooked.

"Maybe you'll end up working in a flower shop. Agatha would find that terrifying, of course. What a silly girl she can be, afraid of a vase of flowers. I never understood it. Agatha says cut flowers reek of death as they wilt and brown. She's terribly morbid, that dear child, which I attribute to her mother."

"Jenny sure knows her own mind," I said.

Margaret was standing silently with her lips pressed together as we talked about Jenny, like we was talking about a lunatic. She went off into Marigold's closet in an adjoining room.

"No lady wants a shiny face." Marigold chuckled with delight at her reflection and brushed some sweet-smelling powder on her cheeks with an enormous puff. "Well, each to their own, I say. There is time yet, so much time for you young people. Margaret and I are having a slow morning today." She picked up a big peacock-feather fan with a base of abalone shell and started flapping it about. "Estelle says we should have air conditioning but I think that's absurd. All you need is a breeze and you can endure any heat. And what we must never forget about summer, darling, is that it just doesn't last."

Since Marigold seemed to be talking to herself, I left her at the vanity and went through the adjoining door. Margaret turned around holding an antiquated maid's outfit. "Jenny sounds like a freak, Fancy. I hope she doesn't come out," she whispered.

"She ain't that bad. You get used to Jenny. She can be kind. You just never know when. Same with being mean. Ma says that's a family trait. Except for Pomeline."

"I just hope they keep Jenny in the city." Margaret held out the black dress with a white apron. "Look what I found yesterday, on the third floor in the sewing room. Or linen room. Whatever it's called. Marigold asked me to go looking for them, for nostalgia's sake."

Margaret carried the maid's uniform on the hanger to show Marigold. She clapped her hands together and tittered like a mindless young girl. "It will be just like the old days. Why don't you try them on, my dears? There must be one that will fit you, Fancy. Go have a look-see. So much nicer than what those cleaning girls wear, dressed like they're going to a gymnasium. Margaret, take Fancy upstairs to change." Marigold was looking at the dress fondly, like it might get up and start moving around the room and fold her clothes, maybe serve her some tea and crumpets.

Margaret bit her lip and went out the door carrying the dress, and I followed her up the stairs to the third floor and past a long row of storage rooms. The nursery had been up there, as well as the room for the nanny and governess, though I couldn't remember those being used in my lifetime. Margaret took out a skeleton key when we came to the room at the end.

"Where'd you get that?" I said, thinking about the key to the Annex.

"Marigold sent me down to get it from Loretta. Loretta said it would be good to humour her." She shrugged. "They're paying me. I could care less. The summer will be over soon enough. That old lady's crazy. You should hear the stories she tells me."

The key turned with a loud click, and she twisted the glass knob and opened the door. The room was large and the air was stale and dry. There was a small deep-set window with a window seat overlooking the back of the house. I reached for the tarnished brass light switch. There was a light fixture on the opposite wall with a pink sconce. I flicked the switch back and forth but it didn't come on.

"Another thing that doesn't work," Margaret said. "Surprise, surprise, with the age of this place. Hector says the whole place needs rewiring."

There was a curious light in the room coming through the window, staining the white walls pale purple. "I guess this was the sewing room. I ain't never been in here." The walls were lined with closet doors. There was a long oval mirror mounted on a stand-up wooden frame, the glass warped and dusty. On either side of the mirror was two of them dress forms, black metal skeletons to pull a dress over. A set of shelves was built into one wall with irons lined up, some books, a stand full of dress patterns and a porcelain watering can with faded yellow lilies on the side. I opened up a cupboard and it was packed with fabric, carefully folded but never used. It was like it had all been abandoned. On the floor was a brittle wickerwork box of embroidery flosses and fabrics and needles, probably my mother's. I could hardly believe my find. There was also a box of wooden frames. I knelt down and started looking through them.

"You might as well take those. Whoever stored it there is probably dead. I'd have figured you and Art would have been through the whole house," Margaret said as she opened up the centre closet, where butler suits hung. "So many doors in this house, and most of them are locked."

Margaret opened up another closet. It was stuffed full of black dresses and white aprons. The upper shelf had white hair bands with a lace detail at the front. "Mrs. Parker said they had a seamstress at one point, when she first married Mr. Parker, to make all the clothes for the staff, and for her and the children." We stood there in front of the big mirror, holding our dresses. "I'm going to put it on if that will make the old lady happy. She's going to give me a reference. And maybe a raise." Margaret took off her skirt and top and stood there in her bra and panties. She didn't mind being undressed, even with her rolls of flesh, her big breasts stuffed into her black bra. "A girl should wear sexy underwear," Margaret said, catching me glancing at her. "It catches a man off guard." She pulled the dress on, buttoned it up and tied the apron. "Go on," Margaret said. "It won't bite you. And it will make Marigold shut up."

I turned my back. It was my first year wearing a bra. I had no choice for in just one year I'd gone from a girl flat as a cutting board to having breasts that reminded me of the naked statues in the gardens that the Colonel coveted. Loretta would have put brassieres on the statues if they'd have let her. She bought a couple for me, a scratchy beige industrial fabric. She said it wasn't right for a girl my age to go jiggling about, although Loretta said nothing about Margaret's bosom. I pulled the dress on and it seemed almost tailor-made for me. I looked in the mirror as I tied the apron. It was then I saw my mother's initials embroidered on the pocket. I ran my fingertips over the stitches as Margaret came behind me and put lace maid caps on our heads. We stood there side by side in the mirror, me puny and short, and her tall and wide, an odd pair if there ever was one. I raised my hand and the girl in the mirror raised her hand back as far off we heard a door slam and we was both startled out of the strange mood that had come over the room.

Margaret took lipstick out of the skirt she had laid over a chair. She circled my lips with it without even asking, and I let her do it. I examined my reflection, and I scarcely recognized myself. I smiled in the mirror and the small young woman smiled back. Margaret suddenly took a deep breath. I looked at her in the mirror, watching myself watching her, or the little maid in the mirror watching her. Margaret's eyes weren't on mine in the glass, or on my dress. She had one hand on my shoulder, and when I followed her eyes they were staring at a face behind us, reflected poorly in the blemished mirror, a young woman's face watching us there in our uniforms, cameo perfect, motionless, just a disembodied head above Margaret's shoulder. *Fancy Mosher*, it said.

The head in the mirror broke into laughter and Margaret gasped. We turned around and there was nothing there. Margaret yelped, and I put my hands over my mouth in fear. A young woman stood in the doorway in the muted light.

"Pomeline! What are you doing here?" I yelled.

Margaret was almost crying.

Pomeline seemed nervous, like we'd scared her as much as she'd scared us. "I'm so sorry. I didn't mean to startle you. What did you think? That I was a ghost? It should be me screaming, seeing the two of you. I'm sure this is Granny's idea. She's lucky you're as patient as you are. She'll be trying to get me in her musty garden party clothes next. Granny's very good at getting what she wants, isn't she?" Pomeline fanned herself with her hand. She was flushed. "It's warm up here. I was looking for some books in one of the guest rooms. My father kept a variety of his things stored up here. I didn't expect to see anyone on the third floor." Pomeline stepped back into the hall, adjusting her dress.

Pomeline had what Loretta called poise, even when she was startled.

"We should open some windows," she said. "Air conditioning is one thing I miss from the city." A drop of sweat rolled down her forehead and stopped between her eyebrows like a crystal-clear pearl.

Margaret was shifting her weight from foot to foot, her arms crossed, pulling the uniform crooked. Margaret didn't know how to behave around a girl her own age, let alone someone like Pomeline. She cleared her throat. "Must be awful quiet out here after living in the city. No television, no friends, nothing to do," Margaret said. "No wonder you go wandering around the house, trying to find anything to keep you from dying of boredom."

Pomeline came back into herself and gazed at Margaret in that same pitying way Marigold looked at people who didn't understand her. "I don't mind at all. I'm so busy with the piano. I'll see you later then, girls. I might have a nap before lunch. I haven't been sleeping well. The party planners are coming out tomorrow and it's going to be busy." Pomeline put her hand on the wall momentarily, like the weight of the whole house was upon her, then stood up, posture perfect, and walked back down the stairs without making a sound.

Margaret sat at one of the old sewing machines. It had a foot pump that she started pressing so that it whirred and clunked. "She might look young but she acts like her grandmother. Who takes a nap at eighteen? Did you hear how she talked to me? She thinks she's better than us because of all their money but she don't fool me like she's fooling you. She's not living in the real world."

We heard a creak from the hall, and another creak and another. We tiptoed to the door and saw Dr. Baker standing on the landing, his hand on the railing. He waved up at us. "Girls. I heard your voices. Now look at the two of you . . ." He looked at us both from head to toe and burst out laughing. "How quaint. You both look so grown up. My goodness. This must be Marigold's doing. You're good to indulge her, girls. And you both look lovely. We need a breeze in here. My God, it's hot as Hades." He too started fanning himself.

"Mrs. Parker thought we might want to wear uniforms," I said. "I didn't know you were out to Petal's End today."

Dr. Baker fussed with his sleeves. "I got here early this morning. I'm out for a few days. Well, I must go check on Marigold." He hesitated a moment, then left.

We stood there until we couldn't hear his footsteps no more. Neither of us said a word to each other but I knew Margaret thought what I did. Dr. Baker hadn't been coming up the stairs—he'd been going down them, trying to sneak by without us seeing.

I went back into the room and put the embroidery basket in the box with the frames and carried them down the stairs behind Margaret.

When we got back to Marigold's room she was resting and Dr. Baker wasn't there. Margaret cleared her throat and Marigold opened her eyes. She put her hands to her lips and pointed at me, staring. She snapped out of it, shaking her head. "Oh my. Fancy, for a moment I thought Marilyn Mosher was standing in front of me. She was young when she wore that, just a few years older than you are now. You are more congenial. She never liked being told what to do, and that's simply part of working here, that you'll do as you're told, and behave properly. It's too bad your mother didn't understand that." Marigold rubbed her face on the stiff side. She gave a cough and took a deep breath. "Let's think of more pleasant things then, shall we? It's just like when I was young," she said. "We'll skip the embroidery today, girls. There's so much to plan for the party now. Never underestimate an old woman. Dr. Baker has found us some professionals to help plan. Ladies he knows in the city. Isn't that exciting? Loretta will be looking for you, Fancy. I kept you too long."

I smoothed my apron and left them there. I picked up the box I'd left in the hall, hurried back to my room and put it in the closet.

The Parkers took their lunch on the verandah. Pomeline appeared to have cooled down. Dr. Baker was laughing and chatting about some fancy event and how the same ladies who had planned it would be planning the garden party. Margaret and I began clearing their dishes. Loretta came out then, with her Lady Dundee cake and iced tea with lemon slices, and we served. Marigold took a bite of her dessert, tasting the whipped cream, smacking her lips. "Now, my cousin Harold and his wife Sakura are arriving tomorrow. Harry is helping me with my will. Estelle won't like *that* one bit but it's really none of her concern."

Pomeline sighed. "You know what Mummy's like, Granny. She's just worried things won't be taken care of."

Marigold reached out and squeezed Pomeline's wrist, the blue veins bulging on her hands, her diamond rings loose on her fingers. "Your mother should have thought more of your father and treated him better. That's what she should have been thinking of. But let's not talk about the past. Pomeline, you are practising all the time. That piano goes night and day. You really must spend more time in the garden again. Cousin Harry will get you doing a few things. Look how pale you are! Perhaps Dr. Baker should give you a thorough checkup."

Margaret cleared her throat and tried to catch my eye but I kept my gaze on the plates I was stacking. Pomeline said there was no need, and Marigold shook her finger at her. "You need to have a social life. I've never known a Parker who didn't like to socialize. Or who worked all the time at such frivolous tasks. You must think of others a bit more. The party will be wonderful for you. Perhaps we can invite some nice young men. Really, darling, I admire your single-mindedness where music is concerned but it's not healthy for a young woman to have no other interests."

Pomeline pointed at me. "Fancy's growing up. Look at her red lips. And look at their lovely outfits. Granny, you have them all done up."

Marigold took another bite of her Lady Dundee cake. "I think they look exquisite. So many happy memories. It's where you choose to focus, isn't that so, Dr. Baker?"

Dr. Baker didn't say a word, just patted Marigold's hand and smiled while Pomeline pushed her plate away.

10.
The Cousins

"'All beneath his eye was a solitude. The strange plants were basking in the sunshine, and now and then nodding gently to one another, as if in acknowledgment of sympathy and kindred . . .' Isn't that just absolutely spectacular? Spectacular, I tell you. A marvellous collection. Hand-painted plates. Truly extraordinary, both the library here and this book." Harry carefully displayed the book, as though he had just hit the treasure trove at an estate auction. He showed it to the swans in the pond but they paid him no mind. He shrugged and turned back to us.

"I was here once as a boy, years and years ago. I wasn't at all interested in the library, in the books. I was mad for the lily pond. It's full of remarkable algae and emerald duckweed and salamanders. And there were always so many fireflies and frogs. It's remarkable how age engenders appreciation. When we saw Jenny in the city I could tell she was a girl who likes books. It's a pity she's not here. She would have a terrific time. 'Rappaccini's

Daughter,' Fancy—that's what this story is called. It's dreadfully sad. Dreadfully beautiful, but sad. That's what happens, of course, sometimes, when science has a relationship with nature: horrible beauty."

That's how Harold Prescott talked. On and on and on, prattling away, with his funny accent and his big booming voice. He was unendingly joyous, whether he was talking about some dusty book or a piece of toast or a blazing sunset. I remember him standing there on the deck of the Atelier a week after they arrived. It was their favourite spot, and Harry and Sakura would come out with notepads and books to take their breakfast. It was mid morning and the gardeners would go by occasionally. Harry would call out to them. He was a botanist, and although he specialized in woodland flowers he cherished the formal gardens. They reminded him of his happy childhood days, he said. It was impossible not to like that man, and it was as though he'd stepped out of some far part of the garden he'd been lost in for years, or from a room up on the third floor where he'd been looking out with a telescope at the stars.

His wife, Sakura, was quiet. We never really knew much about her. She was much younger than Harry. He was the same age as Estelle, as Mr. Charlie had been, and Dr. Baker as well, but Harry seemed perpetually youthful. He had been a bachelor for years before going off to the land where tea was green and cherry blossoms spoke. Marigold described where Sakura came from that way. We got to know Sakura more through her expressions, how she'd shake her head and laugh in her quiet voice when Harry would hold forth on anything that caught his delight, which was pretty much everything. He even drew Pomeline out to the garden for morning tea sometimes. She'd been practising furiously and she was looking more peaked as the weeks passed. To Harry, life was marvellous. Art and I joked that it was his favourite word. And when they weren't off on what he called an expedition, somewhere in the woods or along the shore, he'd be in the gardens. He would have slept in the Atelier if Sakura had let him.

When I was cutting flowers he'd call me over. "Isn't that marvellous, Fancy?" he'd say. Or if I brought out their tea and lemonade he'd insist I stay. "He's terribly convivial," Marigold gushed on the day they arrived, her voice like a little girl's.

Harry liked tomes about history and architecture. He liked maps and atlases. Mostly he liked books about plants and forests and gardens. He had come across that story about a poison garden, and he'd waved us all over as he gave his recitation. It was like he knew it by heart. He even liked Jenny's swans and seemed to think if he spoke to them from the deck they'd eventually be tamed. They ignored him completely. That didn't stop him from trying to gain their favour, and it seemed that morning he was performing "Rappaccini's Daughter" that it was a show for them big white birds and their babies.

"Hawthorne certainly understood the power of plants. But it's so dark. So very pessimistic. Listen to this, Sakura, Pommie. And you too, Fancy. Put that tray down. I can't believe they have a child working here. Aren't there labour laws? From the outfits Cousin Marigold has you wearing I'd say we're in another era so I expect they don't apply at Petal's End. Art, come over and take a break. Those fruit tarts look delicious. Hopefully none of *this* food is poisonous." We all laughed and did as he asked.

"Now listen to this," Harry said. He swept his hand around as he hunched over, acting it out. "'His figure soon emerged into view, and showed itself to be that of no common labourer, but a tall, emaciated, sallow, and sickly-looking man, dressed in a scholar's garb of black. He was beyond the middle term of life, with grey hair, a thin, grey beard, and a face singularly marked with intellect and cultivation, but which could never, even in his more youthful days, have expressed much warmth of heart.' That's the father. His humanity is consumed by his desire for knowledge, for experimentation, experimentation at all costs. A scientist must be governed by a respect for the laws of nature."

Sakura was sketching water lilies with an amused expression. She was illustrating a book, and she kept her notepad with her at all times. We couldn't read the book, the unusual characters running up and down in columns, but she said it was stories, and there was a garden in it, and swans.

Harry wore the same clothes every day. We saw his laundry on the line so we knew he had five identical sets: khaki shorts and short-sleeved cotton shirts. Sakura wore a similar outfit only she had khaki skirts and white linen blouses. He and Sakura insisted on doing their own laundry. Loretta finally gave in. No one told Marigold, though. She'd have had a fit. Marigold was all for being friendly and having us sing in her choir and prance about the gardens, but there was a line. Her humanity was governed by a kindly respect for the laws-of-place, knowing yours and staying in it.

Harry had a funny canvas hat with a long cord. Sometimes he let the hat dangle down his back, the cord pulling on his throat. Art said he looked like he was on safari. He had a knife and a magnifying glass strapped to his belt, binoculars, a small leather notebook and a backpack that he carried, always ready for an adventure. That's what he'd been saying since he'd arrived the week before, how each day was an absolute adventure. Even Hector was around more since the cousins had arrived. Harry made a big deal of Hector's knowledge of cars and mechanical things. He often asked him for help, and Hector lapped up the compliments.

"'Approaching the shrub, she threw open her arms, as with a passionate ardour, and drew its branches into an intimate embrace—so intimate that her features were hidden in its leafy bosom and her glistening ringlets all intermingled with the flowers.'" Didn't he start laughing like someone invisible was tickling him under the arms with a feather. "Isn't that just marvellous? It could be describing you, Pomeline, your enchanting face like a moonflower." Harry beamed.

"Harry worries the garden might be affecting the Parker ladies. That's why they disagree," Sakura said with a rippling laugh. She sounded nervous when she laughed but I don't think she was. It was just her accent. I could never tell with her if she was serious or if she was joking.

"Lord Prescott, Loretta says to ask you if you'd like a packed lunch for when you go off on your expedition." I stood with my hands together.

"Fancy Mosher. How many times must I ask you to call me Harry? You are such a wondrous thing."

"Loretta says we should be calling you Sir."

Sakura and Harry exchanged amused glances. Pomeline giggled.

"Well, perhaps if it were my father here, or even my brother. My father is a duke, and my brother will be a duke. My father is 'Your Grace.' My brother is the Lord Prescott. I'm just the second son, and that's jolly well fine by me. No one looks to you for even the most trifling thing. I can tell you that as a small child the burden and responsibility that would fall upon my brother was clear, and it sent me running through the gardens and the parklands with whoops of joy that nature had arranged for him to come before me, to be the antecedent, so to speak. I can do as I please. Travel the world with my darling Sakura and discover exciting new plants and places. Come here and visit Cousin Marigold, and my simply fantastic young cousins, Pomeline and Jenny. And you charming people. It's wonderful having family to visit. Marigold and I are cousins through our fathers, you know. Her father was a second cousin to my great uncle. And I believe her mother was my great-aunt's father's second cousin twice removed. This makes us the dearest of family." Harry was striding up and down now, using his fingers to map out the family tree in the air. I told him it was confusing and he giggled.

"Marigold's family estate went to her father's fourth cousin as he had no sons, only Marigold. Primogeniture it's called. A dreadful thing if you're a lady, although you certainly won't have to trouble yourself with anything like that in this land. It's a blessing, really. Poor Charlie. He had a great weight upon him, being the only son of the Colonel. Now it all falls to Pomeline." Harry looked away, and it was the first time I'd seen the euphoria wash off his face. Then I guess he remembered himself, the company, and he looked at Pomeline. "I'm sorry, Pommie. Of course he loved you and your sister so dreadfully much."

She looked away and fiddled with the brim of her enormous sun hat.

"It's a great deal of pressure, isn't it, Pomeline, dear child, being the eldest in a grand family? I became a scientist, you see, because I wanted to be useful. I wanted to make a contribution. I don't know if many in my family make much of a meaningful contribution."

"Things are a bit different here, Harry. I've got my mother wanting to get rid of the place and Granny insisting that I keep Petal's End going, and Jenny saying it should be hers because I'll just go and move away. Once she comes out she'll run around and do as she pleases and Mother will make excuses for her and Granny will agree." Pomeline leaned back and her arms fell to her lap, two white, lifeless ribbons dangling by her knees.

Harry took a sip of the iced tea. "It's all about learning to get along, and how to please those we love. We are tremendously honoured you've seen fit to take breaks from your piano to indulge us, aren't we, Sakura? What a splendid girl you are. It's rather magical playing music. It's like bringing those composers back to life, isn't it?"

"I do feel as though they are with me. I can hear the music even when I'm not playing."

Sakura didn't look up from her sketching as she spoke. "I feel the same way about flowers. Even when I'm not drawing them I can see them behind my eyes."

She seemed stuck on the swan's neck, the biggest one. "That's Sweet William," I told her, "Jenny's favourite. He's the same age as us. Swans can live for a long time. There's nothing sweet about William, though. Keep your distance. Swans don't like change and they don't like people. It's their pond, Jenny says, and she don't mind who they scare."

Harry chortled. "Now Fancy, you seem to know about the swans and the flowers here. Do you know much about the flora and fauna in these woods?"

"Well, lots of it grows in there."

Harry started guffawing again. "I took a walk to where you lived with your grandfather. It's a charming stroll. And a charming cottage. I would love to see inside. Loretta tells me he was a terrific painter. That's a very useful occupation, you see. There are so many things you can do as a painter. Your grandfather was a war artist, I hear. What gruesome images they were charged with capturing. But Loretta tells me he then devoted himself to vernacular portraiture. Loretta said he did paintings for families when their loved ones died. That's a wonderful gift, a visual memorial. But there are also artists like Sakura who capture flowers. And Marigold showed me your needlework piece. It's really quite exquisite, almost from another time, such precision. You embroider just as Pomeline plays the piano, luminously. Or, as they would say in 'Rappaccini's Daughter,' *luminoso*! It was such a curious little picture, Marigold resting, with her eyes like that."

"The stitching is exquisite," Sakura offered.

Pomeline yawned, already worn out from the heat that had tiptoed into the morning. "I must get back to the house now to practise. Granny's got the party planners coming again this afternoon."

Harry said, "Well, I would be pleased to help. You have but to ask, dear Pomeline."

They had a brief hug, hardly touching, and Pomeline went off, her dress fluttering as she walked. She disappeared behind a wall of flowers taller than she was.

I gathered up the tray and Art stood. I had forgotten he was there. I hadn't seen Art much in the past two weeks because when he wasn't with the gardeners he was following Harry around, trying to soak up his knowledge. "I better get back and find the gardeners," he said. "We're finishing pruning the hedge maze."

"I've driven you all off with my reading." Harry laughed, clutching the book.

"What happens in the story?" Art asked.

Harry wrinkled his nose. "Well, it's very gruesome. I suppose I haven't shown good judgment. But then I did like the dark tales when I was a lad. You see"—Harry's voice got low and we all leaned forward—"it's an experiment he runs, this scientist, raising his child in a poisoned garden, and she becomes immune to the poison from continual exposure. She is habituated to it. But the tragedy of it is that she becomes just as poisonous as the flowers. All her loveliness is deadly. And there's no cure. In fact, the antidote is what destroys her—the truth, I suppose, of what she has become, and how she can never escape it, through no fault of her own. It's not really a story for children."

"Jenny would like it. She's suspicious of flowers."

Harry perked up. "Is she afraid of them? What they represent?"

"Maybe. Jenny don't like it when her grandmother fills the big house up with cut flowers. She says it makes it like living in a funeral home or a hospital. She likes them fine growing out here, alive in the ground. She says the flowers don't appreciate being murdered. Her grandmother don't understand it."

"She certainly is quite a character, our young Jenny."

Sweet William let out a horrible cackling thrum and Sakura cringed.

Harry pointed. "Such a magnificent bird to look at but they

really aren't friendly at all. I don't know what they were thinking getting a young girl swans as pets. I see they have cygnets. They even chase those off once they get to a certain age. Such a temperamental creature."

"He don't like us talking about Jenny."

Harry cocked his head and looked at me. "Is that so, Fancy? Now, however would you know that?"

Art was looking at me funny. It had just come out of my mouth. But I knew it was true. That swan knew her name.

Sweet William began to gurgle and hiss and paddle along, watching as we walked by the edge of the pond and up the path back to the house.

Loretta sent me right back out to cut some roses Marigold wanted now they were in high season. I snipped them as fast as I could and came back into the tempered air of the big manor home, setting the flowers down in the kitchen. Down the corridor from the back of the house I could hear the piano music. It was not a tune Pomeline had played before. I went and stood in the doorway listening and she lifted her eyes from the keyboard, still playing, talking over the music.

"I don't remember a summer this sweltering, Fancy. You'll be here for choir practice? You have a pretty voice, you know." She gazed down at the keyboard and her hair fell around her. She was drained of colour, almost the same white as the ivory her fingers were touching.

"Everything okay?" It surprised me when the words came out of my mouth.

Pomeline stared at the keyboard for a long moment, and finally she started playing again, lifting her huge luminous eyes. Maybe she was dead. I did think that. Maybe she was the dead come to fetch me. Maybe this was how it was going to be for me. I'd see the dead doing what they did but they wouldn't be alive and no one would know but me. They wouldn't join me for a cup of tea like they did Grampie, or go for a stroll as they did with my great-grandfather. They'd be around forever doing what they did and I could never escape them. I stood there staring at her, waiting for the rest of her to just fade away with the music, for her to become as translucent as the white sheers on the long windows.

There was a tap on my shoulder and I screamed so loud Pomeline's hands crashed on the keys.

"Fancy! I didn't mean to startle you." Dr. Baker took me by the shoulders as Margaret come running down the stairs and dashed into the room and Loretta rushed in from the kitchen. "Now, now, nothing to worry about. I interrupted the ladies here, gave them a scare. I have to go over a few items with our young virtuoso," he said, holding up a list written in Marigold's spidery script. He patted me on the back and stepped into the hall.

Margaret snarled and ran back up the stairs, calling behind her, "Mrs. Parker is expecting the party planning ladies any minute. You scared her half to death, Fancy, screeching like that. 'It isn't civilized to make such a noise under any circumstances.' That's what Marigold said."

Dr. Baker cleared his throat. "Of course. Margaret, let her know all is well. The heat has put everybody on edge."

Loretta brushed her hands off on her apron and I watched her bustle off down the hall on the way back to the kitchen. "Come along, Fancy," she called. "You can help get lunch ready. Come be civilized in the kitchen. Putting your shoes on would be a fine start." She clopped over the wooden floor, the sound fading into the back of the house.

I turned then to Dr. Baker, but he was gone too and the music room door was closed. I could hear his and Pomeline's hushed voices. I took a few steps toward the door and rested my ear on the wood, my hand on the doorknob. I could hear a faint noise and I couldn't tell what it was. And just as I'd known Sweet William was watching us, I turned and there was Margaret standing at the top of the landing watching me, both of us in our ridiculous maid outfits, with a quiet satisfaction.

11.
The Second Coming

THE MIST had blown away and left behind a clear sky and crisp, perfumed air. The heat would creep back as the afternoon hours passed. The event planners were gone and it was quiet again.

Marigold had on a big sun hat and her gardening outfit: a floral skirt, a white blouse and a long smock of an apron. "Well, we'll head off then, shall we, to Evermore? I'll teach you my secrets, my darlings. I'm a bit rusty." She was on Margaret's arm, talking to Harry and Sakura. Margaret was holding a silk parasol to keep the sun off Marigold, and Pomeline carried a dull coral one. It had probably been bright red once but by the time it found Pomeline's long white fingers it was faded.

"Pommie, did you try to call your mother again? Or Dr. Baker? It's time they brought Agatha out to Petal's End. It's absurd, keeping a young girl trapped in the city at the height of summer. You said you'd call, darling, you promised your old Granny."

Pomeline was walking slowly, with her hand on her stomach, like all the activities were wearing on her. "Yes, Granny, I did call, I really did. I couldn't reach anybody. I told you that. I'll try again after dinner."

"We've got everything ready in the Water House, Marigold." Harry came and walked beside her. "Has anyone seen Hector? Loretta was looking for him. I said I'd send him along if I saw him but he's nowhere to be found. That fellow seems to constantly be on the go, doesn't he, Fancy?" I shrugged, and Harry turned his attention back to Marigold, talking about lady's slippers, orchids and trilliums and other flowers of the forest.

Marigold's cane clicked on the stone path. "What a joyful help you are, Cousin. The two of you are just so dear. You really should stay. You can live here. You would die for the cherry blossoms, Sakura. The trees are planted in a heart shape. Did you see?"

We made our way toward the garden but didn't get more than a few steps when we heard a rumbling coming from the wooded lane. A white car emerged, with Estelle at the wheel, enormous sunglasses on, and Jenny in the passenger seat beside her, looking straight ahead like she was gazing through the landscapes of time.

We watched the car pull up to the big steps. Marigold started laughing and clapping her hands, the stiff side of her face twitching. "Well, look who has decided to join us. What a delight." She took to waving like she was at a parade. "Pomeline, I thought you said you didn't reach them!"

"I didn't, Granny."

Just then Hector came out of woods in his pickup truck. He parked it right behind the white car and got out, but Estelle didn't need no man opening the door. She stepped out, the engine still running, and gestured to Jenny to get out, at the same time directing Hector to get the bags from the trunk.

Estelle rapped on the car window so hard it wouldn't have surprised me if it broke, but Jenny kept looking ahead. She knocked again and Jenny put the window down. She turned and looked at her mother. "I'm praying," a low, deep voice said.

Margaret turned her head and stared at the car. She wasn't expecting that. No one ever was.

"Pray later, dear. Now get out of the car and say hello to your grandmother and sister and your cousins." Estelle was tapping her foot.

Jenny turned her head to us, and her grandmother waved again and out she came. She had on an ill-fitting white dress and flat white leather sandals, a white kerchief on her head. She clasped her hands in front of her and ran over the stones to her grandmother, if you could call it running. It was more like a stiff shuffle, on account of her bones being fine and thin. Her mother called after her to be careful but Marigold held her arms out wide, still carrying her cane, and Jenny forgot all about her prayers. "Oh, Granny," she said, her voice rumbling out, "I missed you so."

Harry and Sakura and Margaret were all staring. It was one thing to hear the voice from inside a car but then to hear it coming out of this wispy little creature, that was another thing entirely, something you never got quite used to. You couldn't help but gawk. Art and I were too. She was an odd-looking girl. If Pomeline was the beautiful version of Estelle, Jenny was the crooked version of her father. Her hair was fine like a baby's, sticking out of the kerchief and hanging down her back, not quite blond or gold or white. And she had a noticeable skip in her step that seemed almost like a limp.

"Agatha . . . my darling, darling girl." Marigold hugged her. She took a step back. "Why, you look simply marvellous."

Jenny reached for her grandmother's hand and she swivelled her head around for the view. "I've got a home in glory land that outshines the sun," she said.

Marigold patted her on the head. "Why yes you do, darling."

Estelle smiled and it came off as a twitch in her right eye. "Marigold, it's wonderful to see you looking so well."

Looking back, it's not unfair to believe that Estelle was, in her own rigid way, wanting things to somehow work out smoothly. I remember the stiff hug she gave Pomeline.

"Pomeline, you look tired. Dr. Baker tells me you're spending too much time inside." It was hurting Estelle to keep up the happy look, almost giving her one of her migraines, but she forged ahead, looking around at the property, pretending to admire how grand it all was.

We, the help, stood there while the Parkers got lost in a buzz of greetings with Harry and Sakura, the sun beating down, a few crickets chirping. Jenny turned and batted her eyes at us. She bowed her head and put her hands together. "The holly and the ivy," she said.

Margaret looked off where there was ivy running up the side of the house, next to the climbing roses, and then back at me.

"The holly bears a prickle, as sharp as any thorn." Jenny's head was still bowed and her sister heard her now. Pomeline groaned.

Harry leaned in. "Pardon me?"

"Jenny, now let's not start this." Pomeline shook her head.

"Of all the trees that are in the wood the holly bears the crown," Jenny mumbled.

"Meet Margaret, Granny's helper," Pomeline said.

Margaret smiled. That was a mistake.

Jenny pointed to the car. "Take my bags upstairs, please, Margaret." She folded her hands back together.

Margaret's eyes narrowed.

Jenny lifted her head to the sky and it seemed there were words only she could see. Finally, she looked at her grandmother. "And I'm here now, so Granny won't be needing you any more. I always take care of Granny. Since my father died she's had to rely on me. I do her makeup."

"There's certainly enough work looking after a moth-eaten lady like me, darling. You'll be glad to have Margaret here to give you play time with Arthur and Fancy. Margaret's not a bellhop, darling. Don't be rude. It's so common. Really. And—"

Estelle interrupted. "Jenny, remember your manners, angel. Show how well brought up you are, won't you? Hector has already taken your bags inside. Jenny was making my life a nightmare because I thought it better for her in the city and she didn't agree. Here you are, Jenny, I hope you are happy. Now you can play with Arthur and Fancy. But do take care. You must always, always mind your health. Make sure you wash your hands and use your puffer. I don't know why you refuse to do so."

"It's full of chemicals. I'd rather wheeze."

Art looked at me and I tried not to laugh.

Jenny made an appalling face in Margaret's direction. "It came upon a midnight clear," she said.

"All right then, Agatha. We'll have time to discuss religion later. My, the air is heavy and thick, not a breeze. We're off to the Water House to make rosewater. Will you join us? Cousin Harry and Sakura have been the most splendid company. You should see Sakura's brilliant flower sketches."

Sakura wasn't much taller than Jenny was. She took to Sakura right away.

"You can teach me about the flowers, Jenny." Sakura took her arm.

Marigold caressed Jenny's head. "Remember our special song, Jenny? About the coral bells and lily of the valley? You always have loved the naughty flowers. It's too bad we've missed the lily of the valley. I am thrilled you still use your perfume. It's so precious but so toxic. I worried you might drink it when you were a toddler."

Estelle brushed her hands together. "I don't mean to be rude but I've got to get back."

Marigold brought her dry palms together with a papery clap. "Yes, no doubt you have much more important things to do. You'll be joining us for the garden party? It's in two weeks. Can you believe it's August? Time does fly, doesn't it, Estelle? It seems no time at all since the summer you married Charlie." It was just a statement, but it hung there in the air like something rotting. "You remember how much he relished the reception, the dancing and singing, the paper lanterns on the lily pond and hanging from the trees, lighting up the whole of Evermore? He loved that so."

"Yes, of course, I remember. I remember how much fun you had planning the wedding and reception. And our honeymoon." Estelle's voice was thin as a wire. "David—Dr. Baker—tells me the choir is enchanting, although he says you have them singing the most morose songs. No surprise there. But never mind . . . he says your little crew of servants are dandy singers. Just like before, except you had a choir of soldiers. It's funny how time passes." For a moment, even with them big sunglasses on, Estelle seemed to relax as she stood there across from the rest of us, the car behind her still running. She took out a cigarette and lit it, the harsh smell cutting through the fragrant air. "I'm serious, Jenny, do take care and don't get dirty, and stay out of the sun. And wash your hands if you touch those filthy swans. And Pomeline, make sure your sister does not wear herself out. She needs to go to bed early and do her exercises. You know the routine."

Pomeline coughed in what seemed to be assent. "Dr. Baker says Granny's doing very well, Mother. He says Jenny's fine as well."

"Well, that's lovely, Pomeline, but Dr. Baker doesn't know everything, and there's nothing wrong with you keeping an eye on your little sister."

Estelle stared at Pomeline and Pomeline stared back, her face stained pink from the parasol. She held her mother's gaze until Estelle got in her car and drove away, like she'd never even stopped and got out of the car at all, like we all just blinked and Jenny had appeared.

12.
The Water House

I STILL HAVE not had a glimpse of you. Have you heard the glass wind bells? I hung them there at the edge of the verandah in early June. They tinkled a while ago and I thought you might have been playing with them.

Hector came into the Water House a few minutes after us, giving me a poke in the back as he went by. Art pretended not to notice. "It looks like a kitchen in here," he said. "Like you're going to cook us up some food, Mrs. Parker."

"Loretta was looking for you, Hector, old chap." Harry clapped Hector on the shoulder. "She needs help with a few things."

Art had his hands in his pockets. "She keeps sending us out to look for you."

"I was down to the valley getting parts for old Rolly."

"Well, perhaps you could just check in with her a bit more often, Hector," Harry said. "You know she can't get along without you for long. I can't imagine any of us could."

Hector laughed. Harry knew how to talk to him. It was so easy—just throw out a few compliments, like throwing treats to an animal. "Well, I do my best, you know."

Margaret cocked her hip. "Everyone likes a handyman, Hector."

He winked at her.

Marigold clapped her hands. "Hector will go in and see Loretta when we're done here. I'm sure he'll enjoy this. He's a natural gardener, just like you, Arthur, even though we've got him working on the engines all the time. It's not the same as when we had our own gardeners—these landscape people, cleaning people, party people, all coming in from elsewhere. But at least it's all tended to. I am most pleased you young people are interested in all of this. We'll make soap in a few days, if I don't fatigue."

Marigold was wistful as she touched the items on the table Harry and Sakura had set up: three red bricks, a glass bowl, jar and measuring cup. There was also a water pitcher, a funnel, eye droppers and a row of small glass bottles for the rosewater. They had also scrubbed and straightened the whole place. It was like a mix of a lab, a kitchen and a parlour, with white walls and tiled floors, faded sofas and armchairs in the corner.

"Now then, we'll need rose petals. We can't do a thing without rose petals. Harry, wherever are the rose petals?"

Jenny looked out the window screen past the chimes, in the direction of the lily pond. "I haven't seen my swans yet. How are my swans doing?" She was sniffing the air and stroking the fabric on the chair as she looked at each of us, her eyes landing on Margaret. "I want to see my swans and their new babies. This is taking too long."

Pomeline cleared her throat then and I jumped. She hadn't said a word since we'd come to the Water House. Her tired, pinched face was startling.

Marigold took a deep breath. "Well, Agatha, dear, you didn't have to come with us. You're not even settled in the house yet, for goodness' sake. You have the rest of the summer to check on the swans. Be patient, my darling girl. I've been out a few times myself and I assure you they await your arrival. They only hiss at the rest of us. Right now we'll focus on roses."

"Well, if you didn't want me to come you could have said so." Jenny crossed her arms like she was five.

"I'm sure you're just tired, but there is no need to behave so, sweetest heart. You can be pleasant and stay here or go in the house with Loretta. Let's carry on."

"They're doing rather well, Jenny, gliding about, keeping an eye on things. Cute little cygnets, although I dare say if you even look at the babies the parents come at you like kamikaze pilots," Harry said. "And I'm sure they will be just so superbly delighted to see you, as your Granny says, as they don't seem to be happy to see anyone else."

That made Jenny smile.

Harry walked over and took Marigold's hand. "Marigold, you said to wait to pick the petals so they wouldn't wilt."

"Oh yes, I did say that. It's hard to keep things straight, isn't it, with so many people about. Really, it should be rose petals collected first thing in the morning, still moist, not roses at the end of the day. But we are just learning today so they'll do. There is such an intensity to the scent of hot petals." She laughed. "That's what we're doing. We're evaporating. It's like a wee still."

Margaret chuckled. "You'll like that, Hector."

"Well, we'd better get started if we're going to practise singing as well, Granny." Pomeline was sitting in a chair looking like she was about to fall asleep. "I must do some practising today as well."

Jenny stamped her foot. "We haven't even done the rosewater and you're taking over with the music."

"I'm not taking over with the music, Jenny. You haven't even been here. Don't be silly. We've been working on a few songs for the concert and we really do need to keep practising."

Pomeline smiled at me and Margaret and Art. "It's coming along nicely, though."

Jenny clasped her hands together. "To hear the angels sing."

Margaret was snorting now, trying to hold in laughs. Jenny gave her the eye and Margaret stopped dead. "Jesus smiled at me out in the garden, when I was just a little girl. He smiled at me and blessed me and left me in ecstasy."

No one said a word for a moment.

"Well," Harry finally said, "isn't that absolutely remarkable, Jenny, to have had such an experience. Marvellous. The garden is truly a mystical place, there is no doubt."

Margaret's mouth was hanging open, and Marigold rapped a big metal spoon on the wooden table. "Agatha, I'm so very happy you have the Lord with you. But ecstasy isn't a proper thing for a young girl to speak of. Really, you know better. Now, please don't argue. I hope you didn't travel all the way out to the countryside to stalk about Petal's End suspiring and gloomy. You know better. We're Parkers. Here at Petal's End we'll behave like civilized ladies. Pomeline is right. We really should get started because there is much to do."

The grin left Jenny's lips, vanished, snatched away. She looked shrivelled, her crossing eyes behind thick lenses like bugs pinned to a mat behind a magnifying glass.

"All right, Mrs. Parker," Margaret said. "We'll get some rose petals."

"Margaret, you stay here with me, my dear. Agatha, you look like you could use the fresh air. Off with you. And don't strip all the roses bare. Be selective. Pick the roses that surrender the petals. No ripping and tugging, please. If you get pricked it will be from carelessness. Agatha, do you hear? Mind the thorns. Your mother will be simply feverish if she arrives back at Petal's End and you're torn up. Fancy and Arthur, why don't you take Agatha to my rose garden, the one Charlie and I planted. I used to make rose oil, you know. Distillation only captures a whisper of the scent for particular flowers, and the rose is one of them. It's referred to as a rose otto. Making a concentrated oil is a much more involved process, with a solvent. We call that sort of extraction an 'absolute.' You must extract the solvent after. Oh my, I do digress. Agatha, run along, darling."

Jenny stomped her foot. "I know where Daddy's roses are. I live here. This is my garden, not theirs. Why does everybody keep forgetting that?"

Jenny, Art and I headed off to the roses, with Jenny in the lead.

"Shall come the time foretold," she was singing in her tuneless way.

"And what time is that, Jenny?"

"Oh you'll see, Fancy Mosher," she said over her shoulder, her metal bowl glittering in the sun.

The flowers were so plentiful that even after filling a bowl it hardly looked like we'd touched them. Jenny sat on the stone bench and watched us. She began speaking as though she'd called us together for a secret meeting.

"My mother and Dr. Baker keep causing problems for Granny. He acts like he wants to help but he doesn't. My mother has been in such a nasty mood. I don't care if I get germs and viruses. I'm twelve now. She's been arguing with Dr. Baker ever since Granny and Pomeline left. She says he's out here too much. She says he pays attention to everybody but her, poor Mother. What do you think of Dr. Baker?" Jenny fiddled with her kerchief.

Art and I just kept plucking rose petals.

"That's fine, you don't have to say anything. He's probably got you both brainwashed as well. My mother thinks I'm deaf, not just blind. But I'm not. He doesn't fool me, the good doctor. My mother doesn't fool me, either." Jenny took a handful of petals and started twisting them. She tossed the shreds on the grass and lifted her hands to her nose. She took a long sniff. We always knew Jenny didn't like her mother or Dr. Baker but she had a special hate on for them now.

"My mother is still mad at my father. He promised her she'd get the estate and he didn't keep his promise, she says. *Charlie broke my heart with his lies*. That's how she says it, in her whiny voice. The nerve of her to blame him. It's her fault my father died. And she'd be happy to drive my grandmother to her grave. That's what your mother did to your grandfather, didn't she, Fancy?"

I stopped picking. Jenny was going too far and she'd only just arrived. Art didn't say a word, just continued filling the bowl.

Jenny kept ripping up rose petals. "Well, I didn't mean to offend you, Fancy. It just seems we both have mothers who don't respect us. Does your mother still have her horses?"

"No, she sold them a long time ago. She couldn't look after them. Hector's father has draught horses."

"I always did like a workhorse. Just like my grandmother."

"Well, why don't you be a workhorse and help us out?"

Jenny laughed. She jumped up and threw a few petals in the air. They drifted down on her white sandals, a few landing on my dirty brown toes. She put a rose petal in the middle of my forehead and pressed it with her finger. I could feel how cold her finger was, and when she took her hand away the petal stayed. She did the same thing to Art, and we stood there with petals on our foreheads while Jenny closed her eyes. Then she opened her eyes and answered a question no one had asked.

"My mother would like nothing better than to see this place sold off. She can hardly wait for Granny to die. Half the time I expect to find her up late at night fashioning some sort of spell, putting a curse on Granny. The only time I've seen my mother grieve was when Granny got better from her attack. Granny comes from a strong line," she said. "Like me. I'm a Parker. My mother is not a Parker. It's all in the bloodline, you see."

"Good thing she's got you to take care of her, Jenny," Art said.

"You sound like Dr. Baker. You don't want to sound like him. Trust me." She was whispering now. "And Pomeline thinks she's the best granddaughter because she's older and she never has any problems. And that Margaret, she thinks she's running the place."

"Well, that's just how Margaret is, but she's a hard worker," I said. Art was standing beside me, both of us with our bowls full of petals. It was hard to believe it had come to us defending Margaret.

"Granny needs to be careful who she hires. I will have to stay out here. Pomeline's so busy with her piano she doesn't pay close enough attention."

When we came back to the Water House, Marigold got up from her armchair and ran her fingers through our bowls of petals. "There is nothing that makes me happier," she said. "Once we used copper kettles; however that system was dismantled years ago. But we'll make do with this simple stove-top method of steam distillation. Gather round and I'll explain. It's shockingly simple," she said and then held forth on a baffling process involving sterilization, a big pot, a bowl and bricks, cascades of boiling water and frosty ice cubes, an inverted lid, and most importantly, the exact placement of rose petals in the pot. None of us could make sense of it except Jenny, who kept chiming in with her tips and comments, a self-appointed assistant. Marigold patted her on the head, proclaiming how moving it was to know Petal's End Botanicals would carry on. Harry was beaming and whether he actually understood or was simply besotted with the romance and nostalgia of it all was impossible to tell.

Margaret, of all people, was actually enjoying herself so much she didn't even think to hide it. "I didn't know you could just make this at home with a pot, Mrs. Parker."

Jenny gave her grandmother a hug. She stepped in front of Margaret with handfuls of rose petals and reached down into the pot, packing it as per Marigold's exact instructions.

Marigold pinched Jenny's cheek. "That's perfect, Jenny." Then she picked up the pitcher of water and poured it in. "See how we add just enough water to cover the petals? Goodness, it smells divine already." Marigold's hands shook as she poured but they were still strong. She and Jenny had that in common, tough little fingers. "Now, we'll turn this burner on and bring it to a rolling boil. Arthur, be a good boy and hand me the lid. I remember once when Charlie was quite young and he was helping me. John Lee was here as well. What an eager child. He couldn't wait, and he got his hand scalded. He didn't even cry. You most likely did not whimper either, Fancy, when you got your scar. My Charlie was a sensitive child. His father does not appreciate him. Charlie will love this. He loves rosewater. He's romantic like that."

Pomeline's eyes met mine just for a moment and moved to the scar on my cheek, which my hand had instinctively covered. Jenny and Pomeline exchanged a quick glance before Pomeline spoke. "Granny, you mean it *was* Daddy's favourite."

"Yes. That's what I said. There is no need to correct me. How rude." Marigold went back to looking at her bottles and running her fingers through the leftover petals remaining in the shiny bowls.

It didn't take long and Marigold turned the burner down. We was all fanning ourselves, sweat beading down our faces.

"It's at a nice steady simmer. Now hand me the ice, Harry, please." Marigold poured the ice on top of the inverted lid.

"Now, let's review, children. The steam will rise and hit the cold and at that point will drip down into the glass bowl resting on the bricks at the bottom of the pot. Harry and Sakura, we'll have to leave you here. Every twenty minutes, spoon out the rosewater into the glass jar here, the one we sterilized. When the jar is full, about a quart, it will be done. If you keep going it will be too diluted. Be sure to watch the clock."

"I love how it smells in here." Jenny tilted her chin up, eyes scrunched closed as she sniffed the air.

Margaret crossed her arms. "I thought you hated the smell of cut flowers."

Jenny put her hands over her ears as though Margaret's very voice was giving her a headache. "I don't know how you would know that about me. It's not polite to talk about people when they aren't present. I don't like watching flowers die. A vase is just an urn. That's what they put my father in. He was burned up into ashes. Why did you hire someone so stupid, Granny?"

"Agatha Jennifer, don't be rude. My goodness, look at how you are behaving. You've spent too long with your mother. If you don't mind your manners then you won't be able to participate. Margaret is a fine help. I simply won't have you talking like this."

But the thing is, she didn't make Jenny apologize. I could tell Margaret made note of that.

Marigold clicked her cane on the floor. "Let's head into the house, Margaret. We'll go in and refresh and meet you all in the music room in twenty minutes. We'll make more rosewater tomorrow, don't you worry, with fresh morning rose petals covered with dew. And Margaret, you'll go mad for this rosewater. You can splash it on your face, or better yet, add it to your drinking water. It's soothing for the skin."

"Why doesn't Jenny stay behind to help Harry and Sakura? She's not singing, so she might be bored," Pomeline said.

"I can still come and listen. You can't make me stay out here. You can't make me stay behind."

"I'm not trying to make you stay out here. I don't want you to have a dull time, that's all."

"Well, I could try to sing."

Pomeline stroked Jenny's hair, what was sticking out of the kerchief. "You can turn the music for me." Pomeline knew the music by heart but she wasn't going to tell Jenny that.

Marigold looked over. "Yes, Pommie, you really should include her. You don't do that enough. It's no wonder she feels left out. Everyone makes such a fuss about you and your musical inclination and all the fine things you do, but at the expense of your younger sister. Agatha, we'd be utterly over the moon for you to join us." She blew Jenny a kiss. Pomeline's face sagged but her sister and grandmother did not seem to notice.

Art looked over at me. We knew what Jenny was good at—flowers and snowflakes and her bizarre made-up religion—but no one else truly did. Maybe Pomeline did, the other Pomeline that is, the one we glimpsed at the very beginning of summer, before she got waxen and tired and sat at the keyboard channelling sadness from the air. I don't think it was that Jenny disliked Pomeline, not in the way she disliked Margaret. She did love her sister. But Pomeline was everything Jenny couldn't be, and most of the time Jenny couldn't bear that truth. But in the moment, and I can see it right now as clear as a stone beneath still water, Jenny was happy. When Pomeline held out her hand, Jenny took it and they went into the house together.

13.
Sages, Leave Your Contemplations

SOMETIMES IT feels as though my mind is covered in wallpaper, not of big flowers with golden swirls but pictures of my life, painted and stitched, stretching down endless walls. The music, the scent of roses, the gardens, vases piled with blossoms, big skies, the warm stone walls of Evermore and the halls and rooms of the big house at Petal's End. And the steamy August air with Marigold snoring as she napped in the floral armchair with my mother's embroidery covering, as though she was some wilted flower herself. That was how she was after her first go at making flower water, exhausted.

Here on the verandah now the piano music is as bewitching in my memory as the day Pomeline sat in the stuffy music room. I can see it still, Pomeline hunched at the piano, the late-afternoon sun coming dappled through the leaves outside the long, closed window behind her. Pomeline's eyes were on Marigold as she napped. It was just the two of them. Marigold's face was relaxed as she slept, and Pomeline's creased with concentration as though she was working out a puzzle.

"Time is disappearing," Pomeline said. "There are two weeks until the party. A month until my exams."

The sun went behind a cloud and the room grew dark for a moment, and Marigold and her bright floral dress seemed to disappear into the chair. Then the cloud passed and the room brightened as Pomeline stopped playing and rubbed her hands and did exercises, her fingers long and moving gracefully, each one a creature risen up out of the sea. She told me to sit, that there was no need to stand, that I must be boiling in my funny maid's uniform. I settled in one of the straight-backed chairs along the wall.

The vase of flowers in the centre of the round table was dizzying with colour. The air was oversweet. Down the hall there were footsteps on the hardwood and then murmuring voices. Pomeline rested her fingers on the keys and then delicate melody serenaded them as they filed into the room—Art and Jenny, Margaret, and Loretta coming in with a tray. Behind her, Harry with a box, and Sakura with a sketch pad in her arms. She dropped the pad and I knelt down to pick it up. It slipped far back under a small settee and I stayed on the floor trying to reach it.

Sakura lifted some glistening glass bells from out of the box. Harry said, "Sakura made you some glass wind bells. She didn't actually blow the glass, but her father did. That's what he does. It's an art form passed down in their family. She's painted these blue and yellow flowers on the inside. It's ever so intricate. If you look you'll see they are cornflowers, arnica and coreopsis. Pomeline and Jenny, there's one for each of you." He beamed with pride.

Sakura fanned herself. "Tie them on tree branches or on the eaves, or in a bush, and when the wind blows you'll hear them and see them moving. Traditionally they were hung at the corners of temples to ward off evil spirits." She rocked the glass bells side to side and a melodious tinkling filled the room.

Marigold opened her eyes and saw me still crouched on the floor. She put her hand to her thin lips. "Oh goodness, John Lee, what are you doing in here?" she gasped. "Are you looking for your mother? Go to the kitchen. I tell her to keep an eye on her child but she doesn't listen. The nerve. Look at your dirty feet."

I didn't say a word. No one did.

Harry turned to her. "Whoever could John Lee be?"

Marigold looked afraid, still staring at me. "What are you doing here, you bad little boy?" she said. "You can't come in here. It isn't allowed. Where's Charlie? Is he with you? I hope you haven't got him into any trouble. You and your mother are not even fit to be in the kitchen. Don't you look at me like that, you impudent young bastard."

Sakura set the glass wind bells on the table.

Pomeline stopped playing but the piano music echoed as Jenny skipped over to her grandmother like nothing had happened. "Granny, we're going to sing now. For the garden party."

Marigold was still looking at me like I was my dead brother.

"It's just Fancy Mosher, Mrs. Parker. It's just me," I said, standing up. "See, I'm no six-year-old."

Loretta, who had been standing there like a short, portly statue, put the tray down with a crash. "It's stifling in here." She walked to the windows and opened them. Brisk air flooded into the room.

Marigold relaxed, and she wiped her cheeks. "My goodness, Fancy," she said, picking up a fan on the table by the vase. "You looked just like your brother for a moment. The same eyes and hair. The same bare feet. You Moshers."

Harry and Sakura glanced at me, and at Marigold, and finally at Pomeline, who looked away. Even Loretta was looking at the floor.

No one said anything, so I did. "He's dead."

"Oh how dreadful, how simply dreadful. What a tragedy," Harry muttered.

"It was a long time ago," Loretta added.

"Yes, it was," Marigold said. "He was only six years old. I used to let him play with my Charlie in the gardens but he was dreadfully rough and tumble. He wasn't afraid of a thing, that brother of yours. Your mother was very young when she had him. What a pity."

The thing is, there was no pity for John Lee in her voice.

Jenny didn't know whether to blame me or not. Either way, it was a side of her grandmother she wanted private. She wagged her finger at me like an old lady. "You shouldn't go scaring Granny, Fancy," she rumbled.

Pomeline looked like she was going to throw up. "Jenny, Fancy didn't do anything. Granny, you fell asleep. You must have had a dream."

Loretta poured a glass of water and handed it to Margaret, who passed it to Marigold. She took a sip and laughed. "Yes, I must have had a dream. I have such rich sleeps here." Jenny took the fan but Marigold waved her away. "Agatha, I'm fine. Please, dear."

Margaret snatched the fan out of Jenny's hand. "Your grandmother doesn't need a draft. You're going to give her pneumonia. Don't you know anything about elderly folks? Now give her some space, *Agatha*." Margaret said her name all slow and sticky.

Jenny went over to Pomeline and stood glaring at Margaret.

Harry had been standing there awkwardly with his hands on his hips. Suddenly he lifted them and clapped, short and sharp. "Now, everyone, let's just do a quick practice. It was a long day, perhaps a bit humid to be making rosewater. We'll just do a bit of singing, shall we? I say we need some fun. Maybe a beach fire, later. But for now let's hear your marvellous singing!"

Loretta left to get supper ready. When she went out the door she was moving slow. I worried that the summer of the big return was making her old before her time.

At last we were lined up in our singing order and we began. Jenny joined us the first time and we sang in three-part harmony, except Jenny, who couldn't carry a tune and didn't know the words. She hummed loudly and we tried to sing right over her. We carried on for a bit, Harry and Sakura smiling bravely, waiting for the next clash.

Marigold held up her hand. "Agatha, dear, why don't you turn the music for Pomeline as we discussed? I'm sure that would be a great help. Dear, we've been practising for several weeks now and it's simply too late to join in."

Pomeline nodded. "Jenny, it's not your voice. It's that we've already been practising."

Jenny lunged close to Pomeline, who recoiled on the piano bench, but she stopped as sudden as she started. "That will be fine. I'll turn the music." She put her hand on Pomeline's shoulder for a moment.

Pomeline pointed to the sheet music and started to speak but Jenny interrupted her. "I'm twelve years old. I can read music. You don't have to be able to sing to understand notation, Pomeline. You aren't the only one who can do that. I'm not a baby."

"Could have fooled me," Margaret said in her flat voice.

"Sages, leave your contemplations," Jenny snapped back.

"What's that supposed to mean?" Margaret's nose wrinkled up.

"Don't mind her, Margaret. Just ignore her. Jenny, you're being incorrigible. It was so quiet before you came. We need to get on with our rehearsal, Granny." Pomeline played a chord. "There is much to do and we only have two weeks left. I do need to get back to my practising. I need to be playing for at least six hours a day."

"Angels from the realms of glory," Jenny said. She hiccupped. "Sorry. I'll try, I really will. I'm not good at turning papers. I'm clumsy, with my fragile bones." She held out her arms.

Margaret elbowed me and grabbed a tissue off the table, handing it to Jenny. "Are you going to cry?"

I moved a few inches away from Margaret.

"Sing, all ye citizens," Jenny said, her hands clasped, glaring at Margaret. "I don't cry. My tear ducts don't work." She bowed her head. "I am a vessel of unshed tears."

Marigold looked drained. "It's true. Her tear ducts don't work properly. She uses eye drops and we've trained her to blink. Agatha, if your health problems are interfering you'll simply have to sit and enjoy through the act of observation. You mustn't strain yourself."

"Shall we continue?" Pomeline asked gently.

"Yes, please, I'd be honoured to hear." Dr. Baker had come in so quiet we didn't even notice. He swept in and sat down. "The drive today was long. Traffic in the city. I'll be staying tonight. Jenny, that's helpful how you are turning the music for Pomeline. I didn't realize you were coming out yet. I thought Estelle wanted you to stay in the city with her."

Jenny grimaced but he made out like he didn't notice, looking around the room, his arms folded together, as though she had answered him yes-sir-no-sir-three-bags-full-sir.

"Oh, Dr. Baker, doesn't it bring you back to when Charlie was alive, and the Colonel, when we had the Petal's End Chorus, with all those quaint invalids? They sang with such gusto. They didn't care what anyone thought. I suppose you wouldn't remember the very early days. Your father was the doctor back then. He was so pleased you followed him into the medical profession."

Dr. Baker was listening intently, his chin resting in his hand, like Marigold was telling the most exciting story he'd heard in the last decade, but I saw him rubbing his fingers hard together in his pocket. He turned to us standing there in our choir formation. "Don't they look delightful, Marigold? And you're looking well yourself."

"I'm an old lady, Dr. Baker. I don't need flattery. It is wasted on me, I assure you, as clever as you are with it. It's better spent on Estelle."

Jenny turned to a song and showed it to Marigold. "I want this," she said.

Pomeline looked at the music book and shook her head. "No, I was telling Fancy that I don't like that one. She doesn't like it either, do you, Fancy?"

I was saved having to reply for Jenny seemed about to launch into a tirade. She composed herself, trying to show how agreeable she could be when she wanted. "Well, how about this one? It's one you used to sing just to me, Granny. I know all the words. Then I taught Pomeline so we could sing it in rounds. Remember, Pomeline? I don't mean I have to sing it but can't I pick even one?"

Marigold started singing, Pomeline joining her on the piano. *White coral bells, upon a slender stalk, lilies of the valley deck my garden walk.*

Jenny taught us the few words as though she was the choral director, line by line, everything made right by a song. She kept looking over to Marigold for approval. *Oh, don't you wish that you could hear them ring?* Jenny wasn't allowed to sing but she mouthed the words, trying to look as an opera singer would. *That will happen only when the fairies sing.*

Marigold waved her hands like a conductor and she was grinning, but when her eyes reached mine she frowned.

Jenny looked over at me, fixing a look that Jesus saves for the little lambs. The golden afternoon light left the room as the sun pulled over in the sky and there was nothing but tremulous voices singing in the shadows.

14.
Long Is the Memory of the Mute Swan

ART AND I went down to the kitchen after choir practice and I asked Loretta why Marigold was acting batty around me. It seemed senility had roosted on her. Loretta was finishing supper, pan-fried haddock and lemon potatoes, and she didn't look up as she cut parsley to toss over the fish, talking as she snipped, telling me that it was a sorrowful thing when John Lee drowned, that was all. Marigold felt badly that Ma's child died and she had her Charlie. Loretta was not herself. She was short with me. It was better not to talk about any of it, she said.

I'd already upset Loretta by going in the Annex earlier in the summer, on top of Grampie's letter and the family memento. By this point it seemed like a story Ma and Grampie had made up—the lush Mosher imagination. Anything I was seeing or hearing was just that, put there by adults who didn't know how to deal with grief. Adults who did not understand mourning and who infected little children with their melancholy. I reminded myself the music I kept hearing was in fact just a sentimental song I had heard in the halls and rooms and through the walls when I was small. A child's imagination hears whispers when there is only wind. And moans and groans when it is nothing more than squeaky stairs and hinges.

Later, when Art and I were cleaning up the supper dishes with Loretta, Jenny arrived in the kitchen, saying our names, walking slowly, almost a sashay if it hadn't been so awkward and stiff. We could smell her perfume. She had her glass bells in a box. The Parkers had forever been coming down to the kitchen, for a snack, or to tell Loretta their problems like we all did, to sit with her while she listened, took your hand, put her arm around you, hummed as she went about the kitchen, the way she had that made you feel whatever was going wrong would right itself.

"Let's go out to Evermore." Jenny stood there impatiently. "I want to hang up my wind bells. You two can help me."

"Good evening to you as well, Miss Jenny," Loretta said as she handed me the last plate to dry.

"Oh yes, hello." Jenny clasped her hands. "It smells good. You are the best cook, Loretta."

Loretta wrung out the dishrag, dried her hands on a towel and gave Jenny's cheek a gentle pinch. "Thank you, Jenny. I'm happy to see you eat. There's barely anything to you."

Jenny gave a weird little coughing giggle. She turned to me. "I saw the picture you made of Granny. Why on earth did you make a picture of her sleeping like that? It's not very becoming, although Granny doesn't seem to mind. She says embroidery isn't a realistic depiction but an interpretation."

I shrugged. To me, the face was much improved from my first attempt. I didn't see what she found so disturbing about it.

"Maybe you can teach me to embroider."

"That's a nice idea," Loretta said.

"Granny says you do it like an expert. I wonder what my mother would think if I took up needlework. It's something my father liked." Jenny's laugh boomeranged around the immense kitchen.

Loretta smoothed out her apron. "Dear, sometimes parents don't get along, like anybody. Sometimes we argue with our friends or our sisters. It's just a part of learning to get along. Your father was a good man, Jenny. Oh, I'll never forget what a dancer he was. He'd swoop through the kitchen and twirl me about, and then he'd be out the door and off to Evermore so quickly it was like he was a dream. We need enthusiasm like that around here if we are to be ready for the garden party your grandmother wants, God bless her. Now, off with you. Go hang those bells."

As we went through the hall Jenny glanced into the cloakroom we used, where Margaret had left her orange sweater hanging. A bottle of rosewater we had made earlier was on the top shelf, beside her purse. Jenny didn't stop but her head turned slightly. Her expression was blank, like maybe she hadn't even registered nothing but that orange sweater. Art was calling to us to hurry up and we were both through the door and into the evening.

Outside we heard laughing from the carriage house and we went around. Hector and Margaret were talking in hushed tones, and they didn't hear us coming. It was one of those moments where you should either back up quiet or clear your throat. But we did neither. We stood there at the corner of the carriage house, listening as Margaret spoke.

"*Yes, my darlings, Charlie was a fine dancer. How I love Petal's End. Come along and we'll make some rosewater, some lily oil. How horrible that we do not have fresh morning petals covered in dew. Whatever shall we do with steamy hot rose petals? I'll make you a serum, a deadly serum to put myself out of my misery.*" Margaret cackled. "She prattles on like that all day long making my ears bleed. And she's obsessed with that little freak of a human. And she's so rude to Pomeline. I'd slap her if she was my grandmother. What a hate she's got on for the doctor. Can't say I blame her. I can spot his type a mile away. He can't fool me. No wonder Charlie did himself in. Can you imagine having to live with this lot, day in, day out? They must have drove Charlie to it."

Margaret grabbed Hector and started whirling him around. He wasn't much of a dancer but he played along. A dirty jealousy came over me, but it was nothing compared to Jenny's response, wiggling her fingers fast like they was big spiders itching to coil around their necks and dig in.

Margaret did a dip and Hector caught her and pulled her up close. Margaret reached up to pat her hair down. "Can't you just see that shrivelled biddy dancing with her homo son, talking about roses?"

They kept laughing. Hector lit a cigarette and leaned against the wall and Margaret sat down on the ground just as Jenny came stomping in, pointing her finger. "How dare you!"

They stopped mid laugh and looked at her. "I didn't mean anything by it," Margaret said quickly.

Hector took a drag of his cigarette and stubbed it out in his butt-can. "Margaret, I thought you was going on about your own grandmother. I've been telling Margaret she needs to show more respect."

Margaret's grin shrivelled up. "That's not true, Hector."

Art coughed. "We should go out to the garden."

"Well, I agree with Mr. Man there. I guess you shouldn't be making fun, like I told you, Margaret."

Jenny went bright red and I thought she was having an attack, and she opened her mouth, but Margaret spoke before she could say anything, even one of her weird religious lines.

"What are you going to do? Go and tell her? How do you think that would make an elderly lady feel? Let's just forget about it. I'm sorry if I hurt your feelings. You should be proud of your grandmother." Margaret winked. "Not everyone has time to flounce around in a garden and pluck flower petals and boil them up and make potions. Usually it's kids doing that, but if it makes her happy there's nothing wrong with it."

"To hear the angels sing." Jenny said each word slow and long.

Margaret hurried off to the house and didn't look back. Hector let out a low whistle and rolled his eyes. "You all are just too much for this here fellow. I got work to do."

We watched him saunter away. Then Jenny turned and left, and we followed her to the walled garden. It was still bright as we skipped through Evermore. But Jenny wasn't talking at all, just breathing funny. She stopped. I put my hand on her back and told her to breathe deep and slow. We'd grown up seeing her family do that, and the wheezing settled, bit by bit, the early-evening light falling down tender on us, making Art look so young, and Jenny so old. She worried that if she had an attack she'd have to go back to the city. We stayed there with her until her breathing was almost normal. She licked her lips and we carried on. Jenny wanted to go to the lily pond to see the swans.

A few clanks and bangs came from the Water House as we went by and Harry waved to us through the window. "Come in, children, come in, come in," he called.

Inside, Harry held up a bottle with clear liquid in it. "The garden is simply celestial in the evening. I could stay here all the time. I was just getting the Water House ready for tomorrow, for our second go at rosewater. I can't see how it can go any better than this round. This bottle is for your grandmother." He unscrewed the lid and passed it to Jenny, who took a big whiff and closed her eyes. "Extraordinary fragrance. Truly. I can see why your grandmother is keen, why she wants to continue this, revive the lost art of flower water. The roses in the garden she made with your father are exquisite. What a fitting memorial to him."

Jenny held the bottle. "Take a deep breath, both of you." She passed it under our noses. "This is the essence of flowers that never die. It's their spirit in the bottle, you see." She was very serious about this. "So many memories, and now, all in a bottle."

Harry seemed equal parts enchanted and unnerved by Jenny. He took the bottle from her and put a cap on it. "I see you have your wind bells. If you leave them here I'll hang them for you. Pomeline has hers hung out on the verandah. Anyway, children, Sakura and I were thinking we could go down to the beach and have a fire. I've already been down and have gathered up some wood. It's just a matter of trotting through the woods and striking a match. We'll roast marshmallows and tell ghost stories. What do you say? Sakura has wonderful stories. I've already checked, and even Pomeline will come. And Dr. Baker. What do you say? Fancy?"

I agreed.

"Splendid," he said. "Huzzah! Arthur?"

Art smiled.

Harry crowed with joy. "Brilliant. We shall ring your grandmother so she won't worry and we'll run you home after. And Jenny?"

Jenny did a clumsy spin. As we turned to go out the door she ran back and gave Harry a great big hug, burying her head in his stomach. He was surprised and looked like he was a missionary visiting an orphanage. Her white kerchief hung off the side of her head as he touched the wisps of her silvery gold hair.

"Then it's settled. We'll head down in a half hour. Now on with the three of you to check on those swans. Better hurry before they roost. And be careful. They're not like ducks, those things."

The hedge labyrinth was perfectly trimmed now, towering dense green walls. We weren't supposed to go into it without a grown-up around, certainly not in the twilight. One time Jenny went in and we tried to rescue her and the three of us ended up lost in there. She had a proper attack, and we followed the harsh, strangled breaths until we found her. We called and called for help. Charlie and Dr. Baker found us, and Estelle threatened to ban us from the garden. She tried to blame me and Art. We were just six years old. It was the same summer Charlie died. Jenny told her mother she'd insisted we all go in so there was no point in banishing us. I still remember her hands on her hips, breathless, pushing her mother away. You could never banish Jenny from Evermore.

Jenny slowed down in front of the hedge and Art shook his head. "We're not going in there. It's too late. And we want to go to the beach fire."

"If you do, Jenny, you are on your own," I said.

"You two are cowards."

She didn't know the half of it, of course, of why Art and I might be scared of things in the dark and how not believing, not tempting fate, was working.

I rolled my eyes at her. "You're right. I'm scared. Loretta will skin me alive if I get in any trouble. I'm not creeping around in the dark ever again and getting stranded in this stupid garden."

Never again, the child says, *never again*, but never is a long time.

"Forevermore," Jenny laughed in her disturbing voice. "Stuck forevermore in Evermore. Don't you get it? I'm the only one with a sense of humour." She took off running toward the pond. "Catch me, catch me, catch me if you can." For a sickly child, as her mother called her, she was fast, disappearing through trees and bushes and towering flower beds, only a flash of her white dress and cap, bright, like she was a firefly. We went running after her.

Jenny was standing in the water at the lily pond, her sandals on the bank, the swans at the far end, twisting their bodies around to stare at us. "You kind of look like one of them, Jenny," Art said. I went down to the water. The lilies were closed up tight already. The two adult swans started gliding toward us, Sweet William and Iris White. The babies must have been in bed for the night, tucked up in the swan house.

"Don't worry, they won't hurt you if I'm here. They are mute swans. It's funny because they make so much noise. After my grandfather's peacocks, they wanted contemplative birds. I guess they were fooled. What kind of birds do you like?" She took out a crumbling piece of bread she had jammed in her pocket and threw it in the water, and they came and gobbled it up.

"Oh, I like them all," Art said.

"Fancy?" She kept her eyes on the birds. "I bet you like seagulls. You remind me of a seagull."

I flapped my arms and squawked and she started laughing.

"Well, if I didn't know better, I'd think they knew you, Jenny," Art said. "Maybe your white kerchief is fooling them."

Jenny giggled. "Swans have long memories. They keep in mind who is nice to them and who isn't, but mostly they don't like people. My mother enjoys telling me they eat swans where Granny came from. Sweet William doesn't like Mother." She beamed at her big birds, like she'd had this conversation with them before. "Your Grampie said swans and crows never forget a kindness and they never forget a wrong. He knew as much about birds as Granny does about flowers. Swans live for a long time. Up to thirty years, he said. That way I'd have them right through until I was a grown-up. You don't have to feel bad about them dying when you're a child, the way you would with a dog or a cat."

Old Jake wandered through my mind then, his tail wagging, Grampie there on the verandah in his porch rocker, watching me fill the bird feeders. Wild birds were good pets. They came and went and took care of themselves.

The swans bobbed in the water, cooing as though Jenny's voice soothed them. "Daddy didn't bother thinking what it would be like for his children if *he* died before we were grown up."

The big white birds kept looking at Jenny, and she started trilling at them in this odd way she had, and they trilled back. It was hypnotic, and finally, when the copper chimes in the herb gardens by the Water House started ringing and they hollered our names, we realized how long we'd been out by the pond. Jenny put on her sandals and trotted off, a small girl on a summer's eve. Art and I followed her yet again. I turned and looked over my shoulder, and there on the pond full of the amethyst sky sat the two swans, at the water's edge, watching us as we disappeared into the dark shadows falling down now as night came waltzing in.

15.
The Dead Samurai

IT WAS easy then, as it still is now, to forget that the world beyond the thick forest of Petal's End could be different. While we'd stopped at the big house for sweaters and flashlights, Harry had gone ahead to start the fire. We made a parade of light down through the woodland trail to the beach. It was near dark when we came to the shore and we could smell the driftwood smoke on the salty sea air as we came out of the woods. The remains of the day still lingered in a smouldering red line on the horizon. The island was out there, a black silhouette, a large creature that had risen from the waters, waiting. It was hard to imagine anyone living over there. I remembered Grampie describing how the sky had lit up the night the lighthouse burned down all those years ago, before it was replaced with a steel tower and the automated beacon. Pomeline used to say if there was ever a part of Petal's End she wanted it was the island, that high atop would be the perfect place for a music conservatory.

Harry called out to us as we came over the rocks. "Hurrah, you're here! We can't stay too long. I promised Loretta you'd get to bed early. We have busy days with the garden party so soon. My, we are working you children hard. I hope you don't report us, Dr. Baker, for child exploitation." Harry chuckled and stirred the fire. He was in his khaki shorts, with a wool sweater on. For once his hat wasn't around his neck. He had wool blankets waiting for us on the big logs around the fire. Waves were breaking on the rocks. A thin white line of surf appeared and disappeared in the dark-blue light.

"It's good to see them having some fun, Harold," Dr. Baker said as he sat down on one of the logs.

"Where's Margaret?" Jenny sat down beside Dr. Baker.

"She stayed with your grandmother. Hector was going to drive her home."

"I could have stayed up with Granny and helped . . ." Jenny's voice broke off.

Dr. Baker laughed. "You need to have some fun. Doctor's orders. Margaret's happy to stay late. She's worked out well, I'd say. Your grandmother adores her."

Jenny coughed. "Oh rest beside the weary road."

Pomeline put her hand on Jenny's, her long fingers covering her sister's hands completely. "Jenny, please don't start up with that. Let's have fun." The flames flickered and Pomeline's face glowed. She took a blanket and put it over Jenny's knees. "Let's be proper sisters, shall we, Agatha Jennifer Parker?"

Jenny coughed again and Dr. Baker leaned forward. "Your breathing is a bit ragged. The sea air will be good for your lungs but do stay back from the woodsmoke. Driftwood fires are the worst, what with all the brine in the logs. You need to slow down, Jenny, or your mother will be apoplectic. We don't want that."

The ensuing silence lingered, only the crackles from the fire popping out. It seemed Estelle was speaking to us from far away in the city, looking into a crystal ball where flame and laughter swirled in wheezy spirals of smoke.

"Look, children." Harry was pointing to the east. "Look at the moon rising." There it was, the enormous August moon coming up over the trees at the top of the hill. "Do you really think it's that big?"

"Yes!" Jenny called like she was answering back in church from the Amen pew.

"Well, when it rises, what happens?" Harry asked.

"It gets smaller. Late at night it's like it shrunk."

"Yes, Fancy, that's right. But it doesn't shrink. It's the brain playing a trick on your eye. It's called *the moon illusion*. When the moon is just above the trees the brain puts it into that same perspective. The eye scales it to the objects around it, houses, buildings, that sort of thing, so it looks enormous. And when it rises higher into the vastness of the sky the magnification ends."

"Well, that's not much fun, the betrayal of the moon. Moon, moon, you were once my friend." Jenny shook her fist at it, standing up, her little body wobbling.

"Jenny, really, it's not the moon doing it. It's your brain and your eye." Pomeline giggled.

Jenny ignored her. "Dr. Baker, you didn't know that. What kind of doctor are you?"

"Jenny, don't be rude."

"I'm not being rude, Pomeline. I'm just commenting that our Cousin Harry knows about the moon illusion but Dr. Baker doesn't."

Dr. Baker had that long face that only Jenny could bring out. "Cousin Harry does indeed have a lot of knowledge, but I can assure you, Jenny, I know how the mind and eye work together."

"He isn't your cousin, Dr. Baker."

"I stand corrected, Jenny. What I intended to say is that there are many ways to understand the world around us, and only some of them are scientific. I suppose storytelling offers another kind of truth for certain types of people. They certainly are much more fun, aren't they children? Fancy, you used to tell wonderful tales even if they were rather macabre."

"Not no more, I don't. Busy watching the moon tricking us," I said.

Dr. Baker laughed. "Well that's a pity."

Jenny, for once, agreed with him. "It's true, Fancy, you always told the scariest ghost stories. I remember your Grampie telling the one about the forerunner, the ghost of a ghost. He said they came to remind us that how we live is how we'll end."

"My Grampie's dead. He was full of foolish stories. I don't want to talk about him." I threw a rock in the fire and sparks exploded up. Everyone pulled back.

"Right, then, I can certainly tell some stories. And Sakura loves the traditional stories from her country. *Kaidan* they call them, don't they, darling? All sorts of nasty tales of spirits looking for revenge."

Sakura raised her eyebrows but she didn't say anything, and Harry clapped his hands together. "Let's have some stories and some marshmallows, shall we?"

Dr. Baker had the same fixed smile he did when Marigold told her stories. Harry passed the bag of marshmallows to Pomeline, who shook her head. "I'm not feeling hungry. Too sugary for me, but Jenny loves them. I'll roast one for you, little sister."

"You're practising too much. You barely ate supper," Jenny said.

Pomeline stabbed a puffy white blob with a roasting stick. "Well, I'm not getting enough exercise, I agree with that. I'm getting fat, turning into a slug."

"I hardly think so, Pomeline. You're a gorgeous young woman. But you certainly are practising with sustained concentration. It's good to have a central focus, but you're eating and breathing this. You can't live on music alone." Harry's voice was tender.

"It's hard not to admire such passion," Dr. Baker said. "The Parkers are remarkable people. That's what I tell Estelle, that she should be proud of you."

"The exam will be over soon enough and I want to go to the conservatory. I haven't planned for anything else." Pomeline turned the marshmallow carefully near the coals.

"When is the exam?" Sakura asked.

"At the end of August. And again at the end of September, if I make the short list." Pomeline wrapped her arms around her chest, shivering even with a blanket on her knees.

Sakura looked up at the sky. "Dr. Baker is right. Passion is wonderful."

"How about that ghost story, Sakura? Are they as terrifying as Harold suggests?"

"Harry likes ghost stories. He thinks we are naive because most people in my country still believe the stories, or what they represent."

"Sakura, darling, you're not being fair. I think they're astounding stories, so charming."

Sakura looked bemused. It wasn't a mean look but an endearing one. For all Harry's education, he was the naive one.

Jenny held her hand up as though she was volunteering and glanced over at me. "I still want Fancy to tell one. There are lots of stories about the Mosher family. Fancy's grandfather was nice. I'm sorry he's dead. You might feel better if you tell a story. He called me Jenny Starlight. Mother said that sounded like I was a burlesque dancer. Fancy said it was because my skin is bone white. Samuel Mosher had special ways. Granny was telling me that—"

"Jenny, don't repeat Granny's tales. It's rude. She's talking nonsense this summer. Leave Fancy alone," Pomeline said.

Art poked the fire with a long stick.

I whispered, "Other people can tell stories. The ones about us are just all made up anyways." For the first time it occurred to me that maybe the Parkers had heard more than just rumours about my family.

"I'll tell one, then," Sakura said, breaking the tension. "In my country, at this time, it is the time of Obon. It is a time when we honour the dead. According to tradition, it's when the spirits come to the human world and we make them offerings, so they will return and rest in peace. We go to the cemeteries, where the ghosts dwell. We leave lanterns for them on the water, the ones who have died at sea. If the body hasn't had a proper burial, then the spirit will never rest. My grandparents said you must never swim at Obon, as the water will be full of spirits."

Dr. Baker chuckled. "Well, we'd best stay out of the bay."

Jenny scowled at him. "It's very, very rude to interrupt."

My bare foot grazed against Art's and my cold toes gave him a shock. He took off his sweater and put it on my feet.

Sakura started buttoning up her sweater. Harry used the break to pull out a bottle of wine and plastic glasses. He filled them and handed them to the adults. Then his eyebrows went up as he exclaimed, "We'll just pause for a toast, to days gone by, and to the adventures still to come." He poured glasses for all of us and passed them around. "It's a special occasion. We're celebrating summer! And life. And childhood. A bit of wine is good for the health, wouldn't you say, Dr. Baker?"

"I don't suppose a small bit will hurt. Red wine has health benefits." He smiled at Pomeline and raised his glass to her. The rest of us lifted our glasses and we went around the fire clinking them together. I'd never had wine before, not a drop. I drank it all down. It was sour and bitter and it reminded me of autumn. I coughed, and Harry came rushing over. "You don't drink it like water, my dear. You sip." He poured me a bit more. "It's for sipping, dear, sipping."

Jenny licked her lips. "It tastes sour. Granny gives me sherry and it's much sweeter."

"Granny should not be giving you sherry. You know how upset that makes Mother."

"It's fine, Pomeline, it's medicinal. And we certainly don't have to be reporting that to anyone." Dr. Baker gazed at Pomeline and held up his glass. "Here's to beauty."

Pomeline held up her glass but she didn't look at him. And she didn't take a drink.

Jenny glared at Dr. Baker.

Harry held up his glass. "To beauty."

Art lifted up his plastic cup. "To beautiful stories," he said in his high voice, and we all took a sip of wine, everyone except Pomeline. She set her glass down by her feet. Harry kissed Sakura's head and I wondered how many glasses of wine he'd already had. A glow was burning in my stomach. I took another chug.

"Darling, do continue with your scary tale."

Sakura started roasting a marshmallow. "My mother used to tell me this story. It has music in it . . . you might like it, Pomeline. There was a man named Hoichi. He was known for playing an instrument like a lute, a *biwa*. Hoichi was also known for telling stories, the old stories, of famous battles. This was in the days of the samurai, a long, long time ago." Sakura's soft voice, so rarely heard, was hypnotic. "But Hoichi was blind. And he was poor. Things were difficult for him. He spent a great deal of time at the temple, where the monks enjoyed and appreciated him, and he performed for them often."

Pomeline shivered. Dr. Baker put an arm around her, and the other around Jenny. Pomeline snuggled into him. Jenny sat there like a post and then squirmed a few inches away without taking her enraptured eyes from Sakura.

"The monks eventually invited Hoichi to live at the temple. They wanted to help him, and all he had to do was play and recite for them. One warm night Hoichi decided to enjoy the breeze on the verandah outside his room, overlooking one of the temple gardens. He had glass wind bells and they were making music, calling him out to the cooler air. The priest had gone out to console a grieving family, and the other monks had left to do some work in the nearby village. Hoichi was by himself. He played his *biwa* to pass the time, the music flowing out over the evening flowers.

"The air was tropical and heavy, just as it has been here most nights at Petal's End. Hoichi remained outside. The priest still had not returned and it was well past midnight. The jasmine was sweet on the night air. Then, cutting through his music, a stern voice called his name. 'Hoichi.' He said nothing, but then it said his name again. He was afraid. Hoichi opened his mouth but no words came out. He tried again. He croaked like a frog in your lily pond: 'I cannot see. Who is there?' The man said, 'My master, a very fine lord, has many nobles visiting. He would like you to come and tell the story of the battle Dan No Ura. You must come with me now, and bring your *biwa*. Do not be afraid.'

"Hoichi dared not defy the samurai. He was afraid at first, but then he thought how pleasing it was to be summoned before such an impressive audience. As they arrived, he could hear the murmur of a great many voices. He kneeled and began the story. Stories were told in a different way in that time and place, more like a chant, very formal. The court audience was delighted. Hoichi was told the great lord wanted him to recite for the next six nights, and the same samurai would come for him each night. He was told not to speak of his visits, since the great lord wished to keep his presence in the area a secret. At dawn Hoichi returned and slipped into his room unseen. The wind bells were silent and there was not even a wisp of breeze." Sakura looked around at all of us.

Harry nodded. "It's easy to sneak about in the dark."

Sakura tilted her head to the side and looked out into the dark beyond the fire, like she could see his words out there and she was watching them. "It is easy to think one is sneaking about, though one never knows who is watching. The priest did notice the next evening and reminded Hoichi that going out at night was unsafe. But Hoichi was sworn to secrecy and he could not say where he had been. He knew it was dangerous to break an oath. Now the priest had a bad feeling, so he had the monks quietly trail Hoichi when he left the following night. They lost him on the dark path.

They searched relentlessly for Hoichi and finally heard his *biwa* in the nearby cemetery. They hurried over and found him there at the grave of a famous lord. Death fires burned in the cemetery as he chanted in the howling wind and rain. Hoichi was in a trance."

"Who set the death fires?" Art's eyes were big like the moon. The wine had me more relaxed than I'd been in my life.

"No one, no person sets them. You could say they are the fires from an ill will, from a spirit, from a person or an animal, or even a bird, and they come into this world as blue flame. Hoichi, he was telling a part of 'Heike Monogatari,' the Heike Story. He was telling the part where they lost in battle. And the dead, they appeared as blue fires all around him, listening to him. I wonder, do you understand me?"

Jenny's mouth was wide open. Art put his arm around me and squeezed. Dr. Baker pulled Jenny and Pomeline closer. Jenny brushed him away and moved from the log and sat on a rock. "Well, it's a good thing this fire isn't blue, and we're not sitting in a graveyard." Dr. Baker laughed, but no one else joined him.

Sakura took a bite of her marshmallow and then continued. "They shook him and he came out of the trance, but he was angry they had disrupted him. He seemed crazed, so they marched him home. There the priest asked him for an explanation, and Hoichi told them what he had been doing. Now he feared they had interrupted the dead, and that the spirits would kill him for breaking his oath. The priest carefully told him they would have killed him anyway. They were *onibi*, angry spirits that would kill him after he served them. These were the ghosts of those who had lost in battle and whose families had been ruined. Such ghosts sought revenge upon those who brought about the shame." Sakura put another marshmallow on her roasting stick and held it near the coals.

The fire had burned down. The waves were closer, breaking on the rocks. Grampie had never seemed afraid of anyone who came to see him, but it made me wonder if he knew all the kinds of the dead. And why he wanted to keep me from talking to my dead brother. How he'd said in the letter not to go looking for the dead.

Sakura was glowing in the firelight. "To protect him, they stripped Hoichi naked and they painted sacred passages all over his body, even on the soles of his feet, between his toes and fingers. The priest told Hoichi to sit still on the verandah, and when the dead came to call that night he must remain still and silent and alone. The holy words would protect him. When night came, Hoichi sat for hours until he heard steps come through the gate and all the way to his verandah. The wind bells began to chime.

"'Hoichi!' The samurai called his name three times, angrier each time, and climbed the steps. 'I see his instrument but the only flesh I see are these two ears. I will take them for my master.'

"Hoichi's ears were ripped right off his head but he stayed silent and unmoving on the verandah, bleeding and in agonizing pain. When the priest returned he found Hoichi, only to realize they had forgotten to paint holy text on Hoichi's ears. They sent for a doctor and Hoichi's wounds were cared for. Some say Hoichi lived the rest of his days in fear of the dead samurai sending his dark messengers back for him again. Others say his bravery banished the spirits of the disgraced family for good."

Jenny started clapping. "Sakura, what do you believe?"

Waves were breaking much closer and it was hard to hear Sakura, for she spoke even more quietly now. "Families cast long shadows—"

"We must all remember a fireside story is only that, children. Ghost stories are nothing more than tales we tell to explain what we don't understand," Dr. Baker lectured.

Harry kissed Sakura. "I could listen to her stories for hours. Don't they give you such a splendid frisson?"

Dr. Baker cleared his throat. "I certainly hope we don't have screams in the night up there. It's a good thing we don't have Obon in this country. Imagine that, his ears ripped off. It's a bit gruesome. I suppose different cultures find different sorts of stories entertaining."

Jenny's eyes darkened. "Some ghosts get mad enough they don't ever rest. Certainly ones who are constantly interrupted. And others, like my father. I don't think he's resting. And we might not have Obon but we do have August. Maybe Daddy's come back."

"Jenny! How could you say that?"

"Pomeline, she's just a child," Harry said.

Sakura spoke again. "In my country we think of our ancestors' spirits as part of the family. Just because they die doesn't mean they cease to exist."

Jenny's eyes were circles of fire. "What's wrong with that, Pomeline? You're so uptight. Don't you think Daddy would be angry if he was a ghost? Don't you think so, Dr. Baker? It's why Granny won't let us in the Annex. There's something in there—"

"My prescription for runaway imaginations is a good night's sleep."

Sakura didn't acknowledge Dr. Baker. "Not all spirits are like the ones in my story, Jenny. Some that are angry can be appeased. For example, if they left something unfinished and it is completed they will be consoled and will never appear again."

Art finally spoke up. "Well, my grandmother says some spirits never settle into their bodies to start with. They spend their lives trying to escape."

Jenny shuddered. "That's creepy. Remember the forerunner story, Fancy? Daddy told it to us. He said your mother used to tell him and your brother ghost stories in the kitchen. Isn't it when those men were out walking one night, on their way to a costume ball? Isn't that right? And they saw that thing coming from the sky?"

The wine had made me bolder, ready to fall back into my family ways. "A forerunner isn't no ghost like Sakura's talking about. It's more of a foretelling of something bad that's going to happen, at least that's what Grampie said. He did believe those things he told

Jenny." I felt lighter and more carefree than I ever had before, and my worries fell away. Jenny's sombre attitude made me giggle. "In the story you're talking about it was a brother and a sister who was walking home one evening after they did an errand for their mother, not a costume ball, silly. It ain't no fairy tale. And it wasn't flying but crawling down the road using its legs and arms like a spider would. It was dressed like a woman, but thin as a scarecrow. They ran away but it appeared again in front of them on the road. When they turned to go it hopped onto a wooden fence and balanced there on one leg, one arm pointing out at them, and they went running back the other way screaming. The next day they went back and the fence was so rotten it crumbled away when they poked it with a stick.

"They stuck to what they saw, so the story goes, for it was only dusk so it wasn't no dark night fooling them. Years later when they was grown, the oldest one was dying and she was diseased and on her deathbed. She looked in the mirror and pointed at herself in fear, for she looked just like the thing on the fence that had followed them that night. It was her own afflicted self haunting them under the moon, a forerunner of what was to pass. Her brother swore that his sister on her deathbed looked just like the lady thing that come after them that summer night long ago."

It was silent except for the waves crashing onto the shore. Dr. Baker looked like he had indigestion, and Harry and Sakura clapped their hands as Jenny pointed down the beach. "Didn't your brother die down there?"

Art took my hand under the blanket. I didn't say a word. I finished my wine. My face burned, and I put my finger to my scar and tapped it. I was suddenly tired and dizzy. I felt like I'd been swimming for miles and miles against a current that held me in one place, keeping me from stepping out onto the rocks.

Pomeline looked weary. "Jenny, really, think of Fancy's feelings. There's been quite enough talk of a little boy who has been dead for decades, for heaven's sake. That's enough. All this talk of spirits and ghosts and ruin and revenge . . . I don't mean to be rude, Sakura, as we begged you for a story, but we don't tell such tales. My mother would be appalled."

Harry stood up and began to break up the fire. "You're quite right, Pomeline. It's my fault. It's easy getting carried away sitting around a beach fire in the dark. I think we all need a good night's sleep. We'll rise with the sun for another wonderful day of activity."

Pomeline took Jenny's arm. "Come along. I'm exhausted. I must go back up to the house. And you must get to bed, Jenny."

But no one moved, and the waves were louder now. I saw their shiny heads rising up and flipping over into white foam as they crashed down. Pomeline rubbed her eyes and looked out over the bay. The beacon at the top of Parker Island beamed out, and Pomeline looked away.

I imagined Pomeline thinking about her father, swinging from the ceiling of the Annex. And John Lee . . . could someone that young linger on? I wondered if what I needed was sacred words scrawled over my flesh, to keep me safe. But so far it wasn't the dead that was causing me any fright, just the living.

"We'll head up with you, Pomeline. You do look tired, and deep sleep is what the doctor orders. I'm back to the city tomorrow and need to get a good night's rest myself."

Jenny twisted toward Dr. Baker. "I don't want to go to bed yet."

Dr. Baker could hardly contain his disgust. "Suit yourself then, Jenny, as you always do. Harold, you'll make sure she comes up soon?"

"I will most certainly shepherd the flock back to Petal's End, have no fear," Harry said.

They said goodnight and went over the rocks, Pomeline taking Dr. Baker's arm as they disappeared into the dark night. Harry, Sakura, Art and Jenny kept gabbing as the fire burned down to just the tiniest embers and the sky overhead seemed to get bigger and deeper and darker. I picked up a pebble and rubbed it between my fingers, a worry stone.

"I want to make more rosewater, Cousin Harry. Did you give the other bottles of rosewater to my grandmother? If not, I can take them up to her in the morning."

"It was a small batch and there were only two bottles. Your grandmother gave the other one to Margaret. To thank her for all her work this summer. She says Margaret has gone above and beyond the call of duty."

Even in the muted light I could see Jenny's eyes narrow. She picked up a piece of driftwood and stabbed at the fire.

"We can make more tomorrow. I'm sure your Granny will give you your own. It's only the first batch. The next batch will be the finest. Don't take it so hard, my goodness."

"It's the first batch. It's the most special. And Granny gave the only other bottle to Margaret."

"Well, I'm sure Marigold would have given it to you if she'd had any idea how upset you'd be. Let's just let this go for the night and we'll make more later." For the first time since he'd arrived, Harry appeared exasperated.

It was clear to me that Jenny was thinking of the bottle of rosewater in the cloakroom near Margaret's orange sweater. She already knew and was only confirming what she viewed as Margaret's efforts to displace her, Margaret's trickery. She stood up and started back across the beach. She tripped, but Art grabbed her before she hit the rocks. "Slow down there, Jenny. Don't let Margaret get to you."

Art headed across the beach to his house. "Don't let the ghosts get you," Jenny called out to him.

I watched him disappear into the night. Art, like me, could walk this place blindfolded. He was singing, and I was comforted by his voice even as it faded. Jenny was mumbling under her breath as we walked. I whistled softly all the way up the hill. We came onto the lawn and the house sat quiet, the air warm and sheltered from the bay. There was a small outdoor light on by the door. Harold, Sakura and Jenny went up the front steps, and I called that I was going in through the back.

It was almost pitch-black at the back of the house. The linden flowers were strong on the night air. I heard a scuff. I should have gone in the house but I went further into the darkness. I headed back down the path, to the far door in the wall of Evermore. And that's when I saw it, a shape by the carriage house wall. I was drunk and terrified.

Don't be afraid, it whispered.

Running on the path now, I flew along and it grabbed me. I twisted and kicked it and heard it fall down on the grass before I had a chance to look closely. In the moonlight, when he leaned back, it was Hector sitting there holding his arm.

"Shit, Fancy. Holy fucking shit. What are you, some freaking mercenary running through the night?"

My heart was pounding. "Holy fucking shit yourself, Hector. What the hell are you doing out here at this time of night? Didn't you take Margaret down to the valley?"

He stood up, rubbing his arm. "I took her home a long time ago and then come back to do extra work. Buddy said he could give me a hand. Lots to do for the garden party. I could hardly wait to get her out of the car. It wasn't my fault she went making fun of Marigold, you know. She's got to be running somebody down, that's how Margaret is. She don't ever stop talking around me, giving me her slit-eyed look. You know fat girls. Anyway, I can't get nothing done in the day with them people all around, the gardeners, the city ladies planning out the party like they're putting on some end-of-the-world banquet. I told Margaret she should be more careful with what she says, especially around here where the walls got ears. It was good you come along to get her to shut the fuck up. But I will say Margaret's not a bad dancer, the way she moves her hips." Hector chuckled. "What are *you* doing out here? Now I'm all sore and beat up from you molesting me in the dark."

I am ashamed to say even now what come over me there in that garden with the moonlight flowing down over us, like it seeped through my skin and filled me up with liquid silver. My heart was pounding, and he kissed me, licking the sticky marshmallow bits still on my lips, pressing his body on mine, my back against the cold stone wall. "Well, well, well, will wonders never cease. You've been drinking, Fancy Mosher. All grown up in one evening. Let's see how grown up you are." He pulled my dress up, and went down on his knees. I felt his wet mouth on me. He unzipped his pants and I could feel his hand moving fast. His tongue was hot and hard as the night air licked icy around the edges of my hot flesh.

"That's just between me and you, Fancy," Hector said when he sent me back to the house. "We all need some love to make us feel good. When you're a bit older I'll give you something better than that."

I threw up by the back door. Loretta had left me a bedtime note on the kitchen table beside a plate with a cookie. *Have a snack, get some sleep, and remember to be thankful. God Bless, Loretta.* Through the kitchen windows I could hear coyotes howling and yipping, all stirred up for the hunt on such a deep and starry night. I remember how I reeked, and how dizzy my head was, how badly I didn't want Loretta to find me stinking of wine and vomit and sex, how much easier it had been last summer when Art and I played on the beach and in the forest.

I close my eyes and rock my old body here in this chair but really, I am still that little girl about to go up the stairs when I hear a creak in the hall. The floors are no stranger to me and it's easy to cross them without making a sound. I peek around the corner to see Jenny there in a pink nightgown with Margaret's rosewater in her hand. She's on her tiptoes and her fingers are stretched out straight. She didn't have near as much wine as I did. She crooks her index finger, hooks it around the bottle and pulls.

It was such a pretty bottle, glistening there in the cloakroom in the soft light spilling in from the kitchen lamp that was left on. Jenny moved it forward until her fingers encircled the glass and then she clutched it to her chest. She set it down on the table and took the lid off. It was hard to see and my head was spinning, but it seemed to me she took out another small bottle and tapped a few drops into the rosewater. She shook the rosewater bottle and put it back where she'd found it. Finally, Jenny grabbed the bottle she'd brought and scurried down the hall out the door into the main house as I stood there watching her from the other side of the room, my mouth sour from the wine and marshmallows and from Hector's kiss that tasted of smoke and beer.

16.
The Distillation of the Rose

The next morning I was up early with bloodshot eyes and a throbbing head and out to the garden to cut flowers. I glanced toward the carriage house. It was a different place by daylight. I had bathed first thing, soaking in the claw-foot tub, scrubbing myself. My mouth was dry and my lips cracked. I felt like a child version of Ma. The night before felt like a nightmare, the hazy memory of Hector touching me, of Jenny sneaking around.

When I had finished doing up the vases Loretta came in with lists she must have been writing in bed. She bustled about getting her breakfast, already thinking of her conversations with the party planners and the caterer and the gardeners and the cleaners. I was glad to have her natter on. I poured a glass of wholesome milk.

Loretta waved me out of the house, told me to have a bit of fun after how much we'd done yesterday, to come back for baking once Art arrived, and to pick raspberries. Harry had come into the kitchen as I was slipping out and she'd started in on him in her prim way—he and Dr. Baker should have known better. She still did not realize he'd given us wine, and he was apologizing for that, not for just keeping us up late, but there was no point in telling Loretta if she wasn't putting it together.

I took a bicycle from the carriage house. Hector still wasn't there. I didn't want to be thinking about him right then. I wanted the night to stay in the night. It was Sakura's story I was thinking about mostly, dead spirits who come looking for payment. And my own story Jenny had dragged out—spirits wandering around before their time. It was eerie going down the lane, for the shade seemed darker than it ever had before. I wanted to see Art and I wanted, for the first time, to get away from Petal's End, to leave that world enclosed by the greenwood. The Parkers and Ma had no real use for the bay but I did. It was the first summer we had no time to play on the shore, and being on the beach for the fire, and then being against the wall with Hector, these things had me pedalling like mad for my childhood. I stopped and looked back at the pillars on either side at the end of the lane, the gates open. I whistled as the bike moved over the road.

The stone wall ran around the entire property and I could see as I pedalled where it was beginning to crumble. The wall disappeared into the tomb of forest as the road veered away and then dipped into a hill. I soared into the village, the road meeting the main road by the bridge. I saw Art coming out of the driveway of his grandmother's over on the other side of the village, where their house was perched on the eastern slope that came down to the harbour. The sky and the sea were the same soft blue and the island seemed suspended between them. I waited for Art at the end of the road. Across the harbour were fishermen with their lobster traps. The season was over until the autumn and they were stacking them up. Seagulls swirled overhead in a white funnel and the sky was dotted with puffs of clouds. It was almost high tide.

Art came down the road. He smiled when he saw me. "Just like old times," he said. I couldn't look him in the eye when he said that. I remember at that moment knowing the worst thing that could happen would be Art taking his friendship away if he found out about Hector. No one would approve. Even I didn't approve of Hector. But there wasn't that side to Art, judging people. His torment came from his loyalty.

We rode to the beach and left our bicycles on the ground, running down on the rocks. Art had a camera in his backpack and we took turns snapping photos of each other. Toward the west was where we'd had our fire but we didn't go there. We sat on big rocks until the water came closer, the waves breaking all around, watching our rocks become islands as we stood and peered out across the bay. We waded through the water until the waves got bigger and we scrambled back. I was soaked and self-conscious about the way my dress clung to my breasts. Art didn't look. The balmy wind was strong and blowing our words off, and I don't know why but we kept laughing and laughing, holding hands as waves broke and we'd turn and run before they could catch us. Later, we rode our bikes through the village and back up the hill, finding comfort in our familiar silence until we turned down the lane to Petal's End.

"Did you have bad dreams," Art asked, "about warriors coming for you and ripping off your ears? My head hurt this morning. Grandy knew I'd been sipping, that's what she called it. She was upset. She doesn't know Harry gave it to us. I did have dreams, and not good ones, but I can't remember them."

By the time we got back the lawnmowers were buzzing and there was an army of people in Briar Patch uniforms, white T-shirts and green shorts, with sun hats and tool belts, with wheelbarrows and clippers. We were close to the day of the party. The Happy Helper van was parked with the nursery trucks. We'd been on the beach for longer than we thought.

We were with Loretta in the kitchen when Margaret came in from the garden. I watched her while I swept the floor. She was in her maid outfit and she was blotchy and panting. "Now, Margaret, I don't know what's come over you. Are you ill? Have a glass of water. You must stay out of the sun," Loretta said.

"I'm not feeling so good. All this rushing about waiting on people." Margaret looked at me and Art. "Can you keep that Jenny away from me? She keeps popping up like a damn gopher. I can't take it today. It's giving me the creeps." I shrugged and went into the hallway to the broom closet, peeking into the cloakroom. The rosewater bottle was not on the shelf. I came back into the kitchen and Margaret was now sitting, looking pathetic. I grabbed the pitcher of chilled water from the fridge and poured her a glass. She looked grateful and took a few sips.

Loretta held her hands up by her ears, like she was having a sudden ache. "Please don't keep complaining about her, dear. You have talked of nothing else all morning. I can't take any more unpleasantness this summer. Every time we seem to be getting on a nice path it turns rough. Now take the food up. They're eating in the parlour today." Loretta went into the pantry.

Margaret leaned over and held her stomach. "I'm not used to working hard in this sort of swelter. It's making me dizzy." She went down the hall into the bathroom, and came back with her face wet.

"Marigold's making more rosewater. Your skin is looking real nice." It was effortless lying to Margaret. Lying wasn't a natural ability but it seemed to be coming to me easier as the lies piled up.

Margaret scrunched her face as she rubbed her cheeks. "The nerve all of you have talking about my complexion. What are you, a bunch of fucking beauticians?"

Loretta returned from the pantry. "Margaret, please. Off with the lunch for the ladies. Fancy and Art, take this picnic out to the garden for Harry and Sakura, and find Jenny. And please make sure you take lunch to Pomeline. She'll be in the music room, but she should eat on the verandah and get some fresh air. She's been wasting away these last few weeks." Loretta shut her eyes and clapped twice, like she hoped we'd all have disappeared by the time she opened them.

Art and I went through the door into Evermore. "Do you think Jenny is following Margaret around?" he asked me.

"I'm not sure." Lying to Art felt different than lying to Margaret. One lie will lead to another.

As we approached the Water House, Harry called out to us. "Hello, hello. Fancy, you look as though you barely slept. I hope Sakura's story didn't keep you up all night." Sakura was there beside him, not saying a word, her talk used up by the beach fire.

"Good morning, Art. I guess it's good afternoon. Go in and see what we've done this morning. You can help us later. We have to put them in bags with ribbon." Inside on the counter were trays of hand soap, bars they'd cut from bigger blocks. There was one large brick left to be cut. Bits of crushed dried rose petals lay on the counter where they hadn't finished cleaning. There was a box of small cotton bags with thin ribbon ties.

"We want to plan an expedition. We're thinking about a trip out to the island in the bay. It's very mysterious and downright primeval."

"I got to find Jenny for Loretta. Make sure she gets her lunch. Grampie said that island don't like people coming on it no more. It likes being remote."

"Well, your Grampie certainly sounds like he was an absolutely fascinating man. Jenny's somewhere out here, back by the lily pond. She's been playing in the garden all morning, waiting for the two of you to come back. You are both a fine influence on her. The years of home-schooling have certainly isolated her, but it's never too late for learning social skills and interactions. Oh, and we're ever so sorry for last night. We didn't think a single toast would cause so much trouble."

"I'll run and find her." Before anyone could say a word I took off.

I spotted Jenny over to the east of the garden singing off key to her swans. "Loretta wants you for lunch. There's lunch in the kitchen or lunch with your grandmother or lunch with your cousin and Sakura."

She looked down at my feet. "Why won't you keep shoes on your feet?"

"You sound like Loretta."

"My mother would get mad if I went without shoes. But wrathful is her normal state of being. Imagine if she knew we were drinking wine. You drank too much, Fancy Mosher. You look green."

"Well, your mother ain't here, is she? And if you think I look green you should see Margaret. She's not feeling good at all, complaining all the livelong day."

Jenny lifted her head from my feet, eyes fixed on mine. "Maybe she should take time off," she said blankly.

Art, Harry and Sakura were eating on the table outside the Water House and waved as we came closer. "Well, look what has come forth from the garden," Harry said. "Join us."

Pomeline appeared then, dark circles under her eyes, her skin white like the water lilies on the pond. "Granny has sent me out here to see how things are going. She wants us to hold another choir practice, although I think we sound as good as we'll get. She thinks I need a distraction. If it makes her happy . . . she doesn't understand that I need to practise."

I cleared my throat but they seemed to have forgotten I was standing there. I could have slipped away without saying a word. "Excuse me. I'm going to the big house."

"Hurry back, Fancy. We'll get started on the soaps when you return. See if you can round up Margaret. And stop by the carriage house to get more glass bottles from Hector."

That was the last place I wanted to go but I did as I was told.

Hector was sitting in a chair under the tree beside the carriage house having a cigarette and drinking a beer. He gave me a big grin when I came up.

"They want to know where the glass bottles are, for the rose-water."

"Oh yes, their rosewater. Turning back the clock, these people. Why don't you come over here and sit on my lap and have a drink?" Hector blew out smoke as he laughed. My face burned.

"Suit yourself," he said. "By the way, be careful around your pal, Art. He's thinking about nature this year in a whole different way."

I stared at him in disbelief. It was hard to tell if I was angrier with him or with myself.

Hector stared back. "What's got into you, cranky pants?"

I ran off then, straight for the house. Sweat dripped down my cheeks and into my mouth, salty, making me think of the night before.

"Fancy, is everything okay?" Loretta looked up from her mix ing bowl.

"Jenny's eating lunch with her cousins. She don't want to come in."

"That's fine, just as long as she eats. Girly Miss, how many times do I have to tell you? Put your shoes on. Have a drink and cool down."

Margaret came in then from the main house with a tray of dirty dishes. She put them down with a crash on the counter. "Harry wants you to come out to the Water House, Margaret," I said, walking to the back of the kitchen, not looking at her. When I didn't look at her it was easier to ignore how sick she appeared. "He wants you to help with the soap."

"I said I would help down here. Pomeline is with Mrs. Parker."

"I don't need any help. Go ahead with the others, Margaret. Just walk slow and stay out of the sun. The day will be over soon enough. Mrs. Parker wants all the soaps done up. Honestly, these preparations are enough to give her another stroke. I keep thinking maybe I'm having a heart attack myself." Loretta pounded her chest. "Oh my . . . the weather is getting to us all."

"If you ask me, her freak granddaughters are enough to give her a heart attack. One whining all the time and the other moping about and hammering on the piano all day. Does no one else think Pomeline is sick? It's not just me this place is getting to."

"No one asked you, did they, Margaret, for your opinion, and if no one asks, please keep it to yourself."

Outside, Margaret called after me, following across the yard. "I can't wait for this job to end." She stopped to light a cigarette that she had stuffed in her bra, along with matches. With breasts like hers, her bra was like a purse. She was just like Ma, who kept a photo of John Lee tucked in by her heart. The cigarette seemed to give Margaret a lift. Maybe she was just having an off day. Maybe her being sick had nothing to do with Jenny putting something in her rosewater, I thought. Maybe that whole memory was just some dream or drunken fantasy.

"I'm sick of that four-eyed bitch Jenny telling me what to do, I'll tell you that. Hector says someday she's going to have it out with her mother, with all of them. She likes to scare people. It's the only way she can feel important. Just look at her. You'd think she owns the place."

I didn't like Hector's name coming out of Margaret's mouth. "Well, she *is* going to own the place eventually."

"Hector says it will go to Pomeline because she's the oldest, unless Estelle can get her hands on it beforehand. I guess Jenny takes after her, a thief. You little girls are always up to no good. And you stop following me around too, Fancy. I can hear you.

You're not grown up enough for some things and you should know that."

"I'm not following anybody around," I said cautiously.

Margaret took a few more quick sucks off her cigarette and tossed it on the ground, stamping it out with her kitten heel before following after me into Evermore.

They were just about to get started in the Water House. I sat beside Art at the big table where the soap was piled high on trays.

"Margaret, so glad you could join us. It will go faster with more hands. We'll show you, like Marigold showed us this morning." Harry was fiddling with the ribbons as he spoke and Sakura was clearing some counter space.

Jenny came over and stood beside me, ignoring Margaret. She picked up two bars of soap and handed one to me.

Margaret looked at Jenny's dress. "Doesn't wearing a dress with a floral print make you feel like you're wearing dead things?"

"I told you, it's the smell. Do you have memory problems like everyone else seems to? Fabric doesn't have any smell. Unless you're a servant and you have to wear uniforms like you and Fancy, and then it smells musty which is almost as bad." Jenny wrinkled up her nose.

Harry pointed to the table. "All right then, we wrap each bar, like so. The bar goes into one of these cotton bags, like so. Next we pull the ribbon ends tight and tie a bow, like so, and voila—a charming party favour for each of our guests to take home, to remember the serenity of Evermore, of Petal's End. It's so romantic." The soap was stacked like castles all along the counters.

Art let out a big sigh, and Margaret took it to mean one thing. "And who do you fancy, Art?" Margaret was tying bows one after another in a blur of coloured ribbon.

Art blushed and went back to humming.

"Art loves Fancy," Margaret said, gawking at Art. She thought she was hilarious.

"Margaret," I said. "He's like my brother. Don't be disgusting."

"Oh, I'm just teasing," Margaret said, winking at Jenny, who ignored her. "Art's not interested in girls, not yet. Wait until his voice changes."

"I love the roses," Art said to the soap castles. "I love the gardens . . . the sound of the birds . . . the stars and the sky. And I like fixing engines with Hector."

"And I like all of those things too, Art. You'll be a big tall man with a low voice soon enough. No need to rush any of that," Harry said.

"What's the rest of the story?"

"Which story, Fancy?"

"The story you was reading when you first got here. About the garden."

"Oh yes, what a memory you have, yes, 'Rappaccini's Daughter.'"

"What happens?"

"It doesn't end well. It's not a happy story."

"How does it end? I hope no one loses their ears in it." Jenny giggled.

"Well, you see, as spectacular and exotic as it is, the garden also happens to be, well . . . it's poisonous, as I said before, and his daughter, raised in the garden, is immune to the poisons of the flowers and plants."

"That's a good thing. My mother keeps me in all the time because she says I have a weak immune system."

"Well, Beatrice, the girl in the story, she has a very strong immune system, so even the most beautiful and deadly flower can't hurt her. But she became poisonous to others, as I told you. And when she fell in love, she began to poison her lover. He found an antidote but it overwhelmed her as she was already intensely toxic. And thus Beatrice died in the garden."

Margaret rubbed the sweat off her forehead. "Love can be poisonous all right." She looked at me. Jenny was watching us both.

"Yes indeed, Margaret, that's one interpretation of the story. Love is a complex emotion. Infatuation is an intoxicating thing. I suppose, like anything, we can be corrupted by it or uplifted by it, poisoned by it or healed by it."

Margaret went to put one more piece of soap at the top of the tower and she held it there. She glanced at Jenny and me as she dropped it and the soap castle fell to pieces, the blocks of soap clunking on the table and down on the floor. "Oh my goodness," Margaret said, twiddling her bangs. "That wasn't balanced properly, now was it?"

Harry put his head in his hands.

"Girls. Now please, let's get along," Sakura said. Her voice was level and reassuring.

Margaret seemed so sturdy it was hard to believe Jenny could actually do anything to really harm her. We heard the laughing and shrieking of the party planners as they got near the Water House. Jenny and I slipped out and left the rest of them there. Margaret watched us go.

Jenny held her parasol over both of our heads as we strolled toward the house. I didn't know whether I should be direct and just come out and ask her what she put in that flower water. It was hard to forget Margaret shaking and gasping for breath.

"I know what Margaret did. I've seen them in the carriage house. I watched from behind the corner. It was disgusting. She was on her hands and knees," Jenny said out of nowhere. "I've seen my mother like that. Those sorts of women never think anyone sees. Hector is not your one true love, Fancy. You will know your one true love. My father told me so. He said you'll know when your love isn't true."

Just like that, my pity for Margaret was snatched away with those words. Jenny could do as she pleased to her.

"I long for my one true love. In the winter it's snowflakes. In the summer it's my swans and roses. But there must be more to true love. It's not the kind that makes you bad."

Jenny reached out and with her icy hand she squeezed mine. "All is calm," she said. "All is bright." She let go of my hand and ran up the side steps into the big house. Such a peculiar small girl, holding the handle of that big wooden door as she pulled it closed, leaving me alone like there was no one else on earth but me.

17.
The Boy in the Waves

I AVOIDED MARGARET for the next week and she avoided everybody but Marigold. She was coming late to work and leaving early, walking slow, red hives all over. And I stayed away from Hector. I wanted nothing to do with him—a nineteen-year-old man playing nasty Margaret on one side and a twelve-year-old girl on the other.

On occasion I'd see Hector driving by in his precious Old Rolly or in his pickup truck and he'd wave like not a thing had happened. When he gave Margaret a ride home and she'd wave like the Queen I'd pretend I didn't see them. It disgusted me to even think about them together. I remembered her with the student minister.

Other times she'd be waiting outside for her father to pick her up. Once he drove up quick. The gardeners were leaving and it was noisy and she didn't hear him. I was at the door. Margaret hadn't said a word to me as she stood there blowing out smoke while the trucks went by. Her father's car came and she went stiff, looking at her cigarette with terrified eyes. Without thinking, I plucked the cigarette from her fingers and took a puff. Margaret's father got out of the car. He gave me a once-over. "Smoking's disgusting," he said. "Girls who smoke are disgusting."

I took a drag and blew out the smoke real slow in a haze around my head. It made me dizzy.

"Come along, Margaret."

She looked out the car window and mouthed "Thank you." I gave her a nod.

Hector came to find me later in the day when I was bringing laundry in before suppertime, after he'd been in to see Loretta and she'd scolded him for disappearing all the time. He was burdened down with errands, he said, it wasn't his fault. He went on and on about how much they were expecting him to do, and he had wood to cut, and it was all interfering with the business plans he and Buddy had. He made the mistake of putting his hand on my arm when he approached and I gave him a slap.

"Did Margaret tell you? It don't mean nothing. She'd give it for free to a toothless old man. She's that kind of girl," he said. "Not like you."

"Margaret didn't say a word. The walls got eyes and ears at Petal's End, don't you know, Hector? Remember, I'm my Grampie's granddaughter. I know things." It was like the lies were infecting me. "You keep away from me," I said. "You might have some fooled around here but not me."

Hector took a step back as he spoke. "You're going to turn out no different than your mother, Fancy Mosher. Don't you go acting like you're special, like you're a Parker. You're no different than any of us."

It was easier for me now, with my lust for Hector broken into pieces. I moved through the house in a whisper, wearing my maid outfit. I barely saw Art, who was busy all the time out in the garden. I would hear him singing and I'd join in for a moment before going about whatever business Loretta had sent me out on, taking this and that here and there, slipping through the big house, hearing voices talking and laughing and arguing, the piano music flowing from early in the morning right through to the night.

The choir practices were fast now because we was singing so beautiful and we wanted it to be over. We wasted no time. Jenny stood there turning the pages all demure and proper and quiet. Marigold stately in her armchair, sometimes napping through it or fanning herself, at other times just staring into space, and on occasion looking at me strangely. And me, wondering if I'd see someone, or something, if I looked where Marigold was staring. But when my eyes followed hers I'd see only a hairline crack in the ceiling or a chip in a wooden chair.

It seemed each day Pomeline faded further. She was barely eating. And she was napping now, after her morning practice, and again in the afternoon.

There were five days left until they'd throw open the gates to Petal's End, the doors to Evermore, and people would laugh and children would sing and Marigold would stroll about with her silver-handled cane, tossing rose petals, handing out elegant slices of rose-petal soap and spraying mists of fresh rosewater.

For our afternoon off Art and I had gone out on our bicycles. A cormorant flew by and I followed it on my bike until it was just a dark speck disappearing into the sky.

"What's she doing here?" Art said.

"Don't know," I said. "Hunting, I suppose."

"Fancy," Art said, "I meant there." He was pointing at Ma. She was up the road a bit, leaning on her car, lips painted red. She must have got loose from Ronnie. She had on more makeup than usual and it was all put on as though she had double vision when she did it. Around her neck hung a glittery rhinestone necklace, like she was going somewhere special. She wore a black dress. Ma lit a cigarette and tapped her foot.

My legs were sticking to the vinyl bike seat and when I lifted my thigh it felt like my skin was ripping. I could hear her speaking my name but I planned on biking right by her. *Fancy Mosher, Fancy Mosher, Fancy Mosher.*

"Jesus," Art said. "It's like a bad nursery rhyme. We'll talk to Harry when we get up to Petal's End. He'll help you."

"She'll never leave me alone, not until the day she dies and maybe not even then. You know what she's got in her head."

Funny how the sultry air clasps sound. I heard Ma's voice calling, "Fancy Mosher, you stop. Right now."

I kept going and Art said nothing. I started whistling.

"Fancy," Ma hollered again.

I turned. Art forged ahead but then he gave in and turned too. Ma was beckoning, one hand on her hip, wobbling on her high-heeled shoes.

"How'd I ever end up out of a thing like that?" I whispered. "She's drunk."

"It would seem that way," Art whispered in reply.

She got in the car and started it, backed up and came charging forward, slamming on the brakes when the car was almost touching my legs.

"Get in the car, honeys," she said. She ran her finger softly on my scar through the open window. I did what she said, under her spell. "Put them bikes in the back." She popped the trunk and I put my bike in. I don't know why but Art picked up his bike.

"Art, you go along then," I said, but he put the bike in and got in the car.

"You're looking lovely this afternoon, Mrs. Mosher."

Ma looked at Art as she pushed on the gas and we roared up the dirt road, dust and rocks flying behind us. "Don't call me that unless you want to insult me, Art. Call me Marilyn. Well, I'm glad you noticed how I'm looking. You're going to be a lady-killer when you grow up," she yelled to him, winking, even though it seemed more like she had dirt in her eye. The car swerved near a tree in front of the big stone boundary wall of Petal's End.

"Ma, watch the road."

She hauled on the wheel and we shot across to the other side, almost going in the ditch before she straightened the car out. She grabbed another cigarette. "Don't you go telling me how to drive, Fancy. Don't you go telling me nothing. Just like having your grandfather around. Holy Mother Mercy." All of a sudden she started weeping and took a big breath in, a big huge gasp, and then she stopped. "Forgive me, Fancy. I ain't myself today. Forgive your old Ma."

"So where we going, Mrs. Mosh . . . I mean, Marilyn?"

"Oh, we're just going on a little country drive," she said.

As we passed by the driveway into Petal's End, a small thing glowing in a white dress stepped out, its hands clasped against the fairy-green leaves and the grey stone walls. Ma let out a scream. "Do you see it, Fancy?"

"Yes, I do."

"Praises to Holy Mother Mercy. You got the gift. You believe."

"It's Jenny Parker, Ma," I shouted at her.

"When did she go and die? No one told me."

"She's not dead, Mrs. Mosher." Art was yelling over the car engine too.

"Well, praises, praises, look at that. She ain't dead. I never thought she'd make it to five, let alone twelve. Scrawny, ain't she? Looks like her grandmother does now. I hear she ain't aging well. That's what the cleaners say." Ma pulled over and Jenny came over near the car. She did look like Marigold standing there, like she was turning into a withered old lady.

Ma eyed Jenny. "I thought you was a hobgobbly. Maybe you are and you snuck into Petal's End. Marigold better take care with you running about."

"You shouldn't speak that way about my grandmother." That

was all Jenny said, like us driving up with a crazy lady in a beat-up, swerving car somehow made sense to her.

Ma seemed transfixed, looking at Jenny, a doll that sprung to life before her eyes.

"I've been waiting all day to see them. We play together, you see," Jenny said, her voice stern and low.

Ma laughed, her body jerking. "Oh yes, the Parkers playing with the Moshers," she said.

"How silently, how silently," Jenny said, in a soft voice.

"Well, we're going on a drive, dear Jenny Parker. I'm Fancy's mother." Ma's voice was purring again.

"I know who you are. You've got the Mosher eyes." There weren't a lot of people who could unnerve Ma, especially when she was drunk. Grampie or Loretta maybe. But Jenny was affecting her.

"Get in then, if you're coming. Art, don't be rude. Open the door for little Miss Parker."

Art got out and opened the door for her, and Jenny slid in beside me. She squeezed my arm with her cold, claw-like fingers. "Hello, Fancy."

Art was laughing nervously. Ma pressed on the gas and we zoomed off, pebbles flying, the air getting warmer as we drove away from the bay.

Ma locked eyes with Jenny in the rear-view mirror. "Is your Granny still afraid of hobgobblies, little girl? Because she should be. She should be very afraid. Hobgobblies is coming to get her one of these days, and don't she know it." Jenny didn't seem to take offence. She even gave a twitch in what I thought might be agreement. "You don't need to see the dead if you keep company like this girl, Fancy."

We almost went into a tree then. "Please, Marilyn!" Art yelled, grabbing the wheel. "Please keep your eyes on the road. Why don't I drive? I love to drive on a dirt road."

Jenny leaned forward on the seat. "I could as well. Hector has been giving me lessons in the big car while you've been helping

Loretta. He's also been letting me drive his truck but my legs are too short. Don't worry, Fancy. He thinks I'm five years old. They won't let me do any work around the house or anything at all except play, so Hector takes me along with that moronic Buddy. Hector thinks I'm like a puppy who likes to go for a drive." She coughed from the dust kicking up from the dirt road.

"Jenny, you might want to get out. You can still walk home. There's a door in the wall up a bit and you can walk back on the path."

"She can come along. You haven't seen your mother in a long time, Fancy." Ma burped. "It's almost time, Honeysuckle."

"I haven't seen my mother in a while either. She never takes me on outings. You're lucky, Fancy," Jenny said.

We raced down a hill and as we came up there was a man walking on the side of the road. It was Harry, swinging his arms, long legs striding along, a pack on his back, same khaki shorts and a pair of binoculars around his neck. He was just past where the Petal's End wall turned and ran west through the woods along the southern border of the property.

"Now who is that good-looking man? He looks a bit queer but there's nothing wrong with that," Ma said, staring, almost running him down. "Look at his funny hat. He looks like an explorer."

"It's my cousin, Harry. We should offer him a ride. He's a scientist." Jenny tapped Ma on the shoulder.

"Well, you don't have to get all pushy about it, my God. I never had much time for a man of science."

"Pull over, Mrs. Mosher."

"It's Marilyn. You don't need to go all formal like you people at Petal's End like to."

"Pull over, Marilyn."

Maybe it was not being able to see Jenny's eyes behind her glasses. Maybe it was because she had that Parker way about her. Or maybe it was the creepy low voice crawling out of such a small child. I don't know. Ma slowed right down and peered out the open window.

Harry was out of breath from the heat and Ma was making him trot along there in the full sun beside the car, with sweat dripping off his nose and chin. He had his hat in his hand now that he was jogging. "Very good, then, look at all of you, out for an afternoon drive," he said, voice bouncing with his stride. Finally Ma pulled over. "So kind of you to stop. It's hotter than I anticipated. I've been used to the fresh breezes at Petal's End but when you go inland, well, it's a different climate. You must be Fancy's mother. I was under the impression you were on a holiday . . . of sorts. Have you come back early?" He had this puzzled look on his face, and he kept his eyes on mine like he thought I'd mouth him a secret message.

Ma laughed and pounded the steering wheel as she stared out the window. "You talk like a retarded man," Ma said. "Sure you aren't left over from when they had the mental hospital back up there, one of them crazy choir singers?"

"Why don't you get in, Cousin Harry." It wasn't put as no question. Jenny's voice was loud.

"Well, how kind of you to come and fetch me," Harry said hesitantly.

"Open the door for the man, Fancy. You heard your midget friend. Make room for the man," Ma said.

I opened the door and moved over. Jenny and I were so thin we took up one space together.

Harry got in. He wiped his forehead and leaned forward, holding out his hand. "I'm Harold Prescott, Marigold's cousin. My wife and I are visiting for the summer. What a sensational region, I must say."

Ma looked at his hand briefly then hit the gas and we roared off. She took a drink from a bottle of gin she held between her legs.

"Slow down," Harry yelled. Jenny and I started laughing. She was laughing like it was funny. I was laughing because if I stopped I'd start crying and crying never led to anything good with Ma.

Ma turned on the radio and gospel music came blasting out, and she started talking to Art about the graveyard, about how many Moshers were buried in it.

"Is your mother drunk?" Harry whispered.

Jenny giggled. "You're slow on picking things up. But most adults are. Don't feel badly, Cousin Harry. You mean well. I know you do. Did you know Granny wants to open up the Annex? She wants to renovate it. She thinks my father would want that."

Ma turned the radio down, like she had an attack of manners. "Don't talk about your corpse of a grandmother. We're going to the Flying Squirrel Road on family business, to the graveyard. You can sit in the car, you Parkers. I'll drive you home after," she hollered.

Ma pulled up at the cemetery and the car heaved to a stop. She got out and put her hands on her hips, taking it all in. She took a step forward and her high heels caught on the grass. "This is where my son's buried," she said in a soft voice, looking straight ahead, like there was things in front of her that were listening. "John Lee. He'd be a grown man, if he was alive. He was the first-born and the first to die. No mother should outlive her first-born."

Jenny got out and tilted her head back as though a movement up above had caught her attention. "Risen with healing in his wings."

"Jesus wept. Yes sir, he did, and he also rose. You are a wise little girl," Ma said.

"From the realms of glory," Jenny said. "My grandfather paid for John Lee's tombstone. The finest marble. My father told me so."

Harry tried to catch my eye but he didn't understand. Art looked back at Harry and held his hands up in defeat. Our helplessness seemed to spur Harry on and he jumped out of the car, slamming the door behind him.

Ma lurched off to the rusted gate and pulled it open, the door creaking as it swung. The roses by the garden gate had been chewed off, mangled. The graveyard was surrounded by thick leafy forest and it was shady and cool. I smelled sweet cicely. It was growing all through the ditches, having escaped from the gardens at Petal's End a long time ago. Neither Art nor I had said a word and we were still sitting in back seat of the car.

I guess then Harry thought he'd be a man, take control and be an adult. He followed Ma. "Mrs. Mosher, my dear lady . . ." he started. "I really think you need assistance—"

"Marilyn. Please just call her Marilyn," Art called over to Harry.

"Don't you tell me what to do," Ma spit out—but we weren't sure at who. Then from far up in the branches came a horrible screaming, like it, too, would tell her what to do. The screaming stopped. We had no idea what was hidden in the foliage, and whatever it was, we hoped it would not come down.

Jenny looked where the noise had been coming from, a weird rapture on her face like she was in church, her hands tightly clasped together.

"Don't you think you can go telling me what to do. You could have helped me and you didn't. No sir, you didn't, you just kept what you had to yourself and left me on my own, wondering. I don't need no more judgment." Ma shook her fist. Another scream came piercing down through the air. Art and I got out of the car then and went in through the gate to stand beside Jenny.

"Ma," I called. "Ma. Grampie ain't there."

"You get over here, Fancy Mosher, and you do your job. You wouldn't even tell me if you could see your Grampie. You're stubborn, just like him. I want you to believe. I want you to be a believer."

"Just stay here," Harry said. "Fancy, just stay here. It's all right. Marilyn, perhaps it would make more sense to come back at another time, without the children. I think that's a splendid idea, don't you?" He came and stood beside me, his arm out, like he thought Ma might try to snatch me.

"It's the day," I said. "The same day. All those years ago. It was the day John Lee drowned."

As if in a reverie, Ma touched John Lee's tombstone, talking as she stroked it, telling a story about silver moons and a baby's boat sailing across starry skies, like we weren't there anymore but rather a young boy was sitting beside her on the grass with the shining Mosher eyes and soft tousled hair just like mine. John Lee, she sang, her low aching voice entrancing and holding us as she brought the past to life in a brief graveside moment that plays out for me still.

We could not take our eyes off her as she stood amidst the mid-summer green foliage, smeared ruby lips and sparkling necklace bright against her black mourning clothes. With her peculiar audience of children and a stiff middle-aged man, Marilyn Mosher gave her lament for the dead. I've seen Ma upon a stage in my mind every summer since that moment, and as the words come forth from her mouth with them comes the laugh of a boy who appears on the beach and watches his mother wave to him as she walks down the beach with a tall man. The boy has a toy boat, and he giggles because it looks funny playing in the waves. He follows it, and then he is soaring up and down the waves that cover the steep beach while his Mama is behind the cliff in a shallow cave. This is how Ma recalled it. Her back is against the wet rock, her back going up and down, the skin rubbing raw, absent as the man pushes deeper inside her, and fireworks explode in her belly and travel up to the same breasts that used to fill with milk for the little boy now floating face down in the big waves beyond the surf. The big blue sky and the island out on the horizon watch quietly as he drowns. The other boy who has come to the beach looks up from his rock castle, screaming. There is a woman there collecting amethyst and holding a parasol. She doesn't know how to swim, she cries. The other boy keeps screaming at the water's edge. And Marilyn Mosher comes wobbling, woozy from the gin, over the rocks in her high heels and falls, cracking her forehead open, her hands slipping on the rocks, crawling over them to get to the waves. The other child is in the water trying to reach the boy but the older woman pulls him back. The man from the cave runs to his truck for a rope. The incoming tide brings the little boy closer to the beach and he is caught up on a wave, on the top of the wave, and it breaks and he comes in on the surf, his hands moving like small sea stars as the water pulls back and leaves little John Lee Mosher dead on the beach.

We all knew bits and pieces, of course. It was a story people told from time to time. And people tell parts of stories just as people collect rocks from here and there on the beach, and take them away. But Ma was in possession of the entire thread. In that moment, though, Harry only knew that the drunken mother of the girl the housekeeper named Loretta cared for was out of her mind in a cemetery, telling stories only adults should hear. But the child the housekeeper cared for and the strange girl with glasses from the big house and the boy with the high voice from Lupin Cove, they began to understand how the pieces really fit together.

More screaming came again from up in the ironwood trees, the sound of a harness jingling and clop clop clop as Hector's father, Clyde, came by in his wagon loaded with hay, pulled by a team of four draught horses. One of the horses whinnied. The spell was broken.

"Goddamn peacocks. Stupid man bringing all them animals who don't belong over here," Clyde said, as he tipped his hat and took a drag off his cigarette and watched three peacocks fly down from the high branches, strutting around among the tombstones, their tail feathers fanning out and shimmering against the grey stones as they screamed. Ma turned and looked at the horses.

"Marilyn," he said, nodding at her. He opened his mouth like he was going to speak but then closed it. Clyde sat on his wagon with the reins in his hands.

"You was there, Clyde. You know what day it is."

A look of a pain moved through him, but he ran a hand through his hair and whatever had taken hold of him was gone. It was no surprise to me. Everybody knew what Clyde Loomer was like. He didn't bother even looking at Ma as he called to the horses to giddy up. "You know them horses don't like a woman who cries, Marilyn," Clyde said, and then he continued down the road, showing us the same interest he managed for his son.

Ma wept quietly now, eaten up by a pain I would not know until I was older, when I would understand how that kind of ache never goes away. The clop and the jingle faded off and it was just tearful Ma as she called over her shoulder. "Come, Fancy."

I went.

"Do you see him?"

I wanted to believe and I wanted the dead to find me so I could take Ma's pain away. Grampie's tombstone was behind John Lee's. *Let the dead bury the dead, Marilyn*, Grampie had said to her, not long before he died. *Let them pass*.

I took my mother's face in my hands then, my dirty hands, and I stroked her forehead, my tears spilling down. "I can't help you, Ma. He's gone now. He's gone away in his little boat across the sky." And I whistled for her because I did not have a voice for singing.

Her crying then was something unearthly and I took my hands away from her, my fingers slick with her tears. She bowed her head down and I saw the white roots of her dyed raven-black hair. Art was crying too. I could hear him, calling my name. My heart started pounding and I heard a movement from west down the dirt road, a pebble tossed, and a bird called, the cardinal . . . then stillness. Jenny was admiring the peacocks and Art and Harry were paralyzed with indecision. I saw a flash of white. There was a sound at the edge of the cemetery. I took a step that way. The peacocks were quiet now, eating the flower arrangement left on a grave.

The red bird appeared in the sky, and I took off right through the graveyard, grass soft on my bare feet, weaving through the grave markers, hopping over a few, then over the fence and north through the trail in the woods, in the direction of Petal's End, where Loretta was, where her calm was.

"Fancy! Fancy!" I heard them all calling my name. There was crashing behind me and I kept going until Art called out. I stopped. He was bleeding, scratched from the brambles and shrubs grown in close over the trail. He put his hand on my cheek, where my scar was throbbing, and I pulled away.

Jenny come up behind us, her white dress flying out. She was short and had no trouble ducking the branches. "Heavenly hosts," she whispered as she stopped beside Art. We walked together, single file, me staying in the front. It was cool and dark in the woods.

Art cleared his throat. "You don't think she'll follow us in here?"

"No, Ma don't like the woods. She don't like shadows."

"Harry will take her home. He feels foolish for letting it go on for this long. I can tell. First getting us drunk on his fine wine and now letting us go to the graveyard," Art said.

"I knew the peacocks had to be somewhere. My mother said they died off but I knew she was wrong. They've been living in the forest up here by the cemetery. My grandfather would be happy. Granny will not be. She banished them a long time ago."

We didn't respond.

"It's different, when a child dies, of course. Pomeline says Mother is the way she is because of all the babies she lost. All those babies who died before they were even born. The miscarriages. I guess your mother was the same way, Fancy. We're the same, aren't we?" Jenny pressed. "John Lee drowned." She spoke it as though it was a fact she was reading in a history book or a newspaper.

"Yes, he did too drown," I said, dodging the branches ahead of me.

"My mother doesn't even go to my father's grave. And she won't let us in the Annex. Your mother takes you right to the graveside. Why does she think you can speak with the dead, Fancy? I know about your grandfather."

"Because she's a drunk, Jenny, that's why." Jenny didn't know about being the twelfth. She didn't need to know about that, about believing. The Parkers didn't know any of the true Mosher stories, only their own. But now we both knew who had been on the beach the day my brother died. My mother was in a cave having sex with Hector's father and Jenny's grandmother was helpless on the rocks with Charlie, watching John Lee drown.

"Did either of you hear a noise on the road back there?" I asked.

"You mean Clyde?" Art's voice was worn out.

"No, not Hector's loser dad."

"Your mother and the peacocks were the only things anyone could hear." Jenny giggled.

"I saw something."

Art said, "There was a lot of commotion, Fancy."

It was pointless to talk about it any more. We were getting close to the wall around Petal's End. The trail was sloping down, which meant we only had about another mile to go. We kept going on the trail until we come out into the clearing where the hunting lodge was. Or the ruins, I guess you'd call it. Way back, one of the Parkers built the lodge, for when they'd go out hunting across the mountain. There was a rotting picnic table still, for family picnics, not that they'd had any of those in years.

"This is where it happened to my grandfather," Jenny said. "Stupid man to have a bear for a pet. My grandmother talks about him like he was a saint but he wasn't. He betrayed her. My mother told me. She said Granny deserved it because she was nasty. It is true, that we deserve our punishments. My grandfather would talk mean to Granny, telling her to mind her own business. In front of us. He thought children were like animals and you could say what you liked around them. That's not true—he thought animals were smarter. Grandfather only married Granny because his father told him to.

That's what he said to her. Just like he told my father to marry my mother. 'It's not about love, Marigold. Marriage is never about love.' He told her that. I was just a child but I heard. In the library at Petal's End. Daddy never had enough affection, you see. That's why he was the way he was." Jenny just kept talking and talking, like she was trying to get out five words for every step, as though her words could come out and fit together and it would all finally make sense and growing up wouldn't seem like such a horror show.

I asked Jenny just what she'd been doing with Hector, what she was thinking having him teach her to drive.

"Oh, I followed him back there one day. I got into the back of the pickup truck. It was fun rattling along on the country roads, just like being in a song." She kept walking, her hands clasped together. "He finally saw me in his rear-view mirror. That's the problem with Hector. He doesn't pay attention to details. *I* pay attention to details. He thought he'd seen a ghost and he almost did kill me from how he slammed on the brakes. He has a tattoo of a butterfly. Did you ever notice that? Anyway, I crawled over the other side and ran out of the truck and he came after me, but he didn't catch me before I saw what he and Buddy are growing back there on my grandmother's property. It's pretty, quite tall, and looks like ferns. He offered me a mint. Then he tried to tell me he was growing parsley and sage, rosemary and thyme. He was a moron to think I don't know that song. Or herbs. Hector was a bigger fool to think I don't read and watch the television news when I'm in the city. It's the only thing my mother will let me do. And he made me promise not to tell."

I couldn't help but laugh then, because Jenny wasn't someone you could make to do anything.

"Hector said he'd do whatever I wanted if I didn't tell. It was for medicinal purposes, that's what he said. I told him if he taught me how to drive then maybe I wouldn't say anything. And if he stayed away from Margaret. And now I know how to drive even though it's hard because I am short, you see. And Margaret doesn't go back to the carriage house any more."

Art just kept shaking his head and I was laughing. Jenny seemed pleased and held her hands up like she was doing a benediction.

"Fancy," Art said, "I'm sorry your mother's the way she is."

Jenny answered, like she was nine hundred years old, "We can only endure them. Now we know. I'm sorry. My grandmother couldn't do anything. She was helpless. We should never be helpless."

18.
She Laid Her Snow-White Hand

WHEN WE came out of the woods there was no one outside the big house. Dr. Baker's car was parked out front and Estelle's white car was parked behind it. We assumed they were inside, and we were thirsty but decided to get a drink at the Water House. We weren't ready to see no one yet. Jenny and Art were hovering around me like two weird bats, him on one side, with his squeaking voice, and Jenny on the other.

Art and I sat outside the door of the Water House and Jenny brought out glasses of water. It was the first time I recall her ever doing such a thing. It was late in the afternoon now but we were tired enough for bed, and there was still choir practice yet.

The three of us sat looking at the expanse of Evermore. It was a whole world in behind those stone walls, safe and comforting. The gardens were clipped and perfect. The flower beds were dazzling. The statues, the benches, the stepping stone paths, the foliage, all immaculate. It was a contrast to the shabby graveyard, the forest we ran through, the scruffy dirt road. The screaming peacocks were already a grotesque memory, for when things are strange enough the mind stores them as a story. And in this story the three of us were sitting in the wicker chairs under the awning of the Water House.

There was a tinkle from the tall flowering bushes, where Sakura had also hung glass wind bells. The breeze was strong and lifted our hair in a velvet-soft touch, then it dropped away just as the peace was splintered by a deep angry voice. In a certain sort of summer air a harsh whisper travels intact. Art leaned back and shut his eyes, letting out an exasperated sigh. Jenny stood up and walked down the path toward the sound. We followed her to the Wishing Pool, where I hadn't been since Grampie's teacup had broken.

"Well, I'll have to take care of it. After the garden party, of course." Dr. Baker cleared his throat. "I don't see how you could have let this happen. This is a disaster. You aren't a child. You have to take responsibility for something other than your piano playing, for God's sake, Pomeline."

"Well, you're the doctor," Pomeline pleaded.

"Yes, I am, and that's why I gave you those pills and told you exactly . . . *exactly* what to do with them. All you had to do was take them at the same time. Surely you could have managed that. You Parker women are all the same with your frivolous priorities, only thinking of yourselves. Did you get the days mixed up?"

Pomeline was crying and trying to talk at the same time. "I don't know. It's been hard with Jenny here, bickering with Margaret, with Mother calling all the time and fighting with Granny. And Granny hardly makes sense. It's been difficult to keep track of anything. And my exams are coming, but all that seems to matter is the garden party and Mother wanting to sort out the will. Mother says there is a letter from Daddy that confirms he was going to leave her more, but she can't find it. Granny says it must be a forgery, that Daddy would never let anything go outside the family. She says the entire estate will go to her and pass along to Jenny. It's like I don't even exist to them."

Through the branches we saw Dr. Baker hug her. "You've been under a great deal of stress. Your mother has ruined Jenny, spoiled her rotten. And if only Estelle and Marigold would work things out in a more reasonable way. They're putting me in the middle of it. I'm a friend to them all. I know you're worried about your grandmother but she is a very elderly lady, my dear. You're only eighteen." His voice caught when he said her age. "I'll take care of everything."

It went quiet, other than Pomeline's sobs. Then we heard heels click on the stone path behind us. We ducked into the brush and Estelle didn't see us as she rushed past and flew through the opening in the cedar hedge to where Dr. Baker and Pomeline were standing beside the Wishing Pool. Her finger was on her temple like that deep headache was back.

Estelle's jaw was clenched. "I thought I might find Jenny out here with those servants. We're going to have to search the woods. I knew that if I entrusted her care to you, Pomeline, something would go wrong. You want to play your piano and look at pretty things and sing your days away. And you, David, only encourage her. What the hell are you two doing out here?"

"Estelle," Dr. Baker said, "Jenny will be fine. She's more robust than you think she is."

"Don't 'Estelle' me. You said it would all work out. You say it year after year. And do you see how things are working out?" She turned to Pomeline. "What is it *you* have to cry about? You have your whole life ahead of you, with endless opportunity, and yet you cry like a baby, and David, you comfort her like she's your wife. It turns my stomach. You know *nothing* of being a parent. You act like a teenager with no responsibilities. It's time to grow up. You know nothing, the both of you."

"Because you don't tell us anything, Mother," Pomeline screeched. "It's all secrets and lies and guessing. I hate being a Parker." She ran off, her yellow dress a blur as though she was one of them huge flowers suddenly come to life.

Dr. Baker and Estelle continued arguing about things from way back, not seeming to care about Pomeline's fate. Art and I both put a hand on Jenny's shoulder. She didn't shrug us off but we could feel how stiff she was, and she didn't fight us as we pulled her away and escorted her back to the Water House. I got her a glass of water this time and we sat back down, waiting to be discovered.

Estelle almost went by us without seeing again, but she glanced over and stopped dead in her tracks, with Dr. Baker behind her. "Well, well, if it isn't the missing trio. Honestly, if one person at Petal's End could manage to behave . . . What do you think you've been doing, Agatha Jennifer? What were you thinking, going on an outing to a graveyard?" She looked at me. "You. You are nothing but trouble, Fancy Mosher. Just like your mother."

"Estelle, Harold explained this to us. We don't need to get into it now. Please. Show some compassion."

"Compassion? It would be nice if you showed me some compassion. I'm the only one with any good sense. All of you, every single one of you is encouraging Marigold with this preposterous garden party. And Jenny, that's fine, if you want to ruin your health, you do what you please." She stormed off, arms flailing.

Jenny's lip trembled but that was all. She didn't need no one telling her hush-a-bye, don't you cry.

Dr. Baker adjusted his glasses. "Harry told us what happened. I'm sorry, Fancy. Your mother's friend, Ronnie, came looking for her. Apparently this is the anniversary of your brother's death, and your mother was, well, distraught. You see, a trauma can affect a person for years when there is no resolution. You'll have to forgive her. Harry brought her back here and . . . anyway, it's all been sorted out and they've gone away. We'll just move forward. Time for your singing. There is no better cure than staying busy, keeping to your routine."

Jenny folded her hands together. "And so it continued both day and night."

He flung a look at Jenny. "It's hard on a family with an elderly person who has dementia. And it's hard having a child with brain damage, a child like you. That's what's wearing your mother out, and your sister. You and your grandmother will be the death of them."

"My grandmother doesn't have dementia, Dr. Baker. You're making that up so you can take charge. My sister cries all the time these days. She thinks I don't hear but I do. What a bawl baby. She's full of nerves. You should medicate her like you do my mother and my grandmother." They was testing each other.

"I don't need medical advice from a twelve-year-old, and you can't talk to me the way you talk to the rest of the adults. I won't tolerate it. You have no idea what your sister is going through, no idea at all." He left, no interest in a response.

We'd never seen that side of Dr. Baker before and we were reeling, but then we were the kind of children who already knew that adults weren't to be trusted. It wasn't surprising to find out that he was just like the rest.

Jenny looked ahead at Petal's End, rising up in the baby-blue northern sky. "I don't like that man," she whispered. "He thinks he's the king of Petal's End, but the king died. My mother thinks she's the queen of Petal's End. But she's not the queen."

I didn't dare say nothing, but Art said softly, "We should go in for the practice."

In the kitchen Harry was sitting with Loretta, and they both got up as we came in. Loretta came over and took my face in her hands. Her fingers smelled like buttery lemon cake.

"My poor Girly Miss. Ronnie came and took Marilyn back to the lake, give me strength. She slipped out early in the morning while he was sleeping. He thought she went to town to do errands, then he remembered what day it was. I suppose it's to be expected. I thought he'd have kept a better eye on her on this day of all days. But Ronnie does mean well, and he won't let it happen again. I feel sure of that. Estelle has been in a frightful mood since she arrived. We need to sew bells on your shoes, the lot of you. It's making my head spin." She wiped her hands on her apron and went back to getting supper.

Loretta didn't look at me as she continued. "Harry told me what your mother was saying in the graveyard. I'm not going to deny it. Marigold was there. She was there with Charlie. Your mother was down there with . . . one of her friends. Marigold couldn't do anything. She already felt regretful about John Lee burning his hand that long ago time they were making rosewater. It was dreadfully sad. Charlie was just a boy. He tried to help. The waves were too big. He felt very badly, you see. Adults make many mistakes. We mustn't speak of these things for all it does is stir up the past." She was rolling out pie crust, her back still to me. "Take some cookies and cake out for the children."

Jenny and Art were at the front of the house on the verandah, sitting in the shade. He was telling her about the Perseid showers and she was telling him a story about how the stars were holy lights. The three of us went strolling over the lawn, staying on the stone path, them two still talking about the sky with their mouths full of cookies. We didn't talk about going to the Annex but that's where Jenny headed and we followed. The imposing red oaks and laburnums cloaked the overgrown lawn in shade. They spoke of the big rising moon that was nothing more than an illusion, and I stood looking at the sheer curtains, telling myself there wasn't nothing to worry about inside them windows.

"Let's go back around. We don't want to get in trouble." Art took my arm but I kept looking at the windows quizzically.

Jenny took my other arm and pulled me forward. "What do you see, Fancy?" she asked. "Maybe Daddy is in there."

"Don't say that." Art was like a scared girl. "You're just as bad as Marilyn, Jenny."

I felt as though I had died, standing there terrible cold on that white hot day. Jenny tugged on my arm. She was just being silly, being a child, she had no idea why I was frightened. Maybe it gave her a sense of power, I don't know. The three of us, linked together, ran down that steep bit of lawn and we crept up to the window. There was so many times when it seemed maybe it would all come true, and we was all thinking maybe this was it, that I would see Jenny's dead father dangling from the ceiling, back to tell us why he did it.

From the middle window we heard the fan. Jenny knelt down and peered in the slats. She kept moving her head, trying to get a view. She looked at me and pointed inside, making sure we was looking at the same place. If she could see it too then it wasn't just me. But she didn't seem to see a thing. I realized I'd been holding my breath, and as I let it out Jenny's face changed. Her mouth went round and she was blinking her eyes fast. She fell back, sitting on the grass, and I moved forward.

"Don't look," she whispered.

But I couldn't help myself. Art came beside me and we peered in. That close to the open window we could hear the fan loud but under it we heard a moaning. It was Pomeline, leaning on the desk, gripping it hard, Dr. Baker behind. They were both breathing heavily and the ceiling fan went round and round and blew Pomeline's hair up in golden gusts, his hands on her hips, her dress up. Her face was red and tight, looking crushed.

Dr. Baker grunted and they stopped moving. "Tidy yourself," he said.

Jenny started whispering her funny words. It fell silent inside for they knew someone was at the window. We dashed up the hill and dove into the bushes just as Dr. Baker peeked through the blinds. There wasn't nothing for him to see, for three frightened twelve-year-olds can run fast as a blink. He closed the blind tight, as he should have done earlier.

"We must never tell a soul, not a soul," Jenny said. "No one can know, not that they would believe us anyhow. It would be their word against ours." With that, Jenny ran into the house.

Art was shaking. He was just a boy. I know I was only twelve too but Art was a child in a way I never was. He cried. "I want summer to be fun," he was saying. "I want it to be fun." I didn't bother telling him those times were long over for the likes of us. Art sulked out to the garden. I went upstairs and got cleaned up for choir practice. There was nothing to do but go ahead with the rest of the day.

❧

Pomeline was in the music room. Her eyes were red and glassy but she was calm as she beckoned me over to the piano. "I see you are early for practice, Fancy," she said, glancing away.

I couldn't believe she'd let that middle-aged man touch her.

"Just a few more days, Fancy, then we can all relax. Why don't you and I do a short warm-up, just the two of us?" We began, but before we could get halfway through the first piece Jenny came in, shut the door and sat down in a chair, staring at the huge centrepiece of flowers I had put in that morning. We kept playing until Jenny started impatiently shuffling papers.

"Jenny, could you give us a bit of time here, just a few minutes? We aren't ready for the full rehearsal. Margaret is waking Granny up from her nap. Why don't you go and see if they need help. Margaret has looked so ill recently. The work seems such a strain on her. But she's only my age. I don't understand."

Jenny smiled.

"Jenny, you could at least offer. I am sure they would appreciate it."

"They don't need my help, Pommie. That's been made perfectly clear by Margaret. And it's of no concern to me if Margaret doesn't feel well. She should quit if she isn't able to do the job. I could have taken care of Granny perfectly well by myself."

"Well, that's not true. It's too much work for a child your age to look after Granny. You know that. Dr. Baker thought Margaret would make it easier when Granny insisted on coming out here, and she has been excellent with Granny."

Hearing Dr. Baker's name made Jenny turn red. "Dr. Baker is a horrible man. Can't you see that? Do you think he and Mother are just friends? What do you think has been going on at the house in the city? They think I go to bed at eight o'clock and sleep. They're idiots. I know what they do. I've seen what they do. You think he's special but he's not. He is not special."

Pomeline couldn't get any more white. Her lips started trembling as she looked down at her hands. Before she could respond, the door burst open and in came Marigold and Margaret and Art and Dr. Baker and Harry and Sakura and Estelle, everyone acting like it had been a lazy summer day at Petal's End. Margaret did look ill, and she was clutching her chest.

Dr. Baker lifted up both his hands. "Let's start, shall we?"

Marigold didn't look at me, not once. At least I knew now why she couldn't face me.

"This is such a delightful ballad. I learned it as a young girl . . . One, two, three," Marigold counted, leaning back in her chair and closing her eyes. Pomeline played the chorus and we sang.

It was down by the Salley Gardens, my love and I did meet.
She crossed the Salley Gardens, with little snow-white feet.
She bid me take life easy, as the leaves grow on the trees.
But I being young and foolish, with her would not agree.

Jenny adjusted the sheet music. Marigold's eyes were shut, but whether she was napping or listening, I couldn't ever tell.

In a field by the river, my love and I did stand.
And on my leaning shoulder, she laid her snow-white hand.

No one had drawn the blinds that day. The room was an oven. Sakura got up and opened the window. Jenny elbowed Pomeline in the arm ever so slightly.

"Jenny, stop. Or I'm simply not doing this," Pomeline said.

Marigold's eyes were still sealed shut but her lips fluttered. "Girls. Girls. You are going to be performing for hundreds of people. Please. Get along, darlings, please."

Pomeline looked up at Dr. Baker quickly but he was looking at Estelle, who was looking at the flowers. She closed her eyes and resumed playing.

She bid me take love easy, as the grass grows on the weirs.
But I was young and foolish, and now am full of tears.

We went through the song over and over, until the last bits of piano faded and the room was still except for Marigold's soft snore. Pomeline's fingers rested on the keyboard. Dr. Baker stood up and Pomeline followed his every move, her long golden hair waving down over her shoulders. Jenny reached over, fussing with the sheet music.

There was a knock and a click as the door opened, and Hector was there holding a set of car keys. He leaned in the doorway, his tanned cheek on the dark wooden frame, clapping like he'd just witnessed a miracle. "I just came to tell you I took Marilyn's car back to her house and parked it. I waited until the music stopped. Oh my good God, it's beautiful. I didn't know you could all do that."

Just then Margaret bent over, coughing something terrible, banging into Jenny, who wobbled on her frail chicken legs. Pomeline's fingers were still on the keys, and Hector kept clapping, and Dr. Baker joined in, and suddenly Jenny tumbled into Pomeline's shoulder, one stiff hand hitting the keyboard, the other flailing for a brace, then pulling the heavy wooden cover over, smashing it down on her sister's long white fingers. Pomeline's face crumpled, as it had in the Annex with Dr. Baker behind her, as she tried to pull her fingers out from the lid. Her screams filled the room and poured out of the windows, and I started shivering, and outside the window the glass wind bells were still, for the breeze had stopped.

19.
Labyrinth

THAT EVENING Art and I come out to the Atelier after supper, and Sakura and Margaret joined us with a plate of gingersnaps. We watched the sun sink down in the sky, the swans doing a bedtime glide. Margaret had stayed late to help Marigold, whose screams had fused with Pomeline's, as though her fingers too had been crushed by the heavy wood. If Harry had promised Sakura a romantic summer, an enchanted holiday on his distant cousin's big country property, it had surely gone awry.

"Look how the sun is reflecting on their wings." Sakura's voice was satin smooth on the ear, the way a piece of fine embroidery floss feels on the fingertips.

Margaret took a cookie and went down to the edge of the pond. She broke off a piece and tossed it out to the unmoving birds. "I guess they aren't hungry," she said, turning back toward us. But then Sweet William hissed and lifted up his wings. He came running out of the water after her and latched onto her leg. Margaret shrieked and Art and I ran down to shoo the swan away. It charged all of us and we ran up the bank to the deck.

"Even her pets are wicked," Margaret gasped. Her skin was red and bleeding, but it wasn't a deep gash. She brushed cookie crumbs off her uniform and they stuck to the small wound. "I'm going to go change and get the hell out of here. You might not be aware but everyone is fucking crazy around here. And the adults do nothing. They never do." She was breathing heavily the whole time she talked, and she was covered in sweat. "It was an accident, you know. It was so baking hot in there. My allergies have been out of control the last week, I think. Maybe Jenny felt lightheaded. It wasn't fair for her to say it was my fault she got startled and fell. I didn't mean to bump into her. She hates her sister. I think she did it on purpose but she's never held accountable."

Sakura rested her hand on Margaret's back. "Accidents happen. It was no one's fault. We shouldn't have been in there when the room was that stifling. Pomeline will recover. She was feeling dizzy anyway, from the searing weather and too much practising."

Margaret rolled her eyes and left. We watched her fade into the twilight.

Sakura, Art and I walked across the garden to the gazebo by the labyrinth. The big stone fountain was running. Frothy water, stained pink from the sky, gushed from the grey stone flowers that the angry, chiselled cherub was clutching.

Sakura ran her finger under the water and spoke over the fountain's gurgle. "Harry wanted me to tell you it will be okay. We're going to take you out to the island the day after the garden party. We'll stay all night camping. We can look at wildflowers and collect seashells. I guess it will be you taking us since you've been there before. But nonetheless it will be good for us to have an expedition." She then took our hands and squeezed them. Her fingers were small, like Jenny's, and firm. "You are both good children. I don't think you know that." She went off, floating over the lawn. The sky darkened into hysterical red and orange.

Art walked over to the hedge labyrinth and I followed him. I heard voices far off, so I started inside the maze, trying to disappear. I sat on the bench at the opening. It served as a waiting room for those who were too afraid to go inside.

Art came in and sat beside me. "Do you think she did it on purpose?"

That's what Margaret had yelled directly after it happened: that Jenny did it, that she was up to her tricks again, even to her own sister. She kept yelling it as Art and I lifted the lid off Pomeline's fingers. It was a horrible sight, the blood smeared on the keys and dripping on the floor, her fingers swelling, the skin red and blue. Pomeline's eyes rolled back in her head and she threw up. Jenny was crying out that she was sorry, and Marigold had come over with her cane in one hand, the other hand over her mouth, muffling her screams.

A bird flew through the western sky, a solitary black silhouette. "It's been a long day," Art said.

The darkness inside the hedges made me feel safe, shut away from it all.

"Fancy, the graveyard . . ."

"What about the graveyard?"

"Your mother shouldn't have gone down the beach. She shouldn't have let John Lee out of her sight. But you can't change the past. There's nothing you can do. I don't know what she thinks John Lee can tell you. It's just her guilt talking. It's made her crazy. I think it made your Grampie crazy too. I'm sorry." Art's voice was gentle, which made it lower, a glimpse of the man he would become.

My throat hurt. *Hush-a-bye, don't you cry*. It was all I wanted to do then, cry.

"Do you think she did it on purpose?" he asked again.

I stood up and started walking into the maze. Art came behind me.

"Who?" There was enough going on that it was hard to know who was plotting against who.

"Margaret pushing Jenny. Jenny pushing Pomeline. They're both saying each other did it. It was an accident, don't you think?"

"She did too do it on purpose." Jenny stood at the entrance with a bandage on her forehead, a souvenir of her fall.

"How are you feeling?" Art asked her, ignoring what she'd said.

"I have a headache. Dr. Baker gave me a pill. He's gone off to the city with Pomeline, to have her fingers X-rayed. He's sure they're just bruised. Margaret pushed me. She shouldn't have made fun of my grandmother. She should never have come here. Pomeline's mad at me, as if it were all my fault. I just do what I have to. Doesn't anyone understand that?"

There was no point in any more conversation. I went into the maze and left them there at the entrance.

Jenny called after me, "I won't tell on you."

"For what?"

"For going into the labyrinth. I'm going to see my swans."

"Then I won't tell on you, Jenny," I said under my breath.

"Wait for me here when you're finished," she said, skipping off humming.

I started running farther and farther in. It was stupid to run toward the centre with the light disappearing. It was heavy twilight now, and everything was silhouette and shadow.

"Art? I'm lost."

No reply.

I heard rustling. "Art, speak to me," I called out.

And Art did call to me, his voice muffled. "Fancy?"

"Come find me right now." I heard more swishing. It was not coming from the direction of his voice. Something was shaking the hedges. "Art? You come to me. I'll whistle so you can find me. I'm going to try to go back to the start. I'll follow the sky."

"It's easier if you just stay put." It was impossible to tell where his voice was coming from.

My winding took me to the centre where the roses were. The stars were coming out. And there was Jenny. She was walking funny, all hunched over, shuffling, like she was going to fall over. She was humming. I can hear it still, a tuneless hum. She came toward me. I stopped whistling then.

"Jenny, let's go out," I said.

She looked up but it was no little girl, no Jenny Parker. It had a shrivelled face and eyes like black pits, stringy hair and a horrible leer as it reached out a hand to me, and in its long fingers it held a pink flower. It was still humming away as it tossed its head back and gave a scream that rounded in weird short chirps as it shook its head and lifted its thin arm out in front of its hobbled body, clothes all tattered, palm facing toward its head, index finger pointed up. Through all these years I can still hear the gurgle I made as I tried to call again to Art. The creature lifted an arm over its head and hopped up on the hedge wall, making to pounce down on me, but I darted straight ahead, turning left and right, tripping, my hands grabbing onto the dirt under the hedge, the sharp needles cutting into my fingers. I got up and ran, and it felt like a miracle when I saw the expanse of lawn outside the maze up ahead. I didn't dare look behind me.

Art was hollering from somewhere but I ran straight out onto the lawn, away from the labyrinth. The garden lights snapped on, illuminating the path. Loretta would be on her way out to fetch us for bed any moment. Jenny stood there looking at me, one hand behind her back.

"Don't blame me for anything, Fancy. I'm not stupid enough to go in there at this time of night. After being in the graveyard today I should think you would have had enough of creepy places."

Art came running out. "What was it?"

I went to the fountain and splashed my face with gushing cold water.

"Look," Art said, pointing at the swishing branches behind the maze. A cloud of starlings lifted from the treetops, flying west, east and north and to the dark southern skies, making the same sounds that had come out of the thing's mouth, twisting and turning like a great black current winding through the air, swooping low and then lifting high up and south over the forest, breaking against the sky, a black wave on the twilight blue. They left behind a cloak of silence so thick we did not move, the damp threads of the evening air falling on our tongues. Night was enveloping us now.

This is one of those moments that repeats over and over in my mind now, many years later. With each rock of this chair I see the birds twisting, as though giving us a warning, Grampie speaking to me through them birds.

Jenny held up her hands to the sky, like she was trying to get a scoopful of the stars before they was gone, but it was too late.

20.
Rose Absolute

THEY BROUGHT Pomeline back from the hospital deep in the night and the next day she stayed in her room. It was the first day without the sound of piano music. And Margaret did not come to work. Her father called to say she was unwell, that she had been up all night sick and he was taking her to the doctor. He thought she was having a severe allergy flare. She might not come back to work, he said.

Harry and Sakura came to the kitchen in the morning when Art and I were having a snack. They wanted to make more rose-water for party favours. We were carrying on with the festivities. Pomeline's right hand was injured but it was just severely swollen and bruised. No broken bones, thank God, Harry said. But she wouldn't be able to play the piano for a few weeks. They didn't say she would miss her exams but we all knew she would. She was icing her hand and taking pain pills. Dr. Baker had given her something to make her sleep.

I'd gone up early with a breakfast tray for Marigold. When I took the tray in, she was sitting in bed and she pointed to a table by the window. She talked about the party like nothing had happened, lounging in her white nightgown with a net over her hair, watching me move across the room. Out of nowhere it seemed, she said, "It was a terrible shame about your brother. But fortunate your mother was able to go on and have so many children. I only had one child, one Parker. I had that in common with Estelle."

I was about to point out that Estelle had two children, but before I could she carried on as though she had it sorted out in her mind again.

"She had precious Pomeline, and with the help of medicine she was able to have Agatha Jennifer. She had one miscarriage after another. Did you know that? There was something wrong with her womb." She was looking around her room, like she was talking to someone else. "She lost baby after baby. Charlie was dreadfully disappointed. He was overjoyed to have Pomeline, of course. She was his heart's delight. It was such a pity he didn't care about Agatha the same way. It was as though there had been so many lost that by the time she was born he didn't have any heart left to love her with. For me, there were no babies to lose. I wasn't like your mother having babies like some barn cat, or Estelle with all her dead ones. I can understand why Estelle went to such lengths to have Jenny. We couldn't do that in my day. What I would have given to turn my womb into a nurturing haven. But at least I had Charlie. He wasn't like the other boys. He was a soft boy. His father didn't understand him. He did not appreciate him."

I looked in the mirror and Marigold was looking right at me in the reflection. "But your mother just went on having children, one after another, like she was making cakes, big plump babies, even when it was past her time. There's nothing more distasteful than an old woman having children, when the bloom is long off the rose." I could tell it revolted her. "There was nothing we could do, you see. The waves were horrifically big. And no one could swim. Charlie was traumatized. His father hated how anxious he was after that." Marigold dabbed her eye with a fine cotton hankie, pink roses on it that my mother had probably embroidered all them years ago. I doubt Marigold even noticed when I left the room.

Margaret called in sick the next day as well, and the house was quiet, no piano music, no choir practice. But the day after, we were gathered at the Water House and Margaret came in, drawn and grey, rundown, slipping in quietly as Harry and Sakura put three large pots on the stove. We had collected an enormous amount of rose petals. They were going to refrigerate some to toss at the party. Jenny took one bowl over to the stove and put the petals in the pots. She picked up an enamel pitcher full of water and poured it in, carefully setting the pitcher back down. She peered inside on her tiptoes before she put the lid on top. No one said a word to her. It was like she was taking over her grandmother's job. The water simmered and she poured the ice on the tops.

Margaret stood by the counter near where Jenny and Harry took turns scooping out the distilled water and putting it in a glass container. Despite not feeling well she was making jokes and chatting with Marigold. Jenny had her lips pressed together, as though she was concentrating, thinking on matters of grave importance. She didn't speak at all. Harry and Marigold discussed party details. They'd put a big tent up in case it rained. We'd sing in the gazebo. The waiters from the city would drift through with trays of food and drink. Marigold would welcome the visitors. Jenny could toss rose petals about. Art and I could wander around with baskets of soap and the miniature glass bottles of rosewater and offer them to the guests.

Jenny was on a stool by a big steaming pot. Harry stood by another. Harry said it could have been anyone accidentally brushing up against the knob, it turned so easily from simmer to boil. Margaret had come over to the middle pot and lifted the lid. Jenny sneezed. And she sneezed again, holding her fingers up and squeezing her nose, falling into Margaret, who braced herself just in time on the edge of the stove. Margaret went to take the lid off and that's when Jenny sneezed the last time, and Margaret startled and she fell forward, but this time she lunged over the pot, the sweet, dense steam scalding her face like a lobster shell, her skin blistering before our eyes as though rose oil was forming on her skin, her mouth open wide as she leapt about waving her hands, trying to cool her face off, shrieks coming out of that dark gaping hole, drowning out the gonging copper chimes in the herb garden.

21.
The Garden Party

THAT NIGHT my dreams were shot through with Pomeline's and Margaret's screams, Pomeline's mangled fingers, Margaret's melting face smelling of scalded rose, my mother chanting and bird screech. I hardly slept, and the following day's party was looming.

There was a path of pink petals leading from the house to Evermore the next morning. Harry and Sakura discovered them early and they brought me and Loretta around to see. No one knew who had scattered them. But the day came up behind us breathing heavy and it was so busy no one cared, and no one thought about whether the trail led from house to garden or garden to house except for me. I kept thinking about them open windows earlier in the summer, about the door in the far wall of Evermore that Art and I had come through on our way back through the woods from Grampie's house, and the thing in the labyrinth. I kept sorting through what Grampie said in his letter, but it was of no help to me.

Summer was pressing herself down, digging in with her heels. Marigold missed Margaret, she said, who had been outstanding at bringing her ice water and keeping her fanned. Estelle was there, and she was strangely pleasant, her nursing training taking over, all business, as though they'd hired her, too. She went out to assist, inspecting, helping get the gazebo ready for our choir. Jenny whispered that her mother was calm because after the Margaret Incident, as Estelle called it, there would be no more long summers at Petal's End for Marigold.

Art came over in a white shirt with a bow tie. It was then that the first breaks came in his voice. I watched him ride up on his bicycle with a cap on, like he was a lad from long ago coming by the old pasture where the lane came in, through the fireweed, towering goldenrod and blue star flowers of the borage plant. The summer was turning him into a man as it was turning me into a woman. The season would end and we'd be free of the Parkers, if we could just hang on. But that morning we had the party in front of us, and soon we were in Evermore with the music playing from the gazebo, and back by the lily pond, and all the guests arriving, people I knew and people I had never seen before and would never see again.

The cicadas were buzzing. White gauzy clouds hung in the sky and it seemed we'd been invaded by the world. The party planners dashed about here and there and Marigold wandered with her cane.

"Isn't the music pleasant?" Loretta said. She didn't know what to do with herself. The caterer from the city brought in the food and a fleet of servers, dressed in black and white, moving with the starlings' perfect timing, trays and trays of glasses balanced.

"Must be what a ballet looks like," Art said as a woman with a china plate full of delicate fairy cakes with light yellow icing went by, the tray held high. I took a cake and she swung away. As directed, we were holding out baskets of soap and rosewater bottles and bestowing them upon the guests.

The quartet they had in the gazebo and the quartet by the pond played gentle, almost tranquilizing music. This is the backdrop in my mind, even after the passage of these years. No one could find Jenny. As careful as I'd watched her, she'd still slipped away. We were sent off to fetch her. Not one more thing could go wrong at Petal's End, Marigold said, especially on the day she had been anticipating all summer.

We looked everywhere, even in the labyrinth, a different place to navigate by daylight, but we could not find her. Loretta and Art and I went to the big house to look. We called through the rooms and halls and stairs. We had given up and left the house when Jenny appeared, walking from the carriage house, her white-gloved hands together. Loretta put her hand to her chest. "Oh my goodness, Jenny, don't disappear like that. You'll be the death of me." She rushed back to the kitchen, calling over her shoulder that they were waiting for us at the gazebo.

We took our places to sing. Pomeline, who insisted on playing through the pain, Art and me, Jenny beside her sister ready to turn the sheet music. Marigold stood with her cane like she was the director but she wasn't doing nothing but fanning herself. We were to sing and then Pomeline was to walk over to the side of the gazebo and lead us in a bow. My stomach hurt, and Pomeline gave me a look of desperation. Dr. Baker was laughing and talking, seeming so kindly and wise, busy looking at what he wanted, knowing nothing, you see, of what he did all them years ago when Estelle was a young nurse. He knew not a thing of what he had done now that Pomeline was a young woman who wanted to be a concert pianist. None of us knew then, on that summer day, how all the lies and secrets wove together.

Jenny seemed nervous, like I was, as the people crowded in the chairs on the lawn. We gazed over a sea of summer hats. Jenny held out her bony arm and pulled me to her, Art standing on the other side. Marigold seemed electrified, like the audience had brought a life force out in her. She talked about the history of Petal's End, of the Annex, of the poor soldiers who came, the people who convalesced, of the Petal's End Chorus and how it lived again now in us.

Harry took a step back. He was staying nearby while we sang, off to the side and crouched down, in case we needed him. Pomeline was at the keyboard of the spinet they had brought out for the concert. Her hair was piled up in a mass of ringlets. The bodice of her summer dress was very tight and her sapphire ring gleamed and she began. It was painful to see and hear, but we sang along, and Marigold closed her eyes. When we were finished the crowd was clapping away—oh how adorable, all decked out in their funny clothes. All of a sudden Pomeline started playing her exam piece, "Wedding Day at Troldhaugen." Music coursed through the gazebo, sweet and choppy as her swollen fingers stumbled over the keys, and she cried as she played, for it hurt her.

That's when it happened. Marigold walking over to the side of the gazebo, holding out her arms for applause, taking the bow instead of Pomeline. Marigold bending strangely, the guests thinking she's curtseying—the old lady is curtseying in her big summer gown—and that her expression was leering and off because of her stroke a few years back. But she was not curtseying. Her foot was caught by a loose board, tripping her, causing her to smash down, hitting her head with a thud. In that moment I was beside the lady, Jenny and Art and I were beside her. We tried to get her leg out. Marigold blinked and reached up a claw-like hand and she pointed directly at me. "We must make choices," she said, tears leaking out of her eyes. "Poor little John Lee. But sometimes there have to be sacrifices, even if it brings out the hobgobblies. Do you understand that, darling?" Her runny eyes were wide, as though a ghastly sight was coming at her.

Dr. Baker pushed people aside as Jenny cried with her dry eyes, her shoulders heaving. Art took my hand and led me away from the gazebo and the chaos that had erupted over Marigold. We went to the Wishing Pool surrounded by the polished gemstones from the beach that Mr. Charlie had collected with his dear mother who loved him so. The pieces of Grampie's and my brother's teacups were like mini stepping stones in the bottom of the Wishing Pool, disappearing from view occasionally when the goldfish darted about and made ripples over the water as the afternoon sun fell down. We sat transfixed by the water when we heard someone yell "Fire!" and in the southern sky we saw black smoke looping up in great feathery plumes as the forest behind the carriage house burned. We ran back, and in the pandemonium only Jenny didn't seem surprised or panicked. She lifted her head up and slowly turned it, the blaze shining in her glasses.

22.
The Expedition

HARRY INSISTED on taking us to the island. He said we needed to go precisely because of all that had happened. It would be good for our spirits to get away from Petal's End. An expedition always helped put things in perspective, he said, and perspective brought relief. It would help take our minds off the calamity. The tragedies. The upsets.

They had arrested Hector, arrested him for his big fields of ferny green plants he was growing way back on the land. The police did not know who set the fire. Hector did not tell on Jenny and she did not admit it. She blamed Hector for Margaret being at Petal's End. It was his fault, she had impulsively decided. She was angry, too, that he had laughed alongside Margaret when she made fun of the Parkers.

Marigold was in the hospital. Her fall had caused a heart attack and a broken hip and wrist. Estelle said Dr. Baker wasn't fit to care for her. They'd had a huge argument and Harry had intervened.

Pomeline had just sat in the music room playing, one hand smooth and the other stiff, the music broken and empty. She didn't seem to notice the tumult, just plunked away playing her exam selection over and over as if in a trance. There were to be no exams. The sole focus of her life had been taken away in one moment.

We'd left Dr. Baker and Estelle arguing and we were on the dock at noon. We left in the thick fog that was sitting low over the bay. I sat at the side of the boat looking into the white, thinking about Grampie, hearing him sing to me. *On the wings of the wind o'er the dark rolling deep, angels are coming to watch o'er thy sleep. Angels are coming to watch over thee, so listen to the wind coming over the sea*. The mist was wet and coated my face. My lips were salty when I licked them, and I couldn't help but think of Marigold and her distillations, her rose ottos and absolutes. It was an eerily muted journey.

We were nearing the island when the fisherman who was taking us out cut the engine. He didn't need to shush us. Art and I knew what to do. We'd been out in the boats many times. Harry looked confused, and Art whispered to him that the man was listening for gulls, for the sound of the wind hitting cliffs, for the waves breaking on the shore. He had no radar on his boat and he did as his father and his father before him had done and listened for the island. After a few moments the man seemed satisfied and went back to the wheelhouse to restart the engine.

We veered sharp west and suddenly vast vertical red cliffs emerged out of the fog, daunting and prehistoric. In places, trees and meadow at the very top of the island plunged over the edge in a sheer drop as though the island had been ripped away from the mainland long ago. In spots deep vertical gouges cut into the precipice as though some giant god had raked his jagged fingernails over the cliff face and left his mark. Enormous swells and waves bashed into the cliffs, white foam and spray erupting far into the air. It seemed from this side there was no way up, that the island was a fortress. We rounded the western end where huge towers of rock stood high as buildings. A falcon, perched on top of one of the rocks, lifted up and soared away, disappearing into the mist. We had to journey around the entire island to find the spot on the north side where the wharf and fishing sheds used to be, where the island sloped down.

Finally we came to the beach where the fisherman could row us and our gear ashore and leave the sojourners in solitude. It was hard getting out of the boat. Harry's backpack dropped in the water and his radio got soaked. Sakura tripped and sprained her ankle. It was nothing serious but she had to sit on a stump Harry found and elevate her foot. He got her a stick to use as a crutch. The mist blew in and out. That was a constant out there, the fog rolling in and out, holes opening up in the haze to reveal glimpses of the blue sky before the curtains of mist would pull shut again in an instant and all you could see was what was ten feet in front of you and nothing beyond, there on the island in the middle of the bay. We stood on the barrier beach watching as the boat disappeared around the end of the island. We were alone. Petal's End was gone and the mainland was gone and the gulls cried out.

Jenny was already beyond the beach, over on the grassy area surrounded by buttercups and meadowsweet. Harry and Sakura sent us up to the top of the island, and they put Pomeline in charge. They wanted us to get some exercise while they set up the campsite. They were expert campers, Harry kept reminding us. Harry made us the guides because we had been there before. We were allowed to explore the original lighthouse site. We were not to go near the cliffs. When we came down we would have supper. Sakura waved as we headed off. The fog was blowing in and her long black hair whipped around and then disappeared into the grey mist.

We went up the only path toward the top. The island was surrounded by cliffs on all sides except where we climbed. The path had once been a farm road big enough for horses to haul a wagon up and down, but the island was taking it back now, the boreal forest growing in since it had been abandoned thirty years before. Now it was just a wide and wild overgrown trail, tall enough for children to scamper along but low enough for a grown man to have to duck. Damp ferns brushed our ankles. We moved farther into the dark green light. Art's leg was bleeding where branches had scraped at him. Jenny hummed to herself. Pomeline, beside me, stared meditatively at the trees. And up we went to the tippity-top, the path breaking into what had been a hayfield. It had gone wild, and the grasses were up to our chests. We pushed ahead, through a cluster of trembling aspens. We could see it then, off to the west, the tall metal skeleton of the automated lighthouse. The outbuildings had fallen down. Nothing left but the stone foundations.

Jenny crawled up the crumbling stone wall and into what had been a cellar, now just a jumble of rusted metal and blackened wood. If you pawed around you could find pieces of glass, warped and deformed from how white-hot the fire had been. There was choirs of birds singing on the branches, and late-summer raspberries growing up through the wreckage. Jenny picked a handful. I held up my hand to her, like Loretta. "Don't eat them, Jenny. Ground's covered in mercury from the lens in the lighthouse. Grampie told us that."

Pomeline told her to put them down but Jenny ignored her and stuck out her tongue. "Don't be a fool," Pomeline said. I had never heard her say nothing mean like that before. She walked over and reached down and held out her hand. Jenny gave them berries to Pomeline, dropping them in her white palm. Then Pomeline ate them berries, one by one.

We shuffled uneasily. "What are you doing, Pomeline?" Art asked.

She just laughed.

Pomeline seemed crazed after that. We played tag and hide-and-seek and she had an uncanny energy in her that we had not ever seen before. It was as though the higher elevation was affecting her, the crisp sea air whistling through the hemlocks and pines was revitalizing Pomeline. Her ashen cheeks were now flushed red. The games stopped being games when Jenny was tugging at her sister, pulling at her like she was a small child and Pomeline was her mother. Pomeline ran away from her, up that skeletal metal lighthouse. We didn't see at first from where we were sprawled on the Colonel's helicopter landing pad. We lay there in the searing sun that broke through the mists every so often. We were drained, you see, from the tragedies. We hardly spoke. Art hummed and I whistled. It was Jenny who called out.

"Look," she said, pointing, holding her hand to her forehead to block the brightness out. We did the same, and there was Pomeline up high on the metal ladder, her hair soaring out like a banner, her dress flapping in the wind, and she was laughing. She was not crying, she was not. "Catch me, catch me, catch me if you can," she called out. The weather changed then, a thick grey fog rolling in, dark clouds behind it.

Jenny went over to the old foundation, picked up a small stone and threw it at Pomeline. I remember how surprising it was that it hit Pomeline's ankle from such a distance. Jenny threw another one and Pomeline winced. "Come down," Jenny shrieked. "Come down and don't cause any more trouble. You've been very bad."

Pomeline did come down, quickly, even with her one stiff hand. That's how I remembered it. That is how we all remembered it. She stood there safely on the ground and rubbed her fingers, avoiding eye contact. She ran off to the south through the swaying meadow grasses yelling *Catch me if you can* and we went after her like we was hound dogs on a trail.

As we come to the end of the meadow we saw her, looking over her shoulder. I was screaming by then for she was at the island's edge, and the wind come through them fir trees hanging on the edge, howling, and she dropped down and there was nothing but the foggy sky in front of us. We sprinted forward and she was below the edge, hanging onto a root with her good hand. Pomeline tried to grab hold with the bad one too but she couldn't stand the pain. Slowly, those long white fingers slipped and slipped, each one abandoning her. She was gone before we could even try to help. It started pouring then, sheets of rain coming down heavy in the storm that had blown in on the high tide. Art and I held Jenny back as the rain dampened her screams. I swear it looked like tears were streaming from her eyes just to be washed away by the rain. This is how I remembered it. We was only children.

Even with all them years behind me now, as I sit in my chair with my aching joints and my tired heart, young Jenny cries still. It was long ago but those who walk into the future with grief know the lamentations of the dead never cease.

Part II

Once, far over the breakers,
I caught a glimpse
Of a white bird
And fell in love
With this dream which obsesses me.

YOSANO AKIKO

In my dream the dead have arrived
to wash the windows of my house.
There are no blinds to shut them out with.

SINÉAD MORRISSEY, "Through the Square Window"

1.

The Believers

We drove over the mountain and down to the valley. Loretta wore her mourning clothes, a black dress and black bonnet. She insisted I don a dress she'd sewn for me, just like hers, and she made me cover my hair as well. We were going away, but she didn't say where and I didn't ask. It wasn't a time for talking. Estelle had told us to leave immediately. We packed up our things and loaded them in her car for one of its rare outings. This one was different as it was a one-way trip. We did not talk of Hector and how the only reason the car still ran was from his careful maintenance. When we started driving away from the house it was clear just how little we had. Some clothes and books, Loretta's worn Bible and hymnal, a few toys and knick-knacks, my embroidery basket tucked at the bottom of my suitcase. In our rush I'd left Ma's box of supplies in my room, along with my letter from Grampie.

Estelle was shutting the whole place down. She had berated Harry. His grief draped over him so heavy the man was barely able to walk. He couldn't speak without tears threading through the lines on either side of his mouth. It was his fault entirely, Estelle had said, that Pomeline had fallen over the edge of the island, bashed against those cliffs. Harold alone was responsible for his innocent young cousin being sucked away by the horrible heaving waves and tides, not even a body for her bereaved mother to bury. He was liable for letting guileless children go unattended. It didn't matter the bay had conjured up the storm out of nowhere. He should have done something.

He and Sakura had packed their trunk and left quickly. Sakura embraced us, leaning on her crutches. Harry apologized for not helping, he was overcome as Sakura led him away. Our young faces brought the island back to him, I knew. They went to the city, where Marigold languished in a hospital. Estelle was in charge now, with Dr. Baker at her side, comporting themselves as sole survivors of that summer. It was just what they wanted.

Art and Yvette went to stay with some cousins. We did not keep in touch. Jenny was whisked away after they brought us back to Petal's End. We'd all been taken by helicopter to the valley hospital through a hole in the ceiling of clouds. We were checked over, Jenny, Art and I, and Sakura and Harry, while they looked for Pomeline in the bay, in the atrocious thunderstorm with the churning, monstrous currents of the outgoing tide. We'd all been desperate and parched for rain that summer. The heavens delivered and it arrived in torrents and sheets. Down in the valley at the hospital the sky loomed dark but the air was still. To the north over the mountain thunderclouds and distant flashes cracked through the air.

The police questioned Art, Jenny and me, and we told them that we'd been playing tag, and the gusting winds and rain came. We told them how the sunny afternoon sky had turned dark as night in an instant. After, we'd struggled down to the beach, tripping and falling in the mud. The gale had crushed down the meadow grass, obliterating our trail on the island top. Harry had come back up with me and Art. Jenny had stayed below with Sakura, who could only offer comfort. But we were helpless, all of us. The bay was bashing into the cliffs where Pomeline had plummeted down. Sakura had extra batteries in her pack and Harry used his radio to call for help, but it was slow coming in the storm. We told them this, wailing and shaking. But we did not tell them everything, for we had taken a vow there on the top of the island.

Not for twelve years would we see each other again. We kept this second vow of silence along with the first one we'd made in the garden that summer, to keep what had passed between Pomeline and Dr. Baker a secret. Dr. Baker wasn't as sad as he should have been. I was furious to see flashes of relief in his eyes. In those last strange few days at Petal's End, Jenny walked about with her hands clasped, only speaking in her strange verses, humming, watching, until they removed her.

The nightmares stayed with me for a year, and I had to sleep in Loretta's room with her. The heavy rain and wind would make my heart leap. I would wake covered in slick sweat as though the rain had come in through the roof. My lips tasted of the salt of the sea which seemed to have seeped into my body. Sometimes I would dream of my embroidery wickerwork box I'd forgotten at Petal's End. Other times I would see myself standing over the secret floor compartment in my room at Petal's End where I'd left the letter from Grampie with the flower sachet. I'd awake worried that maybe the peonies had called forth fairies but not the good kind.

They looked for Pomeline for a week. At first they called it a rescue. Then they called it a recovery. They was looking for her body, and they searched that whole massive bay from end to end, to where it emptied out into the ocean, but the natural world had claimed her. We were incapacitated with grief. Estelle only spoke once to me, when she came to the kitchen to tell Loretta we had to go. *At least your mother had a body to bury.* She made a horrible gagging sound like she was going to throw up and she ran out of the kitchen and down the long hall, into the main house. Loretta did not go after her. Later I slunk out to the front of the house, to the door where the mirror was nailed. I stood with my eyes closed and panic crushed my lungs flat. I was sure there was a creak on the verandah behind me and I opened my eyes. Surely this would be the evocation to bring on the memento. But there was nothing in the mirror except me, and behind me the forest at the edge of the property. The dead made no appearance.

Death is such a quiet thing once it has come; however there is nothing quiet about its arrival. At first it feels like the dead have just gone away for a bit, that they'll return. A yearning takes hold of your heart. When Grampie died it seemed if I waited long enough he would come back and take his place beside me on the verandah, or at the kitchen table, surely by his easel. But of course he did not come back. You look for the dead in familiar places. You listen for their footsteps, for their laughter, for their songs. I kept thinking I'd hear Pomeline laugh from down the hall or see her moving through the garden, on one of her solitary walks, resting on a marble bench with her notebook and her pen making her musical notes, her patient voice encouraging us in our singing, and the sound of her melodies cascading from the music room and out the window. Even the sorrow and perversion of her last days of playing, the broken music she had summoned from her crushed fingers and spirit of despair, would have been a welcome sound.

There was no funeral or memorial service for Pomeline Charles Parker. There was only an obituary. It was too horrible, and without the body it seemed she'd just gone away, that she'd forgotten to come home and, eventually, that she'd only ever been a memory, a story told to us once, a fairy who had moved through the garden, as though she was the girl in Harry's garden story, not killed by poisonous flowers but by recklessness, a plague of recklessness corrupting us all.

I worried all the time Pomeline would appear. I had dreams of her looking for us, with that whispering voice singing like a quiet breeze that stirred the leaves of my mind for years to come, asking me where was her body, why was her body missing, why hadn't we brought her home, why had the dead been left behind? *Last night she came to me, my dead love came in. So softly she came that her feet made no din.* The days were a blur, and despite that wicked storm the sweltering dry weather came right back and sucked out every bit of moisture, and the world of Petal's End was as dry as Jenny's eyes. The heat scorched over us as though Holy Mother Mercy was white-hot with wrath, and there was no relief.

Years later Jenny would tell us that jubilation filled Estelle when she closed up Petal's End for there was no one to oppose her. The hired men nailed boards over the windows as Loretta and I left. We passed between the wrought-iron gates on either side of the immense stone walls, gates that would be locked shut for years to come.

❧

As we headed toward the valley my head was heavy and I'd eaten hardly a thing in days. We drove in silence through Lupin Cove and across the mountain on the Lonely Road by them fields of hay and wildflowers. Loretta finally spoke, with her eyes fixed on the road the entire time.

"You know I was a Believer," she said. "The Church of Believers in the Second Coming of the Lord."

That was the full name of the church, but people just called them the Believers, and they called themselves that as well. She said nothing more as we drove along the foot of the mountain on the back road until we were in Believer country, surrounded by big farms that encircled the village. She turned down a long lane and we come up to a big house in front of a huge barn and outbuildings. Two children come out, followed by a woman—their mother—and a man who looked like her husband. Next, the grandmother, an elderly lady—Loretta's mother, as it turned out—stood there in the door with her hands on her heart. All them generations in one house.

Loretta was close to tears as we got out of the car. The man walked over. "Loretta . . . Sister." It was her oldest brother. He didn't say it in a mean way. He was acknowledging her, like she'd been gone on a trip and they was expecting her back.

Loretta bowed her head and said, "Whosoever therefore shall confess me before men, him will I confess also before my Father which is in heaven. But whosoever shall deny me before men, him will I also deny before my Father which is in heaven." Tears then broke through her veneer. Those were the words they spoke to her, she told me later, when they shunned her, when they turned their backs to her and she was sent out from the church and community.

The grandmother came over and took Loretta by the hand as the man responded.

"I tell you, there is rejoicing in the presence of the angels of God over one sinner who repents."

This is how we come to live with the Believers. I saw then that Loretta's kitchen bonnet was a version of their head covering, and how she'd never stopped wearing the dresses. They'd cast her out when she was sixteen, and she kept making her clothes in the same style, just with bright flowered fabric. At first the fullness of her secret was astonishing to me. Then I thought of what she and Grampie had concealed, and the secrets I was then keeping myself—there was no more marvelling.

We lived with Loretta's family in that house. We had two rooms in the attic at first, and eventually they put us in a house down the road where we lived together like mother and daughter. They had me go to the church school and attired me in their clothing. We went to prayer meeting every Wednesday and Sunday. The women would sit on one side and the men on the other in the meeting hall they'd built from divine inspiration. The Believers were as plain as the Parkers were grand, but they both paid immaculate attention to detail. There was no preacher, just elders in the community, men with short clipped beards. You could not do much as a woman. You kept the hearth, tended to the home—you did as told your life entire. The Believers did not take oaths or vows. There was only one bond and that was with God, the Father, Son and Holy Ghost. It was an unforgivable sin to take an oath, for when you undertook this you adopted the dark ways whether you knew it or not. When they talked of this I thought of Art and Jenny, and a fear would come upon me that would take days to settle.

Our first night in the attic Loretta told me how she'd worked as a cleaning lady in the community and she'd been with a man. She didn't say much, just that he was full of flattery and told her she was pretty. She wasn't anything but plain but he knew just what to say. He'd come home at lunch, and she could not resist him. *Don't say a word*, he would say, *not a word*. Her soul had been seized by the burning claws of lust and she'd succumbed and had fallen into sin. That is how she spoke. *I tried to resist. I prayed and prayed but the lust rose up in me, Fancy Mosher, and it hung on me like cherry blossoms hang on the trees in spring.* She talked more and more like this the longer we lived among them, speaking in a funny way, and speaking often of the Lord and blessings and sin. Over time, she said, her belly had swelled up, and finally her mother spoke to her. Loretta was infatuated with the man and he was going to leave his wife, but of course he did not. She put her baby up for adoption by a family outside of the church. The Believers spoke not of the past to Loretta, for that was part of their way as well—what was done was done and the Lord called you forward. You paid mind to living well and therefore there were no regrets to be had, no sins to carry. If you were weak but willing, the Believers would carry you forward until you could walk on your own, and this is what they did for me. We lived with the Believers for three years, and it seemed that Holy Mother Mercy had finally come. I did not speak of her to them for they did not have the beliefs of the Mountain people.

It was a simple life. There were no photos or mirrors. We baked our bread and made our preserves. We cooked the meals and sewed the clothes. We had a modest kitchen garden and not even a posy on the kitchen table. The Believers weren't ones for decoration. It was nothing like Petal's End. It made me think of Jenny's revulsion for cut flowers, but not for long—Jenny receded until she was but a silhouette in my mind's eye.

They worshipped through holy music, but not with musical instruments. These things were of the world, they said, but the human voice was made by the Lord for speaking words of praise and singing words of worship. We were called to raise up those voices in songs of rejoicing and exaltation. They sang in four-part harmonies, voices united. There were no solos. One voice singing alone was vanity. It was not a sin to sing alone but it was what you did when it was just you and the Lord and He would sing with you. Everything with the Believers was an act of worship. The Believers taught the children to read music once they turned eleven and we sang out of the black hymnal and tune book, the *Harmonia Sacra*. They had a youth choir and I sang in it, praising the Lord through song, and it seemed that the very act was purifying, reclaiming me from the summer at Petal's End the year I was twelve. We'd go out singing at Christmas, into the hospitals and the nursing homes. Once during that time I glimpsed Margaret, standing in the back of the room where she worked, all proper in her uniform, and when she turned I saw where she'd been burned. We had been marked.

I knew not to speak of my family memento among the Believers, and in truth it seemed nothing but a silly story, for I began to believe with all my heart in what they were teaching me, that I could know the spirit of clemency and healing. When I sang in the church, or in the orchards picking apples with the other girls, the fear lifted out of me and flew off like a white bird into the sky, getting smaller and smaller until there was nothing left but eternal blue. The letter Grampie gave me had been left behind in my room at shuttered Petal's End, forgotten and entombed. The rare instance the shadow of death did reach out from the mountain and cast itself down upon the valley, I prayed and studied the Bible stories. I sang the hymns and heard the melodies of exaltation, but I did not tell Loretta that sometimes, despite all of this, I would wake in the night and think there was no salvation for me.

My mother did not try to see me, or if she did they never told me. It was later I found out that Ma had finally stopped drinking for good. She had not seen the Light but she was tired and beaten down. Maybe it was Holy Mother Mercy looking after her. I liked to think it was. In church they spoke of fallen angels who lived among us now as dark spirits. I knew Loretta worried that those dark spirits had whispered to Grampie, to the Moshers. She told me I must keep my ears closed to the voices, and if I embraced the Lord then I would be protected, should those voices ever come to me.

2.
A Pale-Blue Dress

When I was fifteen I worked weekends at Spencer's Country Things. It was a sprawling store in a barn on a nostalgic country road. Tourists and city people loved to come and spend endless time and money. We made wooden furniture and sold country-style home decor furnishings. We had a café and served lunch and tea, down-home cooking. At first I worked in the store, ringing in sales. It was there at the cash, ringing in a lady's apple pie–scented candles, where I saw Hector come in from the shop, carrying a new furniture set they were using for a display. I recognized him right away, even though he looked older than his twenty-two years. He'd been out of jail a few months and got the job through the church he was going to, the Greater United Church, the one that ran the Bible School. His eyes met mine and he looked at me in a manner that even going to church didn't take away. Then Hector realized that the teenager in the long dress and bonnet was Fancy Mosher. He blinked slowly, squeezing his eyes open and shut. They called his name—*Hector, Hector, are you all right, boy?*

I told Loretta when I got home and she already knew he was working there. *Everyone deserves a second chance*, she said. *For it is not by chance when paths cross again*. And of course I would not be telling you this story if it had been any other way.

At first Hector kept his distance. Sometimes there is so much water under the bridge it can drown you. We got used to each other being in the store and our occasional interactions. We was different versions of ourselves for we were born again.

The manager, Mrs. Whick, watched us closely. I normally came with Bernice, another Believer girl. In the summer we worked six days a week, Monday to Saturday. In August Bernice came down with summer flu and she took a day off. I covered her shift, cleaning the outdoor tables in the café, and there was a creak behind me. I knew it was Hector from his footstep, but when he spoke my name in his low voice my hands shook. I was the young girl against the stone wall possessed by ecstasy and shame. "Fancy Mosher," he said again. I lifted my head up and looked into his dark eyes. His face was creased as though he'd taken five years on for every one that had passed. "They sent me for coffee," he finally said. I poured take-away cups, with creamers and sugars and stir sticks. There were fresh muffins from the oven and I put them on the tray.

"It's been a long time, Fancy," he said. "I reckon the past is the past." We didn't speak of Petal's End or the fire that ate up his green ferns. He did not ask about the wretched time on the island. He took the coffee and the muffins and his fingers brushed mine.

Bernice came back the next day still with a cough and they transferred her to the shop and kept me in the café, sweeping and baking. Every morning Hector would come by for his coffee, leaning there, telling me about the furniture the same way he talked about cars and their engines. He would always offer me mints from a small tin he carried in his pocket.

Though she professed to believe in redemption, Loretta was not fully convinced. "You can feed a wolf all you want but it always glances toward the forest," she said, which did not seem in keeping with our new beliefs and I told her so, for it seemed he really had changed. Hector was radiant with his new pure ways. He'd join in for the weekly prayer meeting we had on Fridays. In truth it was a staff meeting but the Spencers were religious people and we opened and closed with a prayer, asking for prosperity in our work, and that we might serve the Lord through what we were offering at Spencer's Country Things.

We only talked of uncomplicated matters. Hector seemed grateful there was no question that came out of my mouth about what had happened to him and Buddy, his incarceration. Hector did tell me once when he took the morning tray how he had seen the Light in jail. It illuminated a new road, one he had never seen before, one his father scorned—he knew this road was the one for him to now turn down.

Mrs. Whick had been listening at the door. "The Lord offers salvation to all," she said, patting his shoulder with each word like she was tapping out a sacred rhythm.

Hector started coming to our church, on Wednesdays and Sundays, showing up for the long service. He came to Bible study. He studied for his conversion. Hector wanted to believe, just as I did. He took his baptism as I had, in front of the congregation, baptism by pouring—the method of affusion. The Elder held up the shining metal pitcher. The pure water gushed down over Hector's head. He wept as he accepted the Lord through the cascades covering his face like a moving veil. I had not wept when they'd baptized me, when that veil of water poured down over my eyes. There was nothing pure about me. It did not mean I wasn't grateful to hide behind it. But inside I knew my prayer for cleansing was futile for I was not born innocent.

❧

I wore a pale-blue dress and a formal black headdress. Hector wore a white shirt buttoned up, his beard trimmed tight, in the way of the church, according to scripture. It was autumn. We declared our intent to be married by the Lord-in-front-of-His-holy-witness, the congregation, and to receive their blessing of our union. Our families were not invited for we lived separate from them now, since they were of the world and we were God's people.

Loretta left the house we lived in and went back to her family, and we began our life there as husband and wife. Hector was just as he was at Petal's End—muscles rippling through him from his hard manual labour, the way they do in a young man, his tattoo prominent on his arm. A baby came in me right away. A gift from the Lord, they said.

It all went well and fine until Hector joined the local volunteer fire department. The Elders in the church thought it would be a good contribution to the larger community, and he had all them skills they needed for working on the trucks. The only condition was he didn't do nothing on Sundays. He started as soon as our baby was born and the problems began almost immediately. He'd got a pardon for his crime, and maybe he'd thought he could start fresh in the world we'd left behind. It was the people he took up with, though. Worst of all, Buddy and his idiot laugh. Hector started staying out later and later, saying there was things to be done at the fire hall, a truck to be polished, an engine to be tuned. The Believers weren't idiots. We were trusting and willing to give the benefit of the doubt, but not indefinitely. I knew what he was up to soon enough. If there was an idiot, it was me, not wanting to consider he would go back to his old ways. Hector couldn't stay with nothing for long, moving from this to that. He began coming home late stinking of women, liquor and cigarettes.

At first I didn't say a word in protest, hoping it was a stage he was passing through, maybe from the anxiety of being a father. He would hold the baby all careful like he thought she would break. Hector loved his child in a fearful way. And it made him reckless. The worst moment was when I finally did speak up. I told Hector when he come in late one night I knew about his transgressions. First he said nothing. His lips were moving, like he was counting. Then he lifted up his arm and his fist came swinging into my cheek.

It is a terrible thing to tell.

The baby cried in her crib and a look came over him. Hector knew he'd made a horrible mistake. He walked out and didn't come back. Loretta come by the next morning to pick us up to go down to the church to quilt and I wouldn't let her in. She saw my black eye through the crack in the door. She put her hand on the door and forced it open. The baby was sleeping in my arms. Loretta's sister come to the door followed by the brother-in-law who was driving the car.

The men went later and found Hector. The Believers would work with him, help him find the road again, but Hector was finished. He quit Spencer's Country Things and got himself a job on an apple farm and started living like he was a teenager again, working all week and partying when he wasn't.

The Believers shunned him. They cast Hector out as they had Loretta. He come by the church one day and they knew he was lying when he said he hadn't been drinking. They said unto him: *But now I have written unto you not to keep company, if any man that is called a brother be a fornicator, or covetous, or an idolater, or a railer, or a drunkard, or an extortioner; with such a one know not to eat.*

For two years after he left I lived back with Loretta and her family.

When my girl was three I saw Hector driving through town and he saw me. Such a sad, wistful look come over his face as the car moved along.

I didn't even think about it. I just did it. I took our little girl and I went to find him at the farm. He wasn't surprised. The Believers turned their backs to me because I went to him. Even Loretta wasn't allowed to see me. She wept and said that I could return if I was willing to confess my sins to the Lord.

It was easy falling back into familiar ways. I wore worldly clothes and high heels, dressing like Ma. Hector's friends stopped by, and Buddy joked about how Hector had joined a cult but he'd seen the light and come away. Hector lit into a rage, and they ran out the back. Then he closed the door and pressed his forehead on the wood.

He'd take us to his friends and there wasn't one house we ever visited that wasn't rundown and dirty, weeds where a garden should have grown. His drinking, dope-smoking and scheming friends was either older or younger than him—it was like Hector belonged to no generation. I would sit in the car with our child while he'd go in, remembering when Ma would leave me in the car when I was the same age. Then I'd start walking home and Hector would come after us, sometimes in a rage and sometimes calm as could be.

When the child was sleeping I took to having a drink with Hector, for I discovered it brought a short reprieve to my mind. At first it was just one. But it didn't take long for me to find out I was just like my mother. The authorities come in the night with a paper—what they called an *order of taking*. Hector had been screaming. My girl outside in a nightie on the sidewalk playing, avoiding the arguing indoors. In a flash, our girl had her hands and lips pressed to the back seat window. She was crying, steaming up the window as the car drove away down the dark street. I was drunk running after it and the police came and grabbed me. They took Hector away to jail and they took me off to a shelter for women. They gave our daughter to Loretta, who became her guardian.

It took me a few months but I was able to find my way again. Loretta brought the child back to me. I could not look either of them in the eye for weeks. We lived in an apartment, just the two of us. She started school. I would walk her there each morning and wait by the school doors each afternoon. We were poor and picked fruit, and I made jams and jellies as my mother had done. I did my embroidery again, pretty pictures of young girls by summer streams. I did one of a blond girl in a field of daisies, twirling about, and three little children playing around her. It made me think of Pomeline so I put it away.

Hector come back, yes he did. My girl was just turning six. He wanted to see her. A social worker come to see me. Hector had seen the error of his ways again. This was Hector, you see, believing his own lies for as long as he could. But we all agreed it would be good for her to know her father. She started going to see him on Saturday afternoons. We did that right through the autumn and the winter and into the spring. They sent me to the vocational school to be a personal care attendant. My training was in the nursing home in town, where Margaret was the supervisor. She had an opportunity to turn me away. They sent her a list with the student names on it and mine was there. But she hired me.

She was a hard-looking thirty and I was twenty-two. She had no children and was divorced, for there would be no man telling her what to do. Margaret still had hair hanging down in her eyes and them saddlebags and big breasts that swayed as she wiggled her hips. She did not speak of Petal's End, not then. Margaret did not mention her burn mark. You'd think it was just a birthmark if you didn't know she'd had her face scalded in a pot of boiling rosewater.

It was awkward between us until, one shift, we were folding towels and Margaret said, out of the blue, like she'd been waiting for years to tell me, how she appreciated what I done that day her father drove up and she was smoking. The tension broke, and Petal's End, the flowers and the delicate scent of scalding steam fell away into the soft white towels that smelled of bleach, the towels piled high and perfect like them blocks of soap had once been arranged in the Water House.

My daughter and I moved to a house in the country not too far from Hector. She would visit him most Sunday afternoons. We walked through a field by a brook to get to his house. She adored fishing with him, watching him cast his line out over the water, the fish jumping. When Margaret asked me to start the back shift Hector said he'd keep our little girl for the night. I agreed to try it for that first shift.

I was apprehensive as we walked over to Hector's. The meadow had grown wild and we held hands as we pushed our way through the high sweet hay until we came out onto the yard. I left her there and I went back through the field on my trail, beside the small empty one.

The police came to my door later that day before I was setting out for my shift. She had hit her head on a rock by the brook and had rolled into the water. She'd slipped trying to cast her line. The edge of the brook was slimy. He'd left her alone. Hector had a woman there. She had just dropped by. He wept, saying that he'd thought they'd be just a minute, but a minute was all it took.

She looked so tiny lying there on the hospital table, long dark hair still wet, eyes closed. They sent her away before I could see her again. I was not fit to be a mother. They said Hector came in, beside himself with grief and blame.

A lady at the hospital knew Ma and called her. She came immediately. I didn't recognize her at first. She was no longer a drinker, but her face was heavy and lined. She was an elderly lady finally, even with her hair now dyed red, and her lipstick on her wrinkled lips, her hands withered up like dry ferns. *Don't you tell me not to cry, old woman. Hush-a-bye, I will cry and cry.* She did not say a word and she did not talk of John Lee. *Shush*, I said to her, holding my finger to my lips. *Don't you cry now, Mama, don't you cry. Do you hear me? Just hush up now . . . hush and be still.* For I did not want her to wake my daughter. Ma did not listen. Endless tears spilled from her eyes as though her dry papery skin was just a wrapper for a bottomless pool of sorrow.

Hector went away. I didn't know what happened to him for years. Back home I walked through that field time and time again. Our paths were still there, where we'd beat down the flowers and the hay and clover. But the winds came, the seasons changed, and at last it seemed a small dark-haired girl had never walked through the field at all, that not even I had, for our paths through the meadow were swept away.

Loretta came in with some of the goodly Believers but I could not talk to them. Loretta held me and rocked me and sleep came down and pressed sticky blackness throughout my mind. I woke and she was gone and it was quiet.

I lived there alone. Ma would leave me food. I would not talk to her, neither. I prayed to Holy Mother Mercy that my daughter would heal and that she would come back to me. I called to Grampie but he did not answer. No red bird come, and I took this as a sign she would recover complete. They would not let me have her back. There was a night when I drank so much whisky that I took a kitchen knife and ended up in a hospital and, later, in a place drying out.

The Believers came again. "Girly Miss," Loretta said, stroking my hand. Hideous dry heaves came but no tears, just like Jenny Parker. My mother had stolen them all, I raged. I could not go back to the Believers. There was no salvation for me there. I only wanted Holy Mother Mercy to come. My aim was having my daughter back. The social worker said I had to get a job, had to live clean and straight and narrow. I couldn't bear to live in the house we'd had together. I moved back into town to an apartment. Each day I walked to the gas station and bought cigarettes and coffee, a wiry shell, wobbling in my high-heel shoes. For long enough I'd had my hair covered and I felt safest wearing a sweater with a hood. I pulled the drawstrings tight, hiding as I staggered down the sidewalk. I did not drink nothing stronger than coffee, as tempted as I was. If Ma could be dry then I could be too. We was one in the same, I knew.

It was all I could do to get dressed and walk down that street and get my smokes. I would light one up as I walked home and smoke the rest of the pack throughout the day. It was spelled out what to do in order to get her back, my precious girl, to stay on the straight and narrow, to get a job.

Ma took me back to the hospital. They told me that later. I had not stayed on the clean path as Ma had finally been able to. All the drugs and the drinking. I did not clean or cook. I took up this habit, that when I'd go to the liquor store I'd get a ride home with whatever man would drive me. He'd come in to my dirty apartment. There were times then when I was hungry for warm flesh, for sweating, for the feel of hot skin rubbing together and it didn't matter whose body it was. They'd leave money for me on the counter. It was too much work for me to see them to the door. Then came the time that always comes, where I drank too much and couldn't do what the man-of-the-day asked. His hands flew and smacked. Ma come banging on the door, as the nurses told me later at the hospital, hollering through my window. I was not conscious when Ma came up to the glass pane. She called for the ambulance from the neighbour's. Ronnie was there, waiting in the truck, still driving her around, right to the end, because long ago they had taken her licence away for good.

They sent in a doctor who talked to me about the dark times. They ran the electricity through me and it was hard to remember anything, as though my mind was full of pictures left out in the sun too long. When people talked it was like there was a delay. Their lips would move and words emerged eventually but they was drawn out and distorted.

The doctors had me doing this and that in the hospital. They had programs where I felt like an ancient lady making crafts, singing songs and walking in the gardens. They give me books to read but the words would blur on the page and I just stacked them on top of each other. A doctor would talk to me. I could never remember his name. It didn't matter, he said. He give me a notebook to write things down, for keeping track of my days and what I was thinking about, but I never did so because my mind was a wide, deep ocean with thoughts that would come out of the fog like islands before fading away again.

While I was still in the hospital a lawyer came to visit me. He was young but stooped over, tall and thin, wearing round spectacles. His fingers were dry and white like he never saw the light of day. Raymond Delquist was his name. He was from the big valley town. There was lawyers in every generation of his family. Just like I was born into my family way, he was born into the law. He shook my limp hand. His dry fingers made a swishing rasp as they slid over the paper he put on the table between us. It took me time to comprehend what he wanted. He was saying things like *look after you, a place to go, resting, caregiver, guardian, healing*. He was offering me a job. I could go and work, he said, looking after Agatha Parker. He used her proper name. She was not well.

Jenny had requested me. She was moving to Petal's End for the summer. He wouldn't tell me what was wrong with her. She would pay me more than I could make anywhere else. It would be a fresh start. Raymond Delquist understood we went way back. Agatha had told him we had a childhood bond. I could live there. There were papers I needed to sign. It was hard to follow him. His misty voice made me sleepy. One of the nameless doctors came in and sat with us. He agreed, it was a decent opportunity, he said, to leave the hospital and start anew. The lawyer had the papers there. Agatha needed to know right away. If my mind had been slow before, when he mentioned Petal's End images came cartwheeling through—the island surrounded by cliffs, the lighthouse and storms, the sky full of lightning, Jenny's face in the rain and Art's big hands reaching out. Even in that sterile hospital ward I swore I could smell the deep forest and tangy ocean spray and hear Pomeline scream on a shrieking wind.

Margaret came to see me while I was still in the hospital deciding what to do. She expected me to come back and work for her, she said. A nurse in the hospital had told her that Jenny was offering to take me over at Petal's End. Margaret thought it was a joke and she'd come to laugh with me about it—like that was the last place I would go, or should go.

Margaret was shocked when she realized I had not dismissed it outright. "Don't go up there, Fancy Mosher. You need to listen to me and you need to listen good. Jenny's not right in her head. What do you want to go back there for? You don't owe her nothing. She can't help you. She's just up to something, that mutated dwarf of a bitch. That's plain, isn't it? You're not a girl now. And only bad things happen over to Petal's End. You know that better than anyone. Jenny isn't any different than when she was a kid. No one changes, no one ever does. You think you're some smart, don't you? People don't want to help you. Everyone's just looking for what they can get. That's life. You're an ignorant little fool. Did you really think I wanted to help you get your life back together? Did you really believe that? It's too easy tricking you."

I wasn't even dressed, just sitting there in the hospital lounge listening to her tell me how simple it was to get Hector to stop believing, to come into her big fleshy arms and press himself against her wide hips. My noiseless pain brought a smug look over Margaret's face. It was her, she told me, when Hector went astray. When his precious daughter tumbled into the stream and hit her head, her daddy was in bed with Margaret.

She believed I had done Jenny's bidding. We'd tried to kill her with the poisoned rosewater, but we'd got impatient when it didn't work. If Margaret couldn't get to Jenny Parker then she would get to me. I could reap what Jenny had sown, for Jenny was sealed away in her castle on the mountain. "Hector really did think you believed their preachings," she told me. "He hated you for that. He took all his hate for the Believers and he gave it to you."

I didn't tell Margaret that it was me who fooled Hector, for as much as I wanted to believe I could have a good and simple life, I knew I could not. Even the Holy Mother Mercy Grampie called on had forsaken me. I said nothing to Margaret for it did not matter no more, there was no taking back the past for any of us. Having my daughter returned was the only thing that could heal me. I did not weep or wail as Margaret wanted. She walked toward the door, but before she slipped out I saw her crying. It's a surprise discovering that no matter how satisfying the planning, there ain't no real pleasure in retribution.

That is how I came to leave the valley after twelve years and go back up and over the mountain on the Lonely Road, coming down into Lupin Cove, winding into the village and over the bridge and back up the hill on the other side. Lupin Cove was even further in decline, everything looking shabbier and overgrown, abandoned.

I arrived on a fine June day at the iron gates of Petal's End. Raymond Delquist drove me and he talked only when there was a reason—an economy of words. He was like a Believer in that way. But he did not look like a man who would ever raise his voice in song, and I told him so. His anemic cheeks lifted on either of his lips like the frail wings of a moth. He said his grandfather was my Grampie's lawyer. He said my grandfather was a special man. They had a painting he had done of Raymond's grandmother. She'd been hit by a train. In the painting she was smiling. It made the family happy.

The lawyer unlocked the gates and pulled them apart, using his whole body, and I got out of the car with my bag. "I'll walk in from here, sir," I said.

His hat brim was wide and his face was shaded. "There's a telephone. No answering machine, but there is a phone."

"Probably the same one as before, that old black telephone."

"Agatha has my number, and it's on your contract, should you need anything." He tipped his felt hat.

The leaves closed in on the lane as though it was a tunnel. I took off my shoes and put them in my bag, and as soon as my feet were bare I started feeling better. My daughter was just like me. She loved bare feet. That was the Mosher way. Feeling the dirt between my toes brought me back to life as I walked the lane to Petal's End.

As I ambled along, a long shape moved further down the road. My heart hammered as I saw it was a man with silver hair. He came forward and said my name, his low voice cavernous. The melody of the voice was unchanged even though a great long time had passed, twelve years, since that summer when Pomeline died on the island and the forest went up in smoke and Marigold fell down sputtering her strange words.

3.
Down the Dark Lane

THE SLATE-BLUE eyes in his tanned brown face were the only trace of the twelve-year-old Art Comeau I had known. Before me was a grown man with hot blood in his veins. I saw the muscles move under Art's skin and it made me think for a moment of Hector, but I let Hector bob away in the river of my mind. I stood there with Art on the lane as he took my hands in both of his. Those warm strong fingers cradled my clammy palms.

Art seemed older than twenty-four years, but the same could be said of me. Lines had laid down upon my face as though I'd walked through fine cobwebs. Perhaps my black hair would turn white also.

"Fancy, let me take your bag." He reached for it as he spoke, his hand brushing mine. "I was walking down to meet the car. I knew you would walk down the lane . . . in bare feet. Some things never change."

"What the hell happened to your voice, Art Comeau? Did you start dying your hair? I thought you'd be far away from these parts." I wondered how much Art knew about me, how my life had gone. I knew nothing of him.

"I finally sold my grandmother's house. Jenny offered me a job gardening, a good part-time job. I did a year at the vocational school studying horticulture but then I switched to university."

"You always liked the plants and bugs." I supposed Art would think he was better than me now, me who didn't even finish high school. "What are you going to be? A plant doctor?"

"Actually, I'm studying psychology now. I'm going to be a psychologist, not a botanist like Harry."

Harry. His name a transparent bell between us, which began to ring, then Sakura's voice, a tiny wind brushing up against that bell. I had one of my spells and forgot he was there for a time, feeling the laneway on my feet. In the woods were a few of the broken statue pieces from long ago, covered in mint-green lichen.

"Excuse me, Fancy, are you okay?" I opened my eyes and the man with the silver hair and the deep voice was looking at me. "My grandmother's hair turned like this when she was young too, but she dyed it black. It started happening when I finished high school. For a long time I thought it was on account of all the stress, even knowing it ran in my family. At least baldness isn't in the genes." He ran his fingers through his hair. "Studying psychology has helped me. When Yvette took me away I went to see someone, to talk about things. And when she died her cousins kept me. They were good people. It helped me understand that whole summer, as much as I could."

Anger came up in me. "The only time we could have done anything was back then and we did nothing. I don't want to go talking about that. The past is the past. I'm glad you're all happy and well-adjusted now with your big education and your city accent and your travels. I got things to do now getting my life back in order. Don't you go giving me a hard time, because I can't stand that, Arthur Comeau. You don't know what I been through."

He had the good sense to let it drop. "Jenny tracked me down through the lawyer," he said. "She wants to open up Evermore again, although it's a shocking mess. It would take a crew, but she doesn't want anyone here but us. She's firm on that. She won't let her mother and Dr. Baker on the property. They came by when I first got here. Estelle still wants to tear it down. She says she'll sell the contents to antiquity dealers, auction off every piece inside. The land alone is worth a fortune now. They've been quarrelling for twelve years straight, it seems. Doesn't matter, because Jenny owns everything. But now Jenny's sick, and Estelle says she isn't competent."

"Estelle used to say the same thing about Marigold. Maybe you can tell me what's wrong with Jenny that she needs a caregiver," I said. "Raymond Delquist said he wasn't authorized to give me any additional information. That's how he put it."

"Raymond is a good man and he does what Jenny says. As for what's wrong with her, it goes back to before she was born. Estelle took some drugs so she wouldn't have miscarriages, but those drugs have ended up giving Jenny cancer in her cervix and uterus. They didn't catch it soon enough because she refused to go for regular tests. She said she didn't want doctors touching her. It's spreading all through her now." Art was more like his old self then, long pauses between his thoughts, looking at me to see if I understood. But my face only puzzled him so he explained more, as though that would help. "Jenny wants the gate locked all the time. She doesn't want any visitors." We continued our walk. "You should be prepared, Fancy. She looks aged far, far beyond her years. And she goes by Agatha now. You get used to calling her that but it's weird at first. I've been here for two weeks. If you call her Jenny she won't even acknowledge you are in the room."

"I see. Well, *Agatha's* paying me enough I'm happy to call her whatever she wants, and looking after people is what I'm trained to do."

"I hope so, because she's sick, Fancy. She's doing okay right now, though. Oh, and brace yourself . . . she's doing all the cooking. She says she never cooked in her life but it's never too late to learn something new." Art chuckled. "How's your mother? I hear she's sick."

"I don't know how Ma is. I can do the cooking. And look after Agatha."

The big house was not as I remembered it. The paint was peeling and the shingles were covered in bushy moss. The only thing that hadn't changed was the stone gargoyles hanging there on the corners of the third floor. Most of the windows were boarded up. The grass was waist high and the gardens were lost in a sea of weeds. Thick ivy covered the walls.

The weather is hard on a house that goes unattended for twelve years. It looked derelict. A sea of blue lupins covered the front grounds and flowed around the house. Art put his hand on my arm. I looked at him and he was pointing. Little blue butterflies were flitting about on the blossoms.

I held out my hand hoping a butterfly might come to me but they only fluttered by on the breeze. "I named my daughter after them butterflies, Melissa Blue. We just use Melissa though for there ain't nothing blue about her. She's a joyous thing."

There are still Melissa Blues here now, although I am no young woman. It is a sanctuary for the butterflies and for me as well. They say there are few places left where the Melissa Blue breeds but they do here at Petal's End, where the lupins grow.

Art did not try to force me to discuss anything, as confusing as it must have been following my meandering comments. He was the kind of person who can love the unlovable, and who can accept the unacceptable. He understood without me needing to explain. "It's a pretty name for a little girl. I'm sorry, Fancy, for all you've gone through. For what happened. I didn't think it could get any worse than out there on the island. Or finding Charlie that day. But I suppose it can always get worse." Art told me he'd learned interesting meditation and self-relaxation techniques that could help. He would teach me.

I took his hand. "I got no need of that. But there ain't no need to look glum. Maybe you should try out your psychology on yourself. They had us doing enough of that down in the hospital. I agreed to come here so I wouldn't have to go banging on any more bongo drums like some stupid hippie. Pomeline dying was a tragedy but what's past is the past. This job's for getting Melissa back, you see, Art? And I mean to make the most of it. We can only help Jenny now. There's nothing we can do for Pomeline. You got to remember that."

"I see," he said. "I see, Fancy." But Art didn't look like he could see at all. He hugged me tight and I was like a stick in his arms. He only cried for a moment, his tears stopping as he kissed me on the forehead. "Everything's going to be all right, Fancy."

"Didn't Yvette used to say something about that?"

"All fruits ripe, she used to say."

Art didn't sound as though he believed himself a single bit. Maybe he wanted to, but in the same way he wanted to believe in the moon illusion, that it really was bigger when it rose. I kissed both his cheeks.

And, my dear, you see, when I got to Petal's End I really believed if I did the right thing perhaps I'd capture back a bit of what I'd lost.

4.
Miss Agatha Parker

We came in the grand front entrance. There was a tinkle. Pomeline's wind bells were hanging off the roof of the verandah. The blue and yellow flowers painted on them looked as perfect as when I had first seen them twelve years earlier. Art said Jenny had him put the wind bells up when she found them on a hook in the Water House. Hers were hung in one of the willows by the pond in Evermore.

Art held the door for me, and I tried not to make it obvious as I glanced in the warped mirror still there by the door frame. If he noticed, he didn't let on. There was only a reflection of forest and sky. I realized I had been holding my breath as I walked over the threshold. We went through the great hall where much of the furniture was covered in white sheets. The air was dusty and dank, the way it is when the windows haven't been opened in years and the sunlight has not reached inside. There were dustballs on the floor and cobwebs on the light fixtures. The door to the music room was closed and there was an empty vase in the centre of the enormous round hall table.

When Art and I came into the kitchen, me with my suitcase, the scent of lupins still in my nose, Jenny was there stirring a big pot. She'd made a soup and she had a strawberry-rhubarb pie in the oven. The kitchen looked the same for the most part, except it was a disastrous mess, which I had never seen in all the time I'd spent there as a child. Loretta and I kept it tidy, and I learned to cook and clean as I went. Jenny had the dirty dishes piled, flour dusted all about the table, walls and floor. She stood on a wooden stool beaming like she was going to win a prize at the country fair. She had her face made up just as Marigold always had, with dark eyeliner and bright lipstick, crooked, as though she hadn't thought to use a magnifying glass like her grandmother had. Jenny handed me a cup of iced herbal tea, an elixir for any ailment she claimed. It smelled revolting. I set it on the table and said I wasn't thirsty.

"Off with you, Fancy Mosher," Jenny said. "Get yourself used to the place. I'm making your welcome supper." She wiped her hands on the great big apron. She wanted to be useful, she said, talking like her cousin Harry. It was understandable, seeing she come from a line of people who never did much that was useful in their lives combined. She planned on redeeming herself, she proclaimed from her small pulpit.

Art carried my suitcase upstairs to my old room, which I had requested, and on the way up I asked him why we were here, as it seemed to me Jenny just wanted company. She looked frail and flimsy but not like she was on death's doorstep. It was fine with me, I said, if she wanted to pay for company. It was her money. Art just shrugged, never the kind to say nothing bad. He told me to settle in and went back down to the kitchen.

I thought it might bring up painful emotions being back in my room but it didn't. The pictures I had made at school were still on the walls, but other than that bit of personality it was just the empty chest of drawers and the bookshelf, the single bed, a chair in the corner and the window looking south over the property, over the carriage houses and off to the stone walls of Evermore. I saw the trees rising from behind the walled garden. The lace curtains were rotting and tearing in places.

The first thing I did when Art left was look for the letter from Grampie. I crawled under the bed and found the floorboard, the dust tickling my nose. The metal hook was stiff and I gave it a pull and the board opened up without so much as a creak. But the space underneath was empty. The lavender and peony sachet was there but it was scentless. I had a sudden attack of grief for I was sure I had left the letter, but then, in that moment, I was not at all sure. My mind was confused and I wanted it empty and clear. It was a tricky thing sorting through the past. The anguish it was causing me to go back far in time wasn't worth the bother. In the closet, in the same old spot, I found the box of my mother's old embroidery materials and the frames I'd taken from the third floor that day when Margaret and I had interrupted Pomeline and Dr. Baker's tryst. I didn't have much to unpack, just some clothes and a small pink sweater of Melissa's.

When I came downstairs they didn't hear me, and Art and Jenny were having a serious conversation in the foyer. Art kept pointing at the stairs, and he finally looked over and gave a little cough when he saw me standing there.

Art took me outside for a walk around. We didn't go into Evermore but he showed me how he'd started on the gardens around the front—in the two weeks he'd been there he hadn't done much to the house yet. Jenny was only using the library and the day room and the dining room. The music room was closed up, and so was the parlour.

The welcome supper almost killed me. I swear it was Holy Mother Mercy who kept me from projectile vomiting in that formal dining room. I insisted Jenny let me help serve, and when we came into the dining room Jenny was sitting comfy as can be at the head of the table with candles lit, draped in heirloom jewels and a faded party dress that was too big for her. Jenny was dwarfed by the massive room. She held out her hand to me, as though she forgot meeting me in the kitchen earlier. Stale face powder and the acrid scent of lily of the valley perfume billowed all around her. It was a late supper, and while it was still plenty light outside it was dark in there. The walls were painted a midnight blue, and the buffet and china cabinets were dark wood. Huge portraits of dead Parkers loomed on the walls as we sat there slurping on her soup, which consisted almost exclusively of salt and water. The vegetables had turned to mush. The biscuits were so hard you could have broke the windows with them.

After we choked the meal down, Art served the pie. Jenny said she'd added lemon to give it some zest, just like Loretta did. It made your lips pucker like you was a mackerel on a hook. The crust was so tough I swear she cut out a cardboard box and baked that. *What fine cooking*, we lied to her, and she beamed. At least the tea was hot and strong. She offered to get me sugar cookies she'd made and I said, "Dear God no, Agatha, I'm full enough I think I might perish in this here chair."

Jenny and Art each had a glass of wine. Jenny was taking pills and said she shouldn't drink too much. Or at all, I said, and she just waved her hand like I was a mote of dust in the air. They didn't offer me none. It was understood I didn't drink. I had no trouble with other people drinking, though. They both got giggly and talked about how fine it was to have me join them, like we was at a resort. I thought about my daughter on a constant loop, that's what I did, although it did feel reassuring to be surrounded by the familiar. There was some comfort in it, being back. By then it was twilight and the candles had almost burned down.

They toasted, and I joined with my glass of water. "To friendship," Art said.

"To old times," Jenny said, slurping her wine with the same disgusting table manners she'd had as a child, which no one had ever dared reprimand her for. Art talked about how he wanted to make stepping stones with some of the broken china, probably so we didn't have to sit there in the quiet of the house like the past was going to crawl out of the walls and bite us on the necks. Jenny said she'd knocked a whole pile of dishes over when she was getting used to the kitchen. Art glanced at me then. I knew he was thinking about Grampie's teacup pieces out in the Wishing Pool. One thing was clear—I wasn't seeing no dead like Grampie, and there was no need to speak of it.

I slept deep and long that first night, only waking one time when a night bird sang out. The smell of the room was familiar and I fell back into a heavy slumber.

On my first morning at Petal's End I awoke early and headed to the kitchen. I poked around and saw Art had stocked the pantry. I ate cereal and then began making dough for bread. If I could let it rise I could punch it down and rise it again and bake it before the weather outside heated up too much for the oven to be on. The bread pans had been moved and I rooted around and found them in the cupboards. It was then I noticed pictures sticking out from the bottom of the cupboard stand, photos that must have been misplaced years ago. There was a young woman picking water lilies while her child played by the side of the pond. It took me a moment to recognize that it was Ma and John Lee. It choked me up seeing them, Ma up to her knees in the water, surrounded by all them pretty flowers, and John Lee on the grass by the edge. They was looking at each other, her smiling, and John Lee's head thrown back in a giggle. Ma, younger than I was at that moment. Ma, when she was well, as Loretta had encouraged me to remember her. There was another photo of her with a very young John Lee down on the seashore, him toddling about while she picked through the seaweed, harvesting dulse.

Melissa adored water lilies. Being near a summertime pond made me feel close to her. I became determined to pick them water lilies to remind me of her, and why I was back to Petal's End with the absurd job I had found myself in, looking after Jenny who was weirder than she'd ever been, and Art who'd gone weird in his own way. My attention was fixed on having my daughter back. No men, no drinking the wine or sherry Jenny enjoyed every evening. Not giving in to temptation. It was living life on the straight and narrow, like I was circling round a picture frame, seeing what I wanted in the centre and trying to slip inside with it. Me and Melissa together. Finding the photos of Ma and John Lee made me determined that things would not end up that way for us. I cried and cried over that picture for I couldn't bear how it was making me think about my own daughter. I would not stray, I promised myself.

After I had set the bread to rise I went out to Evermore, but it was nothing like my unchanged bedroom. The walled garden was a tangled-up jungle. The stone walls were the same but it was now a shadow version of the garden I once knew. Of course Jenny had decreed no cut flowers in the house, but I could not resist the temptation to pick the hardy peonies growing happy and splendid without human touch. The pond was dense with fragrant white water lilies. Jenny's pretty glass wind bells were ringing sweet. It was a picture-perfect day. Some of the showy pink lilies bloomed farther out near the swan house on the centre island. Even picking the white water lilies close to the edge of the pond was tricky, but I wasn't about to go in the water with the swans lurking about. I bent out as far as I could and grabbed one by the stem. As I leaned over the glassy pond I screamed, for there was a grimacing face looking up at me from the smooth surface. The water rippled as I fell back on the bank. But the water calmed and it seemed it was only my dark empty eyes staring up from between the lilies. I was spooking myself. I could not trust my own sight. I decided to speak not a word of this to Art or Jenny, because if I told them I was imagining eyes in the water they might go and tell the lawyer, who might report me to the hospital. Then the social worker would know, and that would be the end of me getting Melissa back.

To prove to myself that there was nothing in the water, I tried again. I'd picked lilies with Ma so I was a professional harvester, I reminded myself. But when I grabbed another water lily my fingers were shaking and slippery. I didn't pinch the stem real hard as Ma had always instructed. When I tugged it was like another hand was reaching out from the water and pulling me splashing and wailing into the pond. Once I was in there, the water tingled on my skin. I drifted there on my back. It was quiet but for the birds singing. Then I heard a horrible gurgling noise. Sure enough it was old Sweet William and Iris White followed by a couple of other great big swans and a few babies. The mute swan is an ancient beast. Such long-lived, mean-spirited creatures, their only redeeming feature is their loyalty to each other. Their descendants are still paddling in the pond in Evermore to this day. I fled the pond just as Sweet William starting flapping his wings and skimming over the water like some lunatic set on bashing my face in. I dashed off with my armful of water lilies over the ragged path Art had hacked away. I could hear the faint sound of the wind bells behind me.

After that, those first days passed smooth and steady, each one a card laid down by some expert hand we could not see. Jenny said every evening how pleased she was having me there to help, even though she really wouldn't let me do much for her. Jenny was looking at me queerly from time to time but it didn't seem out of the ordinary, not for someone like her. And in fairness, she had brought me here out of a mental hospital so she had a right to keep her big myopic eye on me. After a few weeks of her observations it was clear she was watching for more than me being delusional or talking to myself. She was always muttering under her breath, and this give her a big range for normal.

One morning we was having coffee on the verandah and her eyes were intent on me with every sip I took.

"Agatha," I said, "it ain't polite to stare. It's giving me the willies."

She laughed like an imbecile, not even trying to be discreet after that.

"I'm terribly sorry for what has happened to you, Fancy. I knew all those years ago that Hector was a bad man but he never told on me for burning down his illegal fields. Good was mixed in with the bad of Hector."

Art stood up. She held her hand up and he didn't move or speak.

"All people do a few terrible things in their lifetimes. One must set those things straight. It's the only way. I hear your mother is doing poorly, Fancy. You must go and make your peace with her." Jenny got up with her cane and went across the verandah and into the house.

For the first few weeks all our interactions were much like that—stunted, convoluted, strange.

Art sat down and put his arm around me. It felt some good sitting together, his musky scent wafting over me as we looked out over the lawn to where the forest began. Shivers went tapping down my spine, maybe from sitting close to Art and from him being kind, from how good his warm summer skin smelled . . . or maybe it was the family heirloom closing in on me, which despite—or maybe due to—my muddled head, I could tell was happening. There was just too much not making sense, too many strange occurrences. I could rationalize and make up stories but something unorthodox was going on. Either way, Art making me excited, and the peculiarities—both scared me. The trees seemed even tighter together, a wall closing us off.

❧

I spent the next two weeks getting the place cleaned and livable, my water lilies and peonies beautiful in the outdoor vase, and trying to figure out a way to take on the cooking without upsetting Jenny. It wasn't just the horror show of nibbling at her meals and then sneaking a sandwich when she was asleep, which I discovered Art had also been doing when we had a midnight run-in. It was that Jenny was constantly in the kitchen watching me, looking at me like she wanted to talk. "Hear that?" she'd ask me throughout the day. Of course I was hearing birds sing and the outlandish racket she'd make with the pots and pans and opening and slamming cupboards. "See that?" she'd ask, pointing over at a doorway or the window. My silence seemed to be interpreted as a sign I was in agreement, as though we had an understanding.

She and Art seemed happy to creep around in the dust and cobwebs. Every evening they drank their wine and we talked about silly things. By day there was barely any conversation, like we were in a monastery. Jenny spent her afternoons reading and sorting through old photos. She was making an album of her grandmother's days at Petal's End, she said. She was off to bed early each night with her sherry and up late in the morning, just as Marigold was. That left me and Art, and we'd go off to the kitchen and clean up, singing while we did so. After, we would rest outside on a bench or in chairs in the sitting room Loretta had. He talked about his psychology and I listened to him, although I couldn't keep up with most of it. But he smelled good and put no pressure on me for anything at all.

Jenny got around with a cane just like Marigold did, but she was more petite than her grandmother ever was. She still wore her kerchief, hiding her bits of hair. She wheezed around the place, her asthma worse than ever. She spent hours in the library with her book, *The Woman Beautiful, or Maidenhood, Marriage and Maternity* by Monfort B. Allen and Amelia C. McGregor. It was Granny's book, she said. It was *full of information on all the marvellous and complex matters pertaining to women together with the Diseases Peculiar to the Female Sex*. She read that much to us.

I can still hear Jenny's thudding and clunking as she walked. She said she had to use the cane because of the horrible treatments her mother had inflicted on her for her illness, treatments that made her wish she was dead more than her illness ever did. Jenny said it was a disease particular to women. She dropped that kind of information into a conversation no different than if she was commenting on the weather. "Oh my, I got a disease in my uterus, pass me the pastry cutter. Oh yes, they gave me such a sinister treatment it burned my skin and made me vomit and made my bones brittle. Where's the sugar, Fancy? I went out to see Sweet William. He was paddling about. He doesn't seem to age. My mother locked me up in a hospital and forced medicine and treatment on me. I love Lady Dundee cake. Can you bake that, Fancy? My Granny died in a nursing home. She never got better. She was crippled up and her face was frozen in a scream after the garden party. Do you think you could make more bread? Mine doesn't rise. It's a shocking shame about your daughter, but it's good you're here with us now. How I adore a fresh dill pickle."

And so it went with Jenny that summer, her talking away and me doing as she requested, but refusing to engage. At least there was no sign of her strange religion, and she was not spouting off any of her funny scripture lines she pulled out of hymns and carols. There was the rare time I would catch myself whistling, but I would stop right away for the quiet house amplified it out of proportion and sent those shivers through my bones.

Since I wasn't running around filling up vases with flowers and doing all the things Loretta had always kept me busy with, there was not much else to do except keep her company, when I wasn't cleaning or hustling her out of the way in the kitchen to stop her from cooking. Jenny didn't want no help with her bathing and she said she didn't need no help with her pills, she just wanted the friendship. Like it used to be, she said, as though in her memory Art and I had been her bosom buddies. Funny how time can draw such different pictures of the past. She also got me teaching her embroidery, although she seemed happier to just watch me do the stitching than try it herself. I was doing up a picture for her of the pond and the flowers around it, and them nasty white swans on the water among the lilies. She liked to do the needlework in the afternoon when it was too sticky to do anything else but sit in the shade. We did the cooking in the morning. Every day she let me do more. We ate in the dining room at that long table, just the three of us sitting there like we was waiting for guests who weren't never going to arrive.

She kept asking if I had seen Ma much. Well, no, of course not, I told her. She said she understood how difficult it could be with mothers. Her mother and Dr. Baker were still scheming how to get Petal's End from her. Jenny didn't ask me much about my daughter. She would start to talk about her and then would drop the topic. I thought that was odd but decided it was because she couldn't have children.

I was stitching one afternoon and she was watching me. "You have good hands, Fancy. You go so fast your fingers blur. And you come up with those designs like I have never seen." I stopped. It reminded me of such a thing Pomeline would have said. I glanced up at her portrait and Jenny's eyes followed me. Together we looked at Pomeline, with her flowing hair and her blue eyes, posed there like she was going to walk right out of the painting. Jenny started shaking and hoisted herself up with her cane. She stood by the door. My needle was still between my fingertips, the white silk floss I was using to make Sweet William come to life was in my hands and the silver thimble capped my index finger. Her breathing got short and wheezy but she held up her hand when I made to get up. I stayed put as she coughed and left the room.

I told Art about it later when Jenny was in bed and he said he'd check on her when she was sleeping. She kept the door open in the night. "In case I need you," she said, "I'll call out for you." But it had been weeks and she hadn't called out once. We kept all them doors open then, connecting the back of the house with the front, just in case, both of those worlds fused together at last. We hadn't said a word about the Annex. When I checked, the key wasn't hanging behind the painting no more. The door was locked up tight, and I didn't know if Jenny had the key or if Estelle had taken it with her twelve years ago.

5.
The Swan House

THE MIDSUMMER air was crispy hot with late-day cicadas buzzing and crickets chirping, the sounds of season change. Jenny liked going out to the pond in the early afternoon, to *sit in contemplation*, she said. She proclaimed it eased her suffering and pain. Counting damselflies, meditating on the water lilies, listening to the frogs croak, watching her swans, all of these activities soothed and calmed her. We did whatever she wanted, seeing we were working for her. There was solace in the familiarity of Art. He stopped with most of his psychology tactics and we just picked blueberries and worked together around the house and garden when we weren't catering to Jenny. It was almost like bygone times. I made muffins, and it gave me comfort, that tradition, using the same pots and spoons and jars and labels, being in the room where Loretta had worked.

August started off with Estelle and Dr. Baker relentlessly telephoning. Jenny wanted nothing to do with either of them.

Finally, after a week of it, I asked Jenny what they were calling about. And why they hadn't been calling before. We were needle-working in the sitting room at the front of the house. I already had three embroideries, finished in July, encased in frames from the embroidery box. Jenny had me hang them in the sitting room.

"Oh, they *have* been calling. My mother never *stops* calling. Those pictures are awfully disturbing, Fancy. The stitching is remarkable, though, just like your mother's," she said.

She must have thought embroidery brought my mother to mind, which it did not. I didn't take the bait, and asked Jenny once more why *her* mother persisted in calling.

Jenny kept studying my pictorials. "How would I know? I leave the phone off the hook. Art keeps putting it back. I take it off again. He thinks my mind is affected by pain medication and I don't know the difference. He means well, so I indulge him."

That explained why the social worker hadn't been calling about my daughter, to check in and see how I was doing. They were getting a busy signal. Jenny said not to worry—if there was anything urgent they'd go through Raymond Delquist at the law firm, as Estelle was supposed to do. That was the arrangement, she said, and it must have slipped my mind. She said it like I was the one with recollection troubles, not her. It wasn't worth arguing about, although she looked primed for a debate.

She sighed and kept on about her tormentors. "They found out I've stopped going down to the hospital for treatments. With all my mother's snooping, it took her long enough to find that out. But my well-being is the least of my mother's concerns. I'm an obstacle, you see. She's threatening to have me declared incompetent. My mother lives to undermine. It's her sole pleasure. I don't want them coming here. They've been waiting for years for an excuse to try to change Granny's will, biding their time. Mother says that I'm possessed by Granny's spirit. Granny thought the same about you, that you were John Lee reincarnated." She didn't need anyone in a room but herself to keep a conversation going.

Jenny fell into a fit of cackles as Art walked in. His arms glistened as he sat down with a glass of ice water. He'd been taking the boards off more of the windows so we could have some light and air. He didn't even bother asking why she was laughing.

"I told my mother what we saw that day in the Annex, years ago. She didn't believe me, not a word. Dr. Baker said I was delusional, making up stories. Well, I told Mother that he was fucking her *and* her daughter, how did she feel about that? She slapped me across the face like I was a lewd shrew. My mother believes only what she wants to. Don't come out here, I told her. It enrages her when I tell her what to do." Jenny rubbed her fingers together like she was doing an invocation. It appeared to me the cancer was the least of her worries—a pestilence of remorse and retribution was growing in her, gnawing on her organs.

As if by divine providence, the phone out in the hall rang then and we all jumped. "Just let it ring," Jenny said.

Art ran his fingers through his hair, his skin brown against the silver. "I have an activity set up for us outside. I thought you might enjoy it. Making stepping stones."

Jenny clapped her hands gleefully. I announced, however, that Art was clearly losing his mind from not having enough to do if it had come to crafts.

"Ain't that nice, Art, making me feel like I'm back down in the valley hospital. Or like we're pretending it's back when they had the soldiers with shell shock. We could go in the Annex and do it there, and bring back more good times," I said.

Jenny folded her arms together. "They don't call it shell shock now, Fancy. It's a disorder. Everything's a disorder, even grief."

I thought of Charlie, but Jenny didn't seem to mind. "There are painful memories in there," she said.

I apologized for being insensitive but Jenny waved her hand. "Sometimes it's easier to forget. But you would know more about that than me, Fancy."

What did she know? Art was drinking his water as though it was the last glass of his life.

"Fancy, your mother isn't well. We can't protect you from that. Ronnie called from the hospital. I think that's his name. It must be short for Ronald. That's a better name. Anyway, he said your mother would like to see you. He's called several times. The busy signal didn't deter him either. It's serious."

"It's too little, too late. She only ever wants one thing from me and I ain't delivering on that."

We set out after lunch for our activity. Art had the materials ready in the Water House. The room still had a slight botanical fragrance lingering in the air. I hadn't been in there since Margaret had her face scalded, but we said nothing of that.

Art started mixing up a big bucket of concrete. He pointed at an envelope on the table and I opened it to find the broken fragments of Grampie's and John Lee's cups and saucers. "I thought you might want them after all this time. You can use them in a memory stone. It's a nice way to put things to rest."

I didn't know what to say. On one hand it was thoughtful, and on the other hand it seemed outrageous, like he was trying to rile me up, to provoke me. Art wanted me to remember while he and Jenny were busy blocking out what had happened on the island. It made no sense.

I poured the china bits out on the table, each piece clinking as it hit the wood. Jenny ran her fingers over them, barely touching, as though she might need to snatch back her hand at any moment.

"My Grampie's teacup," I told her. "And my brother's."

"His paintings are worth a great deal of money now. I've been collecting them. The art gallery in the city wants to do a show, so they have them there," she said. "We could glue this cup together and donate it. Or auction it."

I was speechless.

Art looked up from the concrete. "I think your Grampie would have been surprised too."

"Didn't people want to keep the portraits?"

"When people get old no one cares about the things they leave behind. All these possessions, and as soon as you die the family can't wait to call the auctioneers. Rather humbling, isn't it? My ancestors would be appalled. Anyway, when the value went up on your grandfather's paintings, more people sold them. They were instantly collectible. Such a distinct style. I did some courses in art history. It's folk art, of course, vernacular art." Jenny said that the gallery would like to come out and see where he lived. "I know the place belongs to you but—"

"That's not true," I interrupted. "The place was left to Loretta, and she said we were never, ever to go there again. When we went to the Believers she said it was best to forget life on the mountain." I told Jenny I didn't want to go through the woods to Grampie's and I was glad it was all boarded up. Jenny knew then to let it drop, and Art put two silver bowls full of broken china on the table in front of us.

Art had aluminum pie plates set out on the long table and he poured the concrete in and we made designs. He had some patterns and Jenny used those, and I just made mine up like I did with embroidery scenes, using the bits of broken china. Art's therapeutic session seemed to be working. We went fast, so the concrete wouldn't set on us. Jenny got tired out of nowhere, as she had been prone to. She lost interest. I took her into the house but she refused any help going up all those stairs.

Back out in the Water House, Art was cleaning up. I didn't see the point in mincing words.

"Is it true what she says, about her health, about her mother and Dr. Baker?"

Art said it was true that she gave up getting treatments. She didn't think she'd get better. She still took pain pills but he didn't know how often. She was secretive about that. And yes, her mother and Dr. Baker was phoning. And it didn't matter if all three of us told Estelle what we saw all them years ago, Estelle would never believe it. She would say that Jenny was mentally ill, that she had brain damage from when she was born, that Jenny just wanted to be in control. They had come out a few times for what they called *family visits*, he said. Art was at Petal's End when they had the big fight in early June. He didn't want to tell me earlier, for I was just settling in. Estelle had come out by herself that day and she and Jenny were in the music room. Art ran from the kitchen when he heard screaming from the hall. Estelle even broke a glass lamp. She was irrational, and kept cutting Jenny off, saying she was delusional. Dr. Baker came out with Estelle the next week and he said Jenny was having a psychotic break, with slanderous fantasies.

Art said Jenny seemed afraid of them at that point, of what they might do. It was then she'd retained Raymond Delquist. I pushed, asking him why Jenny was frightened.

Art went about tidying up from our stepping stone project, taking his time before he answered. "You don't need to be worrying about any of this, Fancy," he said.

But I was piecing it together that Jenny had brought me here because she *did* want me worrying about it, that we was all a part of this somehow. Art didn't say nothing when I suggested that. Then he come over and kissed me on both eyes. "Don't you worry, Fancy Mosher." He went back to his cleaning up and I left him there, feeling his lips on my skin all the way back to the kitchen. I brought my stepping stone with me and set it on the grass by the kitchen door to dry.

The next day Jenny wanted a picnic by the lily pond. As usual, she insisted she was fine walking, and as usual, it took us forever just to get there. When we arrived she had to sit down right away on the bench, wheezing away, clutching her stomach. She took to coughing, and I gave her some water from the picnic basket. The swans were floating at the far end by the dilapidated Atelier. She called to them and they gurgled back at her in this low, disturbing way. I had a blanket and put it on the ground where we ate our cucumber sandwiches. She had hardly any appetite, and then she stretched out in the shade, but not before telling me to get her a pink water lily from the pond. Jenny was never too tired to give orders.

That was the last thing I wanted to do, and I told her the lilies was far out in the water and she didn't like picked flowers anyhow. She ignored me and had Art fetch the boat tied down by the Atelier. He had done repairs and painted it—it was the newest-looking thing around. The swan house on the small island in the middle of the lily pond was looking awful rickety too, like a rundown doghouse for a big attack beast. I dawdled at the edge of the bank, adjusted my dress. I didn't want them to know I was afraid so I climbed in. Art paddled us about. He called to Jenny that we were looking for the perfect one. I didn't glance at the water, and I knew Art noticed.

"We don't have all day, Fancy," Jenny said. "I'll need a nap soon. Just pick one. You grew up doing this. Why are you acting all bizarre?"

Nerves came over me again when I leaned out of the boat and grabbed one of them pink floating flowers. The weeping willows hung over us, and it seemed to me every time I got my fingers close to a lily, something underwater pulled it away from my fingertips. A whisper of wind rippled over the surface and the glass bells in the willows tinkled. I thought about when I first got here, the face I thought I saw. The light dappled down through the thin branches and distorted my reflection on the water. My throat was tight and I didn't answer when Art asked if I was okay. I was determined to get Jenny a goddamn lily and I reached one more time for a big fragrant one right by the side of the boat. But as I touched it I saw eyes below the surface of the water, and lips moving as if they was singing. I swear that's what it looked like. I screamed and pulled back with the lily still in my fingers but it wouldn't give. I tugged hard, the boat rocked and over I went. Art almost fell out but he steadied himself as I flailed my way through the water to the island and leaned on the swan house.

"What happened?" Jenny was sitting up on the marble bench now, leaning forward, her hands folded.

"Nothing."

Art was looking at me strangely, and I knew then I would have to tell him sooner or later about the unnatural things happening, how my thinking was all confused. One minute things seemed normal, and then the next it was all wrong, and then back again. They'd think I was crazy. I couldn't stand the idea of Art believing my mind was frail like my mother's and Jenny's. Or him having to report me to the social worker. I remember realizing maybe he could help me make sense of all the confusion with his psychology. I was either going crazy or it was the memento in me, and both were horrible scenarios to consider. But I couldn't trust either Jenny or Art. It was too risky. I had to act like everything was regular and right as robins in the rain.

Art rowed over to the island just as them stupid swans started making low fizzling hisses and picked up lightning speed at the other end of the pond, coming for us. Jenny squawked at them and they stopped dead in the water, turned right around and went back where they came from. That in itself was disturbing. They got right out of the water on the far end of the pond and sat there on the bank.

"They are well-mannered and do as I say. So you two follow their example. Now, since you couldn't get me a water lily, get me the box in the swan house," Jenny said.

As usual, we had no idea what she was on about. She repeated her instruction. Art and I exchanged a glance.

"Are you serious?" I asked.

"Yes, of course," she said.

Art hopped off the boat and onto the island. It was easiest to humour Jenny. That said, there wasn't no way I was reaching inside that swan house. The big white birds was hissing from the far bank. Any second they could come slapping those hard bony-ridged wings at our heads. Art didn't let on the swans were worrying him and he went right over to the small building. He crawled in and come out with a box wrapped up in plastic.

"What's in that?" I yelled over to Jenny.

"Don't drop it in the water," she said.

We got back in the boat and Art gave a couple quick strokes until we reached the edge of the pond. Art tied the boat to a small tree and he carried the box over to her. It wasn't heavy, not for him. He set it down beside her. She tapped it.

"I put it there a long time ago, when I was stronger," Jenny said. She was completely fatigued now.

Art walked down to the Atelier, where he had left a wobbly wheelbarrow, and Jenny didn't put up no fight when Art scooped her up, along with the box, and put them in it. He pushed her through Evermore, her head bobbing, some scary-looking baby out for a walk. Jenny clutched the parcel in her arms. She was singing but I couldn't make out the words.

Jenny didn't offer anything about the wooden box at supper. It took some prying. I asked her what she had stashed away in the swan house. She looked at the candles and at the china in the cabinets around the walls, deep in thought. I can see her in my mind, the soft light making her seem healthier than she was.

"Family photos and papers. And my sister's journal," she said. "I haven't read it yet. I took it before they closed the house up.

It's got a lock on it. I'd have to break it. You know how she liked her secrets. There are other items I've got hidden away. I've already looked at them. Now I know why my mother wanted the Annex torn down. But we don't need to talk about that. You should go see your mother. Ronald called again. He accused me of not giving you his messages. I told him that was most certainly not the case but he kept interrupting me. She's very sick, he said, and keeps asking for you. Your mother won't have much longer. That doesn't seem to bother you. I feel that way about my mother but your mother is a better person, even if you find that hard to believe."

"She's just making it up about being sick. It's always the same with her. Whenever Ma does something nice it's because she wants something. I know what she'll go on about. You saw well enough what she's like."

Jenny took a big sip of wine and wiped her mouth on a napkin. She asked Art if he had any other activities planned. How she had enjoyed the stepping stones, she said.

"Oh yes," Art said, "I have a garden meditation in mind." He seemed happy to change the subject.

It was a distracted conversation, all of us thinking of not just Ma ranting by the tombstone but of what Pomeline might have written in that journal. It was no surprise Jenny had held off reading it. She was as patient as an ancient tortoise, biding her time. Art pressed on about the garden meditation.

Jenny clapped her hands. "I love your activities, Art. It's like day camp. Of course I was never allowed to go to day camp."

"Agatha, you would have loved the hospital I was in. We did all kinds of them therapeutic activities," I told her.

"I spent plenty of time in hospitals when I was a child, time you could not imagine, Fancy."

"Grampie used to say we was all born to die, just some of us earlier than others." It struck me how mean that was to say. What my intention was, I didn't know.

Jenny wasn't fazed. "Your Grampie was a wise man, Fancy. You should think more about what he taught you." She put her glass down, stood up and off she went with her cane, saying good night as she went out the door.

Art and I cleared off the table and did the dishes. He couldn't help himself looking at me and it bothered him. He blushed, and I pretended I didn't notice. My dress fell off my shoulder while I washed the plates. He watched me as he took them off the drying rack and wiped. I let him have a look. It made my heart pound without fear, a welcome change.

I asked Art if Jenny was unbalanced, hiding the journal in the swan house and dragging us out there pretending she wanted flowers. This was getting a bit strange, even for her. Art said he'd talk to her tomorrow. Maybe it would help give Jenny closure, he pondered. That's why people liked reading the diaries of the dead, so they could shut a door. "Not talking about tragic things doesn't mean they didn't happen. We all need closure, Fancy."

Closure. A word I had only ever heard used for roads and bridges.

It was fitting.

6.

The Hobgobblies

THERE WAS one thing about Jenny that never changed and that was how she was full of surprises. In all my life I never knew anyone else like her. That summer when we was all cloistered up at Petal's End she had me believing she needed a caregiver but it hardly seemed that way, seeing as she wouldn't let me do a damn thing for her.

"Fancy," Jenny said, "you are just like Loretta. The house is running smoothly. And you've been so thoughtful to help with the cooking."

"Well, I'm glad you're happy, Agatha. That's what I'm here for, ain't it, not a vacation?" I chuckled a bit because it was funny and all, her thanking me for working for her, which was what her grandmother would have done.

She was staring at me intently then, the dusky evening light bouncing off her glasses. Jenny had not made mention of the journal since the day we brought it back. But she was watching me all the time. If there was the slightest movement in the trees or a creak of the floor she'd turn her head quick and see if I reacted. I would look up from the stove and her eyes would be on me. Then she'd leave the room. Twice I was lost in a book on the verandah and raised my head to see her standing there, like she was waiting. But what Jenny was waiting for I had no idea. Several times she said my name as though she had caught me about to start something, but when I'd ask her what she wanted she would tell me to never mind, the entire while studying me. When I mentioned her behaviour to Art he said we both knew what Jenny was like and to pay no attention to her.

It was mid August when she let out why she had brought me back to Petal's End. We was in the garden after supper, watching her swans cruise over the surface of the lily pond before they retired for the night. I recall how Art stood up and walked down to the edge of the water. His hands were in his pockets, his silver hair looking plum in the sunset light.

"It's lovely having you assist in the house, with the laundry and the cleaning, and of course the cooking. As you know, I'm not well, and I am not going to get better," she continued. "I am mortally ill."

"Yes, I see."

"There have been noises in the house at night. I'm sure you've heard them."

"Is it the hobgobblies?" I said, winking at her, but she didn't react.

She sipped her wine and licked her lips. "Yes, I suppose it is. You know I keep the windows closed, like my grandmother, so they can't get in."

"I have noticed that, Agatha."

"Well, it isn't keeping her out. I can hear her at night, on the staircase. I can hear her going down the stairs and the music room door opening and I can hear her sit at the piano. I can hear the lid opening. She's preparing. She's come back to get us. Given what you have gone through, and of course your family experience, we need you to help us."

"Agatha, this really isn't a good idea. I don't think it's time yet." Art watched the swans shake and twist their long necks, grunting and whistling as they paddled to the island. He didn't turn around. He couldn't look me in the eye, for he had betrayed me.

"Art, you bastard. How could you go and tell Jenny, or Agatha, or whatever it is you want us to call you? I'm not like Grampie. You swore you'd keep that a secret."

He turned then but he looked at Jenny. "See, I told you to just let this alone."

"She doesn't even know what I'm talking about. She's in total denial. An altered reality."

"I do too know what you mean, you freaks. I can't see the dead. Maybe I believed that stuff back when I was a kid. I ain't going chatting with Pomeline. You're out of your mind, Agatha. You're the one in an altered reality. Art's just indulging you."

"I told you this was a bad idea, Jenny."

"Do not call me that, Art. And you, Fancy, you are the one being indulged."

"Everything is a bad idea, just one after another. This ain't just a bad idea, it's an abomination. Grampie used to say what you send out the door in the morning will come back to scratch at the door in the night if you haven't made your peace. I made my peace, but you two have not made your peace with what happened, and that ain't my problem. We all swore over there on the island, didn't we?"

"We did. Pomeline fell," Art said.

"She didn't go *falling* off no cliff. I don't see why you keep pretending it's so. And are you trying to blame me? That's nonsense to put it on me," I said.

Jenny was rocking her head back and forth like she was a wind-up doll breaking down. "We need to go over to the island

and set things right. Art's bought a little boat for me, down in the harbour. We are going to take that out to the island. We'll do a prayer. Just as they did in that story Sakura told us about. Remember? You can call Pomeline for us. Her body was lost at sea. It's August. It's Obon. Her spirit is loose. Don't you remember? Won't you at least go look for her in the mirror at the front of the house?"

There was no way I was going to tell them I'd checked that mirror every day, and right then I swore to myself not to look again, no matter how much I was tempted. "No, I will not look in that mirror. You should take it down. And I ain't going over to the island. You two don't seem to understand some of us have real lives. I have my daughter to get back. I can't go on no ghostly errands for you. What would the social worker say?"

"Well, to start with, I don't know how you think you're getting your daughter back—"

"Jenny, that's enough," Art said. "You need to take a sedative and go to bed. You'll kill yourself."

Jenny bit her lip and went back to rocking her head. "I'm going to die soon enough, so what does it matter? If you won't help me I can't force you to. And if you don't even believe in your own gift there's nothing I can do. She only comes in the night, and we'll be safe with the windows closed. Maybe we should board them up again. We'll be safe . . . for now." Jenny coughed. "But Pomeline's going to do something dreadful, just you watch."

A few days later Art and I was eating breakfast in the kitchen. Jenny was still in bed. She had retreated into herself since her outburst at the pond. She still kept a watch on me, though. While she stopped with the demand to speak to her dead sister, the weight she'd slung around that night did not leave.

We heard a creaking sound in the hall early that morning. Jenny didn't get out of bed until much later. Art and I clutched our coffee cups, suddenly afraid, like we was kids, and we strained our necks to look down the hall. Art stood up and turned around, his arms out, like he was going to protect me.

Jenny arrived, infuriated, in the doorway. "Art, I told you to keep the windows closed. You should never have taken the boards off. I told both of you. And you know how I feel about flowers, Fancy. You know how I feel about cut flowers. You're like a deranged florist, that's what you are. You both know what this means, what you've done. Didn't you even hear the wind bells warning you? Didn't you even hear those, you idiots? Why do you think I had them hanging!" She was thrashing her cane around and her voice was ragged. We told her we didn't know what she was talking about.

"First you refuse to help me and then you act on your own, without even giving me a warning. You want her to get me. To punish me. You went and called the dead, you and your stupid flowers. And you, Art, with your need for therapeutic ventilation. You're helping Fancy. You two were always thick as thieves, one escape after another. But this is no child's play. You want her to kill me."

"I didn't open the windows, Agatha," Art said.

I went scurrying by Jenny in the hall as Art was trying to reason with her—we didn't open any windows at night and no one was cutting flowers and bringing them in the house. No one was doing anything in the night but sleeping.

But sure enough as I come out into the grand hall the door was wide open with a breeze blowing in the screen. The windows Art had unboarded were opened wide. And there on the big marble-topped round table was the huge vase full of glorious, fresh-cut flowers.

Art come barrelling into the room behind me and Jenny came wheezing behind him. "Neither of you did this?"

We made to close the windows and Jenny banged her cane on the floor. "It's too late. She's in the house now and we're never going to get her out again. The point of no return, you imbeciles." She went out to the verandah and swung her cane at the glass bells. They shattered on the wooden floor and she left them there, the jagged pieces, with bits of yellow and blue flowers on the shards.

7.
Pomeline

THERE WAS a pattern now—weird things happening, and then nothing but the normal eccentricity of Jenny and Petal's End. We resumed our routine, the embroidery, Art's group therapy activities. Art was now making a concerted effort to act like a psychologist, and he said his activities would help wake up our true emotions. Sometimes feelings don't need no waking up, I lectured him. Hadn't he seen that already? For a time there was not another word about which was crazier, going in the boat to the island, or Pomeline returning as an avenging ghost. Grampie said to choose your words carefully, that you speak of a thing once and before you know it, there it is, in the room with you, conjured up.

One morning I went out to the garden to look for raspberries. On the way back I glanced toward the front of the house and I noticed there was a path of rose petals leading from the house to the garden, just as there had been the day of the garden party. I walked alongside of it, slowly picking up speed until I was charging back into the kitchen where Art was making coffee. I dragged him out to see. He stood there, holding his coffee cup, squinting from the brightness of the morning sun.

"Look what Jenny's been up to," I said. He shrugged. "She's crazy, Art. That's all there is to it. We're living here with a crazy lady."

"There's no way she could have done this. Jenny can hardly get around with a cane. Maybe *you* did it."

I couldn't believe it. I slapped him right across the face and went running through the path of petals to the front door. I dashed up the staircase and down the hall and into Jenny's bedroom. She sat up in bed wearing a black satin sleep-mask.

"Pomeline?" she cried out, trembling with fear. Jenny's voice made me catch my breath. She lifted the mask up with one hand, the other groping for her thick glasses on her bedside table. She was like some newborn kitten without her glasses, all vulnerable, mewling. "Pomeline," she whispered again, looking over at the door.

"It ain't your dead sister. It's Fancy Mosher."

I would like to say relief come over her but it did not. I moved into the room and went over to Jenny, this trembly thing in the bed in her white cotton nightie. I knew then it wasn't her who put them rose petals down. There was no way she could have got out of bed, gathered them up and scattered them about in the night just to scare me.

We were in such a state that when we heard footsteps coming closer we both shook uncontrollably. We stayed huddled up together until we saw Art in the doorway, and Jenny and I both started laughing. We kept laughing and laughing until Jenny's weird giggles trailed off into a horrible veil of weeping and coughing that draped over the room. I moved to comfort her again, and didn't she start screaming for us to get out and leave her alone to rot and die.

Art gestured to me and I followed him down the stairs. "She's seriously ill. She's making out she's okay, but she's not. She's on powerful pain medication but I think she's taking too much. It's making it harder for her to breathe, and it's messing with her mind. I don't know what to do." His cheek was red from where I slapped him. Art wasn't no psychologist—he was just a young man trying to be a peacemaker.

"Well, I guess that means she's got to stop pretending, don't it, about what happened out there on the island? You can't set the past straight when it's twisted up in lies, and she's running out of time."

"You're right, Fancy. And we're not trying to hurt you. We're trying to help you. Jenny's got this idea in her head, but beyond that, she was trying to help you by bringing you here."

The stress we had been bearing for twelve long years was causing this mayhem. That was what I arrived at in that moment—what happened on the island had damaged us beyond repair. Between the two of them they was making me crazy, Art acting like it was all resolved and, behind him, Jenny acting all creepy and wanting me to do her a séance. After a time I couldn't come up with a single explanation except what I'd been avoiding—it really was Pomeline come back from the dead, set on getting hard, sharp and even . . . until we were all broken corpses just like her.

Jenny now spoke relentlessly of how Pomeline was in the house seeking reprisal. She pointed her finger at me, as we sat having cake on the verandah.

"You need to set things straight with her, Fancy Mosher."

She and Art were drinking wine. It wasn't taking much to get Jenny tipsy. And Art was drinking far more than normal. He'd been doing that the last few nights, when he gave up on settling

Jenny down. He didn't even lecture her about mixing her pills and alcohol, for if he did she'd just deny taking the medication.

"I still don't know what you're talking about," I said. At that, Art put his hand on the table and told me Jenny had found Grampie's letter. This was what was fuelling her.

"I did find it," Jenny said with a slur. "I did. I found it a few years ago when I was here by myself. I would drive myself out and stay the night. I went up to your room and looked through it. Granny kept repeating your name when she was in the nursing home. I wanted to know what she was going on about. When I came out here to go through her things, I found the embroidery you did for her. It's upstairs in my room. I went searching for a reason my grandmother couldn't forget you, and I found the letter. The twelfth-born Mosher can see the dead."

"It's not fucking true," I screamed.

Art shook his head, back and forth and back and forth, like it was some fucking pendulum in one of them grandfather clocks all over this house. He started waxing on about the stress of the many tragic things that had befallen me.

"Tragic things happening to me? What about Jenny? What about you, Art Comeau? You was out on that island too." His head stopped swinging, and he and Jenny shared a look, as they had been doing since I got there, like they had a new secret, not just the old one.

"I can hear the noises, and I can see the flowers and the petals, but I can't see Pomeline," Jenny said. "I can't see her, but I can sense her. Only you can see. Only you can hear her words and talk to her. My grandmother deserved what she got, Fancy, and Pomeline knew what Granny did. Pommie was the one who found out, and she told me. Well, she didn't tell me but I went looking." I frowned, unsure where she was headed. "All those years pretending. Marigold was no better than my mother. She was worse, if that's possible. There's no end to the horrors in the well of evil.

There are no tidings of comfort and joy, nothing to save us all. The only good one was Pomeline, but I was just a little girl and I didn't understand. Children do not always understand that things are more complicated than they appear."

I didn't know what Jenny meant by all of that. We was just kids on that island, that was true. And children understood what lying could conjure. But I didn't understand in the slightest what she meant about Marigold.

"Fancy, I'm so sorry. You have to forgive me, too. And you have to tell Pomeline that I'm sorry. She won't listen to me. I've tried and I've tried. It's my fault. But you and Art helped me."

I wanted to wring her neck. Like we'd had any choice. She always had to have her own way, when she was twelve, and when she was twenty-four. Jenny was drunk, stoned and jabbering on. I asked her what Marigold did but she just kept bawling and bawling, that dreadful tearless weeping. Jenny held out her hands and Art took one. He gave me such a hard glance that, as angry as I was, I reached out and took the other one. Anything to wind her down. Her hands were cold and dry.

"You have to promise me you'll sleep in the hall at the bottom of the stairs. My bedroom door must be shut at night. Pomeline's in the house and she's putting out the flowers and she's going to come up the stairs and get me because of what we did. It was my fault. You just did what I told you to. All will be calm. All will be bright. Calm and bright." She kept saying that over and over again with her eyes shut, her childhood religion welling up. A chill went through me for I thought of what she'd done, all those things she'd done, and pulled us into, and that maybe her childhood religion did have a power we had not ever taken seriously enough.

I could not stop myself from shaking. My thoughts kept drifting to the island, how I could not keep straight what had happened out there—what was truth and what was a lie. Jenny opened up those eyes. She could sense I was starting to believe, not in her, but in the memento. It was an affliction put upon me, just as Jenny was born into her illness. I was a twelfth-born, and my time had arrived.

We sat for a while, holding hands. Jenny's breathing got slower. Her head teetered forward, all that wine and fear. She started snoring. Art put his hand on my shoulder, and when he felt me shivering still he put more pressure into his long strong fingers, and the heat of his skin sent tingles zinging through me. He carried Jenny up to her room and came back down to the verandah for me. He said he'd get blankets for us to sleep at the bottom of the stairs, so we could tell her we'd kept our word. He went off and I cleaned up the dishes. When the kitchen was respectable I went to join him.

I heard a creaking and my bones froze, a chair rocking back and forth outside. I looked out the window—Art in a porch rocker with a glass of wine. I opened up the window and told him he'd scared me. He asked wasn't I scared worse opening up the window and letting more hobgobblies in? I laughed, but then shut it tight. I walked over to the table and poured myself a glass of wine and I drank it right down. I knew it was wrong but that did not stop me, it did not, and I took the bottle out onto the verandah and sat beside Art and poured myself another glass. A glow come over me, and it was as though life was going to be okay again, and it seemed the summer sky that late at night was happy for me, streaks of orange and pink mixed in with the stars coming through. A few bats darted by.

After a few glasses, we went in, giddy like children, lying in our fort of mats and blankets Art had arranged on the floor. A longing for Art went through me, and him being my childhood friend fell away. He was a man, and I wanted him on top of me and inside of me, his smell and marks on my body, protecting me from whatever had come to call at Petal's End. A desperate animal come out in us both. Art grabbed me, and his lips and hands were all over my body, and he was whispering how he'd wanted to do this for years. As my eyes squeezed shut and the swirling nighttime sky surged into my mind I heard something else breathing. Art lunged forward on me one last time before he collapsed. *Shush*, I whispered and he held his breath but the noise was still there. We sat up, naked and slick with sweat. I saw a flash of white at the top of the stairs. He didn't see it, he said.

I went naked up the stairs, quietly down the hall, but Jenny's door was closed up tight. At the bottom of the staircase Art stood at a window he'd opened for some air. He shut it before I could say a word and we lay down on the floor in our burrow of blankets. I realized how drunk I was. My head was spinning as I lurched off into oblivion.

A pounding head and nauseous stomach woke me to the grey light of the early morning. All the windows were open, and on the table in the hall was a huge vase of lilies. My gasp woke Art. I covered my body. The shame was coming over me just as the fear was. Jenny must have done all this. She must have seen us. Art shook his head, reminding me there was no way she could have, not as sick as she was. We wrapped our bodies together and he stroked my face, and in time he carried me up the stairs to my room. I was too sick to do a thing but fall back asleep.

When I came down later there was a note. He'd taken Jenny to the hospital. She had woken at noon in severe pain. He'd told her I was feeling poorly and they'd let me sleep, and would call from the hospital. There was no lilies by the door. The previous night felt like a dream, except for how sticky I was between my legs, and the smell of our sex so thick I could taste it.

I had a bath and went off in the wildwood where we used to pick blackberries. They was still growing, succulent and dark on stiff canes, protected by thick sharp needles, which kept pricking and stinging my wrists and fingers. It seemed the blackberries were plotting against me and I knew I was not in my right mind.

A simple routine would ground me, I decided, so I returned with my bucket half full. From afar the house seemed like a dollhouse, getting bigger as I approached, out of proportion, and looming over me as though it had risen up from a grave. I could not trust anything, least of all myself.

I was the only one in the mansion but it did not feel empty. I did my chores, whistling, and made a blackberry pie. But I could not shake the feeling the house was alive. I rode Art's bike down to the village as fast as I could, to have a break from Petal's End. The lane was quiet and the village was thick with fog. I could barely make out the bridge, and could not get even a glimpse of the beach, but the air was fresh and salty and it invigorated me. I had been hidden away for too long. This was the problem. It had been weeks that I'd been sealed away behind the trees.

I pedalled back with a clear mind and fell asleep on the verandah, until I was startled awake by singing. I couldn't tell if it was my voice, if I was singing in my sleep, and maybe it was me who was cutting flowers and putting down petals, and letting night air in, me that was invoking the dead. Or maybe we were all cracked. I shook my head, still full of hazy images, only I knew they weren't dreams, or at least I thought I did. My memories were colliding into each other. Perhaps I was indeed going insane. This was how it happened—where lies became truth and truth lies, where a memory was nothing more than a made-up story we told ourselves. A deceit we could live with, or live with long enough until it made us sick. Haunted or crazy, they'd never let Melissa come back.

I thought of the letter from Grampie, how he said the dead would find me if I was willing. That they come for truth, a truth the living keep entombed. That didn't make no sense to me as a child of twelve . . . until the summer Pomeline died, and we took our oath on that godforsaken island, and our corruption took form. I was peering through a window in my mind, back to when

I was barefoot and thin with wild long hair and pink cheeks, when we did not know better even when we should have. An overwhelming desire to see the truth came over me for I wanted to be free. I fell to my knees beseeching Holy Mother Mercy to forgive us for what we had done.

8.
The Island

WE DID go to the island that day after Marigold had her fall during the concert in the gazebo. Jenny did look to her grandmother, and over to me, watching fixedly as Marigold's foot went through the wooden floor, in the spot where Pomeline was supposed to stand for the bow. Jenny's expression changed, the flushed fury flooding in as she watched her Granny fall while Pomeline sat at the piano in all her diminished beauty—her sister who had arrived at Petal's End vivacious and elegant. Jenny clenched her fists, and it seemed she would plunge them into her own face for a moment, as though she had failed and had to be punished. Instead, she let her arms fall and she stood mouthing her strange prayers. Jenny reached out and took my hand. I was afraid to let go. Art glanced at me. We both knew—Jenny had loosened the floorboard.

Hector knew, too. She'd come to him for a hammer, he told me when we were married. A hammer to make a dollhouse, she'd told him, for pounding nails in, not pulling them up with the clawed end. I don't think Pomeline suspected the trap was for her. She had rushed to her grandmother's aid, even though the old lady was so cold toward her. There had been such tumult, and more came as the smoke rolled up from Hector's secret meadow. He took Jenny's secrets to jail with him because he was afraid of her. Art and I were afraid of her too as we stood in our finery in the gazebo.

Estelle saw the island as a place we could be contained, exiled to, while she took command of Petal's End. We hoped Jenny would stay behind, that her mother would say she was too frail to come to the island, but Estelle was busy taking over the estate. She was worried the garden party catastrophe would send Jenny into an apoplectic fit. But Estelle was a fool, and that would be her undoing. Frailty in the body don't mean frailty in the mind.

We went out on the boat. That part is true. We were glad Harry and Sakura had taken us away from the calamity of Petal's End, our unusual summer ending fittingly in such an upheaval of screams and smoke and sirens. Loretta and Dr. Baker were just as glad for us to be sent off for a few days. Harry was an expert outdoorsman, a veteran explorer, and he and Sakura had camped all over the world. What could possibly happen to us? You see, that was the wrong question. It was not what could happen. It was what we could do.

The boat headed north in the bay. We did not turn back once to look at the mainland. Pomeline was behaving strangely. She had slowly dimmed as the weeks had passed, her pink cheeks turning grey, as though a disease was taking hold. She was seasick on the boat. All that is true, and we did not deceive ourselves about this. Pomeline alternated two looks that day, either terrible sad or strangely content.

As I remember this my thoughts push me through the window

in my mind and I am back there, on the boat, seeing again what really happened that day.

Pomeline is staring down the bay, the afternoon sun twinkling bright on the waves. I don't know how she can stand to look. *Purify*, as Jenny would say, *the blazing purification of the sun. Holy, holy, holy*. She's been repeating that all morning. Art and I haven't spoken a word to her. I prefer not to look at Jenny for I see Marigold staring at me instead. She keeps her hands folded together. I keep hoping she learned her lesson, that when you set a trap you sometimes get the wrong thing caught in it.

Art asked me how I was while we waited at the wharf as they loaded our camping gear. We heard the adults talking about Hector—he would be in prison for a long time. Jenny slid over and said Hector got what he deserved, and we shouldn't feel bad. Art told her he didn't want to be no part of her games or her secrets or lies and he walked away. Hurt rippled across Jenny's face and was gone as quick as it come. Then we were on the boat. Norman Reilly took us out, a silver-haired man from a big family of fishermen, and his first mate, his eldest son. Norman knew my Grampie. He nods when I go by.

Sakura reassured us that we are not to blame—time would pass and the memory would fade, she said. The gulls cry overhead as they follow the boat. Even in the mist we know the water is calm and the boat glides onward.

The engine is cut. Harry is standing at the side looking into the fog and he calls out to the captain. "What's going on? Why have we stopped? Is there a problem? Are we lost?"

Norman is looking into the mist.

"What's he looking for? Is there a whale? Mechanical problem?" Harry speaks in a strained voice. He don't want no more worries, no more accidents. I know why we are stopped.

He keeps looking at me and his alarm makes me feel queasy so

I hold up my finger to my lips. "Shhhh," I say. "He's listening for the island."

Harry mulls it over. "Listening for the island . . . does the island speak back?"

Norman tells him the island never stops speaking. He lets the quiet take over. Jenny's holding out her arms like she's doing a spell and we just ignore her. I know Norman and his son think she's just another crazy Parker.

I stand with sea legs as the boat sways. We hear seagulls crying and waves breaking on the shore. Norman goes back to the wheelhouse and the diesel engine roars to life. We begin to move forward and then to the west. After a short voyage, there she looms, the island, the mists swirling away, birds soaring as we circle around past massive, ancient cliffs, crevasses cleft deep into the stone running from the top of the island and dropping into the pounding waves. The island rises up in front of the boat, the northeast end the only part not surrounded by cliffs, where there is beach. To the left of the remains of the old fishing sheds is a saltwater pond that rises and falls with the tide. At the end of the pond there's a long rocky spit slithering out into the water, riptides raging where the massive currents of the bay collide.

It's a hard landing. A wind has come up the bay on the incoming tide and the waves are heaving mountain peaks. Norman struggles to keep the boat steady as his son lowers the dory in the churning water. He and Harry load in our gear. Norman says we might want to consider coming back to shore with him as the weather seems moody. Harry scoffs at the suggestion. The son and Harry row to shore and are almost dumped out there on the rocky barrier beach.

Harry is now waiting on shore, his arms wrapped tightly around his body, concerned as the dory lurches back. The rest of us pile in, and we are almost thrown from the boat, feet soaking wet, except for Jenny in her rubber boots, who is tossed off the boat and into Harry's arms. He sets her on the beach and she scampers away. Jenny stands at the top of the steep beach watching us as we haul the gear up. She don't help. Even Pomeline, with her sore fingers, reaches for a bag. Art bats her hand away gently and she staggers up beside Jenny. Neither of them move, staring off over our heads, the island looming behind them as though they're waiting for a photographer to snap a picture.

The engine revs and the boat heads off into the fog, and we are alone. The four of us are gathering up gear, me and Art and Harry and Sakura. Jenny starts singing. I look over and notice something else behind her and Pomeline. Small, disfigured, all in white, and I know it's that thing I saw in the labyrinth, what I had been glimpsing all summer. It's hard to see through the gusting mists. It disappears and there's nothing but two sisters.

Jenny comes scuttling back down, and finally she grabs a bag, Harry's knapsack he'd set down on the rocks. She loses her balance and drops the pack. She falls on the beach as it splashes in the water. Harry is angry, the first time I seen him this way, his face white, biting his lip. He's sick as a ghoul with Jenny. He's fed up with children. He grabs the pack out of the water. When we get up top of the beach to the campsite Harry spreads the gear out and the walkie-talkie radio doesn't work. The batteries are soaked, and so are the extras he brought, and his camera. Harry starts swearing at himself for putting all his gear in one bag. He had no idea it would be such a difficult beach, such a hard landing. To the south, away from the water, it's a whole other world, sheltered, the trees a living fortification. To the north, the water spews violently onto rocks. And off to the east, the beach covered in a mass of driftwood, overlooking the lagoon.

We never talked about how hard it was walking up that beach, how the rocks would roll and shift as though the island was trying to keep us off. We didn't talk neither about the ghost stories of the island, and how just setting foot there was a bad, bad idea. You get your warnings and you heed them or you don't. We did not. All this is the same as before, I swear it is, except for what I saw behind the Parker girls. Art does ask me what's troubling me while we are sitting on a log as Harry continues to curse.

Harry has his hands on his hips and he's looking around at where we're going to set up the tents. Then he looks at me. "Fancy," he says, "you look like you've seen the dead." I jump up and say I'm going up to the top of the island. I'm bored, I tell Harry. But that's a lie . . . I want to find that white thing, and there's no use pretending otherwise.

Harry says we'll just make do without the camera, and the radio. Norman will be back to get us tomorrow at lunchtime anyway. Jenny apologizes, saying she was just trying to help. Then she can't resist adding that Harry didn't pack well for a seasoned camper, and he yells at her. That much happened. Pomeline lifts her finger to her lips at Jenny, which clearly infuriates her. Sakura tells Harry he's taking out his feelings on the kids—he has to get control. She waves us away and says to come back for supper and to be safe, to stay away from the cliffs. Then Sakura trips and sprains her ankle. She sits on a stump and elevates her leg while Harry does deep breathing and hisses in the same way Jenny's swans did. This is true, that the grown-ups on our trip lost control.

Art and I are the guides. We are the ones who have been here before with Grampie. Jenny was never allowed. The air is pungent, almost tropical, thick with wild mint and dewberry. We move into the thick turquoise light. Up we go, up to the tippity-top, the path coming out into what had been a hayfield. It has gone wild, with grasses up to our chests. We push ahead, through a cluster of whispering aspens. We can see it then, off to the west, the tall metal skeleton of the automated lighthouse. The outbuildings have fallen down. Nothing's left but the stone foundations. Jenny crawls up a disintegrating stone wall and over into what was the cellar, now just a jumble of rusted metal and blackened wood. If you pawed around you could find pieces of melted glass, warped and deformed from the raging fire. There is an array of chirps coming from the green. The late-summer raspberries are growing up through the wreckage. Jenny picks a handful.

I hold up my hand to her, like Loretta. "Don't eat them, Jenny. Ground's covered in mercury from the Fresnel lens in the lighthouse that melted in the fire." Pomeline looks over but she says nothing.

Jenny sticks out her tongue.

"Don't be a fool," Pomeline says. She says the word *fool* slow, turning it into a waterfall of sound. She walks over and reaches out, those stiff long fingers opening slowly.

Jenny gives them berries to Pomeline, dropping them in her white hand. Pomeline eats them, one by one. Jenny's mouth drops open, like someone pulled a plug out of her jaw.

Art's arm reaches out to stop her. "What are you doing, Pomeline?"

"There can't be that much mercury."

"Do you think that's wise?" he asks hopelessly.

Jenny screams out of nowhere, "You're just being weird like you've been all summer, upsetting everyone except poor Dr. Baker, him fawning all over you. Why did you have to turn bad like the rest of them? Why did you betray me? I trusted you but you were not trustworthy. You're just like our mother but you were supposed to be different. You ruined everyone's summer. We saw you in the Annex!"

Pomeline rubs her hands together, careful with her injured one. "There's nothing I can do now. I can't change the past. Grown-ups should know better, shouldn't they? Well, I am not as grown up as I thought, Jenny. They never let me be a child. It was always you getting all the attention, and no matter how well I did, no one cared, not after Daddy died."

Jenny opens her mouth. "That's—"

Pomeline growls at her sister. "Don't you dare interrupt me. You listen. Even he changed before he died, as though he couldn't stand to look at me. And it took a long time to understand why. So don't you dare tell me I ruined everyone's summer. Do you think I wanted this, for things to turn out this way?" Pomeline sniggers. She's never done that before.

A seagull circles overhead and squawks. She storms off through another thicket, heading to the wooden helicopter landing pad. The wind is gentle then, sweet with Queen Anne's lace and evening primrose. I look around at all the alders growing, how the island is taking it all back except for that metal skeleton lighthouse. Jenny runs after Pomeline, her white frock flipping up. It would have made a nice painting, her hair swinging, the wildflowers, big periwinkle sky, running apparently carefree. She disappears in the alders. Jenny is yelling at first, and then almost hissing. Pomeline answers in a calm voice, but from where we are Art and I can't make out the words.

A shadow falls over Art and me down in the stone-walled cellar of the lighthouse and we both whip around. There's Jenny, her hands at her chest, with a rose in her fingers. She takes a deep breath and lets it out, saying my name—*Fancy Mosher, Fancy Mosher*—like I'm a fairy tale she's remembering where wolves eat the girl in red and damsels get locked up in towers and smash on the rocks when they let down their long hair. Jenny lifts her hands to the sky, then waves them around as she mutters. "Let's play tag," Jenny says.

Art crosses his arms. "So all's resolved and better between you and your sister?"

"Pomeline is being unpleasant like she says I am. She apologized. But sometimes you can say sorry five times and backwards but it's too late."

We should have known it wasn't right. But they were both off, as Art had been saying, just a few steps over from normal, so it all seemed almost right but not quite.

We walk over to the landing pad where Pomeline is sitting, her eyes closed, soaking up the sun. "Isn't it peaceful?" she says. "You can forget all your cares, as Granny would say, and let them blow away."

I run back over to the lighthouse then and climb up. The metal is fiery from the sun, and halfway up the breeze blows strong and nippy. At the very top there are metal bars over the ladder making a cage to keep you safe. I peer out. The island swirls in mist, as though we're on a mountain. The three of them are minuscule down there, Jenny waving, Pomeline gazing up with her hand shading her eyes, Art putting his hands to his mouth and singing up, just a trace of the song weaving on the currents of the air. It's early evening but we still have time before the sun will start to sink.

"Come down," Jenny screams, hopping about.

Down I go, back into the heady air. Art's at the bottom, and he climbs up as soon as I come down. I sit with Pomeline.

We don't have to wait long for Art to come down. He doesn't linger. "Jeeze, I got vertigo up there."

Then Pomeline is climbing the lighthouse, her dress flying out behind her as the wind picks up. She's sluggish, taking her time with her hands, her stiff fingers.

"Pomeline, we need to be getting down to the campsite." I cup my hands around my mouth and yell it again but she don't look down. I run over with Jenny and Art behind me. Jenny starts screaming that she should stop acting foolish and get off the lighthouse and come down and she is the worst sister ever and she needs to grow up. I'm scared, for Pomeline is ignoring us.

"I know," Jenny yells up at her.

Pomeline looks down.

"I know," Jenny yells again. Then she whispers it, and looks at me. "I know."

Pomeline continues climbing. Jenny has a stomping fit.

"I said come down here. Please, come down. I said please. What more do you want?"

Jenny reaches in her bag. She is furious. No one will ignore her. She takes out a rock she grabbed down at the campsite and she pulls back her arm and hurls it up. Somehow she manages to hit Pomeline in the leg just as she's lifting her foot to the next rung. Pomeline slips and both her feet dangle. She catches herself with her one strong hand and the other stiff one and then she rests on the steel rungs. She turns around, ever so slow, jerky, and faces us, her hands on the sides of the ladder. We can see she is in pain. For a moment I think she's going to jump. Art and Jenny both gasp at the same time. Pomeline shakes her leg a bit before she puts it back down.

It's hard remembering. It seemed we stood forever on the stone edge of the foundation as we looked up. Jenny had that same expression again, angry with herself for not doing what she thought she was supposed to.

Pomeline came down step by step.

Jenny was wheezing. "My turn."

"You aren't strong enough, Jenny." Pomeline was rubbing her leg but she didn't say anything about the rock to Jenny. Neither did Art or me. We was all afraid of Jenny by then. Art and I waited for her to throw a fit. I suppose Pomeline was waiting too. But Jenny just clasped her hands together. The evening sun was falling on her then, and on Pomeline, pink and gold, gilding their faces.

"Harry will be wondering where we are. He said to be back down before supper." I sounded like Loretta. "We gotta head down. It will be getting dark in the woods."

Pomeline reached her hand over to Jenny, stroking her hair, her hand lingering overtop of Jenny's face.

Jenny pushed Pomeline aside and stood up. "I know you're just looking out for me, Pommie. That's what sisters do. Let's play hide-and-seek. You're it," she said. "You were always it."

Pomeline put her fingers, bent and swollen, over her eyes. "One, two, three . . ." She sang the numbers.

We ran through the field to the trees. I suppose we should have fought Jenny on the idea of playing games since we were due back at camp. Pomeline came strolling. We could hear her dress brushing through the grass, and a cardinal sang out. I should have called to mind the drop-off. Pomeline kept going. It was sunny in the meadow surrounded by trees, with an opening in front and beyond that mist on the high grasses.

"Drop-off," I finally did scream. We ran out of our hiding spot. By then Pomeline was over the edge and I stopped dead in my tracks, throwing my arms out. Art smashed into me and Jenny fell forward. I grabbed her just in time and all three of us fell to the last bit of ground near the cliff's edge.

Pomeline did not simply plummet down, hitting her head on the rocks as she fell, the wild waves smashing her against the cliff and carrying her body away. That was the lie we told.

Jenny was on the ground in front of me, Art behind me. Pomeline was dangling from the root of a gnarly fir tree. I got down flat and crawled forward an inch. I saw Pomeline's eyes then, and her long, slender arms trying to hold her body up, the good hand clenched and that damaged hand trembling. Pomeline's teeth bit right through her lip as she forced her fingers to tighten around the root.

"Hang on," I yelled. "Hang on, Pomeline." She stared straight ahead, every bit of her concentrated on that root. We were up so unnaturally high. Waves were crashing on the rocks below and the surging water roared.

Art's hands closed tight over my ankles. "I got you, Fancy. Hold Jenny. She can reach Pomeline."

I clutched hard on Jenny's legs. She took hold of Pomeline's arm with both of her strong little hands and she squeezed. "I've got you, Pomeline," she said. "I've got you. Let go of the root and then we can pull you up."

Pomeline looked at me, not Jenny. She was terrified. "Grab hold," I yelled at her. "Grab hold of Jenny with both hands,

Pomeline. Holy Mother Mercy, would you just let go of the root and hang on to your sister?" My heart hammered as Pomeline gasped in and out, watching Jenny.

Art was trying to soothe her, his voice calm but his hands shaking terribly as he held my ankles. "Please, Pomeline, let go and hold onto Jenny and we will pull you up."

Jenny squeezed Pomeline's arm tighter.

"I got you, Fancy," Art said again. "Haul Jenny back. Right now."

The waves were smashing and thudding below as though the sea was banging a giant drum. But Pomeline wouldn't let go, no sir, she kept holding on to that root. Her eyes were bulging with fear. Finally her hand came free, one held by Jenny and the other waving in the air now.

Art gave another huge pull and Pomeline shifted. She started pleading. "No, no, please, Jenny," she begged, as Art strained to hold me and I clutched Jenny's bony ankles. Art and I were shrieking at Jenny to pull her sister up but it was as though she was frozen. And then this dreadful feeling came over me that Jenny was laughing, not trembling.

"You don't know," Pomeline said.

Jenny straightened out her fingers and her hand was wide open and empty.

Pomeline plummeted through the air and disappeared into the fog, her screams ripped to shreds by the wind.

The dull light of the sun softened our haggard faces as we turned to lie on our backs, and the breeze smelled of smashed flowers and grass. Jenny closed her eyes and a few tears slid down over her temples. Her kerchief was gone now, her wispy hair tangled in the grass. Art put his arm around me. There were scratches on his wrists and I saw the crushed pasture rose bushes behind him.

Jenny was the first one to crawl away from the cliff. We followed suit, though my legs felt like jelly. I started howling at her. Art was crying.

"You told her to let go," Jenny whispered. "You shouldn't have done that." She pointed at me. "You should have warned her about the drop-off."

Art stepped forward. "Okay, okay, it was an accident. It must have been an accident. It wasn't your fault that you couldn't hold her."

Jenny brushed off her dress as if she'd been doing some work in the garden. It was stained with dirt and grass, ripped in a few spots. "You didn't do anything to help, Art. It's your fault. You shouldn't have told her to let go, Fancy."

We kept arguing in circles, interrupted only by our sobs. Jenny said that if we told on her she'd say I had squeezed her ankles, that Art had shaken me and her, that it was our fault entirely for she was too weak and helpless. We'd be locked up in an institution for juvenile delinquents and never see the outside again, for they'd experiment on our brains. It was true—we was implicated. It would be our downfall, for it would make no sense if we tried to explain. We had both begged Pomeline to let go. But we could have never imagined that Jenny would do what she did. I had seen the truth in Pomeline's despairing eyes, that Jenny did indeed let go of Pomeline's arm and let her tumble down a cliff. Jenny insisted she didn't mean to do it, and we wanted so badly to believe her. Maybe that's why we took that vow—we were children, and children could not be that wicked. If we said nothing, if we protected Jenny, she might be able to come back from whatever dark place she was caught in, a place she had swept us to as well.

We moved through the forest shaking and silent all the way back to camp, where Harry waited with Sakura. About halfway down the steep trail tremendous rains came pelting from the sky, and the fierce gusts almost knocked us over as a thunder and lightning storm moved in—the first one we'd seen all summer.

They sent out a helicopter and a boat for us when Sakura discovered spare radio batteries, but they could not find Pomeline's body anywhere in the turbulent ocean. It was swept away. It was this that began to stalk us, a shadow that grew longer with each year that passed—the kind of shadow that belongs to the dead who have come to call.

9.

The Dark Rolling Deep

My belief that facing the truth concerning Pomeline's death would end the madness was mistaken. It did the exact opposite. The sounds coming from all corners of the mansion seemed much louder—each creak, the hum of the refrigerator, the drip in the sink and the wind outside. When I would busy myself with housework I'd then hear a quiet singing, but the singing would end at the exact same time I stopped my work to listen closely. Pomeline had followed us back to Petal's End. There was no other explanation. Jenny was right. Art could go on pretending but I was finished with that.

It was late and Art and Jenny still weren't back from the hospital. Art finally called and said they'd be there all night doing tests. "If Estelle calls," he said, "just tell her Jenny's sleeping. Tell her to call Raymond Delquist if she's got anything to say." He didn't tell me much more. There was a moment when he asked if I was okay where I wanted to say *We need to talk about the island*, but before I could utter a word came a soft click . . . what sounded like someone picking up the receiver somewhere in the house. There was a prolonged silence on the phone line while Art waited for me to reply and I listened to my own heavy breathing.

"Fancy?" Art said.

"Well, goodbye then," I said to him, and hung up.

Shaking and raw, I went to the front of the house. The phone was where it always was, in the parlour on a table, where it remains to this day. The receiver was on the hook. I picked it up and put it to my ear. "Hello?" I trilled. "Hello, hello," like I was answering myself. It was my brain from drinking again, I told myself, no question about it. My little girl came through the window in my mind then. I could hear her laughter, feel her delicate hands. I saw Pomeline falling over and over in the mist.

I was overcome with dread that my mind was collapsing. It seemed the past was slipping out of my eyes and taking form in front of me. My screams snapped down the hall, an endless rope cracking out and snaking through all the corridors and over stairs, then back at me from every corner of the house. Suddenly I was running in the kitchen and there was Melissa looking at me with great big dark water eyes. It was a mirror I was staring in. I took to laughing. My lips were moving, the lips on the Fancy Mosher in the mirror, and I peered up right close, put my fingers on those cold lips, and they were whispering *Grampie, Grampie, come and help me*. His voice singing *Hear the wind blow, love, hear the wind blow* and I don't know if he was singing in my memories or if his voice was coming right out of my lips. *Hang your head o'er and hear the wind blow.* I closed my eyes and hung my head down and his voice was ringing in my ear. *On wings of the wind o'er the dark rolling deep*. There was breath on my neck, and the soothing balm of turpentine and beeswax. I felt his fingers gentle on my shoulder. *Angels are coming to watch o'er thy sleep*. My eyes opened and I was hoping he'd be there behind me, his hand on my shoulder, but there was only me in the mirror.

I was resting in my bed still hearing Grampie's voice but I didn't trust it. Just what sort of messenger would be standing over me if I fell to sleep? I prayed out loud for Holy Mother Mercy to come and relieve me, to guard me. Far off I could hear the wind bells in Evermore, and then a breath smelling of decaying flowers brushed my lips as a dark shape leaned over me. But before I saw what it was, the night closed in and took me away.

10.
The Lady on the Beach

IT WAS them birds that woke me the hell up. Before my eyes were even open I heard chirping and I thought how I'd like to shoot them out of the branches. I was acutely aware I was turning into Ma, with a thought like that. She didn't never see a thing wrong with killing something for food, or if it was eating your food. Right before the car accident there was a groundhog in the garden eating up her lettuce and she shot it dead. If she had just the right amount of drinks in her to stop her hand shaking, she had a deadly aim.

Drinking was the least of my worries right then. It was early dawn, when the light was still thick and dark. The bed spun and I fell asleep again, my fear lessened knowing the night was over. I closed my eyes and it was like Grampie was still singing to me, and this time I believed his words. Melissa's pink sweater was in my hands as his voice became my voice and I sang my daughter her lullabies, the same songs Grampie sung to me. Then it was late morning.

The curtains weren't shut and I looked out. The thing was there, on the grass, and then on the path to the kitchen door. Then it was gone. It only took me a moment to fly down all them cold wooden steps and I stopped when I reached the kitchen, feeling like I'd been kicked in the gut. There was a colossal bouquet of flowers on the table. And in the main house, in the front hall, another huge vase. I gathered them up and ran out the back door to find petals scattered about, as though we was about to have a ceremony. I took my armfuls of flowers and tossed them in the humus pile. On the way back to the house it seemed a thousand eyes were upon me. I kept waiting for that horrid thing in white to peep out, but it did not. I didn't know what was worse—seeing it and being terrified, or not seeing it and thinking I was crazy.

At first, pretending things was normal seemed like it might fix everything up. I made coffee. I made biscuits and I hummed and whistled the whole time, every song I knew, keeping the creaks away. And yes, it seemed like there was something else in the house singing and whispering. I'd run down the halls screaming for it to come out but there would be only silence. Then when I'd go back to the kitchen I would hear it again.

Twice I went up to Jenny's room. I could hear it in there, breathing heavily, warbling. The first time I snuck up the stairs and down the hall the door was closed, and I put my eye to the keyhole. There was a flash of white and I damn near pissed myself, but I was stubborn. I looked again and did not see a thing, but I heard the singing, and I rested my ear against the keyhole. The words were muffled and a puff of cold breath filled my ear. The glass doorknob rattled, and right before my eyes it began to turn, and my mouth opened to shriek and to this day I have no idea whether I did. The doorknob clicked. I wasn't waiting to see what might pop out to throttle me. I grabbed that doorknob and pushed the door open with all my force. The window was wide open and air blew in, the white curtains dancing. You try at moments like that to tell yourself it was the curtains and the breeze. You cling to any explanation, anything so you don't have to believe. I felt a rush of relief as I stood in the room.

Just as my heart rate was finally coming down, the doorknob swivelled when my hand was not on it and that click was more like a bang, and yet again nothing materialized. Art and Jenny were playing a trick on me. That was the reason for all of this. It was a punishment for refusing to help them with my memento.

I ran back up to my room and I took out Melissa's pink sweater and the embroidery I did for her—but they'd gone and messed with it. I couldn't imagine Art would do this, torment me so. The pictorial I did for my daughter to hang in her room—Jenny had gone and changed it. There was the house and all them flowers in the garden and such a peaceful babbling brook and ducks paddling, and butterflies in the air, but in the water there was a girl, a little girl with dark hair and a cute dress, face down and legs and arms fanned out. There was a man kneeling by the edge of the brook and his face was screwed into a scream. Jenny went and made it a horror show. It felt like it was burning my fingers.

I put it down and went through the upstairs hall connecting the back to the main house, through the door and over the carpet back to Jenny's room. The door was open but the windows were somehow closed and the white curtain hung still. Her big wardrobe, which was kept locked, loomed over me. It wouldn't open. I pulled and pulled on the door but it would not budge. So I went out to the carriage house and I got an axe. There's lots of things you learn growing up with a wood stove and one of them is how to use an axe, and yes, I did, I chopped my way right through that door.

I took out the photo albums Jenny had been working on and I opened one to find black-and-white photos, a young woman in what they called a bathing costume, a short sleeveless dress with bloomers. She had on a swimming cap that looked like a bonnet. She had won a prize ribbon. She stood by a big pool. It was a very young Marigold. My ears filled up as though I was crashing through the air. Marigold had said she couldn't swim. It was why John Lee drowned. There wasn't a thing she could have done, she said. But she lied. I threw the album down.

I jumped then, for Art was standing in the bedroom door with Jenny beside him. She hobbled over to her bed. "I need a nap," she said, as though it was just another day and I was having a little episode there on the floor. Jenny looked at the axe and the broken door, and then at me. She perked up and cleared her throat as though she had just remembered she was supposed to deliver a sermon.

"He was my grandfather's son. John Lee was my uncle. The Colonel couldn't keep his hands off the maids. That's what my grandmother told me as she lay there in the nursing home. She thought she was making her confession to me, that telling me would set her free. 'Forgive an old lady,' Granny said. 'You and I are the only ones who understand how important the time-worn ways are, Agatha. We are the only real Parkers. We have a duty.' She thought I'd feel badly for her, of course. That Marilyn Mosher was such a temptress. That's the word she used. As if it was your mother's fault. But Marilyn was just a teenager, Fancy. She didn't know better. That's what I told Granny. She was crippled up lying in the bed, looking pathetic, but she still didn't want to die. Can you imagine that? She refused to accept that her time had passed. Her shock that I felt compassion for a piece of poor white trash like Marilyn Mosher. She felt a bit of remorse later, but she still felt justified, vindicated. She thought she'd righted something unnatural—your brother. That crumb of remorse . . . that's why she let Loretta have you here."

Art went over to the bed. "You really should just stop talking and get some rest." He was starting to cry. Jenny was not through holding forth.

"No, Art, I want to tell you both. It must be illuminated. My grandmother couldn't see what all this meant, that we, in fact, were unnatural. We were the abomination. Granny thought showing her mercy to Marilyn would put things in their natural order. That's why she did what she could for your Grampie. Because she could fool herself. She even fooled herself when I came in with her precious botanicals, and she drank what I gave her. I needed to make sure she would never recover. It took Granny a few weeks to figure out what was making her feel bad, but by then it was too late to do anything. Poor old lady, sick and breathless, like stupid Margaret was. You remember that, Fancy?"

I stood up from where I'd been sitting on the floor, and my cheeks burned. Jenny held my eyes.

"They were just the same, those two, so vain. I remember near the end whispering into Granny's ears that the white flower bells were ringing but it wasn't fairies she was going to hear singing on the other side. Her eyes were popping out of her head. They thought I was dry-eyed at her funeral because of my condition, but even if I could have cried I would have had no tears for that wicked woman. Guilt never repairs anything, does it? I did not feel badly for her. I do not feel badly for any of them."

Art started to speak, and Jenny cut through the air with her arm. "I am not finished, Art. Don't cut me off. I am not dead yet. Someone must restore the natural order, I realized. What I felt looking at her was horror over what I did to Pomeline, how I made you two go along with me. We were children. My grandmother was not a child. She was selfish, just as my mother is. They smelled it on each other. And my mother can smell it on me. I reek of it. I am no longer a child. I'm the only Parker left."

Jenny collapsed back onto her bed, dry weeping, looking for relief when there was none to be had, and her hands dug into the bedding, hanging on tight as though she might fall.

Art stepped forward then. "Jenny is exhausted. They sent her back home. There's no hope. She's on a new medication to help with the pain. That's all they can do for her now. It's making her delusional."

Jenny waved at him. "I'm not delusional, Art. How deep is your denial? Aren't you the psychologist?" she hissed, and her anger seemed to steady her as she sat back up on the bed.

I was too confused to process what they was saying. It was in one ear, out the other. I held up the embroidery picture of Melissa. "You don't have to go and ruin me and my daughter just because you want to destroy your whole family. What did we ever do to you that you'd change my picture like this? You just tell me what. Even dying young don't give you the right, Jenny Parker, to go and wreck things so everyone has to suffer. There ain't enough suffering in all the world to satisfy your thirst for it."

"I didn't change anything. You're the crazy one, Fancy. I don't know what you're talking about. I'm trying to make things right. I am trying to confess."

"It's just the way you are looking at things that is changing, Fancy. Your mind is clearing," Art said.

"Oh stop with your psychology, Art!" I shrieked. "The only thing that's changed is I got no patience no more, not for any of you. Look what you done to Melissa. You put her in the stream face down. You want everybody dead. You are suffering because of your mother and whatever she took that went and made you all cancerous and deformed in your organs, Jenny. But that's not my fault. You want us all to *suffer* just because you suffer. You're no different than Ma. You're jealous because Grampie gave me the memento and no one else, but I ain't using it, not to make selfish people like you and my mother happy. No, I am not." My throat hurt, as though I'd breathed the smoke of a thousand beach fires, fires burning up the words of a thousand ghost stories. The rage was all through me, deep in my bones. I pointed at Jenny and I could feel a vibration in my fingertips.

She drew back, but then softened, like she was suddenly feeling terrible sorry for me. She was up and down like the tides. Out crawled her low, raspy voice. "Fancy, Art saw your mother. She's in the hospital. Ronald was there in the lobby. Isn't that what you said, Art? You should go and see her. She doesn't have long. I've been telling you all summer and you act as though you don't hear." Jenny started coughing.

Right then I decided I should go and make peace with my Ma. That or be just like Jenny and spend the rest of my life senseless with regret.

11.
I Found You in a Picture

RONNIE WAS outside the hospital having a smoke. "Well, looky who decided to think of someone other than herself." Ronnie took a hard drag on his cigarette, sucking it right down to the filter. He dropped it on the ground and crushed it under his heel. He sized me up with a look that offered no mercy. "Fancy Mosher, come to see your mother? Look at all the trouble you caused her. I wish when she had that car accident that you'd been thrown clear and hit a tree so hard that was the end of you. But you're like an earwig, Fancy Mosher. You don't stop crawling no matter how hard life stamps you down. Marilyn tried her best for you. Tried helping you with your baby. Tried helping you in the hospital. But you just had to have your own way. At least your mother could admit what she did, but look at you . . . still hiding out in your goddamned fantasy land so you don't never have to grow up and take responsibility like your mother did. If you come to give her even a bit of grief, you turn right around and march your ass back over the mountain to Petal's End and rot away with those two other freaks."

Ronnie hocked and spit out a big yellow glob and wagged his finger right in my face.

"You were born strange, just like them Parkers. And don't you go telling me it's your mother's fault. I knew Marilyn like no one else ever knew her. I always loved the woman. I waited my entire life for her."

He went white because he realized he was talking about her like she was already gone. I knew then Jenny and Art weren't just trying to get me out of the house. Ronnie cried like Jenny, no tears coming out of his eyes.

"None of you appreciated her. And your Grampie weren't the saint you like to believe. Not that I believe in any of that horseshit, but he could have at least pretended and give the woman some peace. And you, you could have done the same. She's up there now believing to her dying breath that her dead baby boy's going to eat her alive when she passes." A great large noise come out of him, this big whooping sob. He sucked it right back in and waved me away without letting me say a word.

People were looking at me as I ran through the hospital corridors but it made no difference. On the ward an attendant took me to her room. He asked when the last time was I seen Marilyn. He couldn't hide his shock when I said not for six months. She was gravely, gravely ill, and I should prepare myself. The cancer was all through her now.

I took a deep breath and went in. The room was full of the prettiest bouquets. Ma lay in the bed and didn't her eyes open wide. She'd gone yellow. She held out her hand and I went to her crying like a child. She comforted me as the dying always comfort the living.

Ma took my hand and said they took a biopsy off her liver. "When will you get the results?" I asked.

"Fancy, I ain't getting out of here. There's no getting better for me."

"Sure you are, Ma," I said. Ma always got better. She was like me, an earwig. She didn't never die, no matter how hard you stomped. She stroked my cheek with a puffy finger. Though she hadn't been smoking there was a faint smell of nicotine soaked into her flesh.

"I did you a picture," I told her. Out of my purse I took her needlepoint wrapped in a towel. I unwrapped it for her, shaking because it had changed—it wasn't a lady bending over, making a bed with a little boy beside her. It was a lady lying on a bed, and she had a yellow face, and there was a boy holding her hand. Ma started crying in such a gentle way, and it plays in my ear even now, as though I've opened a music box.

"Oh Fancy, thank you. You saw John Lee. It was just me all these years wanting to change what happened, the old me just tormenting the life out of the younger me. The past don't change—just how we look at it." She paused. "You're the one who needs to know how sorry your Mama is, Honeysuckle. Your Grampie was right taking you away, giving you a chance, because I couldn't do it."

I held her hand and kissed it. Then I took out my embroidery of Melissa by the little brook and showed her how Melissa was lying with her face in the water, how Jenny went and wrecked it. I burst into tears.

"It's okay, Fancy baby," she said. "You did the best you could. Accidents happen, terrible, terrible accidents, and we can't take them back. If the dead come looking for you maybe all they want is for you to let them go." She pulled me close and we stayed like that for a moment, until I heard Ronnie clear his throat. I didn't even know he'd come in the room. A nurse come in next and Ma cradled my head. "It don't matter now, Fancy," she said. "John Lee forgives me. I see from your picture, and he'll be there to greet me. You found your gift, Fancy, in your pictures." She sang faintly and I could just make out the words, *Baby's boat the silver moon, sailing in the sky.*

Ma gave a soft moan and the nurse said she needed her meds. It was time to leave. "Farewell," I whispered, but she didn't open her eyes. Ronnie nodded at me. It was the best he could ever do.

The sun was setting in the west by the time I was driving up and over the mountain. A sultry breeze blew in as I looked over to the island. Long shadows fell on the road. There was no consolation for me.

I understood now it wasn't Jenny who went and changed my needlework. It was like that the whole time. I would check the others as soon as I got to Petal's End. That kept hammering through my head as the car came down the hill into Lupin Cove. I drove over the bridge and turned up the road and at last down the long lane to Petal's End. It was dark in the forest and the car headlights shone a dim beam directly in front. A deer ran into the road and stood there glaring at me. I slammed on the brakes and squeezed my eyes shut. There was a crackling of branches as the deer moved on, and I opened my eyes. That ghastly white thing was right on the hood of the car gawking at me, its fingers scraping against the glass windshield, long stringy hair, grimy and dirty. It was too dark to make out its features but I could hear its piercing singing through the open window. It was Pomeline, I was sure. She had come back to punish us.

My foot pressed hard on the gas and the car lurched ahead, throwing the creature into the ditch with limbs flailing. I screeched into Petal's End and parked in front of the big house. Art came out on the verandah and folded me into his arms, and I whispered that Jenny was right, Pomeline had come back to get us. It was her opening the windows and cutting flowers and laying out petals.

She was furious we were lying. She'd make us tell the truth, each one of us.

"It's bedtime, Fancy," he said, patronizing me. "I shouldn't have let you go down to the hospital alone. I'm sorry. I'm not thinking straight. None of us are."

I had no time for this and brushed past him right into the sitting room, turning on all the lights as I went. I wanted to see my pictures, but none of them were there, where I had kept them. I ran down the hall to the Annex. The door had been unlocked and opened, inviting me in, terrorizing me. Art was behind me and he kept telling me to calm down, that I needed to have a nice cup of tea, he'd make me a pot. It was all overwhelming, he said, too much for me, too many people passing away. He started crying, and I realized I was as well.

I turned back then and went right up the stairs, taking them two by two even in my high-heeled shoes. Down the hall, Jenny's door was wide open and she was reading by lamplight. Art was behind me still saying I needed to just take a time-out. Jenny placed her bookmark and closed the book. She was waiting for me.

"Why didn't you tell me earlier about what Marigold did if you knew for so long? That John Lee was your uncle, that your Granny let him drown?" I was sobbing.

"Oh, *now* you listen to me," Jenny said. "She killed him. She stood there and watched a child drown. It's no different than if she had shot him in the head. It's no different than letting Pomeline fall down over the cliff. And it's no different than how Granny stood there as my father died. Remember? When you came down the hall and found us? My father was wiggling around like a helpless spider caught in a web. My grandmother did nothing. I was too young, too weak, to help. Even so, when I rushed toward him she stood in front of me, and her strong arms scooped me up like I was nothing more than a kitten rolled up in a quilt. She screamed and cried, yelling at Daddy that it was his fault for not being the right kind of son. He was to blame for not being a real man like his father wanted him to be. It was his fault John Lee died because she did it all for him, but he was like the rest—ungrateful. He had wasted the life she gave him with his perversions. Being stupid enough to marry Estelle, letting his father down.

"Daddy finally stopped moving. I kicked Granny in the shin and ran free. I was trying to hold his legs up so he could breathe. But the dead can't breathe. Then you and Art came along and you found us." Jenny took a big breath of air, wheezing violently, then continued. "When Marigold was dying she told me that John Lee had come back for her, she could see him. It was him that tripped her in the gazebo, and she said that you saw him, too."

"But I didn't see him. I saw you. It was you." We was both hollering, and Art came right in the room and shouted for us to calm down. He was going to have us both committed to a mental hospital if we didn't get a hold of ourselves.

I needed answers. I ran back down to the Annex and right into the big room at the end where the curtains blew long and white. There was nothing but the wires in the ceiling, no chandelier any more, no Charlie Parker hanging with his eyes bulging. But on the walls Jenny had hung every embroidery picture I done, and they had all turned bad, every single one. I saw all my stitching, intricate and perfect, but they was all distorted now, serene pictures from a child's imagination turned into nightmares on display. Jenny had made the room into a revolting art gallery. The space had been many things over the years—a chamber of wrongdoing.

I looked at my embroidery of Grampie on his sofa, but he wasn't napping with his arms hanging down like they did. Grampie was lying there dead, in the same position I found him in, his arms crossed over his chest. The small miniature of Marigold wasn't of her napping but of her lying there dead. And there was Pomeline, but she wasn't sitting in a field of white flowers while we ran around laughing. She was falling through the mist as we thrashed about in the flowers screaming. Each a memento of a time to come.

While I am the one who can capture those moments, it is how each of us lives that guides the needle in my hand.

Art had come up behind me without me noticing. "We should go sit down and talk." He was desperate now, his low voice breaking.

He told me this was how they always looked, that my perspective was finally getting clearer, that being cooped up in this house alone was changing how I was able to comprehend. We were ignoring things because it was all we could do. Art looked exhausted as he went on about stress and lack of sleep and worry. I looked over at the embroidery of Jenny by the lily pond with her swans, and she was in a lawn chair in her kerchief with her eyes open, a pink flower in her hand. That one wasn't no different, at least, but it was the only one. I wondered why. I had a tantrum trying to figure out what I was seeing, and Art slapped me right across the cheek. My head flew back. My skin, my scar especially, was burning. There was stars in my eyes, but I was suddenly calm, like he'd knocked the panic out of me and what was left was a dull fear.

There was a thud. Art held his hand up to his lips, which at first I misread as guilt from hitting me. But his eyes revealed that he could hear it too, the steps in the hall, the wood creaking. Then running, and a bitter laugh, the door slamming. I threw on a light switch by the door and we hurried out in the darkness but there was nothing there. We heard a crash upstairs and ran up. Jenny was on the floor in her nightgown.

"Was that you running around down there, listening, spying?" She was groping for her glasses. I kicked them out of the way. "What kind of game are you playing, Jenny Parker?"

Art moved past me, picked up Jenny's glasses and handed them to her and helped her up. "We need to stop this," he said.

Then came that shrill singing and we all heard it, almost no tune, words we could not make out. Rushing into the hall, I pointed as a shimmer of white descended the stairs. It stopped, waiting there at the bottom in the semi-darkness. Art came out behind me with Jenny at his back, as fast as she could be with her cane, leaning on the door frame. "There," I said, pointing.

They looked and said in unison, "Where?"

They did not see, but they could hear it singing. Jenny furrowed her brow and listened closely to the words, and then she started singing almost perfectly along with it, ". . . *with one star awake, as the swan in the evening moves over the lake*."

"I've been hearing that song since I turned twelve," I said. "Whatever it is, it's at the bottom of the stairs singing. Can't you see it?"

They both shook their heads, but they kept their ears cocked. There was not a doubt in my mind that it was Pomeline.

As it disappeared, I put my hands to my eyes. It was time for me to face Pomeline. Art was shaking his head. He wanted me to stay in the house. But when he realized I would not stay, he said he wasn't going to let me go alone. He took a lantern from the kitchen and we went out outside.

I remember standing on the stepping stone mosaic made with the broken teacups. Art turned the lights on in Evermore. The door was closed, and that seemed to reassure him. He was still hoping it was stress that was breaking us—and that if it was closed nothing could have gone inside. Art opened the door. We walked along the path holding hands and we could both hear the loud tinkling of the glass wind bells. We heard the humming surround us, and Art kept shaking his head as though that might send the music off on the breeze. The night air was toasty but still I shivered, and my scar tingled. There were no lights near the pond but the bright moon reflected on the water. Art whispered that maybe it was just one of them wood creatures we had believed in when we were children. That was easiest to believe, I suppose, that a childhood story had come to life.

I left Art there on the path with his lantern and went down to the pond's edge. Bats ricocheted all about. In the moonlight I saw petals scattered on the water and I knelt down there on the bank. The humming all around me became song blending with the bells:

My love said to me, "My mother won't mind.
And my father won't slight you for your lack of kind."

That song I had heard so long ago in the Tea House, and in the Annex, the ballad Pomeline had been playing early that summer in the music room.

She stepped away from me, and she moved through the fair,
And fondly I watched her move here and move there.

Cold, vile-smelling breath blew on my neck and the scar on my face blazed as I sensed her lean forward over my shoulder.

And she went her way homeward, with one star awake,
As the swan in the evening moves over the lake.

"Pomeline," I said, "we're sorry for what happened. We were only children. You must go away. You can't stay here any more. You should never have let Dr. Baker touch you. That could only ever have led you to heartache, don't you see?" The breath was in my ear, relentless, unsettling. I heard Art calling to me as though he was far off in the brambles.

Last night she came to me, my dead love came in,
So softly she came that her feet made no din.

It came ever closer, and there was its image in the moonlit pond.

She came close beside me, And this she did say:
It is deep in the pond, the place where they'll lay.

There were gleaming ponds in its eyes, glassy pools with moons and white swans, and I saw then it was not Pomeline back from the dead to haunt us. A disfigured version of Jenny was reflected there, singing her lifeless tune. The swans came squawking out for me at that moment, as if on cue, and I stood up and turned to find nothing but Art back on the path, coming toward me, his voice clear and loud, the lantern swinging in his hand. We looked behind us and the mansion was completely illuminated, every room in the house. We ran back, screaming Jenny's name.

Jenny was in her room reading when we came rushing in, the same as before, as though she was expecting us for an appointment. I sat at the edge of her bed with Art. I did not know how to tell her it was not Pomeline who was haunting us, but Jenny herself, that she was that little white thing that had showed itself to me throughout the years. She was so unsettled in herself for all of her days that her spirit started rising early. I had told Art all this as we came in the house. And all the while I had been thinking of the man in the shade of the sugar maples at the Tea House the last two weeks before Grampie died. Grampie said in his letter it was the memento stirring in me, and I understood that now, the ghost of a ghost. Grampie had begun to rise, and, perhaps because I was a Mosher too, I had sensed him even as such a young girl.

I looked at the photographs Jenny had there on her bed. She'd taken them out of an album bound in black velvet. "This is what my mother has been looking for," Jenny said. She laughed grimly. "Granny must have taken them and tucked them away so no one could ever find them. That's why they were afraid of her. Now my mother knows I have them." Splayed out were unholy black-and-white photos of Dr. Baker and Estelle, much younger, naked and doing things in positions I had never imagined.

Art carefully pulled out Pomeline's journal. It had weathered poorly in the swan house, warped and mildewed from moisture. He tried to read it aloud but couldn't get words out. Art handed it to me. He and Jenny listened while I read. It wasn't no journal entry I was reading, but words to a song, lyrics, about a girl who found out that her love was a ruin, and poisonous, the girl whose baby was ill got. Her lover had spurned her, he had turned from her, had been with her mother, although he was her father, and the man who dangled, choked and tangled, was, *la la la*, not of her blood.

It was poetic, a ballad she might sing at the piano wearing a pretty summer dress as the piano keys tinkled the melody, but nothing could make sentimental the fact that Dr. Baker was her father, and the father of the baby that died with her when she crashed down in the surging waters and was bashed into them red rock cliffs. Jenny explained to us, as we sat there in utter shock, that Estelle never told Dr. Baker, and he was too wrapped up in himself to even think Pomeline wasn't Charlie's child. Estelle didn't let Pomeline know, at least not until the damage was done.

I thought of the Pomeline of that summer, the bright Pomeline who wilted before our eyes, with her drawn, tired face and tender stomach, the Pomeline with no one to turn to but three children who held her over the pounding waves and tossed her away into the sky.

There was a gust then at the window and the white lace curtains blew in and pulled out. Jenny gazed at the two of us with her big, pleading eyes. She did not know until it was too late that some things you can never take back. And we were only children. We renewed our pact in that dishevelled and cluttered room never to say a word about what happened so long ago. Pomeline was now a part of memory and the island and the moody water forever circling it. We linked our hands together and as we took our vows

Jenny whispered, *Peace on earth and mercy mild.* She took her hands away from us and clasped them to her heart.

We did not discuss that night. Raymond Delquist came over each day in the week that followed to meet with Jenny. She was getting weaker and was not expected to live beyond the autumn. On good days she could walk around, and on bad days she would lie in bed or sit in a chair. She was quiet in a way she had never been previous.

I still saw the thing in white. I could hear it singing in the night, and I could see it flitting through the garden in the twilight, and peering in the windows. But there was no longer fear, for I understood that some spirits who knew they would be passing would show themselves to me. Their stories would find their way into my bones and my fingers, and into my needle and onto the muslin. Quaint and final, once I put the last stitch down and encased it in a frame. This was the memento as it stirred and came to me.

They took Grampie's house, piece by piece. They rebuilt it in the art gallery in the city, the Tea House, even with his sign. They had a bench right outside the house, like it was on the lawn instead of in a gallery room. I went there once, watching people coming in and out, as though we'd never lived there, those Moshers who saw the dead. They took my embroideries too, and they called it *grotesque art*.

The one of Jenny and her mother and Dr. Baker by the pond in Evermore is in the exhibit. No one but Art knew it was stitched before they found them there. I sat on that bench and looked at it on the white wall beside our little house now in this big stone art gallery in the city. While the ghosts of ghosts found their way into my needle, in all my years holding the memento it was only ever Grampie and Jenny who I saw beyond my pictorials. Perhaps

Grampie's war horrors and Jenny's childhood malady and agony conjured up some part of them seeking witness to their lives and suffering . . . and to their end. I thought of the day of my mother's funeral, when we come back to Petal's End after she was put in the ground. I stood by Art on that late-August afternoon when the sun was already far around in the sky. I wore a black dress from the closet at Petal's End and I wore black everyday thereafter, to remind me we have to fear but what we let hide in the shadows. We threw dirt on Ma's coffin and we laid down flowers by her tombstone beside John Lee and my grandparents. We left Ronnie there, alone, as he wanted to be. Jenny paid for the tombstone but she did not want to come to the graveyard.

Down the dirt road we drove back to Petal's End. For a moment I thought I could hear Ma saying not to call her fucking Mrs. Mosher, and Jenny reciting her peculiar chants, and I glimpsed that white thing in the white dress with the hands clasped, standing by the side of the road as we turned into Petal's End. Lifting her head, and eyes full of the pond, swans and ripples. Art said later I spoke out as though in a pulpit, proclaiming, *There ain't nothing mild about mercy . . . when you call for Holy Mother Mercy she don't always come alone. In the shadow of her skirts comes Sweet Sister Vengeance.*

When we come through the wildwood, back from the funeral, there were petals from the house to Evermore, the path laid out, and Dr. Baker's car was parked there in the driveway, the keys still in the ignition, as though the car was waiting to be moved back by the carriage house. We ran across that trail of petals, crushing them into the grass and gravel. The door to Evermore was locked from the inside. Art got a ladder so we could go over the top and then down from a tree. We followed the petals to the pond.

Jenny was in a lawn chair, her eyes open behind her glasses. There was a teacup broken at her feet, a pot of tea on the table beside her, the swans at her side. In her fingers was a long-stemmed rose. And face down in the pond, like you had been in the brook, Melissa, were Dr. Baker and Estelle, their legs caught in metal bear traps that had been thrown in the water some time before.

Later it was reported that the swans had beat Estelle and Dr. Baker in the head, hit them hard with their massive bony wings, beating them as they protected their cygnets. Estelle and Dr. Baker had stopped in their tracks from the shock of seeing Jenny sweating profusely, her face mottled and red. And in that moment the swans had attacked them and they had fallen into the pond and stumbled into the traps below the surface. There they drowned as Jenny sat before them in her lawn chair and sipped her mortal petal tea, every wicked blossom she could find, the foxglove and monkshood, brewed and steeped in silver, and sipped from a delicate china cup. She wore all the horror of her life and death. Her wind bells hung silent in the weeping willow tree.

After Art called the police, there was sirens and vehicles and a commotion that hadn't afflicted the estate since the final garden party twelve years earlier. Of course we knew the truth, for it was in my embroidery.

Art took me away to my room where I slept deeply, for a long time. Petal's End went to the Nature Conservancy, with us to live there as long as we wanted, Art and me, and our children, the sweet ones with their own now, who will come and find me here, for Art has been gone some years. In the picture you see how he fell in the flowers along the stone wall of Evermore, the hoe still in his hand.

I wonder if you've been here all this time, Melissa, as I've told this story of the years you knew, and the years that were taken from you. It was your favourite time for a story, when the evening came. The stitches I put in now, of the old lady in the rocking chair on the verandah—they show a wrinkled woman who looks asleep, but if you look careful you see she is still and her arms hang down, that she has fallen into a sleep she will never wake from, her eyes gazing ahead. There is an embroidery hoop on the verandah floor, and the little girl stands by the mirror and she is holding out her hand. Below the picture is stitched in finest silk floss:

On the wings of the wind o'er the dark rolling deep
Angels are coming to watch o'er thy sleep
Angels are coming to watch over thee
So listen to the wind coming over the sea.

I see you now. I am a twelfth-born Mosher, and when the dead appear in the mirror by the door it is time. Holy Mother Mercy sending you, perhaps, a gift for carrying the memento all these years. We walk through the meadow, leaving a path behind us in the tall grasses. The wind blows the path away and there is only an untouched field of sweet hay and late-summer flowers swaying under the enormous singing sky.

Acknowledgements

Ongoing gratitude to the fiercely talented Kiara Kent, literary editor with the heart of a dramaturge. Thank you for such intellectual elegance, rigour and devotion to the novel. Endless thanks also to associate publisher Amy Black for kindness, wisdom and guidance.

Thank you to Kristin Cochrane, Susan Burns, Catherine Marjoribanks and the team at Doubleday Canada. Thanks to Mr. Five Seventeen who beautifully carried the world of the story into book format. Special thanks to Maya Mavjee, the first to believe in this novel, and to Lynn Henry. Thanks also to Lynne Reeder for salty Nova Scotian encouragement along the way.

My gratitude to artist and dearest friend Marie Cameron. *The End of Spring* graces the cover, a painting inspired by a photograph I took of a dead bird which fell on my door step during the writing.

Deep appreciation to Kent Hoffman and Mary Lynk for expert guidance through various forms of storytelling and understanding the power of voice. Thanks to the Box of Delights Bookstore in

Wolfville, Nova Scotia and the Writers Federation of Nova Scotia for steadfast encouragement.

Abiding appreciation for Sara Keddy's affection for the old mountain and valley ways. Thanks Dana Mills and Meaghan Franey for those literary coffees. Thank you Melanie Little, Madeleine Thien, Barbara Lipp, Yvette Doucette, Millie & Maurice Laporte, Pat Acheson, Scott Campbell, and Waldo Walsh & Judy Noel Walsh at Birchleigh Farm. Thank you to Dr. Beverley Cassidy; to Dr. Chris Toplack for research on DES; and to Lois Hare, ND, for discussion of deadly flowers. I would like to also acknowledge the support of the Woodcock Fund through the Writers' Trust of Canada.

Thank you Atsuko Tomita Poirier and Sarah Jane Blenkhorn for sharing their knowledge of traditional Japanese ghost stories and cultural practices. Thanks also to the work of Lafcadio Hearn, a 19th century writer who wrote extensively in English about Japanese culture and ancient texts. Thank you, Joan Levack, for unwavering encouragement from the very start, and the life changing vintage floral card table. Thanks to the effervescence that is Sheree Fitch.

Thank you Dan Conlin, helpful historian and big brother—for traditional Nova Scotia ghost stories told by island beach fires.

Gratitude to Gwenyth Dwyn and Bruce Dienes for never, ever doubting, not even once, and for your sea of kindness and love of eccentricity. A profound thanks to Joceline & Martin Doucette for the espressos and everything else.

And of course, sparkly thanks to my marvelous son, Silas, with me through the long journey of the book. Thanks to sweet Milo and Angus, and to the loving miracle that is Andy Brown—he has kept the home fires burning, the graphic novels flowing and the lamp glowing in the long dark nights.